I0613255

CONCESSIONS AND BETRAYALS

William Wesley

Enfield Press

Copyright © 2023 William Wesley Fields

All rights reserved

No part of this book may be reproduced, or stored in a
retrieval system, or transmitted in any form or by any means,
electronic, mechanical, photocopying, recording, or
otherwise, without express written permission of the
publisher.

ISBN: 978-1-7372565-2-6

Library of Congress Control Number: 2023914017

For Paris

Tragedies are resolved in one of two ways:
The Shakespearian way
Or the Anton Chekov way.
In a tragedy by Shakespeare
The stage at the end is littered with dead bodies.
In a tragedy by Chekhov
Everyone is unhappy, bitter, disillusioned, and melancholy,
But they are alive.

Amos Oz

Disclaimers

Concessions and Betrayals is a work of fiction. While many actual persons, places, and events are included in the narrative, all names, characters, and incidents are products of the author's imagination or are used fictitiously. To assist readers, glossaries of historical figures, arcane wartime agencies, and petroleum industry terminology have been appended.

Introduction

In a world beset by disparities, global warming, and zealotry, the genesis of the Arabian oil industry may seem irrelevant. Saudi Aramco is the most powerful institution among the oil producing countries. Al-Saud are international symbols of excess. Jihad has disseminated widely from the cradle of Islam. And human disasters all over the Middle East and North Africa bear the fingerprints of governments in the West.

But our dilemma can't be blamed on any particular cabal. The root cause is the proliferation of our innately destructive species. We chopped down primeval forests for shelters and fires. We mined coal to the detriment of our atmosphere and well-being. We hunted whales into oblivion to illuminate the darkness we still fear. Survival strategies of clans and villages have been overtaken by global companies and autocratic nations, dividing us by geography, race, religion, and self-reference.

If we are to save ourselves from our differences we must learn how we are bound together. To prevent irreversible degradation of our environment or a holocaust of our own making, we must find common cause. There have never been more human beings living on our planet. But only a handful remember the events in the Persian Gulf that transformed the entire world. This historical novel - a true story, by and large - is about those encounters.

Before compelling evidence of climate change, before the explosive dawn of the atomic age, before the end of the British Mandate in Palestine, before countless coups, the Gulf Wars, or 9/11, Franklin Roosevelt came to believe that he couldn't defeat the Axis powers without crude oil from a desert kingdom no older than his presidency. Thousands of Italian expatriates and starving Arabs joined hundreds of Americans to build the first refinery and marine terminal at Ras Tanura. The synergy between those Arabs, Europeans, and Americans fueled the end of one millennium and the beginning of another. Without intention, they catalyzed the cultural, economic, and scientific conflicts that threaten us all.

CONTENTS

Part 1 - Across the Arabian Sea

San Francisco, 18 May 1944

The electric train on the lower level of the Bay Bridge was packed: everyone over the age of 18 who wasn't fighting was working. Outside, the morning fog concealed everything but the top of Coit Tower. In the late spring, the marine layer advanced through the Golden Gate at night and didn't retreat until the middle of the afternoon. San Francisco only needed to be blacked out for cocktails and dinner.

Hank Simmons, the tallest passenger in the coach, was reading the front page of the *Chronicle* over the shoulder of a balding man. The headline above the fold read "Allies Take Monte Cassino." He wondered how long the war in Italy might last if Kesselring wouldn't surrender a monastery with a view.

When the Key Line coaches were full they were stifling, even if you were a head taller than the rest of the commuters. The sailor leaning into Hank was asleep on his feet, close enough to catch whiffs of cheap rye. He still missed the fresh smell of the bay on the ferries between Emeryville and the Embarcadero that had been taken out of service when gas rationing began.

When his wife wanted to needle him, Gloria would ask, *What's the point of working in an oil refinery if you can't get more gas?* If he felt like playing along, he would correct her. *He didn't work in a refinery, he ran the marine terminal at Port Richmond, the busiest gas station on the west coast.*

But the real answer wasn't a joke. They had a young son named Peter who he could watch grow – so long as he kept filling up tankers for the war in the Pacific. Hank had been working for Standard Oil of California since graduating from Berkeley as a chemical engineer. Unlike most men his age his draft exemption didn't change after Pearl Harbor.

Hank wondered why he had been summoned to 220 Bush Street, literally in the shadows of Standard's headquarters. Rockefeller himself had commissioned 225 Bush to look like the Federal Reserve Bank in New York. The government might have more gold but it didn't control the world's largest oil reserve. The Arab Layer was rumored to be so massive that Standard had partnered with Texaco to develop the concession before the shooting started in Spain.

The ground-floor windows at 220 Bush still read *California Arabian Standard Oil Company*. A pair of painters in white coveralls were scraping off the old lettering and cleaning the glass with turpentine. From his mundane post on the Long Wharf, Hank had always liked the distant concession's nickname more than its acronym: *Calarabian* sounded like something out of *One Thousand and One Nights*. The new name for the joint venture, the Arabian American Oil Company, had been announced a few months earlier. The buzz was that Abdulaziz, the founding king of Saudi Arabia, their partners from Texas, and the US State Department were all happier with *Aramco*.

At that point in the war there were a lot more jobs in the oil patch than experienced operators. The lobby was still packed with oilmen who could smell money. Hank recognized them by type if not by name. The upstream men - the drillers and the pipeline builders - had borrowed ties to dress up worn leather jackets and heavy pants. The downstream men - the accountants and the marketers - had pressed suits and clean shaves. The geologists were huddled in one corner - brainy types with beards in expeditionary gear - looking like they would rather be anywhere but downtown. Hank chatted with a couple of other Standard engineers he knew. Sooner than most, he was escorted to the office of Fred Davies, the concession's president.

Davies wore a tailored double-breasted suit and rimless bifocal glasses. He stood to shake hands with Hank, maintaining his no-nonsense demeanor. The president's grip was brief but strong, like a high school wrestler pinning an opponent for two seconds. He didn't seem to like being shorter than Hank, jabbing at one of the chairs on the other side of his desk until the younger man sat down.

"I've been hearing good things about you, Henry."

The only person that called him Henry was his mother, without affection. "You can call me Hank, sir."

"All right, Hank. Pendleton tells me you're a solid man as far as industrial processes and organic chemistry is concerned."

"Thank you." There were a lot of ways to make a fortune from petroleum, but Hank knew that shooting his mouth off wasn't one of them.

Some strangers he passed on the street assumed Hank was violent by nature. Most engineers didn't look like they could crush skulls. Davies, the president of Aramco, knew otherwise.

"Pendleton tells me you've shown a real knack for handling the working men at Richmond."

"I learned a lot from him."

Hank had only been on the job a few months when Pendleton started inviting him to meetings with shop stewards that had nothing to do with using a slide rule. The refinery manager had always ordered the big kid from Berkeley to take off his glasses before sitting down with the pipefitters or tanker drivers. When meetings started,

Pendleton would be deliberately vague about the young engineer's title. Like most near-sighted people, Hank had to resort to a squinty stare to see tradesmen who were more than an arm's length away. The union leaders, without prejudice, assumed he was company muscle. Regardless of what side of the table you were on, only tough people lasted in the oil patch.

The way Pendleton taught Hank to play the game, it was always the refinery manager who took the hard line. Whether it was lunch breaks or overtime pay, Hank never spoke until the moment came to offer the compromise that he and Pendleton had worked out in advance. Soon enough, the foremen in the refinery trades were going Pendleton one better. They would seek out Hank (wearing his glasses and carrying his clipboard) to solve problems as soon as they arose. Hank kept getting promoted and the grease under his nails kept getting harder to see.

Davies asked, "What do you know about the global supply of petroleum?"

"I know that the US was the biggest producer before the war, even more now."

"That's right, Hank - sixty percent or more. What would you say if I told you that the best minds at the Petroleum Administration in Washington have concluded that America can't produce enough crude oil to win the war?"

"I'd say we better get on the ball, sir."

Hank had heard the scuttlebutt. The proven reserves of Standard, its sisters and the independents in the continental US had been maximized. The Caribbean Basin was looking tapped out too. The only exception was shale that would be prohibitively expensive to reach. The American oil industry was barely producing a million barrels more than the four million that Roosevelt had been sharing with the British since 1940. The Arab Layer on the Persian Gulf was their ace in the hole. After four years of exploration, Max Steineke,

Standard's best geologist, had figured out the deep dark secrets of the limestone. Then the war in North Africa halted development. The only debate between the US government and the oil industry was how many billions of barrels were in the Middle East.

Davies leaned in and lowered his voice. "The War Department has given us priority to build a refinery to process 50,000 barrels a day in Ras Tanura. And the boards of Standard and Texaco want Aramco to export ten times that much crude by the end of 1945. We need your help, Hank."

The younger man could feel his throat tighten. The president of the Saudi concession might as well have had red, white, and blue stripes on his Brooks Brothers suit. He could only nod as Davies continued.

"We are opening up drilling on the Dammam Done and elsewhere in the concession. Ras Tanura is the best location for a refinery complex and terminal on the Persian Gulf. There was a tea kettle built there in 1939 but it was only designed to handle about three thousand barrels a day, enough for our crews and the royal family. We had to shut it down after the Italians bombed Dhahran."

Hank nodded again. He was struggling to imagine how Standard could build a refinery as big as Richmond in a year and a half. The Persian Gulf was still bracketed by epic conflicts all over Europe and Asia.

Davies continued the pitch. "I used to run Bapco, our operation on the island of Bahrain. There's already one submarine pipeline that connects Ras Tanura with the refinery there. But we'll need a bigger pipeline to move another 50,000 barrels a day to Bahrain. The rest will be stabilized or refined and shipped out on tankers for the war in the Pacific.

"It's still hush hush but the War Department priority means we will have enough steel to build out Ras Tanura as well as the feeder lines from all the new drilling sites. We've hired Bechtel to build the plant and the terminal. Steve Bechtel is already there. His partner McCone is a wizard when it comes to fabricating steel."

Hank nodded without speaking. Bechtel and McCone were legendary among Berkeley's engineering alumni. He knew Standard had been one of the Bechtel family's best customers for a generation. Consortiums led by the Bechtels built the Bay Bridge, the Hoover Dam and a host of other big projects in the West. Now Bechtel and McCone were building Liberty Ships. But Aramco's plan for Ras Tanura, as Hank continued listening to Davies, sounded far bigger than the refinery that Bechtel was building in Bahrain.

"We want you to run the marine terminal at Ras Tanura, Hank. We need you there as soon as possible to coordinate construction with Steve's men. Our plan is to get the pipeline to Bahrain working first. We want to sign you up for three years at $10,000 per year."

Hank was stunned by the thought of a five-figure salary. But three years in Arabia? In the middle of a world war?

"What about my wife and son, sir?"

Davies nodded, "I know you're a family man - that's good. But we evacuated all the families from the American Camp in Dhahran after things got rough. The first group of wives won't be going back for a few months."

"I see."

Davies frowned. "We have a lot of housing to build for new employees, along with everything else we need. Let's just say we hope to have enough for everyone's families by next year."

"I understand," Hank said. Only fanatics contemplated what the world might be like by the end of 1945. Davies changed the subject.

"You'll get a month's leave for every year of service, travel expenses included. We will be bringing in teachers for the younger children soon. And the company pays for the education of the older children back here in the States, top prep schools."

Hank nodded as he wondered how much Peter would grow in a year. Davies broke back into his thoughts.

"Of course, most of what you earn overseas is exempt from income tax. And your annuity program will accelerate with service in Arabia. I'm sure you'll want to talk this over with your wife. But understand, Hank, I'm not asking you to do this for the company. I'm asking you to do this for your country."

Davies stood and shook his hand again, a three count this time. Hank knew that there were other people in the lobby waiting to hear the same pitch. He waded through the crowd and wandered back down to the waterfront. He glanced at the Mechanics Monument on his way through the triangular plaza where Bush met Market. Tilden's super-humans wrestling with a punch press had been the only survivors downtown after the earthquake and fire. Clad in shop aprons, the working men looked fine in bronze. But Hank knew what they smelled like in real life. As a kid in Martinez, he had shared the dining room in his mother's boarding house with a whole platoon of refinery workers.

For a long time, Hank paced along the Embarcadero, trying to sort his thoughts about Aramco. Every pier was like a beehive: crane operators and longshoremen grappling with cargo, taxis and trucks battling for parking spaces, mothers kissing service men goodbye, girlfriends hugging them for making it back. For Americans, the war was as much about petroleum as anything. FDR's oil embargo in the summer of 1941 had been the pretext for the Japanese attack on Pearl Harbor. Hank felt like he was finally getting into the fight without being in the line of fire.

Montclair, 19 May

At the end of his work week on the Long Wharf, Hank took a Key Line train from Richmond to Oakland, shopping in the village after getting off the bus in Montclair. Like any good provider, he had been giving most of the stamps in their book of food rations to Gloria for her mother's cook in Palo Alto. With the stamps he had left, fresh meat was out of the question. But Friday was still Fish Day around the bay, whether one was Catholic or not. Military provisioners were less interested in local mussels than pork and beef. Hank made do with a local fettuccine that wasn't as good as it had been before the Italian family who founded the company were forced to sell.

He had been living like a bachelor Monday through Friday in the foothills of Montclair, the only part of Oakland that Gloria would consider when they were looking for their first home. He decided not to discuss his transfer to Ras Tanura until Friday night. Their new ritual was catching up over dinner about everything they had missed during the week.

They had met at Berkeley: she had never shown the slightest interest in chemical engineering and he had never understood her fascination with primitive societies. They had second languages they seldom used with each other: her French was cultured and well-travelled; his Italian came from a fishing village on the wrong side of the bay.

The summer before their engagement, while he was working at a refinery near Martinez, she had sailed with her advisor to the French colony of New Caledonia to study the indigenous Kanak. After Pearl Harbor her professor recommended her to Owen Lattimore, a China hand from Berkeley who became the director of US propaganda in the Pacific. Before Peter's first birthday in 1942, she was drafted (unofficially) by OWI, the Office of War Information.

Gloria was one of a handful of Caledonian specialists in San Francisco translating American military imperatives into white lies for the local tribes and French colonials. The capital city had become the busiest port in the South Pacific after the US entered the war. When New Caledonia became the staging area for the campaign in the Solomon Islands, every faction in Nouméa wanted to repel the American invasion. To accommodate her long hours at the Presidio, Gloria and Peter had been spending weeknights at the Palo Alto home of her parents, who adored their only grandson.

Gloria was no more interested in cooking than she was in refining petroleum. One of the few things they had in common was growing up in homes with live-in cooks. Gloria, like her mother, thought of the kitchen as a wing from which the house staff periodically appeared with food and drink. But Hank had grown up feeling like the kitchen in his mother's boarding house was his refuge. Their cook, Giulia, was the only woman he had genuinely loved (including his mother) until he met Gloria. Like Giulia, he cooked as if he was Sicilian. On Friday nights when his wife and son returned to their home in Montclair, food and love were synonymous.

Gloria and Peter arrived at the bungalow just before sunset. Hank's love was like a banked fire that burst into flames when they came through the door. His son looked like a boyish version of his wife and she looked like a million bucks. She was taller than most men, even taller in her heels. Part of their attraction had always been that neither had to

10

compromise their physicality. The padded shoulders of her suit made them look even wider than they were. Peter had wrapped himself around Hank's legs by the time Gloria crossed the living room to meet his embrace. Her green eyes dared him to adore her again, auburn hair falling away from her long neck.

Hank savored her perfume as they kissed - *Joy*. Somehow, four years after the fall of France, Gloria hadn't run out of the fragrance by Jean Patou. But late afternoons in May were chilly when the fog rolled in and his wife was even chillier. Playing host in their own home, Hank had devised a formula for Friday evenings: for every day they had been apart, he allowed an hour to rekindle his relationship with his wife. He spent the first part of it playing with Peter, who was as guileless as his mother was illusive. She helped herself to her first martini from a batch he had ready in the kitchen. (The first time he ever made Gloria laugh was when he tried to convince her that her favorite cocktail was invented in Martinez.)

Hank had learned everything he knew about New Caledonia from Gloria on the nights when she made it back from the Presidio. The ebb and flow of hydrocarbons that he was loading onto Armadillos - the tanker class of Liberty Ships - never seemed as interesting as the latest international incident in Nouméa. Since she had been staying with their son in Palo Alto, the weeklong debrief made for longer and more entertaining meals. As usual, the night after his Aramco interview Hank did more listening than talking. Gloria became more animated as the martini pitcher emptied. Like a good host, Hank served his wife dinner and fed his son as the OWI version of the news continued.

The sixth governor of New Caledonia since the fall of France seemed less adversarial - now that the invasion of "la mére patrie" was imminent. Most of the US Navy vessels that irritated the colonials in Nouméa had moved on with the war. The remaining US Army units were either medical or logistical. *Caldoche accusations continued - Americans were practicing a new form of slavery in the Pacific, preferentially hiring the indigenous Kanak instead of colonials of French descent.*

After dinner, Hank bathed Peter while Gloria cleaned up the kitchen. They put their son to bed together. Hank's newest pleasures was listening to Gloria read The Little Prince to Peter in French. At other times of the day, he read the English version to their son. Hank's mind wandered as he thought of an aviator stranded in the Sahara. In any language, Gloria's bedtime voice enthralled her husband as much as her son.

"Ce n'est qu'avec le coeur qu'on peut bien voir; ce qui est essentiel est invisible pour les yeux."

Peter traced the illustration done by de Saint-Exupéry of the fox sitting beside the little prince.

"What is essential is invisible to the eye?"

Hank was amazed at the ease with which their little boy could switch between languages, grateful that Peter inherited Gloria's facilities as well as looks.

She kissed her son's forehead as his father said, "It means the things you know in your heart are more important than the things that you see and hear."

Peter nodded seriously. "Like I know you love me even though we only see you on weekends?"

Hank's eyes welled up with tears, only able to nod in agreement. Gloria winked at her husband as she hugged Peter.

"Exactement, mon coeur."

After they tucked Peter in, they returned to the kitchen table. Gloria poured them both another dash of wine from a jug labeled "burgundy." When the French wines they could afford began to disappear in 1940, she had sneered at the local plonk Hank had grown up with - sturdy varieties from the north bay that Italian families could legally ferment at home during Prohibition. The longer the war lasted, the less Gloria complained about table wine from Sonoma.

"So tell me about your interview with Calarabian."

Hank didn't bother to correct his wife. She could get used to the new name of the Saudi concession along with the rest of the world.

"Bechtel's building our first refinery complex at a place on the Persian Gulf called Ras Tanura."

When she repeated the name, she made it sound more exotic and alluring.

"Ras Tanura."

"You're mocking me."

"You know how I feel about getting trapped in some dusty corner of the oil patch."

"They want me to supervise the construction of the marine terminal and then manage it."

She aimed a puff of her first cigarette of the evening at the light above the kitchen table.

"So, what did you tell them?"

Before Peter, they had often played cards to pass the time, especially when their feelings for each other were failing them. Gloria never wanted to be the first to show a card. If she wanted him to go to Arabia, she wouldn't declare it. If she wanted him to stay, he knew she would reveal her terms, one by one.

"I told them that three years was a long time to be away from home during a war. It would be at least a year before you and Peter could join me."

Gloria offered him a patronizing gaze, as if she would ever leave her work at OWI and her parents looking after Peter to homestead in a desert kingdom.

"How is an emancipated woman supposed to live in a tribal patriarchy? Arabia is the cradle of the most repressive religion in the world!"

"They're offering a lot of money."

13

"Oh?"

Gloria's father was a wizard in property law whose clients included Standard. His studied endorsement of Hank's proposal had carried the day despite her mother's vehement reservations. During the Depression, her family had acquired a lot of real estate while many others were losing theirs - including Hank's. A lot of money to him wasn't necessarily a lot of money to Gloria.

"Ten thousand a year. Plus, an accelerated annuity and free tuition for Peter when he's old enough to go away to prep school."

Gloria nodded agreeably.

"There's no income tax on overseas earnings, either."

She egged him on as she took the last drag off her cigarette.

"And I get a month off for every year of service in Arabia."

His wife laughed, the smoke beginning to burn his eyes.

"It would take you that long to get back here."

"But someday - maybe even next year - we could meet in Europe, just like we've always talked about."

Gloria shook her head. She and her mother had dashed across the continent before their wedding, before the fall of Poland. Hank was sure his future mother-in-law spent most of their time in Paris trying to talk her daughter out of marrying him.

"Europe will never be the same."

Hank rued the sadness appearing on Gloria's face. He feared the possibility of being unable to save his wife from her own melancholy. Motherhood and another world war had confirmed her worst suspicions about the fate of women in the twentieth century. He was terrified by the memory of the afternoon he came home from work to find her disheveled, their infant son screaming in his crib in the next room, his sodden diaper dirty, his formula bottle empty, as if she hadn't been near him for hours. That was the night he called her mother to come to Peter's rescue, as well as Gloria's. His son hadn't begun to thrive until he was under the care of her parents and their staff.

A few months after they were both well enough to return to Montclair, the job offer from the Pacific division of OWI had hit Gloria like a bolt of lightning. His wife was far happier working at the Presidio than she would ever be as a housewife in the hills of Montclair. With both of his parents working wartime hours, Peter was lucky to have his grandparents. Gloria thrived on the complexity of the New Caledonia desk, insulated from the mundane. But two years on, Hank felt like it was his turn to save the world.

"They say we may not be able to win the war without tapping the reserves in Arabia. I don't think I can turn this job down."

Gloria studied his expression. No one knew him better, even if it meant that he was powerless before her. Another moment passed before she reached across the table and touched his hand.

"Of course you can't."

He looked into her eyes and saw what he wanted to see. They had always been at their best without words that could betray them. The war had added to their need to disappear into each other when all else failed. As their son dreamed of the desert and the stars in the next room, Gloria and Hank re-enacted their own fairy tale. She became his magical Beauty and he became her devoted Beast. When Peter awoke on Saturday morning and found a trail of clothing between the kitchen and their bedroom, he slipped in next to his father without waking his mother.

Washington DC, 4 June

When he got off the train at Union Station in the federal district, Hank began to understand what it meant to be an American rather than a Californian. Men and women from all over the US, some in uniform, the rest in business attire, rushed by. Most of them looked purposeful, lost in thoughts about assignments all over the world. The rest were smiling, even laughing. Everyone, including Hank, seemed to know that they were in the most important place at the most important moment of their lives. Washington was the only major capital that remained unscarred by world war. Instead, global conflict electrified the District of Columbia.

Wearing the same suit he had worn on all the way from Oakland, Hank walked down to the Capitol Building. Then he hiked up the Mall to the Washington Monument. He didn't blink as he went past the White House on 15th Street, gawking like the big kid that he still was. The Aramco office was in the Shoreham Building, just beyond Lafayette Park.

Hank wasn't the only man on his way to Arabia. A lot of them were in the waiting room of an unmarked suite one story above the Aramco office. He recognized a few of them from the lobby of 220 Bush. The secretary directing traffic didn't have much to say, checking names off a list. It was another famously humid late-spring day in the District. The sweat from Hank's hike across DC had dried during the wait.

He had shaved before getting off the train but now desperately needed a shower and a clean shirt. Finally, the secretary with the salt and pepper beehive called his name.

Hank entered an unadorned office with a wooden desk and two unpadded chairs. There was a fan turning overhead but even less air moving than there had been in the waiting room. There was one window looking south towards the Treasury Building. A man about his own age beckoned Hank to sit. He introduced himself as Rod Berglund without saying who he worked for. He had a dossier on Henry Simmons Jr. that was surprisingly thick.

Berglund continued to read, leaving Hank to stare at the top of his head, the fair hair freshly trimmed around the ears and slicked back. He wore a bespoke suit of charcoal grey with a lighter pinstripe, a junior Dean Acheson. Berglund turned another page and then looked up at Hank, his irises the color of ice. A blonde eyebrow went up.

"Your father committed suicide."

Hank acknowledged the observation without elaborating, a painful fact that couldn't be changed.

"Arabia is a hostile environment. You'll be thousands of miles from your wife and son. Do you think that you'll be able to take it?"

The cold blue eyes were fixed on Hank, who couldn't hide a sneer. Berglund reminded him of fraternity boys at Berkeley who were born on third base but acted like they led the league in triples.

"I've been running stills at five hundred degrees since I was seventeen."

Berglund turned another page. "You're from Martinez?"

"That's right."

"Your mother has been harboring an Enemy Alien within the Evacuation Zone."

Hank knew what he was talking about but only shrugged. "I haven't lived with my mother for years."

17

"Giulia Amalfitano lives in your mother's boarding house."

His mother was a terrible cook. Keeping Giulia after his father's death wasn't a luxury but a necessity: the boarding house would have failed without her. But Giulia wasn't just the culinary star of their establishment - she had raised Hank like one of her own.

"Does your file say that her oldest son died at Guadalcanal? Or that the younger one just landed at Anzio?"

Berglund was enjoying their seated shoving match. "It says that Mrs. Amalfitano is a non-naturalized Italian national who lives at your mother's home address on Alhambra."

"Joe DiMaggio is from Martinez. His parents are non-naturalized Italian nationals. Most of the fishing fleet in San Francisco Bay lived in my hometown and all of them were Italian. Some of the immigrants - like Giulia - were too busy working and raising their families to learn English or take a citizenship test."

Berglund leaned into his next few questions. "Is Mrs. Amalfitano a fascist sympathizer?"

"Her family left before Mussolini came to power. Otherwise, they might have starved to death, like a lot of southerners."

"Is she a communist sympathizer?"

"She likes Roosevelt. Does that count?"

Berglund didn't try to hide his amusement as he turned the last few pages. Hank took a deep breath to collect himself. Davies had already promised him the job at Ras Tanura. The Aramco personnel office had been vague about the interview in Washington DC. But Hank was beginning to get the idea.

The Enemy Alien Act had been passed in 1940 when "America First" still seemed like a reasonable political stance. After Pearl Harbor, FDR had signed an executive order that covered Japanese, German, and Italian nationals living in the US. The Evacuation Zone laid down by the Army at the Presidio included most of the coastal towns in California -

Monterey and San Pedro as well as Martinez. The majority of the commercial fishing vessels in the state were operated by Japanese or Italian families. The Island Hill neighborhood overlooking the marina was entirely Italian, as were most of Hank's teammates in high school.

In the beginning of 1942, the FBI had shown up at Giulia's home a few blocks away. She had been a widow since her husband had disappeared on a trawler in the Gulf of Alaska. She and her two boys were told they had to evacuate inland. The agents took her radio and told the Amalfitano brothers they could either enlist or be locked up. Giulia pretended to move but spent every night in the basement of the boarding house. By the end of 1942, tens of thousands of Japanese Americans were interned. But a month before the elections in November, the government proclaimed that Italian Americans were no longer enemies. Giulia continued to live (illegally) with Hank's mother. Every three months she reported to the local authorities from a fake address outside the zone.

"I understand you speak Italian, Mr. Simmons."

Fond memories helped him relax. "I picked up a lot living with the Amalfitanos. Giulia got mad when her sons taught me to swear like a *napoletano*. My teammates used their first language to call plays against schools that only spoke *inglese*."

Berglund's final question was a lob. "What was your favorite sport?"

Hank eased back in his chair, feeling like he was earning a passing grade. "High hurdles."

"Sprints?"

"I wasn't fast enough for sprints."

Berglund was grinning at him. "You wore down your competitors."

"That's right. I cleared a lot of hurdles just to get here. I love my country. And I love my work. I'm going to give Aramco everything I've got."

19

The Army and the Navy would be his only customers at Ras Tanura. They had a right to know if they could trust the man who was filling up their tankers with the world's most combustible distillates. Berglund extended his hand and wished him luck. Hank shook it like a gentleman, happy thinking they would never meet again.

Washington DC, 5 June

The Lafayette Building on the first block up Vermont from Lafayette Park was a monument to the New Deal. Most of the agencies inside were newer than the structure, creations of the war effort. The alphabet soup in the lobby obscured their singular activity: conducting trade between the US government and private industries. One floor was the home of the Petroleum Reserve Corporation, a market maker for the oil majors and their smaller competitors. On another was the Export Import Bank, which was more than convenient for the co-owners of Aramco.

On the hottest morning of the month, an olive-green sedan with a white star on the side was parked at the corner. A balding businessman with a heavy overcoat draped improbably over his left forearm dashed out of the Shoreham Building and handed his leather suitcase to the uniformed driver. He spoke with a Scottish brogue softened by decades in San Francisco.

"Take me to the Air Transport Command at National Airport."

James MacPherson had joined the Production Board for Petroleum in the first few months of 1943. His patriotism was underwritten by Standard, which continued to pay his salary as vice president of Aramco. He had an office in the Pentagon but spent most of his time shuttling between the agencies in the Lafayette Building and the oil lobbyists on K Street. After a last-minute meeting with Captain Berglund, the new military attaché in the US legation in Jeddah, he was excited to be leaving government service and getting his first look at the concession in more than a year.

The fastest way to get to Arabia was the Air Transport Command. Mac, as he was universally known, had hoped to go through London and reconnect with friends and enemies in the oil patch. But the Northern Atlantic route had been overbooked for weeks. Fortunately, Aramco's workers had priority on the Middle Atlantic route, his secretary arranged his flight to Bermuda, the first leg to Dhahran.

The ultimate monument to the Roosevelt administration, the Pentagon, loomed beyond the ATC ramp. The interior of the C-47 had spartan aluminum benches on the inside of the exposed fuselage. MacPherson, the last passenger to board, got dirty looks from the men who had been sweltering while they waited for the VIP. The only seat left was next to an oversized young civilian with dark-hair and horn-rimmed glasses. MacPherson nodded to him as he sat down, still clinging to the winter coat. He checked for the lined leather gloves in one pocket and the handful of cigars he had stuffed in the other. A sergeant from the flight crew pointed at the one he had been smoking in the stop-and-go traffic.

"Put it out."

MacPherson, a veteran of the Egyptian Expeditionary Force, tried a convivial tone. "This was hand-rolled on the thigh of the last virgin in Havana!"

The sergeant only smirked. "You're on a military aircraft. All passengers have to follow Army Air Force regulations."

"See here - I helped procure the aviation fuel for this flight!"

The pilots were revving the twin engines. The sergeant was losing his patience. "Don't try to pull rank on me, Mac. I was the head bouncer at the Copacabana!"

MacPherson saluted, then took a cigar cutter from his pocket and snipped off the burning tip. The rest went back in his mouth as he looked up at the younger man sitting beside him.

"How do you think he knew my nickname?"

"They say non-commissioned officers know everything."

"True enough in the Great War." He extended his hand and said, "James MacPherson."

"Hank Simmons."

MacPherson echoed the name like a boon companion's - *Hank Simmons!* Berglund hadn't told him that their man was as big as an oil rig. Seated and bespectacled, he still resembled a chemical engineer. Aramco had plans for Hank - far bigger than the assignment he had been offered in San Francisco - but it was too soon for Mac to reveal them. Instead, the wolf remained mutton.

"Call me Mac. Where you headed?"

"Standard is transferring me from California to Aramco."

"I'm heading to Dhahran for a look see. Where are they sending you?"

"I'll be setting up the marine terminal at Ras Tanura."

"Excellent! I'm transferring back to Aramco myself!"

Hank had never been on an airplane but tried to remain nonchalant as they taxied and took off. By the time they reached the cruising altitude of the unpressurized C-47, he was looking enviously at the oil executive's lined gloves and heavy coat.

(Hank would later chide himself in his first letter to Gloria for not remembering that air temperature dropped inversely with altitude, the opposite of core temperatures underground.)

Mac read one thick document after another from his briefcase. He sensed that Hank was finding it impossible not to peek, as if he was reading newspapers on a train. His undeclared mentor decided it was time for his tutoring to begin. The older man brandished a memorandum signed by Harold Ickes, the Secretary of the Interior, along with the presidents of Standard, Texaco, and Gulf. He started half-shouting to be heard by Hank over the engines.

"Ickes is a dangerous man, one of those left-wing bureaucrats with more ideas than common sense. He thinks he's smarter than everyone in the oil business just because FDR appointed him as Petroleum Administrator!

"I've spent half the war lobbying against the worst of his ideas - like having the government buy out our concession in Arabia. Have to give him credit for the Big Inch, though. Moving product from Texas to markets on the east coast without barges or tankers wasn't feasible until the U-boats started picking them off. The bloody underwriters stopped insuring our cargos!

"Now he wants to build a pipeline more than a thousand miles from Al-Hasa to Palestine to supply Europe. The route parallels the kingdom's northern border, then runs through Jordan and Syria. No one knows for sure where the bloody Iraqi border is!"

Bermuda, 5 June

After they landed at Kindley Field in Bermuda, the Copacabana sergeant announced they would be laying over until morning. Their next stop would be one of the British airfields in the Azores. When Mack asked about hotel accommodations, the sergeant pointed to a Quonset hut with a wooden sign "ATC Passengers."

Hank lengthened his stride on the long walk from the C-47 to the transit hut. Mac fell in beside him, double-timing to keep up.

"Hank, how tall are you anyway?"

"Six-six, sir."

"If you were a horse, you'd be more than nineteen hands!" Hank frowned as Mac chortled around his cigar.

They arrived at the Quonset hut. Inside, it had the charm of USO centers throughout the British Empire: the sandwich platter was empty, the coffee was cold, but the tea was piping hot. The oilmen stood outside and watched the clouds gather for a squall. It was their first chance to chat without shouting over the Pratt and Whitney engines. Mac was already hoarse but amused himself by continuing Hank's first day of training in the cutthroat business he was about to enter.

"Do you know how much we pay for the crude oil you'll be pumping?"

Hank shook his head. The Long Wharf in Richmond wasn't like most gas stations. The only thing that mattered was the volume of product flowing through the pipelines. Men like Mac, who had advanced through Standard's finance department, collected the cash.

"We pay the Saudis four shillings for every ton we export."

"How much is that in dollars?"

"That's a good question."

Hank watched the smoke from Mac's cigar merge with the low clouds rolling over the airfield. Timing was as important as the tale for a raconteur.

"The price was pegged to the New York market when we signed the agreement with King Abdulaziz in 1933. Suleiman, his finance minister, would only accept payment in British sovereigns. At the time, it worked out to twelve cents a barrel. Then the Federal Reserve devalued the dollar to help get international trade going. That pushed the Saudi royalty to twenty-two cents a barrel. That's the current exchange rate in London. But in Jeddah, where the Saudis do most of their government exchange, it's twice that."

"Sounds complicated."

Mac smiled around his cigar.

"It's actually quite simple, Hank. When we started negotiating with Suleiman, the kingdom's treasury was literally a chest. He kept it locked so that no one knew it was usually empty. But the king is a truly great man. It took generations for his family to conquer the other sheikdoms in Arabia. They won and lost Arabia twice. The third kingdom was only a few months old when we started negotiating the oil concession. But no matter how much it costs us to turn dollars into gold, the peg is still the price of oil in 1933."

Mac was smiling around his cigar like a cat after eating a pair of canaries. The best time to expand crude oil reserves had always been at the bottom of the market for refined products.

"Along with Texaco, we've put more than a hundred million into the kingdom so far. And we'll spend a lot more than that in the next few years. But Aramco will control the largest oilfield in the entire world, Hank. And our production cost per gallon will be lower than our competitors. We'll make the Saudis rich. But we'll be richer."

Talked out, Mac yawned. They headed into the Quonset to inspect their sleeping quarters. The Scot threw his overcoat over one of the cots and stretched out. Hank was too keyed up to sleep. He headed for the civilian passenger terminal looking for a postcard to send Gloria. It was easier to find one than to pay for it. The elderly Bahamian woman behind the counter sighed when he tried to pay with an Indian nickel, then put a few pence from her purse in the register and took his coin for herself.

The wind was up over Castle Harbour. Hank walked on the white sand along the perimeter of the airfield. Being on an island in the middle of the Atlantic was another first, something to write about in the countless letters and postcards that followed. He missed Gloria and he missed Peter but he was in awe at the water's edge. The stars had never seemed so close or numerous. The moon was so full that it looked like it was falling out of the sky.

Bermuda, 6 June

Hank was dreaming about Gloria when Mac's voice intruded on a tender moment on a weary couch. "Our boys are landing at Normandy!"

The smell of Mac's first cigar of the day cut through Hank's disorientation. He didn't remember falling asleep in the transit hut. He tried and failed to adjust his stiff neck before slipping his feet into his shoes on the slab floor. As sore as he was, only one thing mattered to Hank as they headed outside: not so far from Bermuda, D-Day had finally arrived.

The oilmen hurried to queue with the military passengers for their flight to the Azores. Millions of gallons of everything would be needed by the Allies and the oilmen couldn't wait to do their part. Everyone on board the ATC flight was solemn: not so far away, Americans were jumping out of C-47's under heavy fire and landing on beaches where Germans had been dug in for years.

By the time they landed on Terceira Island, beyond the Luftwaffe's reach, Hank was feeling guilty. The RAF ground crew at Lages Field greeted the passengers on the ATC flight with nervous energy, the intensity of Normandy coming ashore. While their plane was refueled, most of the Americans scattered, along with their thoughts.

Mac stayed on Hank's wing. The older man had spent his life trying to draw attention to himself. The younger man had spent most of his trying to fit in. Hank enjoyed Mac, the kind of Scotsman who didn't need a bagpipe so long as he stayed at the front of the parade. Mac's favorite phrase announced to his audience, large or small, that they were about to be blessed with another nugget of worldly wisdom.

"As you know, Portugal is officially neutral. But Salazar is a bloody fascist, as bad as Franco. At the beginning of the war, the only combatants he allowed in the Azores were Nazi U-boats. The generals in the Pentagon wanted to invade the islands on their way to North Africa. Salazar saved his own ass by pulling out a British treaty that was four hundred years old!"

Mac nodded at a bench in the shade outside one of the RAF hangars. After Hank sat down, Mack continued sotto voce, "Our concession partners from Texas supplied Franco with all his fuel during the Spanish Civil War."

To prevent Mac from being overheard, Hank said, "I know."

The story had made the cover of *Time* magazine. Torkild Rieber was a Norwegian tanker captain who had risen through the ranks of Texaco, building the global refining and marketing network that Standard lacked in the Persian Gulf. He had been chairman for a decade when he made the bold decision to invest in California Arabian in 1936, before the big strike in Dammam. But Rieber's tankers also supplied the Royalists in Spain under false flags. Texaco marketers in Europe spied on the Republicans, who were as desperate for petroleum as their opponents. In one case, Texaco had tricked the crew of a Republican tanker at Marseilles into leaving the ship, then put on board another crew that delivered it to the Royalists.

The chairman of Texaco denied being a fascist, though Franco didn't pay for everything Rieber delivered. By the summer of 1940, France had fallen and the Texaco board -

withering under criticism from Washington and London – had forced Rieber out.

The Copacabana sergeant let out a whistle that would have stopped a dozen cabs. He waved for the passengers to return. Everyone scrambled back aboard. During the flight, Mack continued Simmon's off-the-record orientation by letting him peek at the documents he read from other concession executives:

A memorandum to Standard and Texaco from James Terry Duce, another Aramco VP splitting time between the War Department and the Shoreham Building. Senator Truman was making a name for himself on a Special Select Committee investigating their fuel oil contracts with the Navy for fraud and abuse.

A report to Standard and Texaco from a third executive, Max Thornburg, advising the Secretary of State on petroleum markets. Distrust between the US and British governments was an obstacle to a new international commission regulating production (and prices) after the war.

Marrakech, 7 June

After their third day on the metal benches in the ATC transport, Hank and Mack reached the coast of Morocco as the sun descended. The passengers took turns looking through the portals in the C-47 as they approached the ancient city of Marrakech. At dusk, the long shadows of the walls around the medina were disappearing as the oilmen disembarked. The Menara airfield was on an arid plain with the Atlas Mountains in the distance.

Hank felt like he was back in California until he heard the muezzins calling the faithful to prayer from every minaret in Marrakech.

Mac said, "*Salat al-Maghrib*. We think of sunset as the end of our day. But it's the beginning of a new day for Muslims. Quite apropos, Hank. We're entering their world and must live on their terms. The Saudis are Sunni - Wahhabists, the most conservative branch. By God, we're paying our Arab workers to pray! All work comes to a halt at mid-day for *Salat al-Dhur* and again in the middle of the afternoon for *Salat al-Asr*."

The American military police posted at the entrance to the airfield wouldn't allow Mac to hail a taxi and take Hank into Marrakech. ATC passengers in transit were required to remain on the airfield. The Aramco VP was crestfallen.

"Hospitality is a requirement of all Muslims, but I prefer its interpretation in Marrakech."

The Americans settled down in barracks built from mud bricks, another first for Hank but (as he would soon learn) the norm in the kingdom. As he wrote out another postcard to Gloria, Hank listened as Mac rambled on.

"The Berbers assimilated invaders from all over the Mediterranean. Marrakech is far more worldly than Riyadh."

The older man wasn't fooling Hank: Mac was just sore that he couldn't go to La Mamounia, an elegant French hotel outside the old city. Denied a chance to visit one of his favorite watering holes, the Scot passed time by criticizing the colonial attitudes of the English.

"As you know, Hank, the key to success for American oil companies in the Middle East will be our willingness to treat our clients as equals rather than as coolies."

Hank watched the ash grow on Mac's last cigar. The older man dozed off after the scattered chants of the muezzins at Isha. Keyed up in Morocco as the Allies continued the invasion of France, the younger man hardly slept at all.

* * *

The following morning, Hank and Mac boarded another ATC flight to Algiers, where they were only on the ground long enough to refuel, before continuing to Cairo. The C-47 played tag with the coast of Algeria and Libya throughout the day. From one of the few cabin windows, Mac pointed out how close El Alamein was to Alexandria.

Shaking his head, he said, "Rommel could've taken Cairo if he hadn't exhausted his men and run out of gasoline."

Their plane descended over the Nile's Delta. The broad green agricultural belt was a shock to Hank's eyes after hours over the desolate coastline at the edge of the Sahara. Bayn Field, newly built east of Cairo, was crowded with other Allied aircraft. Across the tarmac, dozens of American and

British bombers and fighters being ferried to the Pacific were tied down. Armed guards marched up and down the line.

Hank and Mac tried to confirm details of their next flight to Dhahran via Iraq and Basra. But civilians weren't going to Arabia until the ATC could clear a backlog of military passengers stuck in Cairo. All around the airfield were the tents of US Marines and British Army units from Sudan and South Africa. Most of them were headed to the bleeding edge of the war in Burma. It was early evening before the two American oilmen gave up on their next flight and turned their attention to finding a room at one of the European hotels along the Nile.

In the taxi, Mac was philosophical. Cairo was a good place to kill time until they could catch another flight. For Hank, the ride to the central district was like a Warner Brothers double feature. The Army Air Force had built the airfield on the flats between the city and the Suez. He could trick himself into thinking he was in Arizona until the taxi left the military base. Then the fresh asphalt gave way to a road that looked like it was built by Romans. It narrowed and zig-zagged through souks and crumbling neighborhoods of low buildings made of concrete, stucco, and mud. Everyone seemed to live behind heavy wooden doors.

Mac said Cairo was a young city by Egyptian standards, only five thousand years old. Poor people from villages up and down the Nile clung to the edge of the modern capital. In the souks, flies covered chickens waiting to be slaughtered. Everything from camel meat to mutton hung from hooks. Baskets bigger than the seats in their taxi were filled with grain, salt, peppers, cumin, and cloves. Bolts of heavy cotton fabric shared space with bright silks and lace. Most of all, there were throngs of hungry-looking people. The children wore little more than rags. The men wore tattered thobes. The women covered their heads and dressed in shapeless skirts or robes. Pockets of laughter among friends and family interrupted long stretches of Arab men and women passing each other without expression.

Traffic slowed to a stop for an old man with a wooden cart pulled by an ox. Children pressed against the windows of the taxi begging for coins. The taxi driver honked his horn. The sound drew more children to encircle the old English sedan. A few steps away from the taxi, Hank could see the mothers of the children, keeping watch as they begged. It took an hour for them to reach the entrance to Shepheard's Hotel, Mac's first choice for the night.

The last several blocks before they reached the Nile Corniche brought them to another city, a more familiar sphere of European grandeur that was shocking to Hank after the poverty in the outer reaches of the old city. Attendants in spotless white uniforms opened both passenger doors of the taxi. Two more bellmen took the oilmen's suitcases from the boot. The lobby was filled with American and British officers in dress uniform. Well-dressed European and Egyptian women were everywhere.

At the front desk, a mustachioed Egyptian in a dark suit told them the hotel was completely full. Mac's *baksheesh* - a five-dollar bill - only yielded a phone call to the Windsor Hotel. They were assured rooms were available at the Windsor and Mac led the way back to the taxi station outside. It took their next taxi half an hour to reach the hotel, which was smaller than Shepheard's but substantial. Mac recognized it as the officer's club from the first war. Another fiver at the front desk earned them two rooms. The bellmen were as polished in their service as the staff at Shepheard's. Hank took his first bath and stretched out in the first real bed he had seen since leaving California.

Cairo, 10 June

Hank saw less of Mac after they arrived in Cairo. The Aramco VP encountered friends from the oil patch and old mates who were now senior British officers. On their third day waiting for a flight, Hank made plans to meet Mac for lunch before he left the Windsor for another reunion.

The younger oilman was adjusting to some aspects of life as an expatriate. Thousands of Europeans stranded by the war were biding their time in Cairo. Hank had learned the route from their hotel to his rendezvous with Mac. By mid-morning he was walking through Tahrir Square, passing the American University on his way through the business district to the Nile Corniche. He crossed one of the bridges to Gezira Island built by the Turks, the French, and their pocket kings. The north end featured blocks of modern apartments that ranged from Art Deco to Second Empire. Foreign embassies punctuated the residential splendor of wealthy Egyptians. In Zamalek, at least, kings and colonials had succeeded in turning Cairo into Paris on the Nile.

The heat of early summer was punishing the city. Among the palaces and museums on the south end of the island, Hank found respite in the gardens of Al Horreya. Light wafts of wind passed over the muddy water. He settled onto a shaded bench near the river and opened the book he had brought along, *Seven Pillars* by T.E. Lawrence. Used copies of the memoir had been in every book shop on Telegraph Avenue. As a kid he had heard about Lawrence of Arabia on the Lowell Thomas radio show. On a date in high school, he had seen the newsreel coverage of the adventurer's death after a motorcycle accident.

Mac arrived and registered his disapproval when he saw what Hank was reading. "You can't believe everything that bender says about the Turkish campaign, laddy."

Hank closed the book without protest as they started across the park to the restaurant. Beyond it was a dock for tour boats. There was something reassuring about the sight of the British Embassy and the US Legation on the other side of the river.

"As you know, Lawrence was backing the losers. Hussein bin Ali Al Hashimi was the last Sheik of Mecca from his lineage. They may have descended from the Prophet and been Custodians of the Two Holy Mosques for a thousand years. But after the war our man, Abdulaziz Al Saud, chased Al-Hashimi out of the Hejaz."

"The Western Province," Hank said.

"Quite right. Lawrence had two enduring accomplishments. He showed Churchill how to screw the French when they redrew the map of the Levant and Mesopotamia. And he helped Hussein's sons, Feisal and Abdullah, become the kings of Jordan and Iraq. Not that either country has any cultural or historical meaning to the Arabs. If Lawrence and the Hashemites had their way, the British would have gotten the oil concession in Arabia as well as the rest of the sheikdoms. I knew good men who died so Lloyd George and that lot could claim the Ottoman Empire. The reason - apart from more money - that Abdulaziz chose the Americans was that he didn't trust the British!"

Hank wondered if his companion thought of himself as a naturalized American or a dyed-in-the wool Scot. During their journey, Mac had flashed passports from the UK as well as the US.

"The Crown had another military advisor on the other side of the Arabian peninsula with the Saudis, St. John Philby, a linguist from the Raj who stayed with Abdulaziz after the war. He was more of an adventurer than an officer - the first European to explore *Rub' al Khali*, the Empty Quarter. Philby converted to Islam, at least for business purposes. The king gave him his second wife - Lebanese, I believe. Philby convinced him to take the Standard offer over one from the Iraqi Petroleum Company. As you know, the British government is the majority owner of IPC."

Mac gave Hank the high sign to whisper in his ear. He was a foot taller than the older man. Having killed some time at the Giza Zoo, a pitiful if historical attraction, Hank felt like a giraffe listening to a wildebeest.

"It was top-secret during the negotiations, but Philby was on the Standard payroll, our spy in Riyadh."

The maitre'd at the restaurant seated them at a table under a canopy. They watched the muddy green river flow north, some traditional watercraft under sail, smaller ones being rowed, gas rationing a fact of life on the Nile. For all its history and centrality, no one had found petroleum in Egypt.

Their waiter brought them gin and tonic, which Mac insisted was safer than the water in Cairo. It was telling for Hank to hear the Aramco VP speak of the British as their enemy. That was the way Standard and Texaco seem to think of them: allies in the war effort but opponents in the region. As big as the ramp-up would be in the kingdom, their British competitors would make plays of their own in the Persian Gulf. To outsiders, the oil business appeared to be about instant wealth: the next gusher, the next millionaire. To insiders, it had always been about eliminating rivals who couldn't be cut in or bought out.

Mac lit another cigar, the gin and the river liberating his memories of the Great War.

"I marched behind Allenby from the Suez to Jerusalem, carried a backpack and a rifle the whole way. Lawrence's Arab Alliance may have made it to Damascus before the main column. But that's only because Allenby took his foot off the gas. The Turks were in full retreat and their German advisors couldn't make them stand and fight. The Ottomans may have been ruthless but they weren't going to die for Palestine."

Their waiter appeared with cups of tomato soup. Next they shared a whole fish from Alexandria that had been seasoned and grilled to perfection.

"As you know, the fall of the Turks simply meant there were fewer hands reaching for oil profits. We got a sliver of the pie when Gulf Oil was forced to sell its concession in Bahrain as the price of entry into the European cartel."

"The Bahrain Oil Company?"

"Quite right, my boy. The sheikdom is a British protectorate - an island, really. I'm on the concession's board because of my British citizenship."

The waiter had taken away what was left of the fish and served them tangerine sorbets. Mac ordered sherry for them both. Hank watched the wooden boats float by between Zamalek and the Corniche. The waiter returned with their sherry.

"There's too much money to be made in this part of the world to leave it all to the English."

Hank smiled at Mac: Scottish by birth and sensibility, British when it served his interests, but a big American oil man most of all.

Cairo, 13 June

Hank and Mac finally caught an ATC flight to a British airfield west of Baghdad. After changing planes and refueling in Basra, they began their final leg to Dhahran. Even then, looking through one of the portals of the C-47, the Arabian peninsula appeared endless to the impatient engineer. The kingdom was three times the size of Texas and Al-Hasa, the Eastern Province, was immensely flat.

"You can see why we've spent the last year haggling with our own government about who's going to build the pipeline to the Mediterranean," Mac said. "It's a straight shot for a thousand miles."

Hank began to doubt that the Earth was round. Over the horizon, a tectonic thrust had formed the Red Sea and the mountains of the Hejaz, tilting the rest of the Arabian peninsula towards the Persian Gulf. He became aware they were being watched.

A driller named Powell had boarded with them in Cairo. He was a thick man with a weathered face covered by a worn fedora. Hank sensed that Powell hated Mac's accent without recognizing it as Scottish. Men like him hated those with clean hands who claimed to be oilmen. Every time the Scot said *as you know*, contempt appeared on Powell's ugly face.

Hank had known a lot of men like Powell that weren't wildcatters. They were ranch hands from the rolling hills around Martinez that picked on Italians. They were refinery workers transferred to the night shift in Avon for making trouble during the day. They were Teamsters in Richmond who didn't drive trucks. Onboard the C-47, Hank was glad that Powell wouldn't work for him in Ras Tanura. If he did, he knew he would have to fight the driller or fire him.

A lot of wildcatters thrived beyond the reach of civilization. They hated most people and they hated most social structures. There were no more frontiers in the Lower 48. Men like Powell struggled to make a living by hunting or trapping. Wildcatting afforded them a way of inflicting an acceptable form of violence upon Nature. They could make good money if they could pipe a hole a thousand feet deep. They could shoot anything that moved in the wilderness as they drilled. And they could make a lot of money if they knew how to lure crude out of its hiding places. Powell was such a man. And the Eastern Province was just another wild place for him to conquer.

The last hour between Basra and Dhahran dragged on. From one of the few windows in the transport, Hank and Mac took turns looking at the desert below. In the late afternoon, the only signs of life came from the drilling rigs. As soon as the Saudi crude reached the surface, its gases were being flared off. The fires looked like torches marking their descent into Dhahran.

Mac looked troubled by the waste. He said, "Saudi crude is sour. We have to burn off the hydrogen sulfide before we can pump the feed anywhere."

The airstrip built by California Arabian was being expanded to share with the Army Air Force. Hank's first step out of the C-47 was like a punch in the face: 100% humidity with air temperatures close to 120 Fahrenheit. After freezing aloft for days in unpressurized planes, the feeling in his body was like dropping ice cream into a deep fryer.

A contingent of local executives picked them up. There were no limousines in Dhahran. The pitted Ford station wagon that carried them to American Camp had been shipped to the concession before the war. They raced through the desert with the windows down. Mac wasn't the only Aramco VP in the Eastern Province. The other was Floyd Ohliger, a pioneer from California Arabian who had been running the concession when war broke out in North Africa in the middle of 1940. Ohliger still looked freckled and baby-faced, as if he had never set foot in the deserts of Al-Hasa.

Mac introduced Hank to the welcome committee. He was too tired to remember names other than Ohliger's. Everyone seemed to know, without saying so, that Mac, the only other VP in Arabia, had been sent from the States to look over Ohliger's shoulder. The Scot had made his name in San Francisco as a numbers man and Standard and Texaco were spending immense amounts of money in the kingdom.

The roads through the desert flats were graded and paved with oil to keep the dust down. When they arrived at the American Camp. Mac's bags were taken into the VIP suite, which looked little different than the other prefabricated bungalows. In Dhahran, luxury meant not having to share your bedroom or bathroom. Hank was taken to one of the bunkhouses for new arrivals, the fourth in a room designed for two. The blessed feature of each room was a swamp cooler that dropped the gulf air to eighty degrees. His guide pointed to his bunk and he collapsed into it, sleeping through the rest of his first day in the kingdom.

Dhahran, 15 June

At first glance, Aramco headquarters reminded Hank of the Standard operation west of Bakersfield. Instead of dry marshland, where the Kern River disappeared, the Persian Gulf was a few miles east. The smell of the sea was thick in the boiling air. In every other direction, all Hank could see were rocky plains. Machine shops and clusters of prefabricated offices and single-story housing for workers dotted the desert floor. Warehouses fabricated from corrugated metal were the largest structures in camp. African soldiers with rifles and white robes stood guard at the gates. Overhead, a banner in Arabic celebrated the union of the Americans and Abdulaziz, the founding king, as Allah's blessing. General laborers in familiar oilfield attire covered their heads with ghutras.

After striking oil on the island sheikdom of Bahrain, geologists like Davies had been fascinated by the domes on the Arabian mainland. With their binoculars, they could see the classic silhouettes associated with petroleum deposits. The formations the Arabs called *jabals* were visible around Dammam, less than twenty nautical miles away. Farther north on the Arabian peninsula, oil tars bubbled on the sands of Kuwait, another sheikdom under the protection of the British.

In 1933, after a negotiation that was more like a crooked poker game than an auction, Abdulaziz chose Standard over the British bidder, IPC. California Arabian spent the rest of the decade mapping the uncharted Eastern Province. They perfected core drilling to explore its subterranean geology. They began drilling around the foot of the jabal in Dammam. It had taken four years to make their first big strike at unprecedented depth, Dammam #7. But within a few years of small-scale production, the beginning of WWII prevented Standard and Texaco from recouping the millions they had invested in Arabia.

Hank's first night ended when he was awakened by Fajr, the pre-dawn call to prayer from Saudi Camp. All four of the new arrivals in the bunkroom were unsettled by the sound of lilting Arabic at the beginning of their first day in the concession.

Powell bit off a chew of tobacco before sitting up in his bunk. For the wildcatter, civility meant spitting the worked-out chew tobacco from his mouth into an empty Coke bottle. All the new men shared a dormitory bathroom with half a dozen other bunkrooms in the temporary building. After washing up in silence, Hank and Powell and the others went looking for the Dining Hall.

The early summer sun was still low in the eastern sky. But the refreshing feeling of Hank's shave was extinguished by the heat and humidity. Arab workers were beginning to appear in the concession headquarters. If there was a ditch to be dug or masonry to be carried, an Arab was doing it. But inside the American Camp in Dhahran, the domestic chores in the bunkhouses and the kitchen were being done by male foreigners. The cooks were from the oil patch in the Dutch East Indies, displaced by the war.

The cultural legacy of the Hundred Men, the hardy oilmen who sat out the war in Dhahran, was egalitarian. Rank appeared to have little meaning and few privileges in

American Camp. One exception was that the drillers had their own table service. Their schedules demanded it. If the company had learned anything about the Arab Layer, it was that foremen drilling new sites had to pay attention to the lacunae in the limestone, day and night, to forestall the kinds of problems that had taken years to solve.

Powell filled a tray with food and abandoned Hank for a couple of wildcatters he had worked with in the Panhandle. For the next few days, he steered clear of Powell. Men like him left a trail of broken people behind them: women who made the mistake of taking his money, men who made the mistake of drinking with him, rig workers who made the mistake of thinking he would treat them fairly for an honest day's labor. Arabia was just another godforsaken place where Powell could earn top pay.

The breakfast spread in the Dining Hall comforted men who were thousands of miles from home. The coffee was from the highlands of the British colony in Kenya, savory and strong. The only place in the Eastern Province where non-Muslims could choose bacon or ham was the American Camp. Fresh eggs were flown in from India. Malay cooks carried platters of pancakes. The end of the cafeteria line had plenty of butter (on ice) and jars full of maple syrup and honey.

Dhahran, 19 June

Hank's first week was classroom training that Aramco had polished over its first decade. The concession managers weren't trying to teach experienced drillers, refiners, or engineers how to do their jobs. There were no rookies in the kingdom. For many of the new hires, the most significant orientation was to the concession work week. To honor Al-Jumu'ah, the Islamic day of congregational prayer, Friday was the only day off in a six-day work week. It was a practical decision since all Muslims were expected to attend the mid-day prayer on Friday. The lunch break was aligned with Salat al-Dhur, the mid-day prayers. All work stopped in the middle of the afternoon for Salat al-Asr. Workdays began early to minimize the sun's effect but drilling was more open-ended. Crude oil under tremendous pressure in the ground knew no schedules.

Speakers from every division warned them about their conduct. For Hank, the most memorable was Tom Barger, the head of government relations. The lanky Dakotan had a winning smile and spoke with understated confidence about everything that mattered in the concession. Mac said he was a mining engineer by training but a polymath by nature: surveyor, explorer, biologist, hunter, hydrologist, and linguist. He was second only to Ohliger in diplomacy with the governor of the Eastern Province, Saud bin Abdullah bin

Jiluwi, who ruled on behalf of his father's first cousin, the founding king. Barger was a welcome guest in the palaces of Al-Saud in Jeddah and Riyadh. But the warnings of Aramco's rising star were passionate.

"Interactions with your fellow Arab workers are crucial. In Arab culture, the sheiks see themselves as servants to their tribesmen. Aramco wants to serve our Arabs workers.

"Most Arab tribesmen don't think of themselves as Saudis. Most of the people of the Eastern Province are still nomadic. Few Bedouins can read or write their own language. They've survived some of the harshest conditions in the world for centuries. The *bedu* are immensely patient with Allah. They're proud of their ancestors and traditions. Things that might seem innocent in the States may insult them.

"The kingdom is a theocracy. The only constitution is Sharia law. The Saudis installed Wahhabism, a more conservative form of Islam than the one practiced in Mecca since the Dark Ages. Most of the villages along the gulf practice Shia Islam, which the king tolerates. But our rights as Christians aren't protected in the kingdom. In fact, we aren't allowed to practice any religion but Islam in the concession.

"Never touch an Arab worker. Consult with your superior before any harsh discipline. Honor all their religious practices, even if they disrupt drilling and operations.

"Aramco is counting on you to do your job well. We're all working overtime to get our jobs done. We're guests in the kingdom. The livelihood of every employee depends on how each American behaves. Protecting the concession - and winning the war - is everyone's job!"

Dhahran, 1 July

A Jordanian, Ammar bin Qasim Al Hashimi, was assigned to be Hank's secretary and interpreter. Since most of the residents of Al-Hasa were illiterate, clerical work was done by men from other parts of the Muslim world. Arabs and Pakistanis educated in British protectorates accounted for most of Aramco's office workers.

During their first meeting at Aramco headquarters, Hank's new assistant looked too civilized to last long in the desert. He was taller than nomadic Arabs and wore prescription glasses, a rarity beyond the ruling Saudis. His ghutra was different than most of the headdresses Hank had seen in Dhahran and he dressed in western khakis with a white shirt. Most of the Arabs working around headquarters were barefoot; Ammar wore sandals on tender-looking feet.

Hank and Ammar traveled to Ras Tanura in a pre-war Ford sedan that they picked up from the automotive shop in Dhahran. None of the four tires matched. The mechanic who handed him the keys proudly said that he had rebuilt the cracked cylinders with scraps of tubular steel.

The road between Dhahran and Ras Tanura was no more than an ancient camel track that had been rolled and oiled. The terrain along the gulf was barren and flat, monotonous even for a newcomer. A Bechtel road crew was widening it for the countless cars and trucks to follow. Shards of flint were being used to fill the ruts. In the hills to the north, Bechtel was opening the first quarry for the aggregate rock needed for cement and stronger roadways.

A province floating on crude oil should have been able to produce enough asphalt to pave the entire coastline. But the tea kettle in Ras Tanura hadn't been designed to produce it. All the petroleum products needed in the Eastern Province were still being shipped on barges from Bahrain. One of Aramco's first goals was to get the tiny pre-war refinery back online.

As they drove, Hank's head began to spin. At first, he thought it was because he was thinking too much about the company's goal of producing half a million barrels of oil a month. He put his worries about timelines and material aside and turned to an introductory conversation with his new assistant.

"Were you born in Jordan?"

Ammar eyed him warily. "I am Hejazi, born in Medina."

"You're a Hashemite?"

Ammar nodded. He seemed surprised that an American would know about the branch of Islam displaced by Abdulaziz and the Ikhwan, his army of Wahhabi zealots.

"Your family followed Hussein and his sons to Jordan?"

Ammar gazed at the whitewater in the distance. "It was safer there."

Hank's assistant was an advanced practitioner of the art of being cordial and cautious at the same time. The American was learning that Arabs wouldn't speak against Al-Saud to strangers. Men like Ammar thought of themselves as members of their ancestral tribe, not Saudis.

"Were you raised in Amman?"

"Yes."

"And you learned English in school?"

"Yes. A British school, with instructors from Cairo."

"Are you a citizen of Saudi Arabia?"

48

Anger flashed across Ammar's face, then receded. "I am a guest of Al-Saud, like you. Would you like to see my visa?" He started to pull a Jordanian passport out of his breast pocket.

"No. No."

There was silence for a long time, the wind coming through the open windows of the Ford like a furnace blast. The American decided to make the kind of gesture that distinguished his countrymen from the British in the eyes of most Arabs.

"You can call me Hank."

Ammar nodded and repeated his name politely. But it still sounded something nasty he brought up from the back of his throat.

In Dhahran, Hank had learned that there were four different characters in Arabic that equate to *Hha* in English. H alone had an entirely different pronunciation - *Heh*. Ammar was just the first of many Arabs that Hank would meet that politely repeated his Christian name as if they were spitting it out. He pulled over to the side of the lonely road, having spent his first week in Dhahran being told how important it was to avoid offending Arabs. His second week had been a crash course in Arabic for managers and foremen. But he still resorted to pantomime to teach Ammar how to say his name.

Hank inhaled slowly through his nose and smiled patiently as he took off his glasses. Then he gently clouded the lens with his breath, repeating the American English version of his name as he cleaned them with a handkerchief.

Hhank.

Ammar earnestly repeated the first name of his new boss, borrowing a softer diacritic from the Hejazi dialect.

"Very good!"

Without taxing the rebuilt engine, Hank pulled back on the road. Ammar seemed to reassess him as they continued

49

north. They were from different worlds but were no longer complete strangers. Ammar was still guarded, but less so. Like most Arabs who had only dealt with the British, he seemed accustomed to being patronized. Hank knew there had only been a few Americans in the office where Ammar worked in Manama.

"You studied law at the American University in Beirut?"

Ammar became somber. "Until the war."

The conflict in North Africa had brought an end to Ammar's studies. Mac had spent hours talking to Hank about the region and the war on their way to Dhahran. Less blood had been shed in the Middle East than elsewhere but starvation and suffering were still widespread. Britain and the US had struggled to prevent famine in Arabia without allowing each other to gain a political advantage in Riyadh. In 1943, before FDR approved the kingdom for Lend Lease, the US sent wheat for the kingdom through the British, who kept the wheat and sent the Saudis rice they didn't want.

"It must have been a blessing when Bapco recruited you for Lebanon."

"*Allah karim.*" Allah is generous.

"And you were working as a clerk in Bahrain before they transferred you to Ras Tanura?"

"They thought I could be helpful to you because I am familiar with the pipeline."

The first submarine pipeline from Ras Tanura to the Bapco refinery in Bahrain had been finished before the US entered the war. Since then, most of the royalties paid to the Saudis was for crude oil pumped to Bahrain, where it was refined into fuel oil and gasoline for the US military. Hank was grateful that Ammar knew who was on the other end of his telephone calls to Bapco.

The drive to Ras Tanura was the American's first prolonged exposure to the fury of early summer on the Persian Gulf. In Dhahran, the bunkhouses, offices, and Dining Hall had all been equipped with swamp coolers. Now Hank was getting parboiled at fifty miles an hour. His ears began to ring. His head began to feel like it was being squeezed. About the time he caught sight of the tea kettle, Hank began to taste bile mixed with bacon and eggs from breakfast in the back of his throat. The combination of the heat and the puny scale of the only refinery in Saudi Arabia was making him nauseated.

Ras Tanura made Dhahran look like San Francisco. The Aramco complex was little more than trailers and sheds with one row of prefabricated bunkhouses and offices. In a neighboring fishing village, there was a small mosque with a minaret no taller than the tea kettle still. Clustered around the mosque were mud brick dwellings and a wider swath of shelters made from scraps of wood and palm fronds, barastis. Hank had spent hours with Vukovich studying the plans. He had imagined that there would be more to see around it. Apart from the tea kettle, the only other sign of the petroleum industry was a small wharf that he could make out at the end of a south-facing spit of sand. He was seeing double by then; there were two wharfs bobbing side by side on the grey-green bay.

Hank pulled over to the side of the road and half-fell, half-crawled out of the car. The heat rising from the oiled road burned his hands and knees. Flatbed trucks loaded with barrels of crude oil and building supplies zoomed by. Ammar looked at him in confusion and then alarm. The American's pallor added to his assistant's anxiety. He dashed around the back of the Ford, opening a canteen of water that he offered his new boss.

"Drink, Hank."

Hank threw up his first sip. His breakfast began to cook a second time on the crust of oil spilling over the edge of the roadway. Time slowed down. The waves of nausea in his gut kept time with the soft splash of the waves in Tarout Bay.

When he began to feel like he might survive, he looked at the foamy surge a few meters away.

Ammar convinced Hank he could cool off faster if he stepped into the sea. He walked beside the long-legged American as they slowly entered the waves. The water was as warm as the baths that Gloria made for Peter when he was a baby. Hank ducked under a wave and then cleared both sides of his nose. In the distance, flying fish scurried on the surface of the bay. His head was still throbbing but there was only one horizon now. The strange world stopped spinning.

Ammar walked him back to the Ford, his arm around his boss's back, whose legs were still wobbly. He helped Hank into the passenger seat and drove the rest of the way. As soon as they began to gain speed over the last few kilometers to their camp, Hank began to feel better; the flop sweat on the back of his neck dried, the numbness in his hands and feet ebbed. By the time they arrived, the American's clothes were no longer dripping with sea water. He finished one canteen of water and then another.

In the concession's medical terminology, the episode would be called *moderate hyperthermia without permanent organ injury*. But for Hank, it was just the first day of work in Ras Tanura.

Ras Tanura, 2 July

Before they left Dhahran, one of the Pakistani clerks had given Ammar a map showing the location of Hank's quarters in Ras Tanura. His new boss would share a bedroom in a bunkhouse with only one other American - a privilege when most slept four to six in a room. When they arrived, both bunks were empty. Ammar helped Hank lay down on one, his legs extending beyond the metal frame.

"Why don't you take the other one?"

Ammar had shaken his head. He could tell that Hank was still ill from the heat. "It is not permitted. I must go to Saudi Camp."

"Sorry, you're probably right."

Ammar made sure that there was fresh water by Hank's bed. He went to the Dining Hall in American Camp and asked the Chinese cook for saltine crackers and a sandwich in case Hank's appetite returned that evening. Then he wished him a goodnight after promising to return the following morning after the Fajr prayer.

The Saudi soldiers guarding the Aramco complex looked indifferently at Ammar as he walked by on his way to Saudi Camp. The encampment's name was a misnomer. Few of its residents were kinsmen of Al-Saud. Most were Arabs from nomadic tribes in the Eastern Province. The rest were Muslims from other countries like the Pakistani clerks. The grounds were little more than a few unfenced acres on the edge of the old fishing village. There were no permanent buildings. Apart from coastal Shia, most of the men in Saudi Camp were Bedouins who slept in black tents they had carried with them from other parts of the province. For the most part, the bedu lived with friends and relatives from their own *wadis,* the oases visited by their tribes for generations.

Ammar knew his fellow Muslims might offer him shelter for the night. But they would not trust him or welcome him for long. He was *hadhari*, a city dweller, corrupted by western ways. To be bedu was to believe in a simpler life, closer to Allah and the teachings of the Prophet. Most of the men in Saudi Camp thought this was only possible in the desert, moving as one needed with one's goats and camels and as few possessions as possible. To be hadhari could lead to being no better than the Christians in American Camp. Were it not for the drought that killed so many of their animals, most of the men in Saudi Camp would never have left their homes for Aramco.

Apart from the tents, the only structures in Saudi Camp were the barastis. Ammar came to a cluster occupied by other clerks and interpreters. Many of them were British-educated Muslims from Karachi or Hyderabad. A face or two he recognized from Dhahran or Manama. Since most of the bedu laborers were illiterate, Ammar hoped he would have fewer differences with educated men from other countries. He didn't speak Urdu. Most of the Pakistanis spoke little Arabic. It was easier to communicate in English, which they had all learned in colonial schools.

During the Maghrib prayer at sunset, Ammar met another Hejazi named Mohammed who invited him to be his guest. His host offered him water from a clay pot and shared his supper of rice and dates. Mohammed told him that he had taken over a barasti that had been abandoned by day laborers who quit arduous jobs in Ras Tanura. The Arab workers were leaving the concession even faster than the Americans, many of whom lasted only a few weeks in Al-Hasa.

Ammar and Mohammed shared their bewilderment at being back in Arabia. Hashemites who remained unwelcome by Al-Saud in their own province didn't trust their acceptance on the other side of the kingdom. They still felt a lifetime away from their homeland, the Hejaz, even if Abdulaziz had united every province in Arabia.

Mohammed had been educated in Jordan like Ammar. His family had lived in Jeddah for generations before. They were about the same age, though Mohammed was plumper and had thinning hair. He worked for Tommy Lanier, the refinery manager who shared a bunkroom and office with Hank. Mohammed described Lanier as a terrible human being. Ammar reported that Hank - praise be to Allah - was not yet terrible.

Ammar had brought his bedding with him in the Ford from Dhahran. He spread it on a fraying mat of woven reeds that the barasti's previous occupants left behind. He and Mohammed ate and drank, laughed at a few jokes about the *Mericans*, and soon fell asleep.

Palo Alto, 2 July

A few leafy blocks from the Stanford campus, Gloria and Peter had taken over the north end of the second floor of her parents' home. Her son slept in the room in which she had grown up, her mother having taken inordinate pleasure in eradicating the vestiges of Gloria's childhood. She had been given the guest bedroom, a larger suite with a bathroom she didn't have to share. From the windows overlooking the street she could see Hank's Oldsmobile in the circular driveway. The white convertible reassured Gloria, easing her sense of entrapment living with her parents again. Before she met Hank, it would have been unthinkable for her to become a working mother and a single parent. Now her future - as well as Peter's - depended on whether the war ever ended and her husband returned from Arabia. In the meantime, Hank's car was the key to her escape plan. If the Japanese invaded or she simply couldn't stand her mother another minute, Gloria took comfort in knowing that she could grab Peter and leave.

Having struggled through the early years of the Great Depression, Hank took pride in being "a good provider." Despising her own caste - the *haute bourgeoisie*, her parents most of all - Gloria was annoyed by her husband's euphemism. But after he boarded the train east in Oakland, she had been grateful when she climbed behind the wheel of his convertible to see that he had (illegally) topped off the gas tank at the refinery in Richmond. In a small way, it made her fall back in love with Hank: his concern for Gloria and Peter had overridden his law-abiding nature.

Because of her work at OWI, Gloria had known as well as Hank when gas rationing began that the real US shortage had been rubber. The Japanese had seized the rubber plantations in the East Indies and Americans had to make do with the tires they had. Two years later, most of which the Olds had spent in their garage in Montclair, the tires still looked new. But to Gloria's alarm, her husband's pride and joy burned a third of a tank of fuel between Oakland and Palo Alto. The original quota in 1942 for private automobiles had been four gallons per week. Hank had proffered the recent cut to three as proof of the necessity of developing Arabian oil. Now that the Olds was with Gloria and Peter in Palo Alto, she kept the tank topped off, rarely taking Hank's car out of the driveway.

Americans weren't celebrating the Fourth of July for the third year in a row. There would be no fireworks displays for Peter. Patriotic citizens like Gloria were expected to show up for work on Tuesday - especially if they worked for government agencies like OWI. She had set aside Sunday to spend with her son, promising to take him to Lake Lagunita, the western frontier of the university campus. Despite the heat of summer, there was still enough water in the reservoir for Gloria and Peter to rent a canoe and while away the afternoon.

At the last minute, Peter begged Gloria to let her father's golden retriever come along. She found it impossible to refuse her only child. Her father let the dog hop into the back seat of the convertible after she promised to look after Ranger as well as Peter.

When she was younger, Gloria would have avoided the sun so close to the summer solstice because she was prone to migraines. But one of the curious blessings of motherhood was that Gloria had become less sensitive to the bright lights that triggered her worst headaches. Day trips with Hank in the convertible had become one of their most reliable pleasures as young parents. Through trial and error, she had learned to wear sunglasses, a wide-billed hat, and fortify herself with seltzer and iced coffee before venturing out on summer days. And it *was* a glorious day: the top down on the Olds, the Mission Revival architecture of the central campus looming beyond the Arboretum, the wind washing over her and Peter, Ranger luxuriating with his nose in the air.

Her parents had met at Stanford, the kind of alumni that never ventured far from campus, a shrine to their enlightenment and love, like a couple from Harvard and Radcliffe who could only live in Cambridge. They had married while her father was finishing law school; Gloria had been born the following year. Her mother was the youngest child of a surgeon from Paris, a republican who had escaped the Commune and gone on to great success in San Francisco. Her father was a *Californiano*, his career in property law inspired by the Spanish land grant his family lost after the Gold Rush.

Gloria had always loved the foothills covered with scrub oak surrounding the west side of the campus. Leland Stanford had relentlessly added thousands of acres to the stock farm he set aside for a university in honor of his son. Lake Lagunita was a manmade reservoir that dated to the original ranch. In 1943, when record rainfall in the valley, it saved the entire campus from flooding. She parked near the wooden boathouse that had collapsed during the Water Carnival a few years before the war. Canoes were still available to rent from a shack at the edge of the lake. Peter climbed in first, pulling Ranger in behind him. The aging attendant handed two paddles to Gloria and then gave them a shove off the muddy shore.

Peter gamely pulled at the first few inches under the water's surface, choking up on the handle of the paddle that was nearly as big as he was. He reminded Gloria of Hank in so many ways, always ready to pitch in, happy to be part of any team, large or small. Ranger barked at the geese and gulls that came and went, landing just long enough to drive the dog mad again. A breeze off the Pacific came up. In the distance Gloria could see fog clinging to the coastal range, adding to the pleasure of the afternoon.

"I wish Daddy were here."

"We miss him, don't we?"

"Yes. Can I draw him a picture of the lake?"

"No dear. It's against the rules with V-mail."

"What's V-mail?"

"It's a special way to send letters to soldiers and workers overseas. You can't use crayons or paint with watercolors."

"But that's not fair!"

"If you tell me what to say, I can write him a letter. What would you like to tell him?"

"Dear Daddy."

"Yes?"

"Mommy and I and Ranger are having a good time at the lake."

"That's good. What else?"

"I wish you were here to paddle for me."

"Me too," Gloria laughed.

"I hope you have fireworks on the Fourth of July. They won't let us have any here."

"Anything else?"

"Please come home soon. I miss you and so does Mommy."

Gloria placed the paddle across her lap. The canoe began to drift. Peter turned to look at his mother. Clouds were gathering in her mind.

"Why are you crying?"

"I'm not crying, dear. I'm just a little sad. Would you like to explore?"

"Yes!"

The west side of the campus beyond the reservoir was still wild. The reeds were still green at the water's edge but the tall grass on the hillside was golden dry, fairy-like spores wafting across the lake, the onshore breeze building off the unseen ocean. Peter and Ranger bolted for the tree line. None of them recognized the poison oak that was just beginning to turn from green to amber and red.

Gloria needed a moment to herself. She would dutifully transcribe Peter's words to Hank. She would fold the sheet of V-mail she would post to Hank's APO in Dhahran, then tuck away the secret she couldn't share with her son or her husband - or her parents, for that matter. By the time Peter and Ranger were back in the canoe, she had composed herself. The wind at her back helped her paddle to the east side of the reservoir. She welcomed the fatigue she felt by the time she turned in the canoe. That night she had less than usual to say over drinks and dinner with her parents, then went to bed early. But she slept poorly, as she seemed to most nights since Hank's departure. Weekends were usually better, her mind and body giving way after the long days at the New Caledonia desk, and all the hotels and taxis and last-minute dashes to the Transbay Terminal.

Two days later, the only fireworks were invisible, erupting from the angry rash covering Peter's arms and legs. He even had poison oak on his face and neck. But after her mother bathed her grandson in oatmeal and Gloria slathered him with calamine lotion, at least there would be another amusing letter to Hank, another distraction from the truth that only she could know.

Ras Tanura, 5 July

There had been less to celebrate on the Fourth in Arabia than in the States. The concession offered the Americans hotdogs and hamburgers to go along with their beer. And there was no shortage of fireworks on Tarout Bay: Aramco set off a barge loaded with roman candles from Bombay. But the evening made Hank yearn for Gloria more than ever. When he fell asleep, he dreamed about taking Peter to watch the San Francisco Seals play the Oakland Oaks. Then he was awakened by the call for the Fajr prayer ringing out from the only mosque in Ras Tanura. Muslim clerics who condemned all other electrical devices made exceptions for the battery-operated bullhorns they carried to the minarets.

Lanier, the refinery manager with whom Hank was sharing a room, had worked in Mexico and Venezuela before Texaco transferred him to Ras Tanura. When he arrived with Ammar, Lanier was in Bahrain, dealing with his counterparts in the Bapco refinery. Alone for the first time since arriving in the kingdom, Hank had slept like a rock. Then Lanier showed up and flopped into the other bunk. It didn't take long for his roommate to figure out that Lanier was always looking for a reason to go Manama. The British and Bahrainis offered the refiner better selections of whiskey and women.

The string of prefabricated wooden bunkhouses in the American Camp had been hauled up the coast from Al-

Khobar in 1939, when California Arabian began exporting crude oil from Dammam. But a few weeks after D-Day, there weren't a thousand ships off the coast of Ras Tanura. Half a dozen Aramco refinery workers were sleeping in bunkhouse cubicles meant for two. The sheer numbers of sweaty bodies were defeating the swamp coolers. On the other side of the fence was an even more spartan encampment for the builders arriving from America. The only shelter for Bechtel's men were surplus British Army tents that weren't designed for the desert. Vukovich seemed to enjoy complaining to Hank that his living conditions were the worst he had endured since working on the Hoover Dam.

After being spoiled in Dhahran, Hank was losing weight eating at the American Camp at Ras Tanura. The kitchen was an open-walled shed with a tin roof. Aramco was hoarding all the decent cooks for its headquarters and dispatching the rest to the concession's hinterlands. His breakfast was a hardboiled egg, two pieces of buttered toast, and three cups of Kenyan coffee.

Unlike California in wartime, Hank commuted to work by car. The marine terminal, like the rest of the new refinery complex, was going up at the far end of a miles-long spit of sand extending south into the bay. As he drove slowly with the windows down on the unfinished road connecting the main installation with the construction site, Hank savored the feeling of being at sea.

The currents in the northern end of the Persian Gulf flowed counterclockwise. The prevailing winds also blew from north to south along the Arabian Peninsula. As a result, the finger of sand at Ras Tanura lengthened and widened every year. But the same natural forces filled Tarout Bay with sandbars that blocked the entry of keeled vessels. Bechtel was hardening several miles of the sandspit before building a causeway into the gulf for tankers to safely anchor. Then the new refinery and tank farm would be added to the complex at the south end of the point.

Hank's office was a full-length Airstream trailer on the old wharf that was rapidly becoming his home away from home. One end was an office he shared with the refinery manager, Lanier. The other end looked like a sleeper car on a train. The two men were moving towards a tacit agreement that Lanier could snore alone in the bunkroom they shared in American Camp if Hank could sleep in peace in the Airstream. In the middle of the trailer was a proper bathroom with metal fixtures: a sink, a toilet, a shower stall. Best of all, there were swamp coolers at both ends.

Ammar was admiring the splendor of the Airstream when Hank arrived in the Ford. As disorganized as he was proving to be in the office, Hank felt lucky to have the Jordanian as his translator everywhere else. After his first day touring the construction site, the American realized that the dialect of Arabic he had been taught by his Lebanese instructor in Dhahran was useless in Ras Tanura.

There were plenty of Americans and Arabs standing around on the wharf, which predated the war like the tea kettle and the feeder line from Dammam. The men from Saudi Camp seemed lost in their own country. Many of them looked too hungry and sickly to work at all. Some were ready to fight each other for something to do. Others seemed happy to be paid to do nothing at all. Dozens of Bechtel tradesmen were easily identified by their shiny new hardhats, trying to make sense of an impossible situation.

In a snafu worthy of its time, the Americans hired by Aramco and Bechtel were arriving before the precious steel approved by the US government. The same was true of most of the lumber and equipment needed to build the refinery, marine terminal, and a host of ancillary structures. As difficult as it had been for Mac and Hank to reach the Eastern Province by air, it was easier than shipping materials across the Atlantic and the Mediterranean, through the Suez Canal to the Red Sea, and around the Arabian Peninsula.

The more Hank saw of the rudimentary facilities in Ras Tanura, the more he questioned Aramco's plan. Job One was firing up the tea kettle. Job Two was putting the pre-war pipeline to Bahrain back into operation. Then the checklist continued ad infinitum; the new feeder lines from the drilling sites, the refinery product lines, the tank farm and the marine terminal. The plan called for Ras Tanura to begin operating on a larger scale in early 1945, when the new submarine pipeline to Bahrain was supposed to pump tens of thousands of barrels of Saudi crude to the expanding Bapco refinery.

Ammar followed Hank to the gulf side of the construction zone. The design called for a new causeway extending a kilometer into the gulf that would be the base of a T-shaped terminal that could simultaneously accommodate multiple tankers. But that morning, the original wharf facing the bay was only capable of handling small barges. And refined products were still flowing from Bahrain to Ras Tanura rather than the other way around.

Vukovich was offshore on a floating pile driver, installing the deep-water pylons at the future junction of the causeway and terminal. Lanier was at the water's edge, his bandy knees exposed between khaki shorts and long woolen stockings. Unlike the pioneers from California Arabian, he wouldn't be caught dead wearing anything as practical as a ghutra on his bald head. Instead, he wore a pith helmet, like a British colonial, his shorts hitched up to cover a flourishing pot belly.

Lanier was yelling at the Arab skipper of a *dhow,* one of the wooden boats with triangular sails favored by pirates and pearl divers. It was loaded with granite from a rocky point north of the bay. The boat had a crew of five along with its skipper. All of them were standing on the port side of their vessel, its bow nosed into the sand. Lanier and the skipper were both pointing at a red line painted on the side of the dhow.

The skipper only spoke Arabic. Lanier abandoned English for Creole, which didn't work as well in the Persian Gulf as it had in the Caribbean. Neither Lanier nor the captain of the dhow had much interest in what the other was trying to say.

Hank introduced Ammar to Lanier. Mohammed was already translating for his boss.

"I'm paying that A-rab by the load for that rock he's hauling. I measured his boat and calculated the tonnage he could carry without sinking. I had him paint that red line on the side. That way everybody knows when they have a full load."

Hank began to understand why the entire crew was leaning over the port side. Their combined weight made the dhow heel over until the red line was submerged. If the crew were centered on the keel, it would have been obvious that their boat was only carrying a partial load of rock for the jetty. Like any good pirate, the dhow skipper was trying to get credit for five silver riyals that Lanier had agreed to pay for each boat load of rock.

Hank knew that Lanier had already fired two Arab-speaking secretaries. Hopes were high in Dhahran that Mohammed would last longer than an Iraqi and a Pakistani who preceded him. In Arabic, he yelled down to the dhow. My boss says he will only pay five riyals for a full load!

Hank didn't need to be fluent in Arabic to understand the skipper's answer. He was pointing at the red line on the side of his boat and saying that the refinery manager had agreed to pay five riyals if the dhow was loaded to that level.

Ammar and Mohammed both waved at the crew, yelling at them to move half the crew to the starboard side of the dhow. When the men on the dhow finally shifted to the other side, the red line was a foot above the surface of the bay.

The skipper extended both of his arms in dismay; he had technically complied with his verbal contract. Hank could hear the mocking tone of the captain's words as he gestured at the open sea, Did the Merican want him to go back for more rock?

Mohammed translated. Agitated, Lanier said, "Hell no! That'll just waste more time. Tell him I'll pay him three riyals to dump that load. Then he can go back and get a full load."

Mohammed relayed the message. The men of the dhow shook their heads and sadly began tossing the rocks onto the sand. Hank could hear them grumbling to each other about the Mericans. Ammar murmured to Hank that they were complaining about Lanier being no more honorable than the British. His American boss shook his head and moved on.

Hank spent the next few hours pacing off the dimensions of the marine terminal, as if he could walk it into existence. Because of the length of his legs, it was more natural to walk off meters than yards. The Bechtel plans showed all of the major dimensions in both the British and American standards. Ammar struggled to follow Hank's footsteps in the sand. The tide was rising as they walked. Most of the spit was disappearing into the bay.

"Ammar, what does Ras Tanura mean?"

"Ras means point. Tanura means petticoat."

"Petticoat Point," Hank muttered.

Another crew appeared in a different dhow loaded with rock as they climbed back up on the wharf. Lanier glowered as they unloaded, using his binoculars to confirm that the red line painted on the side was fully submerged. But a new crew meant different tactics and other forms of trickery. The Arab sailors unloaded their chunks of granite, some bearing barnacles from their previous home. Too hastily for Lanier, they began to push off.

"No, no, no!"

The skipper looked up, raising his arms as if he could not comprehend the refinery manager.

Lanier looked at Mohammed and said, "You tell that bastard that if he wants to be paid five riyals, he better unload every god-dam rock on that boat."

Out of the refinery manager's view, Hank grinned at Ammar. He had to admire the ingenuity of the dhow's crew. They had hidden half of their load under mats in the bottom of the dhow. The skipper had decided the best tactic was to only unload half of the rocks in his dhow and aim for more round trips each day to the other beach.

Lanier turned to Hank for sympathy. "These mothers are going to steal us blind if we let them. This is your goddam causeway. Take over!"

Lanier retreated to their office, not to be seen again until dinner in the Dining Hall. Ammar and Hank spent the rest of the afternoon under the shade of a tarp lashed to the footings of a crane. The jetty was being built by hand, one rock at a time. Dozens of Bechtel road builders stood watching, useless until their heavy equipment arrived. Other barges would eventually be brought in from Bahrain and even Basra.

Hank thought back to his interview in San Francisco. Davies had pitched Ras Tanura as their country's strategic effort to fuel the final stage of the war. As he watched it progress at an excruciating crawl, Hank missed his wife's embrace, his son's laughter, and the fresh breezes from the Golden Gate at Port Richmond.

The two-stroke outboards on the dhows started sounding like farts to Hank, who was getting woozy in the heat and humidity. The captain of one of the wooden vessels continued a shouting match with Ammar. The sun was angling across the bay, the tarp above Hank's head no longer protecting him from the rays bouncing off the sea. He prayed for the announcement the Asr prayer so he could flop into his bed under the swamp cooler in his Airstream. As the minarets remained silent, he grew impatient for Ammar's translation.

"What is he saying?"

"He says that the Mericans are crazy to move rocks from the beach where Allah placed them to another."

After another ferocious summer day in Ras Tanura, Hank looked at Ammar and shook his head.

"He's probably right."

Ras Tanura, 9 July

There were only two American women in Ras Tanura, both nurses wedded to Aramco employees. Mrs. Vogel was married to Dr. Vogel, a package deal. The other nurse had fallen for a pipeline engineer while they were stranded together earlier in the war.

Gloria and Peter were half a world away. Hank warded off despair by reconciling with the massive amount of work needed to reach the goals of his country and the concession. Longer days shortened lonely nights, but delays at Ras Tanura vexed him most of all.

Steve Bechtel and Floyd Ohliger had agreed that it was best for the builders from America to have quarters of their own. When they started arriving in late spring, the only shelter that the oilmen had to offer were surplus British tents. The refinery, marine terminal, and tank farm couldn't be built until the steel arrived. The competition between Bechtel and the drillers in other parts of the concession for steel was fierce. While they waited, tradesmen sweltering all night in the ventless tents started scrounging for scraps to construct their own barastis; lumber was easier to find than steel.

It was clear to Hank that family housing in American Camp was at the bottom of the list of projects needed to get Ras Tanura operational. Like a military recruiter, Davies had lied to Hank to get him to sign up with Aramco. There were scores of more senior American staff - many of the Hundred Men - who had been waiting longer for the first crack at housing for their wives and children. Even if there were family housing in Ras Tanura, Gloria had made it clear that she wouldn't leave her work for the OWI or Peter's grandparents in Palo Alto.

There was little reason to think, when Hank could be dispassionate about it, that he would see his family until the middle of 1945, when he would be eligible for his first leave. Even then, the status of the project - and the war - would take precedence.

That night, laying on a cot in his office that allowed him to stretch out more than his bunk at the other end of the trailer, Hank re-read the first letter from Gloria delivered to his APO in Dhahran. He didn't entirely regret missing his son's first case of poison oak. He could imagine Gloria battling with her mother about whether to soak Peter all night in an oatmeal bath or dry out his rash with calamine lotion. His wife and his mother-in-law were too much alike to yield to each other. His son was the only member of the family they both loved. Gloria's V-mail seemed even more guarded than her work or military censors required. Hank wasn't convinced she missed him, no matter how many times she wrote it. The cot in his office was close enough to the swamp cooler for him to feel every bead of sweat on his skin. Trying to sleep, all he could think about was falling in love with Gloria again.

* * *

By the time Hank had been an upper division student, he was off the night shift at the refinery in Avon. Commuting daily from Martinez to Berkeley became less practical as his laboratory blocks grew longer. The most convenient housing near campus were fraternities. His size and skills made him an attractive recruit for Greek athletics. Tau Kappa Epsilon took pride in membership based on merit rather than race or wealth. In Hank's case that meant TKE needed a center on their basketball team.

At a Saturday night mixer with Tri Delta, he had been nursing a beer with his TKE teammates when he became aware of being watched. The entire purpose of Greek life was socializing - especially at events when fraternities and sororities dissolved in alcohol. Hank was used to gawkers because of his height, used to sisters whispering to each other about where he ranked in their inventory of future husbands. But Gloria was sitting alone, smoking cigarettes, fending off Hank's housemates from TKE one by one.

The most beautiful woman in the room didn't pretend she wasn't looking at him. But the feeling Gloria evoked in Hank was that he was being observed as much as desired, a handsome specimen at the zoo.

A record came on, the Fred Astaire version of "I Won't Dance." Most of the Greeks took their cue and began to pair off. Gloria remained seated across the room, legs crossed, keeping the beat in open-toed shoes. Hank threaded his way between the dancers and introduced himself. Without sharing her name, Gloria looked up at him with detached curiosity. When Hank asked her if she wanted to dance, she shook her head with false gravity.

Sweating in Ras Tanura, Hank still didn't know why he hadn't accepted defeat and walked away. Then Gloria uncrossed her legs and stood up, enjoying how close they came to being eye to eye.

"Do you want to go for a walk?" she had asked.

"Of course." Gloria took his hand and led him outside. Hank could still remember the surprising warmth of her touch. The evening was fresh enough to give him goosebumps. Still not knowing her name, he tried a few more words. "You've been watching me. It was getting unnerving."

"I'm an anthropologist. We study primitive behavior."

"You don't seem like most of the Tri Delts."

"I joined to appease my mother. She was in the Stanford chapter. My parents will never forgive me for going to Cal. Please please tell me you're not going to law school."

"I'm going to be a chemical engineer."

Relieved, she finally introduced herself and asked, "Do we have chemistry?"

"There's usually some analysis required." Only little guys could get away with being socially aggressive. Gloria stuck out her lower lip, feigning disappointment. Hank could barely keep himself from kissing her before asking, "You don't agree?"

"Not at all. It's instinctive, like the birds and the bees."

"So, you believe in ectohormones?"

"I've never heard of them but I'm sure I do."

"Ectohormones are only a theory, you know. No one's proven that biological behavior is mediated by chemical messengers."

Hank could still remember the look in Gloria's eyes when she said, "Maybe you will."

For ten blocks, he had to keep both hands in the front pockets of his trousers to hide his arousal. Under the streetlights, they walked back and forth on Piedmont Avenue, up and down Bancroft Way, occasionally circling back to check on their brethren. Hank would have followed her all night; Gloria seemed just as entertained by him. Their first encounter lasted longer than the mixer they left.

His life changed forever when she kissed him goodnight at the front door.

Over the next few months, Hank was interested in whatever she was willing to say, while she measured his every word, as if they were filling each other's hand in a card game. She had grown up in a world of privilege that she had come to disdain. He had grown up trying to replace everything he had lost as a child. She was the only person he had ever met who seemed enthralled by his father's death. He was the only person she had ever met who thought her father's legal work for Standard was interesting. Like most engineers, he believed in a world of rational design. She was a double major in anthropology and French who was disappointed by the world after *fin-de-siècle*. He had no idea who Rimbaud, Verlaine or the rest were. She had no idea how many hydrocarbons were in crude oil. Before they met, Hank thought of volatility as a physical property of molecules. Then Gloria became the most alluring and unpredictable creature imaginable.

As their graduation approached, she became anxious, the only Tri-Delt without an engagement ring. She hated the idea of remaining tethered to her parents. But she was even more intimidated by the notion of making her own way. Abandoning the bourgeoisie lost its appeal as reality loomed. He became the shelter from the storm on their horizon. If she was an unstable element in the atomic table, he was the iron that bound her. He proposed to her after she gave herself to him wantonly and repeatedly. If her parents seemed indifferent about their engagement, his mother felt vindicated by it, back among the kind of people she deserved. Most important of all, Giulia loved Gloria and Gloria adored her. At their wedding, his mother and his protector sat side by side in the front row. His mother beamed at Gloria in all her cultured beauty. Giulia gazed at Hank as if he were hers alone.

Palo Alto, 5 August

After years of standoffs, motherhood had redeemed Gloria in the eyes of her parents. They were almost as happy with her government service as they were with their first grandchild. Once she began working at the New Caledonia desk at the Presidio, they were astonished that she could juggle her obligations. The depression that plagued Gloria after Peter's birth gave way to global cataclysm; like mothers everywhere, she would do whatever was necessary to keep the war away from her son.

Gloria's father was proud of her commuting to the city Monday through Friday, even if she looked worn by the time she returned to Palo Alto. Gloria's mother was gratified that she enjoyed being around Peter more than she had as a full-time mother. And when her mother was with a gaggle of friends, she had a new expression when asked about Gloria's work for OWI, arching a penciled eyebrow and closing an imaginary zipper over her ruby-red lips, as if what went on in New Caledonia was top-secret.

What could be better than a live-in daughter with an exotic job at the Presidio and a grandson to dote on when she was away?

Hank had been in Ras Tanura for a few weeks when Gloria announced that she needed to spend Saturdays at their own home in Montclair. The fuchsias would die if not watered. Someone had to deadhead the roses and geraniums. The

74

weeds had to be pulled before they took over slopes that Hank had planted with ivy. The cute little bungalow in the hills above Oakland had to be opened to prevent mildew. Her parents wholeheartedly agreed, proud of their only daughter's newfound practicality. If Peter stayed home with them, Gloria could spend as much time in Montclair as she needed to protect (Hank's) investment.

The first Saturday in August, Gloria slept in after her long work week and then boarded a train from Palo Alto to the Transbay Terminal, where she connected on the Key Line to Oakland. What her parents didn't know - would never know, she hoped - was that Gloria was joined in San Francisco by a co-worker from the New Caledonia desk, Thierry de Lataillade, who accompanied her to Montclair. His bona fides as an OWI propagandist were impeccable. Thierry had arrived in the French colonies in the Pacific after escaping arrest in Marseilles and then Algiers for financial schemes based on elaborate lies. Early in the war, he had been thrown out of Nouméa by the last Vichy governor for supporting the Free French.

Before they became lovers, Gloria asked Thierry if his politics had anything to do with the money he owed prominent supporters of Marshall Pétain. He had become indignant without denying that he swindled some of the wealthiest Caldoche. But after being deported from New Caledonia, he had saved the lives of real French patriots when their ship, flying an Australian flag, was torpedoed by a Japanese submarine. Staying afloat was one of Thierry's many talents; his sense of timing was another. After a week on a life raft, he had arrived in Auckland within a month of Pearl Harbor, when Americans needed heroes as much as the British colonials in the Pacific.

The OWI recruited Thierry because of his familiarity with the racial and cultural sensitivities of the French in Nouméa. Gloria was the countervailing force on the other side of the station, the expert on the native Melanesian tribes, the Kanak. As a con artist, Thierry was well versed in appealing to French egos, the subtext for most of the statements from the US military. Gloria's assignment was to eradicate his most offensive colonial phrases before they could be heard by the larger indigenous population on the American radio station. As his counterparty, she had been cautious in her professional dealings with the Frenchman at first. But as time went by their debates about messaging the Caldoche and the Kanak began to feel like intimate spats.

More to the point, the longer that Gloria worked for OWI, the harder it became for her to reconcile the whole truth from half-truths. The problem extended far beyond the Pacific branch. The OWI managed government communications on the homefront as well as overseas. Republicans (like her parents) were increasingly uncomfortable with how her agency defended FDR's takeover of the domestic economy. But no one in Washington or the Presidio seemed to have any doubts about telling the French and the Melanesians whatever was deemed to be in the best interests of America. The New Caledonia desk's mission was duplicitous: soothing French sensibilities about the US presence in their colony without inspiring the Kanak to demand independence. Gloria had lost count of the misleading announcements and proposals they had delivered in the name of the war effort. Realities that she wanted to translate into nuanced French were edited or deleted by their superiors. Thierry, a lifelong fraud, was happy to be legitimized by the Allies. He was far less attached to their work product than Gloria. As her doubts grew about her role at the New Caledonia desk, Thierry was uniquely positioned to console her in ways that her husband couldn't.

There were collateral benefits working for the OWI, after all. The Resistance smuggled out the newest books and periodicals from France, most of which De Gaulle dismissed before handing them over to the intelligence services of his allies. Thierry, whose mother was Algerian, had given Gloria a rare copy of *L'Étranger*. Albert Camus had been a new arrival on the French literary scene before the war. She was amazed that the philosopher had been able to publish his first novel in occupied Paris. Somehow the Nazi and Vichy censors thought the hypocrisy of colonial Algeria reflected only on the regime they had replaced.

Thierry knew that Gloria would respond to the story of an atheist condemned for a meaningless murder. Part of the Frenchman's appeal to the American woman - lost in a sea of illusions, clinging to her marriage like a life preserver - was that he couldn't have been more different than her husband. At one of her Friday-night reunions with Hank, when she mentioned how much she liked Camus, he shook his head. How could the French be so enthusiastic about life when they claimed to be so indifferent? Her husband lived in a world of black and white, while Thierry and Gloria worked in shades of grey, some hues more appealing than others.

The oldest form of propaganda were the lies that lovers told each other. Like other idioms they gained power through repetition. Gloria had surrendered to Thierry's while Hank was still working in Richmond. By then, the first cup of coffee of the intra-mural combatants had turned into gallons, every drop of which would have tasted better in Paris. One shared cigarette had turned into a stolen carton. Long walks on Lovers' Lane at the Presidio were replaced by hectic encounters - *cinq a sept* - in downtown hotels. A raven-haired prostitute who had seen Gloria with Thierry in a seedy lobby winked when she saw them again on Geary one night.

Since they were only together on weekends, it had been easier for Gloria to hide her affair from Hank. And when Aramco offered her husband a job in Ras Tanura, Gloria's gesture of wifely generosity belied her sense of guilt. The only one who really suffered when Hank left was Peter and her parents helped her make up for that. But the truth was that her husband's transfer allowed her to open her arms to her lover, the ultimate indulgence.

When Gloria and Thierry reached the front door of the bungalow in Montclair, she showed him where the key was hidden. Inside, the shuttered home had trapped the heat of summer. They didn't open the windows until they had stripped off their clothes, explored each other's bodies at their leisure, and made love on a divan handed down by her mother. She kept the shades drawn on the windows, hiding their nakedness from hillside neighbors, if not the sounds of their pleasure.

Gloria had had no other lovers as a married woman, though loyalty meant less to her than her husband. For all his size and strength, Hank had always been a careful, predictable lover. Thierry, the interloper she invited to their home, was savage by comparison. But Gloria was frightened only by the degree of her own excitement, her own need. Afterwards, when she and Thierry were both exhausted and covered with sweat, Gloria found a robe in the bathroom and finally opened the windows and screen doors.

Sunlight filled the bungalow but no breezes blessed them. She turned on the fan in the kitchen and made a pitcher of lemonade to share with Thierry. Then Gloria put on Bermuda shorts and a light muslin blouse to water her garden. Thierry smoked out of view on the back porch, listening to her hum along with the radio, watching her pluck wilted flowers in her bare feet. Then they made love again before Gloria took a bath, returning to Palo Alto as early in the afternoon as she could tear herself away. Thierry took his time cleaning up the mess they had made, showering and dressing before closing the windows and drapes in every room, hiding the key by the front door on his way back to San Francisco.

Ras Tanura, 10 August

As more Americans quit or got fired within weeks of arriving and the delays in crucial materials for drilling and refining continued, the brass in Dhahran decided to address the only problem they had a chance of solving. The lack of decent housing in the most ferocious month of the summer in the desert was threatening the plans of the oilmen as well their builders.

By the end of their first week, all hands in the concession - including the drillers - had put up a dozen new buildings in the Bechtel annex of American Camp in Ras Tanura. Ferguson told the cooks to break out the beer on Thursday night, after the workers in Saudi Camp began to make their way home for their day off. The food in American Camp was no better than usual, corned beef has and boiled potatoes, but the Americans washed it down with beer imported from Bahrain that lasted longer than second helpings from the kitchen.

After dinner everyone was happy enough until sunset. But as the evening continued, wildcatters from Oklahoma and refiners from Texas weren't mixing well with welders from California or carpenters from Oregon. Anthropologists like Gloria could explain why rednecks descended from Scots Irish might clash with recent immigrants from Europe, but no one cared once fists were flying. Her husband happened to see the first few sparks.

Hank was listening to a geophysicist from MIT complain about his blisters when he saw Powell begin clenching his fists. There was something about a particular riveter that he didn't like. How many beers Powell drank was irrelevant. The wildcatter was having too good of a time after going too long without being able to give the ragheads at his drilling site what they deserved.

The pushing and shoving between Powell and the Bechtel man, whose name was Wisniewski, wasn't the problem. Then the Pole broke off a bottle of beer. The loud chatter in the rest of the room turned into a roar as the two men circled each other in the middle of the room. Cochrane, the teetotalling geophysicist with blisters, was the first to exit. Wisniewski drew first blood, slashing the wildcatter on his left shoulder. Powell was enraged by the sight of it and pulled a switchblade out of his boot. He stabbed Wisniewski in the belly. The Dining Hall lapsed into silence as the Pole went to his knees and then collapsed.

The rest of the crowd drew back into the corners. Four men from Aramco's security unit suddenly appeared, all wearing matching khaki, all bigger than the ATC sergeant from the Copacabana. Each of them carried police-style billy clubs. They were on Powell, sodden with beer and blood, before he saw them. He didn't go down with the first strike but went to his hands and knees after a shower of blows from all four of the men standing over him. By the time they had knocked him out, Dr. Vogel was asking for help rolling over Wisniewski to evaluate the stab wound to his belly.

Ohliger and Ferguson herded the rest of the men out of the Dining Hall as quickly as they could. The security detail helped the Vogels carry Wisniewski to their new medical clinic. Barger waved for the other two to pick up Powell and follow him out a side door.

Hank looked at Mac and asked, "Where are they taking him?"

"I don't know, and you don't need to know. The concession agreement makes it clear that we are all subject to Sharia law. The enforcer isn't a man to trifle with: Jiluwi, the governor of Al-Hasa, a trusted cousin of Abdulaziz."

"What will happen to Powell?"

"It depends on whether the man he stabbed lives or dies. If he's lucky, Barger will have the legation branch in Dhahran hide him until they can arrange an exit visa. But the Saudis don't subscribe to the sovereignty of foreign embassies. If our doctors can't save the man he stabbed, Powell could be the first American beheaded in the kingdom."

Ras Tanura, 17 August

After another week, all hands had produced neat rows of prefabricated housing for Bechtel's construction workers. Although fenced off from Aramco's encampment, everyone expected the concession to annex it when Bechtel moved on to other projects. Both sides of the fence had new cinderblock buildings for bathing and cooking. To celebrate, Steve Bechtel had lamb chops and T-bone steaks shipped in from Australia. A truckload of goats was brought in for Saudi Camp, where another cinderblock kitchen had been built. The culinary equipment for Arab workers, however, was somewhere between the US and the Persian Gulf. The Yemeni cooks roasted the goats over open fires as they would anywhere in the kingdom.

The brass from Dhahran joined Lanier, Ferguson, and Hank for the occasion. Bechtel, their host, sat at the head of a table in the Dining Hall. Their Chinese cooks served the chops and the steaks with fresh corn on the cob and mashed potatoes. After the fiasco with Powell and Wisniewski, beer wasn't on the menu for most of the Americans. But Lanier was inconspicuously pouring authentic mash whiskey at the executive table.

"How are plans for Ramadan going, Tommy?" Barger asked.

"Rama what?"

82

Ferguson was instantly cross.

"We talked about this, Tommy."

Ohliger leaned in, sitting across the table from the refiner.

"You can't schedule a regular work plan for the Saudi workers this month. They're all fasting from sunrise to sundown."

Lanier became defensive. The Kentucky bourbon was not having the effect he intended. "I already need three A-rabs to do one man's work back in the States."

Barger tried a lighter touch, as usual.

"We have several years of experience with Ramadan. The change in workload is just a reasonable accommodation. The real issue is that they're not allowed to drink water during the day."

"Or fornicate," Mac added.

Everyone but Ohliger chuckled.

Hank listened as the other men chatted. Mac had explained the depth of the challenges facing Aramco en route from Washington. More than a decade after signing the concession agreement, Abdulaziz was still waiting for royalties to change the lives of his poor subjects. There were too many emirs in his alliances and too many princes in his extended family. The war had decimated his traditional source of revenue, a tax on pilgrims to Mecca from around the world. Early on, Roosevelt had relied upon the British to look after Arabia, as they had for many decades. Even though they depended on Lend Lease to prevent the collapse of their own economy, the UK still claimed dominion over the Persian Gulf.

In the meantime, the people of the Eastern Province were still starving. The sunken eyes and thin limbs of Arab workers in Ras Tanura made Hank wonder if the company could do enough. Arabia was the poorest, most backward place he had ever seen. Many of the men from Saudi Camp didn't look healthy enough to work. Before Aramco opened clinics in Dhahran and then Ras Tanura, the coastal villages had relied on occasional visits from American medical missionaries. Abdulaziz probably owed his life to the Methodist surgeon who treated a dental abscess before it could spread to his brain.

Over dinners or drinks, the Volkers told Hank that the Arab workers were hosts to multiple equatorial parasites. Blindness due to trachoma was endemic. Everyone seemed to have malaria. Intestinal parasites appeared to be extracting the caloric value out of every morsel the local population could eat. The mid-day meal Aramco was hosting in Saudi Camp was an exception to the company's policies against non-salary benefits for its foreign employees. But it improved the concession's chances of getting a full day's work out of the Arabs.

Taif, 19 August

The bespoke pinstripes that Rod Berglund had been wearing when he interviewed Hank Simmons in Washington were in mothballs at the US legation in Jeddah. Along with his superior, Colonel William Eddy, Berglund was in bedu attire at the wrong end of a caravan headed for the summer palace of Abdulaziz. The US foreign service officer who had opened the legation in Jeddah – James Moose - had just been recalled. Protocol required a decent interval before Eddy assumed his new diplomatic cover, Envoy Extraordinary and Minister Plenipotentiary. In the meantime, the founding king had invited his new American friend to join him in Taif, unaware that Eddy was the senior agent of the Office of Strategic Services in Arabia.

As stifling as the heat on the first day of their journey was, Berglund was engrossed in his first look at the kingdom's interior. The junior agent had been working on Wall Street when he was recruited by the OSS and posted to Eddy's staff in Tangier in 1942. Before the Allied invasion, their secret network of Arab merchants, Berber thieves, and European prostitutes had co-opted the Spanish police and Vichy military. Berglund had enjoyed Tangier before he had to share it with hordes of other Americans after the successful landings in Morocco. For more than a century, the US legation in Tangier had been part of a romantic milieu of artists, degenerates, and spies. On a fair day, one could see the coast of Spain while walking along the Corniche. Like Wilde, Berglund thought of himself as a man of simple taste, and the best of everything had been affordable in the medina. Best of all for the international lawyer, everything in Tangier but Bilal, his hammam boy, could be expensed to secret accounts.

Berglund's reverie evaporated on a desolate stretch of the unpaved road to Mecca. Since his transfer from OSS Cairo earlier that summer, Jeddah had been filthy, mirthless, and suffocating. Even so, the new military attaché was happy to be reunited with Eddy, who had known Berglund's father since their college days at Princeton. His boss had been born and raised in Lebanon, part of a family of missionaries from New England who outlasted the Ottoman Empire. Since Eddy's forebearers were never allowed to proselytize in the Levant, they had established themselves as secular educators in an illiterate Arab sphere.

After serving in the Marine Corps during the Great War, Eddy had been an English professor at the American University in Cairo and then president of Hobart College. One of the reasons the Arabist was so respected by the Departments of State and War was that he had returned to government service before Pearl Harbor. On the first leg of their journey from Jeddah to Taif, the seasoned intelligence officer passed time as an avuncular professor, with Berglund as his only pupil.

"The pilgrimage to Mecca is one of the five pillars of Islam: the faithful are expected to complete the *Hajj* at least once in their lifetime. Since Lawrence destroyed the Turkish railway, Jeddah has been the only portal of entry for tens of thousands every year. Until this war began, the duties and taxes from the five days of the pilgrimage were the most reliable source of revenue for Abdulaziz."

Berglund looked through the open window at the empty landscape. Mecca was ninety kilometers from the Red Sea on the western slope of the Hejaz range. At mid-day during summer, the vehicles carrying the royal provisions had the rutted track to themselves. Al-Saud owned or gifted most of the cars and trucks imported into their poor kingdom. Occasionally the caravan passed an Arab townsman in a donkey cart or a few bedu on their camels. The third Saudi state was only a few months older than the American oil concession on the other side of the Arabian peninsula.

Eddy continued. "Abdulaziz has been exchanging personal letters with Roosevelt for some time. Like most sheiks, he's too proud to beg. But his ministers have been burnishing the art of pitting the British against us for bigger subsidies. Meanwhile, the lobbyists for Standard and Texaco have convinced the White House and the Pentagon that they can't afford to advance the Saudis more royalties than they already have."

"That's rich."

Both men knew that the US government had sent their best geologist to conduct a seismic survey of the Arabian oil concession the year before. DeGolyer had confirmed that the Eastern Province was floating on the largest petroleum reserve in the world. But Aramco had been forced to shut down exploration when the Italians bombed their headquarters in Dhahran. While Eddy was developing the relationship between their government and the founding king, Berglund had been delegated a novel form of restitution by the Italians.

The trucks pulled off the road to Mecca for the Asr prayer in the middle of the afternoon. The proximity of the holiest place in Islam seemed to heighten the fervor of the Arabs like a gravitational force. Then the American diplomats watched the drivers and soldiers set up their encampment, stopping again for the Maghrib prayer at sunset. Most of the men in the caravan of trucks were townsmen from Riyadh or Jeddah. Over a meal of flatbread, dates, and fresh camel milk, the drivers and soldiers bantered with Eddy, who seemed as cheerful as if he was still a boy among his friends in Sidon. The Arab dialect that Berglund had learned in North Africa was useless in Arabia. Like any subordinate, he still laughed along with Eddy through the early evening hours, never reaching for his flask of gin until the others were asleep on the ground around him. The last thing he remembered was the echo of the Isha prayer from the minarets of every station on the pilgrimage ahead.

The following morning, after Fajr, the caravan continued on the road to Taif in the mountains. Their route paralleled the path of the five days of the *Hajj*. Eddy pointed out the three battered pillars where the faithful had been casting stones at the Devil for centuries, followed by the vast but empty encampments around Mina, Muzdalifah, and Mount Arafat, where Mohammed had offered his final words to his followers. The canon of Abraham and his sons shared by Jews, Christians, and Muslims was more important to Eddy than it was to Berglund. Having seen the architectural marvels the Moors left behind in Spain, it was hard to think of the rubble around Mecca as anything other than evidence of a failed empire. But the OSS and their British counterparts were operating on the assumption that the Persian Gulf was going to change radically after the Axis powers were defeated.

Berglund and Eddy became more subdued as the heat increased and the terrain steepened, the rutted road narrowing as Mecca receded from view. Hopelessly, Berglund watched their driver wrestle with the wheel of the big American sedan on washed out switchbacks thousands of feet above the desert floor. By mid-morning, he was relieved when the caravan came to a halt: one of the trucks at the front of the line had to change a flat tire.

Scattered a few meters from the Buick were the desiccated carcasses of a small herd of goats. Beyond the swarm of flies hovering over the dead animals, the rocky road gave way to a steep ravine. There was no vegetation for miles. In April, Eddy had been the first American official to visit Riyadh, the capital city in the center of the desert kingdom. Berglund knew his boss had been alarmed by the extent of famine he had seen. Thousands of starving Arabs were being fed from the palace kitchen every day. It was traditional for sheiks to provide for their tribe. But the long lines of bedu abandoning the desert for Riyadh deeply worried the missionary's son.

"You see, Rod? Our British friends think the drought is just a Saudi ruse to get bigger subsidies. If they ever left their consulate, they'd know the shortage of water on the Arabian peninsula is very real. The people in this country are in a desperate situation."

The summer palace proved to be the exception to Eddy's assertion. As Berglund and his boss approached Taif, they passed streams where water still flowed and terraced gardens of verdant roses and pomegranates. There were orchards of almond trees and dates. Beehives on the slopes filled the air with the smell of honey. After the cruel journey from Jeddah, they took pleasure in the cooler breezes from the Shafa Mountains and the aroma of Taif's fruit and flowers. Berglund felt as if he had somehow left the Arabian peninsula. The king was a devout Muslim with few indulgences beyond the company of his wives and courtesans. But he took great pleasure in exotic fragrances. The oil from the roses of Taif were treasured in Paris and Rome as much as they were by Abdulaziz.

Berglund saw a medieval stronghold whose fortifications were still marred by battles between the Hashemites, who had ruled over the Hejaz for a millennium, the Ottomans who had occupied it for centuries, and the ancestors of Abdulaziz. Taif was a special place for the founding king. His army of zealots, the Ikhwan, had laid siege to it in 1926. The son of Hussein, the last of Al-Hashimi to rule Mecca, had fled their mountain stronghold before the Ikhwan arrived. The male citizens of Taif were massacred for their loyalty to Hussein and their more moderate beliefs; Abdulaziz had indoctrinated his warriors in Wahhabism as he trained them for *jihad*. Over the next few years, the Ikhwan had used the mountains around Taif to stage the conquests of Mecca and Jeddah. Then Abdulaziz united the Hejaz in the west with the Najd in the north and Al-Hasa in the east to establish the third iteration of the kingdom which bore his tribal name.

Eddy and Berglund were greeted with great formality by the king's emissaries and escorted to rooms facing the private gardens of Shubra Palace. Berglund was taken aback by the king's residence, the only modern building of any consequence in Taif. The Turks had borrowed its squarish, five-story design from the Romans and decorated the interior with Italian marble, luxurious window treatments from Europe, and exotic hardwoods from the Far East. Shubra Palace looked like a fancy bordello.

The wardrobe for the American visitors to Taif was delivered by an assistant of Yusuf Yassin, the king's foreign minister. Like many of the king's advisors, Yassin wasn't a Saudi. Despite their finely crafted gifts, Eddy warned Berglund that they could count on Yassin, a Syrian by birth, to oppose anything that Europeans or Americans suggested. Like Suleiman, the finance minister, Yassin's real skill was pitting infidels against each other to the kingdom's advantage.

Berglund had been studying Abdulaziz with Eddy as his tutor. Throughout the first half of the century, the young ruler had been an avid consumer of information from neighboring Kuwait, Iraq and Jordan, wary of the foreign nations nibbling at the edges of the Arabian peninsula. Abdulaziz was an uncommon ruler who encouraged opposing views, trusted his own judgement, and turned sheiks from rival tribes into supporters (if not kinsmen through marriage). Before choosing the Americans for the oil concession, he had navigated between the Turks, the British, the French and the Germans from the relative safety of Riyadh. But as worldly as he was, Abdulaziz had never traveled farther than Kuwait, where he had been exiled in his youth.

Berglund, a clotheshorse at heart, enjoyed putting on Yassin's gifts. Unlike the heavier attire they traveled in, his new *thobe,* a full-length tunic, was soft and lightweight, made from the finest Egyptian cotton. His new *bisht,* the outer robe favored by nobility and wealthy merchants, was made of translucent silk. It reminded the OSS officer of the slip worn by his favorite contact in Rabat, a French courtesan who hated her Vichy clients. On his head was the same style of *ghutra* worn by Saudi courtiers.

One of the minor emirs informed Berglund and Eddy that the king would welcome them after the *Majlis,* the open council at which Arab sheiks received the petitions of their subjects. They were escorted through the Italianate corridors to the largest hall in Shubra Palace, gleaming with crystal candelabra. The king's throne was to one side, rows of gilt-covered chairs lining the other walls. Saudi men from all walks of life filled the room. Some wore simple clothing like the travel attire worn by the Americans. The Saudi ministers and princes were conspicuous in finery matching the garments that Yassin had given Berglund and Eddy.

The military attaché was surprised by the king's stature and girth, reminding him of an Ivy League tackle going soft with age and wealth. Like Eddy, the king had problems with his lower limbs from battle that had worsened with age. As he walked Abdulaziz leaned on an ivory cane in one hand, the other locked around the arm of his second son, Prince Feisal, with whom he shared penetrating eyes and a hawkish nose. Unlike his son, the king smiled easily, enjoying the company of his many visitors, unfazed by his acquired infirmities. Berglund watched and Eddy murmured commentary as Abdulaziz graciously received men from all over his kingdom.

A man who had traveled all the way from the southwestern border complained that the Saudi authorities were not protecting his sheep from Yemeni poachers. The king offered compensation and vowed to increase the troops guarding the border.

The owner of a date grove in Taif whose daughter was betrothed to the son of a wealthy farmer demanded justice after the cancellation of their engagement. Women were not permitted at Majlis. Gazing kindly at her homely father, the king seemed incurious about the reasons for the breakup. He promised to meet with the groom's father and speak to the petitioner again.

A local merchant demanded payment for a shipment of imported wheat that the king's provisioner refused because it was weevil-ridden. The king said he hoped that his country would be able to grow enough wheat to feed his people in the future. He nodded at his American guests and said he was grateful for their experts at the new agricultural station in Al-Kharj. In the meantime, he referred the grain merchant to the local emir who oversaw Shubra Palace in his absence.

A carpetmaker from Medina appealed the ruling of the ulema which held that his recent financial losses didn't qualify for relief from paying *zakat*, the tithe Muslims of means paid each year for the less fortunate.

Eddy elbowed Berglund. The king was famously impatient with details and figures. The well-dressed carpetmaker had fat hands and a double chin. As he droned on about *nasib,* the modest amount of savings not subject to charity, Abdulaziz turned stern for the first time.

Did he not see the greater suffering of so many of his countrymen? Is a man who once had a thousand riyals not wealthy if he still has nine hundred when so many of his fellow Muslims have nothing? Had he forgotten how blessed he was to have his health, a home for his family, and a business whose doors remained open?

When the Majlis ended, the hall emptied and the Americans were ushered into a less imposing chamber. Yassin, Suleiman, and several of the princely emirs of Al-Saud sat together on one side of a less imposing throne, with Eddy and Berglund on the other side of Abdulaziz. The king beckoned to Eddy to join him, clasping hands as if they were lifelong friends. Eddy introduced Berglund, who the king greeted warmly, entertained by his attempt to speak Arabic like a North African.

The greetings and salutations of the American diplomats to the members of the court that Abdulaziz introduced took a quarter of an hour. *Peace be with you. And with you. How are you? I am well. Praise Allah.* Yassin, despite his welcoming gifts, seemed stern. Suleiman was stone cold sober, though he was rumored to be a habitual drinker. The crown prince, Saud, was absent, a blessing according to Eddy. Feisal, the second son of Abdulaziz, was reserved in his father's presence.

Unlike authentic diplomats, Eddy didn't expect Berglund to take notes. Nor did he allow the translators of the Saudi ministers to come between him and the king. The new American minister seldom quoted Abdulaziz directly in his cables to Cairo or Washington; Berglund suspected their most important conversations were private. In Taif, with so many members of Al-Saud listening, each with their own agenda, the two old warriors engaged in their own form of statecraft, revealing little while affirming the growing affection of each country for the other.

The king's attendants served tea in cups with delicate glazing that matched the blue and red flowers of Taif. Abdulaziz waved for Eddy to be served first; his guest waved it off in favor of their host. Berglund tried to avoid the gazes of the courtiers when he was served after Eddy, declining the camel's milk. After everyone had been served, there was little conversation during the first round of tea. Berglund knew that good manners required him to slurp his cup. The conspicuous sound of happy sipping by the emirs and their guests filled the chamber. Another round of tea was served and enjoyed uneventfully. The third round was a good sign, according to Eddy, an indication that the American diplomats were truly welcome by Abdulaziz.

Berglund watched as another servant placed a shallow brass pan over a small open fire in the center of the chamber. He spooned coffee beans into the pan to roast them. Then he removed them from the heat and ground them together with cardamon in a mortar. The coffee was then placed into a handcrafted brass coffee pot filled with steaming hot water. When it was ready, the coffee were poured into cups that were even smaller than those used for tea for the king, his guests, and his courtiers.

Business was not discussed in the kingdom until after the second round of coffee. Abdulaziz and Eddy continued to exchange pleasantries as if they had known each other far longer than a few months. Berglund strived to follow their conversation in Arabic.

I look forward to meeting your wife and daughter, the king said.

Unfortunately, my wife will not leave the mountains of Lebanon until summer ends in Jeddah.

Allah requires our patience then.

Eddy and the founding king exchanged wry smiles. Abdulaziz had benefitted from the medical services of missionaries earlier in his life and found the treatment of women by Christians peculiar. Berglund knew that the king would happily provide a courtesan for Eddy's comfort in Taif; he was almost as sure that Eddy would never accept the offer.

It will be our pleasure to welcome you to the legation in Jeddah. My wife has asked me if you would consider an exception to the prohibition against musical instruments.

94

Of course, my friend.

Mary loves to play the piano and will have few ways to amuse herself in the legation. Would it be possible for her to have her piano shipped from Cairo?

To the consternation of the more devout members of Al-Saud present, including Feisal, the king agreed.

If our guests in the European quarter of Jeddah have telegraphs, so shall they have pianos!

Eddy placed his right hand over his heart and bowed.

You do me a great honor, your highness.

Abdulaziz made a trifling wave with his right hand. Berglund found it hard not to stare at the gnarled knuckles and battered bare feet of the founding king. The effect of being in his presence was oddly like the feeling Americans - except for some Republicans - had about FDR. Abdulaziz seemed to be full of optimism, goodwill, and humor.

Yassin and Suleiman became impatient when a second round of coffee became a third before Abdulaziz allowed Eddy to speak of more serious matters.

It is rumored that I have you to thank for my promotion.

The founding king's heavy brow furrowed quizzically; great rulers didn't celebrate their most subtle victories.

Thank Allah, who bestowed many talents upon you - and President Roosevelt.

Eddy winked at Berglund. Like most Arabs, Abdulaziz preferred to avoid direct confrontation whenever possible. He had been disappointed by James Moose, the scholarly diplomat who opened the US legation, spoke Arabic, and appreciated the region's culture. The king's ministers were frustrated with Moose and his counterpart in the British foreign service, Stanley Jordan, who spent most of their time arguing with each other rather than increasing their support for the kingdom, impoverished by drought and war. Nor was Moose any more willing than the British to journey to Riyadh, the inland capital that Abdulaziz preferred to the filthy seaport of Jeddah. After Eddy arrived in Arabia as a military advisor, the two old warriors had taken a liking to each other. They both preferred desert encampments to palace intrigue. Eddy's promotion had become inevitable in April, when the Saudi ambassador to Britain complained about Moose to a senior US diplomat visiting London.

Their first evening in Taif, Eddy and Berglund witnessed the king feeding the entire city from the palace. Berglund's first royal feast was literally eye-popping. The cloudy looking globes were still in their sockets when the roasted lamb was served on a platter with mounds of rice and herbs. A local emir popped out the delicacy and gave it to the military attaché, who endured a few bites. The next day was far worse, ceaseless wrangling between Eddy and the king's ministers about the extent and timing of US aid.

On the long ride back down the mountains from Taif to Jeddah, the Americans debated how to triangulate between Abdulaziz, Aramco, and their own country.

"The king is still trying to make his kingdom more than a tribe of tribes," Eddy said.

"Have to give him credit for getting so far on the strength of personal relationships," Berglund agreed. "He'd make a great managing partner on Wall Street."

Eddy gazed into the distance, trying to catch a glimpse of Mecca as their car rounded another treacherous turn. "We need to get Abdulaziz in the same room with Roosevelt."

Berglund nodded at the enormity of the idea. Getting their commander in chief within a thousand miles of the founding king would be a feat. After all, there was still a world war to win and a campaign for an unprecedented fourth presidential term. But two days in Taif was enough to convince the military attaché that his boss, the best Arabist on the home team, was right.

Ras Tanura, 20 August

The Prophet received the first revelation from the archangel Jibril in the scorching heat of summer. The first day of the month of its annual observance, one of the Five Pillars of Islam, was a Sunday, the second day of the Aramco work week. Schedules had been adjusted as much as possible for the rigor of the season. The heat and humidity that afternoon on Tarout Bay tested the Prophet's most faithful followers.

For Hank, the cumulative effect of the gulf air on exposed metal was more dangerous than a daytime fast. There was a valve on the pipeline for crude oil being pumped to Bahrain that had to be replaced before it failed. He had decided he couldn't defer work on the submarine line any longer. Each bolt on the valve was the size of a man's fist. Two Arab workers with an oversized wrench were trying to loosen a lug nut on the valve, which looked like the wheel of a ship. Another pair of Arab workers were on the other end. As they wrestled with the huge wrench, one pair of men dangled in mid-air trying to use their combined weight to turn the bolt, encrusted with five years of rust. Hank's mind was wandering back to the Mechanics Monument in San Francisco. Then one of the men who had been hanging in mid-air collapsed on the pier.

His co-workers cried out in dismay. They shouted his name, *Ismael*.

Ammar was half a step ahead of Hank. Ismael wasn't drenched in sweat like the rest of the men. His skin was strangely cool, ashen, and mottled. His breathing was shallow. His pulse was weak but too fast to count.

Four men picked him up and headed for the medical clinic on the edge of American Camp; two would have been enough for the job. Barely fifty kilos, Hank could just as easily have thrown Ismael over his shoulder like a fireman.

The clinic was at the near end of a long row of prefabricated buildings assembled just a few weeks before. The air inside was cooled by a new swamp cooler that purred in one of its windows.

Dr. Vogel was on duty. He wore a short-sleeved white shirt and fresh khaki pants. Quickly he listened to the unconscious man's heart and lungs. Laying on his back, Ismael's abdomen was so sunken that the doctor could easily feel the rounded bones of his spine. The doctor checked his pupils and seemed satisfied with how they reacted to the penlight from his pocket. He spent another few moments inspecting the rest of Ismael's eyes. The white areas - the sclera - were unusually clear, as if there were no blood in his patient's body. The doctor checked his blood pressure; it seemed to take a long time for anything to register.

His wife appeared and placed a few pillows behind Ismael's neck and head. A few more were placed behind his lower legs. Dr. Vogel asked Ammar for his patient's name. Mrs. Vogel began to call him gently as she offered him a sip of water.

His co-workers erupted in protest, speaking directly to Ammar. He interpreted for the Vogels.

"It is Ramadan. He is not permitted to have water now. The sun is still in the sky."

The doctor looked at Ammar and nodded in understanding. He knew from his years as a missionary that it was useless to challenge the beliefs of the people of Al-Hasa. He whispered

98

to his wife, who left the room and then returned with two bags of ice. She placed one on the back of Ismael's neck. The other filled the convexity of his empty stomach.

Everyone took turns calling his name. *Ismael!*

Without asking permission, the doctor began searching for a vein in his patient's arm. His wife fetched a glass bottle of intravenous fluid from a cabinet in the next room. He inserted an intravenous needle, saw blood return into the syringe attached to the needle, then nodded to his wife to attach the tubing to the sterile fluid. Half a liter disappeared from the bottle over the next few minutes. Then Ismael opened his eyes and mumbled something in Arabic to the doctor, who looked at Ammar.

"He wants to know if he is dead."

Vogel smiled and said, "Tell him he is very much alive."

His co-workers were all relieved. *"Allahu akbar!"*

Allah was greater again. The doctor turned to Hank.

"He's certainly anemic, as most of them are. It's likely he fainted in the heat. A pity that they can't drink water during the day."

"So, you think he'll be okay?"

"We'll watch him until sundown to make sure he doesn't get worse. I'll give him another liter of fluid intravenously. After that, his friends can take him. He needs to drink as much water as he can this evening, eat a light meal. It would be wise to keep him out of the heat for a few days."

"I'll make sure he stays home."

Dr. Vogel told Ammar to bring him back the next day if he wasn't improving. Hank and his assistant nodded in agreement.

Ras Tanura, 21 August

After the Maghrib prayer, Hank asked Ammar to take him to see Ismael in Saudi Camp. He was embarrassed by the lack of progress that had been made in the fenced off area for Arab workers. The only new building was the cinderblock structure intended to be the kitchen for the midday meal. The appliances and culinary equipment were still on one of the cargo ships headed to the Persian Gulf. Little else had changed. Unlike the neat rows of prefabricated structures for Americans, Saudi Camp remained an Arab version of Hooverville, a hodgepodge of tents and shelters made from scraps. The encampment seemed larger every day; the Arab workforce was growing faster than the American.

It took Ammar a few minutes to find Ismael. The only geography in the jumble was tribal. There were dozens of Ismaels among the hundreds of Arabs arriving in Ras Tanura. Ammar's breakthrough was finding another man who worked with Ismael in the marine terminal.

It was Ismael from Abu Sahbal, one of the villages of Al-Hofuf, who had collapsed earlier in the day. Inshallah he would recover.

Ammar continued, now looking for the tents of the men of Al-Hofuf. They found them on the eastern edge of the encampment where the gulf breezes were freshest.

Ismael lived in a simple tent of classic bedu design. It was dark by the time that Hank and Ammar knelt to enter. By the light of a single candle, Hank could see that life had returned to Ismael's eyes. He sat beside three other young men that he introduced as his cousins. Beaming, he welcomed Hank to his tent. They were just about to begin *Iftar*. All they appeared to have to eat was the traditional evening meal, dates from their village which they told Ammar were the finest in Al-Hofuf. Ismael offered them first to Hank.

The American was embarrassed that hungry men with so little to eat would offer to share it with him. But before he could say no, Ammar said - in English - that they would be honored.

Hank took a date from a weary bronze platter and said, *"Shukraan."*

Ismael smiled and said, *"Shukraan liziaratikum."*

"He thanks you for your visit," Ammar explained.

"Is he feeling better?"

"Hal tasheur bitahasun?" Ammar asked.

Ismael smiled and said, *"Alhamd lilah."*

Hank nodded in approval. Whatever came to a Muslim - good or bad - came from Allah.

Ismael offered them small cups and filled them with water, another tradition of Iftar. Hank accepted it and sipped, hoping that it was from one of Aramco's own wells that filtered out parasites and bacteria. It tasted fresh and sweet. Hank smiled back at Ismael.

Ammar translated as their visit continued. They were the first members of their family to leave Abu Sahbal. Hank had heard of Al-Hofuf - the largest inland oasis in Arabia, if not the world. Their tribe had pastured their animals there for generations. Like others in Saudi Camp, they had taken jobs with Aramco only because their family's camels had died during the drought. The money Ismael and his cousins were making was feeding their extended family. Because of the great distance, they took turns at the end of each week taking their earnings home for their families to buy food.

Before leaving, Hank told Ismael that he should rest at home for a few days. A look of fear appeared on his face. Speaking too quickly for Hank to comprehend, Ismael lodged a protest with Ammar.

"He thinks you are firing him for being too weak to work."

Hank thought better of laughing.

"Tell him that I will pay him to rest. He is welcome to return to work next week if he feels better."

The American offered his right hand. Ismael clasped it with his. Each of his cousins shook his hand as well.

Shukraan. Shukraan. Shukraan. Shukraan.

It took five minutes for Hank to leave their tent. Because the month of Ramadan coincided with a new moon - and because there was no electricity in Saudi Camp - Hank and Ammar walked in darkness through the jumble of shelters. The only lights came from the perimeter of American Camp. Moved by the encounter with Ismael, Hank was silent for a few minutes before asking his assistant a question.

"What is the name of the predawn meal during Ramadan?"

"Suhur."

Hank looked in the direction of American Camp. "Let's go find one of the cooks over there and make sure that Ismael and his cousins have some decent food for Suhur."

"Only for them, Hank?"

Hank stopped and frowned at Ammar. When there were Americans or Saudis nearby, Ammar referred to him as *Mr. Simmons*. If they were in the presence of lesser Arab workers, he was *Sahib*. But when they were alone, his assistant had developed a knack for using his nickname to pose ethical challenges.

Being called *Hank* by Ammar was almost as humiliating as being called *Henry* by his mother; admonition disguised as affection. Hank took a deep breath, then another. It was hard to be angry with an employee who prayed five times a day and saved your life his first week on the job.

102

"No, goddam it. For once, let's get enough food for everyone in Saudi Camp to eat like Americans."

Ras Tanura, 25 August

The first Friday of Ramadan brought an end to the first week of light duty. Most of the Americans were happy to have a day off, out of the late-summer heat. Aramco brought in feature films from the US that circulated up and down the coast. But watching Fred Astaire dance with anyone other than Ginger Rodgers wasn't entertaining. News reels were helpful to keep up with the real war. But features about *Mom and Dad Buying War Bonds* or *Kids Starting a Victory Garden* just reminded the men in American Camp how much they were missing. It bothered him even more to think that such features were from the domestic side of Gloria's agency, the Office of War Information.

Hank preferred the other six days of the week. Working long hours meant less time missing the wife he loved and the young son growing up without him. Fridays were just days to feel sorry for himself in his Airstream. He couldn't drink enough beer to forget Gloria's kisses or Peter's laughter. In his office he could usually get BBC broadcasts from Baghdad or Basra. The Brits were big on American bands like Benny Goodman. That night they were more boisterous than usual: the German commander had surrendered Paris; de Gaulle was still speaking when Hank was getting ready for bed.

Every day there was an ATC flight into Dhahran with a mail bag and another carrying letters from the Americans back to the States. Hank's letters to her were subject to screening; one of the consequences of Aramco's strategic value. It didn't bother him if someone from military intelligence read his letters home. He wanted everyone to know that he still loved Gloria and Peter. The day before he had finally received the first letter from Gloria in weeks. It was even vaguer than the one before.

A day later, Gloria's letter was still bothering him. The most tangible evidence of her state of mind was that she had leased their home in Montclair. On the face of it, the decision was reasonable. His wife and his son were living with her parents in Palo Alto. Now that he was in Ras Tanura, it made little sense for the house to sit empty seven days a week. There was still a mortgage to pay and the price of rentals near San Francisco had skyrocketed during the war. In the letter announcing her decision, Gloria complimented herself, as if she had always been interested in their finances.

Even though she had only agreed to a year's lease, it disturbed Hank to think that his family didn't have a place of their own while he was in Ras Tanura. But there was little to gain from second-guessing Gloria in his next letter - it would only give her another reason not to write back. The kid who had been raised in a boarding house had never been more secure financially, living in a company trailer, eating three complimentary meals a day, saving most of his fat salary tax-free. In Palo Alto, his father-in-law was picking up every tab, strengthening his claim to his daughter and grandson. Hank would rather have been paying full price for everything Gloria and Peter were consuming.

Every night in Ras Tanura, Hank put his head on the pillow about the same time his lovely wife was getting out of bed in Palo Alto. Thinking about what Gloria was doing kept him awake all hours. On the gulf in summer, nights stayed uncomfortably hot in his trailer berth. The swamp cooler in the office never seemed to keep the sweat from building up on his body, even when he tossed off the top sheet and stripped down. Fortunately, Fridays were when Lanier hopped on a launch to Manama to find what he needed in some filthy cathouse. Some of the other men Hank worked with in Ras Tanura were making the most of Bahrain, whether they were married or not.

That night, when there were no more blueprints to check, no more slabs or junctions to inspect, he drove to the point and headed up the beach beyond American Camp. The waves lapping at the edge of the gulf gave him some peace, as did the ridiculous number of stars. In the Persian Gulf, the heavens offered an unfamiliar perspective, a new meaning he couldn't make out. Long after the Isha prayer echoed around the point, Hank was still wandering north on the beach. When he was tired enough he started back for the Airstream, where he slept restlessly until the Fajr prayer.

Palo Alto, 25 August

On a sunny Saturday in late summer, it didn't matter that the swimming pool was unheated. For Gloria's father, it was enough to have been the first household on the block to install one. He was the kind of man who was more attached to his personal regime than his family. Rain or shine, he began every day with twenty laps. But when Gloria and Peter moved back in, she was grateful that her father taught him to swim. Now her son was the kind of water bug who didn't get out until he was so tired that he had to be dragged out. After a hearty dinner, Peter would be asleep before "Your Hit Parade" was playing on the radio in the den.

It was the first Saturday of the month that Gloria hadn't spent with Thierry. She had hoped that their time together in Montclair would restore some form of normalcy to her life, a chance for them to escape the despicably convenient hotels in between the Presidio and the Transbay Terminal. But almost as soon as they began to spend Saturdays at the bungalow, the pleasure she took from being alone with Thierry was overshadowed by darker self-hatred the other six days of the week.

From the beginning, Gloria had refused to make love with Thierry in the bed she shared with Hank. The only other bed in the bungalow was Peter's tiny twin, which was less sturdy than the living room furniture or the kitchen table. Thierry found her bedroom taboo comically impractical. When he accused her of being too American, Gloria offered no defense. But there wouldn't have been anything funny about her neighbors discovering that Thierry wasn't her husband. She was having trouble sleeping for the first time in years. On the penultimate weekend in August, returning to San Francisco on the Key Line, sitting alone in a coach loaded with soldiers and sailors, Gloria had silently excoriated herself. When the servicemen tried to pick her up, she ignored them so completely that they told each other that she must be crazy. Without saying so, she agreed with them.

How could she have believed a professional liar like Thierry when he said he loved her? How could she possibly have chosen her own home for their assignations? It wasn't that Thierry had already taken another lover. Gloria knew that was inevitable as soon as their affair began. It was that Hank had never done anything to justify her betrayal. He was only guilty of being naïve, methodical, and devoted. Hank would be crushed to learn that he had been cuckolded while serving his country in Arabia.

By the time she changed trains and reached Palo Alto, Gloria had decided to rent the bungalow in Montclair. If she were too weak to break off her affair with Thierry, she could at least restore the sanctity of her family's home. Decent housing was becoming impossible to find at any price near the city. The following day she ran a listing in the Oakland Tribune for what she considered an extravagant amount, trying to sabotage her own escape plan, only to receive a handful of solid offers.

As she spent the last Saturday of the month by the pool with Peter and her parents, tenants were moving into the home she had profaned in Montclair. Her father, sipping his first gin and tonic of the afternoon, sitting under a broad umbrella, began speaking to her as if she were a client instead of his daughter, the undeclared adulteress.

"Have you decided how you're going to invest the net rental income, after you pay the mortgage?"

Gloria was startled, lost in her thoughts as she sunbathed. She was thinking about Hank, who was probably exhausted after another day working in 120-degree heat and 100% humidity. As far as she knew, Thierry was looking for another matron at the Presidio with a husband overseas.

"I hadn't thought very much about it. What would you advise, Daddy?"

"I suppose you could buy war bonds. But having the money tied up for ten years is a little too patriotic for my taste."

"I see. A regular savings account then?"

"Those are paying less than two percent a year. Railroad stocks are booming. You could earn twice the interest banks are paying just from dividends."

"Really?"

"Once the war's over, I think the shares to own will be General Motors, possibly Chrysler and Ford. It's never too early to start investing for Peter, you know."

It pained her to be reminded that she had a son as well as a husband. But her heart began to mend when she looked at Peter. He was out of the pool, still dripping wet, scooping potato salad with celery stalks. Her boy wasn't so little anymore, playing hard and growing fast, never seeming to gain an ounce of fat. Some day he would probably be as tall as his father. She only hoped he would be as good a man. Gloria resolved never to spend a penny of the rent, even when she stopped seeing Thierry. Her parents looked so peaceful together by the pool in the shade of the umbrella. She wondered if she still had a chance to grow old with Hank.

"Can you arrange for your broker to set up an account in Peter's name?"

Her father smiled at Gloria as he poured her mother's second gin and tonic. "Why, my dear, I already have."

Part 2 – Mission to Asmara

Dhahran, 28 August

James MacPherson, the visiting VP, had never heard of *Monsun Gruppe* before he arrived in Dhahran. But everyone waiting for tubular steel, drilling equipment or even kitchen gear learned the hard way that the shooting war as close as Aden. More than once, the sinking of a Liberty Ship pushed Aramco and Bechtel farther behind their construction schedule. Even though the Allies had control of the North Atlantic and the Mediterranean, one last group of U-boats had slipped around the Cape of Good Hope. Using Japanese bases in Malaysia, they patrolled the Indian Ocean. British tankers from Iraq and Iran were ripe targets for the Nazi submariners. So were the high-priority US cargos headed for Ras Tanura. The Allies couldn't eliminate the last U-boat fast enough for Mac.

Before the *SS John Barry* could reach the Persian Gulf, she was sunk in the Arabian Sea, ruining the last payday of the month. Like Abdulaziz, the Arabs in his kingdom had never accepted any form of payment other than silver or gold. Out of necessity, Mac had helped Ohliger, the VP running the concession, to cobble together the kingdom's first paper money. The men of Saudi Camp had been skeptical on payday until merchants in Dammam and Al-Khobar that were already doing business with Aramco began accepting their scrip. Arabs began to use the paper money up and down the coast, whether they worked for Aramco or not. It amused Mac that Aramco was floating the kingdom's economy just like the British - even though the US government said it opposed old-world colonialism.

A week later, *Monsun Gruppe* struck again, sinking the eighth Liberty Ship destined for Ras Tanura. It was a bigger blow to construction than the loss of the *John Barry*. The shipment included the oxygen generating equipment for Bechtel's welders and all of the kitchen equipment needed for Saudi Camp. The loss of thousands of feet of tubular steel was painful for Aramco, adding to the delays for the refinery project. But the biggest shortage of all in the Persian Gulf had nothing to do with U-boats.

The American oilmen and the Pentagon had always known that the biggest obstacle to building Ras Tanura would be the dearth of skilled labor in the Middle East.

Mac had shared many secrets with Hank during their journey from Washington to Dhahran. But he had kept one that involved Hank. Along with James Terry Duce, the other Aramco executive on loan to the War Department, Mac had keenly followed the progress of British and American military construction up and down the Red Sea. There were 50,000 Italian colonials - most of them ex-POWs - trapped in Eritrea, the capital of their fallen empire in Africa. The Italians were better builders than fighters and had been earning testimonials at the Pentagon. That they could be had for a fraction of what tradesmen were paid in the UK and the US wasn't lost on Aramco.

Ohliger and Barger had broached the subject of allowing foreign laborers into the kingdom with Abdulaziz in April. The founding king had been noncommittal, complaining about several hundred Italians he had already locked up, suspected war criminals who had crossed the Red Sea to avoid British justice after retreating from Ethiopia. The Italians were despised throughout the Arab world because of atrocities against Muslims in Libya - long before Mussolini. A decision about whether the Saudis would permit them to work in Ras Tanura would take as long as any other contentious issue between the Americans and Abdulaziz.

Mac hadn't known that D-Day would arrive while he and Hank were in Bermuda. But he knew that the Italians would inevitably build the first refinery and marine terminal. That was why he and Duce knew they needed someone like Hank as liaison for Aramco in Eritrea. Someone who understood both sides of the Ras Tanura project had to reach out to the Italians under British control before SAG approved their entry into the kingdom.

Berglund, the OSS agent under cover on the legation staff in Jeddah, had signed off on the Californian in Washington DC. Mac had known he was the right man for the job by the time they arrived in Dhahran. The Scot liked to think of himself as an impresario and Hank was going to be the star of his next international production.

Dhahran, 5 September

Hank was summoned to a meeting with Ferguson, the project manager for Ras Tanura, near the end of Ramadan. He assumed the subject was the resumption of regular duty by their Arab workers. But when he arrived at Ferguson's office at Aramco headquarters, Ohliger and Barger were waiting for him along with Mac, who beamed at him like an uncle. The others were more solemn, the loss of another Liberty Ship still sinking in. Ferguson waved Hank to the last empty chair.

"We wanted to bring you up to speed on something we've been working on, Hank. But we need to keep this between ourselves for the time being."

Hank looked at the four most senior executives in the concession and thought he was in the wrong room. They gazed back at him like an admissions committee about to announce a scholarship he didn't remember applying for. Ohliger spoke first.

"Once our government gave us priority for the steel, the biggest challenge for Ras Tanura was getting skilled labor. Every weld has to be perfect. Every subsystem has to withstand erosion from the gulf, multiples of sea-level air pressure, and five hundred degrees in the stills."

Hank nodded politely, waiting to be told something he didn't already know. Ferguson went next.

"Obviously, sending back two men back to the States from every five we bring here isn't helping the cause. The king's ministers in Riyadh know they've issued hundreds of exit visas to Americans who either quit or got fired this summer. And they know the longer it takes for Ras Tanura to come online, the longer they have to wait for their royalties to spike."

Ohliger continued.

"Our military have been using Italians from Eritrea to build facilities on the Red Sea since last year. So have the British. They've gotten good marks for their work. In April, Tom and I went to Riyadh to ask the king if he would permit us to use them in Ras Tanura."

"There's more bloody Italians in Asmara than Africans," Mac said.

Ohliger picked up the thread; Hank still didn't understand that he was the needle.

"Tom and I went to see the king and requested permission to use the Italians in Ras Tanura. He told us he would consider our request. But we heard nothing back until this month. We're used to the Saudis trying to pit us against the British for money or information. Now we know Abdulaziz asked the British envoy in Jeddah what he thought about Aramco hiring the Italians."

"We don't think the king or his advisors have any idea how many ex-colonials are in Eritrea," Barger said. "Stanley Jordan, being the pain in the neck that he is, would never admit how badly the Crown wants to get rid of them. He acted like he was doing us a favor when he told our guys in Jeddah that the British government wouldn't object if we start recruiting in Asmara."

Ferguson didn't care about the political back story. The project manager for Ras Tanura was getting impatient with his own meeting.

116

"Hank, the reason we called you in is that we believe that the Saudis are going to approve the Italians building the refinery complex. But until it's official, none of us can offend Abdulaziz by going to Eritrea. We need the better part of two thousand skilled laborers - ASAP - to finish Ras Tanura before the end of next year. There's no chance in hell they're all coming from the States."

Mac's eyes locked on Hank's as Ohliger leaned in.

"We understand you speak Italian, Hank. We need someone who's sympatico to go to Asmara and start screening applicants. As soon as we get the word from Riyadh, we're going to start signing them up. You could save us a huge amount of time."

"And money," Mac added.

"The problem, Hank," Barger cautioned, "Is that the Saudis will insist that we abide by the concession agreement. The king won't tolerate us paying foreign workers more than his own people. Perceptions matter too. His ministers are going to pounce if it looks like we're treating the Italians better than the Arabs."

Ferguson was ready to wrap things up. "Hank, you grew up working in refineries. You have the technical background and management experience needed for every aspect of this project."

Hank was feeling oversold. "I hope you understand that I'm only fluent in Italian when I'm swearing."

Mac hooted. Barger chuckled. Ohliger cracked a smile. But Ferguson remained serious.

"You grew up with them in your hometown, Hank. We know that one of them might as well have raised you."

Hank was startled. He had never mentioned Giulia to anyone at Standard or Aramco. When he glanced at Mac, the oilman who knew everything looked back at him like the village fool. Hank could understand why the US military had to clear him to work in Ras Tanura. But he was troubled by the idea of intelligence agents from his own country sharing information about his loved ones with Aramco. Privacy seemed to be another casualty of war - even in America.

Ohliger stuck out his hand. Hank stared at it for a moment before shaking it. The concession administrator seemed as anxious to close the deal as Ferguson.

"This is our best chance to get Ras Tanura going on time and on budget. You know what kind of workers we need. We've got a plane ready to take you to Asmara first thing tomorrow. Mac has an expense account and some cash for you."

"Carte blanche, laddy."

Hank's eyes bounced between the two Aramco VPs, whom he had never seen look happy at the same time. It didn't make sense to turn down the company's appeal to get the refinery and the marine terminal done. But something about his mission to Eritrea made Hank uncomfortable in a way that working in Arabia didn't. The other executives rose to offer their congratulations, his stature seeming to match his importance for the first time in his career. Mac patted Hank on the back like one of his own.

Ras Tanura, 6 September

It took Hank longer to work through his punch list with Vukovich than to pack his bag. Ammar drove him back from Ras Tanura to the airfield in Dhahran. The Jordanian seemed relieved when Hank told him that he would be working temporarily with Vukovich: Ammar loathed Lanier as much as Mohammed. But Hank's assistant seemed troubled when he wouldn't reveal where he was going or when he would be back.

The C-47 that Aramco leased from ATC had been reconfigured to seat fewer passengers in more comfort. The flight path to Jeddah took Hank over Riyadh. He could easily make out the Najd, the massive plateau forming the central province. The capital, Riyadh, wasn't impressive from 10,000 feet, sitting in a series of wadis where seasonal water flowed out of mountains to the west. An hour later, still crossing the arid peninsula, Hank realized what he had read before arriving in Al-Hasa was true. *There were no rivers in the kingdom.*

As the hours passed and the engines droned, the mind of the only passenger wandered. When he had been a kid, before a growth spurt turned him into a man-sized adolescent, Giulia had loved for Hank to read to her. Like many of the women of her generation, she could barely read Italian. Although she spoke enough English to get by, she depended on Hank to read the recipes his mother found in magazines for Giulia to

119

serve. He liked to keep her company after school, doing his homework at the kitchen table while she prepared dinner for the boarders. He was always hungry and she was entertained by anything he read aloud. She feigned interest in Geometry and seemed genuinely curious about American History. But her favorite was *One Thousand and One Nights.* Giulia loved Scheherazade, the resilient bride who delayed her own execution by telling her husband, the jealous king, tale after tale. Her favorite was the story of the old fisherman who netted a *jinn* in a bottle. But when her husband was lost in the Gulf of Alaska, the fisherman's widow cried as she clung to Hank.

By the early afternoon, the mountains of the Hejaz loomed on the cloudless horizon. The Aramco plane descended over the Red Sea to Jeddah, a smallish rubble. Hank got off the plane to stretch his legs while the C-47 was refueling. The mid-day weather in late summer on the Red Sea was somehow worse than the Persian Gulf. He found a patch of shade under a corrugated metal shack housing the aviation fuel pumps. The ATC crew tried to maintain their flyboy composure while a Saudi ground crew scattered to look for a ladder that reached the wing tanks.

Hank was beginning to feel like an Aramco bigshot, flying alone on a secret mission. A Jeep pulled up with the blue flag of the US State Department on the radio antenna. The last man he expected to see in Jeddah jumped out: Rod Berglund, wearing the khakis of a naval officer instead of pinstripes. Hank's inquisitor in Washington held out his arms like a long-lost friend.

"Hank old boy!"

"What are you doing in Jeddah?"

"Officially, I'm the military attaché in the US legation. I think you know my boss, Colonel Eddy, is our new minister to Arabia."

"Congratulations, I guess."

"Unofficially, I'm your tour guide to Eritrea."

Berglund grabbed a knapsack from the Jeep and sauntered towards the shade. He shook Hank's hand before seeking out the pilot of the C-47. While the Saudis finished refueling, the military attaché had more to say to the ATC pilot than to Hank. The pilot glanced at his passenger as Berglund kept his back to him. It bothered the Aramco man to be the only one of the three who wasn't on active duty. Not being privy to Berglund's secret pained him even more.

The ground crew hurried to finish in time for the C-47 to reach Eritrea before dark. Berglund threw his knapsack into the cabin and joined Hank in the padded jump seats that made the troop carrier more like an executive aircraft. His uninvited guest seemed to enjoy the luxury even more than Hank.

"This is much better than my last trip to Asmara. Two days on a British corvette, eating terrible food in a Royal Navy mess."

They took off and headed south by southwest over the Red Sea. Hank felt like he was looking at a page from a living atlas. The water below the plane filled the fracture between the African and Asian Plates. Anthropologists like Gloria thought the region was where human life began. But from the air, there was little evidence that their ancestors had survived.

The radioman gave Hank and Berglund headsets so that they could hear each other over the engines. They left their seats to look out the window portals that dotted the cabin. Hank looked down at the shape of the barren coastline. He knew that Eritrea sat at the north end of the Great Rift Valley which opened on the Red Sea with a spray of islands. The ATC pilot descended and circled a modern harbor that suddenly appeared. Berglund's guide began.

"That's the Gulf of Zula. The Italians seized the port of Massawa in the 1880's. At the time, the British were happy about it. Their partners in the Suez Canal, the French, were being too selfish about the southern entrance. Mussolini built the modern port in the early thirties, a fascist version of the New Deal. Then he invaded Ethiopia in 1936.

"You probably know how poorly the Italians fought in North Africa, even though Rommel damn near took Cairo. Then the British got their ass kicked by the Germans in Greece. So our friends needed the East African campaign to rebuild their self-esteem. They pushed the Italian forces out of Libya and hit them again from Sudan. The main objective was to get them out of Ethiopia. Lawrence of Arabia had a cousin name Wingate - even crazier than he was - whose irregulars put Haile Selassie back on the throne in Addis Ababa. A lot of Wingate's commandos were Zionists from Palestine that he called the Gideon Force. The British bombed Massawa when they rolled up Eritrea in early '41."

Below the C-47, ships scuttled by the Italians were being salvaged. Massawa was now an Allied base protecting the southern entrance to the Suez. The damage to the harbor itself seemed light to Hank.

"It looks like the Italians are damn good builders."

Berglund smiled. "The best is yet to come."

Asmara, 6 September

The C-47 began the ascent to Asmara, which had been built on an inland plateau to escape the equatorial heat and the humidity of the Red Sea. Berglund pointed out a tramway in the port. As they flew west the Americans followed the pylons for more than seventy kilometers. Gondolas that had carried all the supplies between Asmara and Massawa still dangled from triple cables hundreds of feet above the rocky ground.

Berglund said, "That's the longest tramway in the world - plus seven thousand vertical feet from beginning to end."

As they approached the airport, Hank could see the city of Asmara set back from the escarpment. North and south, the plateau extended to the horizon. The ATC pilot circled the airfield before landing, the damage to the runway from British bombs still visible. The patched surface and thinner air made for a harder landing for the Americans.

After three vicious months in the Persian Gulf, stepping off the plane in Asmara was like a weekend at Lake Tahoe. Hank savored the clean crisp air.

"Feel like you're back in California?"

"I wish," Hank said.

"Dallol is a hundred kilometers south of here," Berglund said, the sun setting behind him. "It's even farther below sea level than Death Valley. They're neck and neck for the hottest place on Earth."

Their host, Major Tottenham, arrived in a Jeep driven by a Sudanese *askari*. The driver looked more like a warrior than the British officer. Europeans had relied on Africans as proxies in their wars against each other for generations. Tottenham reminded Hank of the kind of Englishmen that Mac despised in Cairo, enjoying war at a comfortable distance. The only difference was that Tottenham's colonial home-away-from-home was Asmara.

Berglund introduced Tottenham as his liaison from a branch of British military intelligence called MI2b. Hank thought better of asking what the abbreviation meant. Then Berglund introduced him as a "big oil man" from Ras Tanura, enjoying his own double entendre.

Tottenham looked up at him and asked, "Are you from Texas, Mr. Simmons?"

"No, California."

"I thought all American oil men were from Texas."

Berglund hopped into the Jeep. "Wrong, Major!"

Tottenham seemed to enjoy rubbing Americans the wrong way. They said little as they headed for their hotel near the headquarters of the protectorate. The air rattling through the open vehicle was almost cold. The terrain around them was high desert that reminded Hank of Nevada. But there were no camels in Las Vegas, no hooded goatherds in Reno. On their way, the dirt roads became cobble-stoned before growing into wide boulevards. All of the Italians in the city seemed to be out for a chat or an evening stroll, oblivious to the Eritreans they passed.

Unlike Arabia, women and children mixed with men on the streets. The African women walked without masks covering their faces. Their clothing looked cooler and lighter than burkas, even though they were still draped from head to toe. Despite the hardships that war had brought to the Horn of

Africa, Eritreans smiled easily at each other as they went about their daily lives. Structures ranged from modern to shambles but were all made from masonry and stone. The central district was filled with buildings that looked like they belonged in Italy.

Berglund resumed the travelogue from the back seat.

"Eritrea was the center of ancient Abyssinia. Orthodox Christians have been here since the first century AD. For a thousand years, they've been living alongside Muslims, outlasting the Ottomans. The Italians brought in the Catholic Church and - less officially - Yemeni Jews."

Hank's attention was drawn to many of the western comforts that Arabia lacked: movie houses, cafes and bistros, parks and plazas where friends and families gathered. Mussolini had envisioned Eritrea as the centerpiece of his colonial empire. To prop up employment and commerce in Italy, he had sent forward-thinking architects and city planners to reinvent Asmara. The final phase of the Art Deco masterplan had been disrupted by the wars in Africa and then Europe.

Their hotel, *Albergo Italia*, dated to the early colonial era when the constitutional monarchy in Italy had been more robust. Smaller than the grand hotels of the Nile Corniche, the interior was still elegant, its Eritrean staff gracious. Hank and Berglund checked into well-appointed rooms and met Tottenham for drinks on the terrace. The early evening was delightfully cool.

The Americans found Tottenham at a table in a quiet corner of the grounds, surrounded by bougainvillea. He had ordered the first round of gin and tonic. The British officer seemed to be warming to the task of entertaining his guests by the time they appeared in fresh clothes. But he remained patronizing in small ways that annoyed the new Aramco liaison.

"So tell me, Mr. Simmons, how may we be of service?"

"We expect that King Abdulaziz will approve the use of skilled Italian labor to finish our project in Ras Tanura. I was sent to explore the possibility. Since our military and yours have used the Italians on construction projects since last year, I'm hoping you can help me find good candidates."

Berglund broke in.

"Hank, the Major and I don't want to tell you who to hire. But we have some pretty strong opinions about who you should *not* offer jobs."

Tottenham feigned confusion.

"This project at Ras Tanura seems exceedingly complex. Your company is already building a new refinery in Bahrain, a stable British protectorate. And there is a great deal of well-priced petroleum in Iraq and Iran."

Berglund smirked. "Since the Crown is the majority owner of IPC, would the American Navy get the same price for fuel oil as the Royal Navy?"

Tottenham waved at the waiter for another round as he gazed impassively at Berglund.

"I'm afraid that's above my pay grade, Captain." Then he turned back to Hank. "Why bother to spend so much to increase production so far from home, Mr. Simmons?"

"Our military is entitled to its own supply chain, Major. Last year the US government almost took over our Saudi concession. At this point, the Pentagon is our partner and only customer. However you slice it, my company outbid our competitors on your side a long time ago."

Another pitcher of gin and tonic arrived. Glasses were refilled. Tottenham took a few sips, looking blandly at the Americans.

"Mr. Simmons, I hope you understand that Italy is in the middle of a civil war."

"The Major's right," Berglund said. "The expatriate population of Eritrea is the Reader's Digest version of the entire country. The southern half of Italy is under the control

126

of a unity government supported by the king and the pope that remains unpopular. The northern half is a fascist rump, supposedly ruled by Il Duce but controlled by the SS. The southerners are mostly monarchists. The northerners are mostly fascists. The partisans fighting in the mountains are communists. And both sides are under-paying ordinary Italians for the only work available in an economy destroyed by the war."

Tottenham added local color to the colloquy.

"The resistance here were fascists, small groups of Italian officers and Eritrean *ascari* who were still making trouble a year after the official surrender. There were a lot of desertions and deaths during the campaign. Tropical diseases killed more Italians than we did. Captain Berglund and I have a hard time knowing whether the Italians we interview are really who they say they are. It's easy for the hardcore *fascisti* - the Blackshirts - to assume the identity of a soldier who died anonymously in the deserts or the mountains."

Berglund stared at Hank and shrugged. "We don't really know who's loyal to Mussolini or Stalin or King Victor Emmanuel."

Tottenham sipped his gin and smiled quizzically. "Mr. Simmons, we can't say with any certainty if you could trust *any* Italian with a box of matches in your new refinery."

Berglund looked annoyed by his British counterpart, stuck in a long-running debate that neither officer seemed willing to concede. But Hank's tour guide couldn't resist another swipe at Tottenham.

"It's impossible for the Allies to repatriate the Italians in Eritrea while the war is still going on. But there's no more work to be done, militarily speaking, in East Africa. The unemployment rate here in Asmara approaches fifty percent. And the Crown doesn't want tens of thousands of Europeans on the dole."

It was the first time Hank felt like Berglund was trying to help him instead of just playing games with a rube from the oil patch. But Tottenham didn't want to acknowledge the obvious. Instead, he said, "Getting a bit chilly out here, don't you think?"

Hank had to agree. Like a radiator that had boiled over too many times in Ras Tanura, he had never thought he would freeze again. The three men moved to a private room off the main dining area inside the hotel.

Berglund looked at Hank with a winning smile as they passed through the lobby.

"I hope you understand that the British Army and the American Navy are counting on the Arabian American Oil Company to pay for all of this luxury."

"Of course. Our pleasure."

Tottenham beckoned to the Eritrean sommelier and said, "In that case, we'll have them open the 1932 Brunello."

The Italian colonials had defended their cellars better than their capital. The meal began with a Negroni cocktail, another first. Supper at the *Albergo Italia* was unlike Giulia's home cooking. She was a southerner like most of the Italian fishermen in California. Hank had grown up eating the simpler food of Campania and Sicily. Asmara's cuisine reflected Mussolini's center of power in the north, Milano. It was just as well that Hank couldn't easily calculate how many East African shillings their delicious meal cost: a lovely minestrone, clams from Zula drowning in butter and garlic, *risotto alla Milanesa*, *asa bucco*, and a summary plate of pungent local cheeses. Nor would he remember how he made it to his room upstairs.

Asmara, 8 September

Hank and Berglund sipped fresh espresso on a soft morning, sitting on a second-story terrace at their hotel. As he had since Giulia served it as a childhood treat, Hank added milk and sugar. Cappuccino was somehow more American. Major Tottenham had arranged for them to meet Alberto Pedani, the chief engineer for public works under the old regime. He arrived with Tottenham and two superfluous military police.

Pedani was a middle-aged man in a frayed but spotless white shirt, his leather belt pulled tight on loose trousers. The chief engineer hadn't been eating as well as the Americans. A look of mutual disdain passed between the Italian and the British officer when Tottenham introduced him. Pedani seemed to have already met Berglund, whom he greeted neutrally. He was more collegial with Hank, a fellow engineer who surprised him with a few words in Italian, gazing up at the younger American as if he were a building that had mistakenly been constructed with an extra floor.

Tottenham said, "Mr. Pedani has been a very able manager of the projects we have asked him to help us with over the last year."

Pedani ignored the compliment. "It is easier to build airfields and seaports when one is doing so a second time."

"Asmara is a beautiful city," Hank said.

"We were very proud of her."

The chief engineer spoke of the place where they were meeting as if it no longer existed. The precision of his accented English was polished by three years of unwanted occupation. Hank continued trying to charm the most important candidate for Ras Tanura.

"Mr. Pedani, we flew over the cableway connecting Asmara with Massawa, an incredible design. It's even more impressive that you were able to construct it in such an isolated part of the world."

Pedani bowed slightly and said, "Thank you. I wish I could demonstrate it for you but the Major has removed the diesel engines from the line."

Tottenham turned to the Americans and dissembled. "Precautions. Reparations."

"Alberto," Berglund broke in, "We've been telling Hank that there are lot of good people here that are hungry for work."

Pedani said, "They are simply hungry. Mussolini was a mistake for Italy. Fascism was a mistake for Europe. My countrymen here in Eritrea are ready to move on."

"Not all of them," Tottenham objected.

Pedani shrugged. "I am not religious man, Major, but the nuns used to teach us that we were all sinners."

Hank didn't want to be sidetracked by Tottenham. "Mr. Pedani, the Arabian American Oil Company is beginning the largest industrial project in the history of the kingdom. We're building a refinery and marine terminal complex in Ras Tanura. We need you and your men to help us."

Pedani remained calm, listening carefully. "How many men?"

"Hundreds then thousands."

"What kind of jobs?"

"Every trade you needed for the roads and buildings here in Asmara. Every welder and pipefitter you have. Every longshoreman and crane operator from Massawa. Plus your own cooks, drivers and doctors."

Pedani remained reserved. "What will you pay?"

"You will be paid in silver at the same rate that we pay our Arab workers."

Pedani smiled for the first time. The Italian engineer was the kind of man who smiled when most men could no longer hide their anger.

"But not what you pay Americans."

"Our agreement with the king requires us to train and hire his people whenever possible. It also prohibits us from paying workers from other countries more than we pay the Arabs."

"How will we live? Will you provide us food and shelter?"

"We only provide one meal to the Arabs during work hours. We are just beginning to build Saudi Camp in Ras Tanura, very basic facilities for cooking and sanitation. We can't offer extra benefits to foreigners under our agreement the king."

Hank knew that Pedani had negotiated contracts with the US military in Eritrea and Egypt. He had the demeanor of a man inured to lies who expected the most important parts of the Aramco offer to be concealed.

"We must buy our food from you?"

"We will only charge you what the company pays for your food. It will be deducted from your pay. The rest will be paid in silver - just like the Arabs."

"Is there a bank in Ras Tanura?"

"Not yet. We expect the American banks will be opening branches soon in the Eastern Province."

"Until then, we would bury our silver in the sand?"

Hank was feeling like he was back in Richmond, trying to toss lobs to a union leader who only wanted to play hardball. He looked to Berglund for help. The white shoe lawyer turned intelligence officer feigned ignorance.

"Mr. Pedani, I'm here to explore the possibility of us working together. I can't make you a firm offer for work until we have the approval of the Saudi government. But we expect that soon. In the meantime, I would like your opinion about the best tradesmen and professionals in Asmara."

Pedani gestured at Tottenham and said, "As the Major can attest, we have many thousands of good men who need work. Forgive me, can you tell me a little more about what you would pay them?"

"Most of the work will be paid at D-5 level, a little less than five hundred East African shillings per month. And we pay thirty percent more for overtime work."

"But American workers are paid more for the same work?"

"In order to get them to come to Arabia, we have to pay Americans more than they can earn at home. But in all honesty, Mr. Pedani, if we could get enough Americans to Ras Tanura, I wouldn't be here. What we're offering you is a chance to make hard currency while helping to end the war."

Pedani flashed his mirthless smile again. "The war is already over for us."

Berglund leaned closer to the Italian. "But not for your families."

The engineer nodded in accord with the American officer, then turned back to the oil man. He seemed sad as he gazed at Hank.

"That is why my men have to send their money home."

Asmara, 10 September

His last morning in Eritrea, Hank fell back asleep after the Fajr prayer echoed from the minarets, drowsy after his last indulgent night until he was reawakened by church bells. Through the window of his hotel room he could see Eritreans walking in the direction of the Enda Miriam Orthodox Church. The men and women as well as their children were all dressed in white from head to toe. After months in the kingdom, it was disorienting to be back in a land where Christianity could be openly practiced.

The bells ringing from Our Lady of the Rosary - a building constructed by one of Pedani's predecessors - reminded him of his childhood in Martinez. As a schoolboy, Giulia had taken him to mass on Sundays. Even though his mother had lost faith after his father's death, she allowed Hank to accompany her housekeeper. The boy who became an engineer appreciated the rituals of the mass, the stained-glass windows, and the smell of incense that reminded him of Scheherazade. He had been confused by the Holy Trinity but found it easy to think of Giulia as the Blessed Mother. He believed in her unconditional love more than the Holy Ghost.

After a few days in Asmara getting to know Pedani, Hank wasn't surprised that the Great Mosque and the Synagogue, like the Christian churches from the colonial era, merged tradition with modern architecture. The chief engineer of

Eritrea was a visionary, a twentieth-century Renaissance man. He hadn't built Asmara to honor Mussolini. The public buildings merged the best of Africa and Europe and dignified the lives of everyone in the city. The aerial tramway may have been futuristic but it was also pragmatic, sustaining the isolated population when neither a railway nor a road were feasible. As Hank flew over it again, then had a second look at the port of Massawa, he was confident that Pedani's men could build the Aramco complex in Ras Tanura. But there was a lot to ponder on the long flight.

How could he defend paying the Italians a third of what Americans were earning for the same work? How would the Italians react to the higher standards that they would see in American Camp? Would the Saudis be angered if Italian Camp evolved into something like a working-class neighborhood in Asmara?

Most perplexing of all, how could he deposit pay for Pedani's men in Italian banks when half of their country was still controlled by the Germans?

Before Hank left Asmara, he had had one last luxurious breakfast at *Albergo Italia* with Berglund. The military attaché had been cryptically optimistic about a payroll scheme connecting Italy and Arabia. Berglund implied that the OSS had agents monitoring the flow of cash and precious metals through Switzerland. He spoke vaguely about an undertow of Nazi wealth flowing out of the Third Reich as its troops retreated and its industries collapsed.

Hank was the only passenger on the C-47 headed to the concession headquarters. In his briefcase was Pedani's list, written in the engineer's precise script, of the best-qualified workers in Eritrea. Alongside each man's name was the address of their next of kin in Italy. Berglund had stayed behind to do another round of investigation of Pedani's men with Tottenham. When he arrived back in Dhahran, Hank went looking for Mac. It was late enough in the day that

Aramco's administrative offices were closed. He found him in the Dining Hall of American Camp, where the VP was kibitzing with a table of operations managers. Drilling was outpacing refining throughout the concession, which only increased Hank's sense of urgency. They walked the dusty roads of Aramco's headquarters after dinner, Hank trying to stay upwind from Mac's cigar.

"I was hoping you could help me sort a few things out, Mac."

"Of course."

"I'm feeling good about the Italians as our skilled labor but I'm struggling with how to pay them."

"How's that?"

"It's the opposite of the Saudi situation. They don't want silver or gold. They want their net pay to go to their families in Italy."

"That should be easy enough in the south. Rome is under control of the Allies. The Bank of Italy should be settling international transactions. I'm sure they'll be happy to have dollars or pounds flowing into their economy."

"But a lot of the skilled workers and most of the managers - almost all of the engineers - are from the north."

"There's no war in Switzerland, my boy."

Hank stopped in his tracks.

"You have to understand, Hank, Standard of California is just one of many companies whose biggest shareholders are the Rockefellers, including Chase National Bank. The Chase branches in Paris and Vichy France have continued operating throughout the German occupation. The managers - Frenchmen, of course - have done a very good job of keeping the Nazis happy. Neither of us probably want to know what that entailed."

Stunned, Hank fell behind Mac as he strolled with his cigar, enjoying their new scheme. Then the younger man closed the gap in a few long strides as the Aramco VP mused aloud.

"We can route payroll through neutral countries like Portugal or Spain. The industrialists in Germany continue to do business through the Swiss. IG Farben is the second biggest shareholder in Standard of New Jersey. As you know, the US government was none too happy that New Jersey protected Farben's synthetic rubber program. They didn't even stop selling Farben tetraethyl for aviation fuel until Pearl Harbor."

"I had no idea."

"Big oil is big money, my boy. The Mellons don't just own a bank and a steel mill. They own Gulf Oil. Once SAG gives us the green light, we can accommodate the Italians. The only challenge will be the last mile."

Hank tried to take in everything he had heard. Mac kept the rest of his thoughts to himself. Both men were counting on the OSS to make sure that their payroll made it from Swiss banks to families in provinces still controlled by the Nazis.

Asmara, 8 October

Hank's sense of prestige shuttling between Asmara and Ras Tanura on the company's C-47 dissipated as the weeks passed. The British insisted on working Monday through Friday in their protectorates while Aramco adhered to the customs of Islam, working Saturday through Thursday. As a result, Hank had worked every day for a month.

In the Eastern Province, Barger was laying the groundwork for entrance visas for the Italians. The concession's official policy had always been that they didn't bribe government officials. Hank was grateful that he didn't have to deal with an astounding number of emirs and bureaucrats with particular needs.

In Eritrea, the British were even more maddening than the Saudis. Tottenham was using the vetting process for exit visas to flush out the Italians the British wanted to expel. Berglund was camped out at *Albergo Italia*, haggling with his counterpart about which incorrigibles should be locked up or dumped in Arabia. Like most bureaucratic conflicts, the intractable decisions were deferred until the first wave of Pedani's men began working for Aramco. Berglund and Tottenham seemed to agree that fascists were more marketable than communists.

Hank had flown to Asmara on Sunday in order to be back at British headquarters when Tottenham opened his office on Monday morning. He met Berglund on the terrace for cocktails before dinner, preparing for another meeting with Pedani. Hank was ready to let off some steam after thirty straight days of work, his first gin and tonic in a week, and the milder weather in the mountains of Eritrea.

"I'm getting tired of every key man I want to hire being a suspected war criminal with a false identity."

Berglund was in a more philosophical state of mind, having avoided late summer in Jeddah, softened by the comforts of Asmara, and inured to the intransigence of their British allies.

"Eritrea was a protectorate before Pearl Harbor. For the last year, both armies have shed a lot of blood on their way up the Italian peninsula. Both country's military intelligence service thinks they have better information than the other's. The people that Tottenham and I work for are already looking beyond the endgame with the Nazis. They're political appointees who remember that Hitler and Mussolini got elected opposing the Bolsheviks after the Great War."

"What does that have to do with building a refinery and marine terminal in Ras Tanura?"

"The Allies exist in name only at this stage. One of the only things Washington and London agree on is keeping Uncle Joe from turning the continent red after the war."

"You're saying that all this rigamarole isn't about Arabian oil?"

"Not bad, Hank. This is just a prelude to what's going to happen all over Europe. Once the Germans surrender, we'll have to feed and house the losers as well as their victims. But it's tossup whether the Italians are going to restore a constitutional monarchy or create the next Soviet satellite."

More than once, Hank had heard Tottenham insist that Mussolini had dumped young leftists who were too talented to kill in Eritrea. The Major suspected that Pedani was a communist but the proof was still behind enemy lines in Torino, where the chief engineer had been a university student. Hank didn't really care. He needed the Italians to build things, which put him at odds with Tottenham, who was more interested in tearing people apart. He tried to be rational with Berglund.

"The empirical evidence at your military bases on the Red Sea is that Pedani knows how to get the best out of his men, regardless of their politics, and deliver projects on schedule."

Berglund leered. "That's because he has two families to feed: one here in Asmara and another one outside Florence. It's hard to be too egalitarian when you're a bigamist."

The next day, after another meeting at British headquarters, Pedani asked Tottenham if he could treat the Americans to his favorite *gelati*. It was typical of Pedani to insult Tottenham in small ways; the Major dismissed the MPs without being included in the invitation. Berglund declined the offer, which the Italian seemed to expect. Hank was happy to be Pedani's only guest as they waded through one of the busy thoroughfares in central Asmara. He was curious about the rumors about Pedani's wives that he had first heard from a leering Tottenham.

Pedani pointed out the Lady of the Rosary cathedral and the Asmara Synagogue; public monuments to the progressive glory that had been Italian East Africa. Hank was just as drawn to *Cinema Impero*, an Art Deco showplace with a queue of Europeans and Eritreans lined up outside. Movies, like secular music, were taboo everywhere in the kingdom except American Camp.

Hank had started skipping desserts at the hotel. Aramco hadn't sent him to Asmara to get fat. Pedani went into a gelateria gleaming with plate glass and white tile and asked his new boss what flavor he wanted. Hank was carried away by his first taste of the chocolate. On the hottest days of summer, Giulia had churned her own recipe at the boarding house. But the gelati in Asmara was the best he had ever had.

Pedani ordered hazel nut and beckoned for Hank to follow him outside. The two engineers were now on a first name basis. While there were four H's in Arabic, both the letter and the sound were absent from Italian.

"*Anka*," Pedani had asked him, "What is the top level of the Aramco pay scale for its Arab workers?"

"For daily pay, D-6."

"What about monthly pay for salary men?"

"M-8 goes up to about a thousand shillings a month."

"We will need this for the capos in each of the trades. Also for the doctors. Do you agree?"

Hank looked down at the world-weary Italian, who seemed oddly anxious.

"That seems reasonable, Alberto."

"In Aramco, do you have the expression, *top man money*?"

"Maybe you should explain, Alberto."

The other engineer shrugged. "For the very best man, sometimes it is better for the company to pay their true value without the other workers knowing. That way everyone is happy."

"How much would you suggest?"

Pedani shrugged again. "Perhaps two thousand shillings a month."

Hank laughed. "That's a lot of money, Alberto."

"But still less than you make, *Anka*."

He conceded Pedani's point but had one of his own to make. "Do you mind if I ask you a personal question?"

"Of course, *Anka*."

"Do you really have two wives?"

The chief engineer shook his head seriously. "Only one - in Fiesole. But I do have two families: two girls in Italy and two boys here in Eritrea."

Hank scoffed as they continued to stroll, savoring his gelati. Pedani looked up at him with an expression of unfamiliar earnestness.

"No wonder you need so much money."

"You must understand, *Anka*, that divorce is impossible in my country, part of the corruption between the church and the *fascisti*. If it were possible, I would marry the mother of my children here in Asmara. But I am an honorable man who will look after my first wife and my daughters, whether we are married or not. It is very difficult for them in the north. That is why it is so important for my men to be able to send their pay to their families. They are trapped between the Germans and your armies."

Hank offered Pedani his hand and - *confidenzialmente* - twice the top monthly scale for the chief engineer. The Italian's final request was that Aramco send half of his pay to his family in Fiesole and the other half to his family in Asmara.

San Francisco, 12 October

The hottest time of year in the city was after summer officially ended in the rest of California. The American southwest was a desert, after all, and by early fall the region heated up so much that its dome of high pressure extended to San Francisco. Despite being bordered on three sides by the Pacific, the city would be defenseless until the early winter storms arrived from the Gulf of Alaska. It was the only time of year when the military gabardine at the Presidio was too hot, when even the best-dressed San Franciscans shed their woolen coats and jackets. There were a few swimming pools at the Presidio for the troops and larger ones at Letterman Hospital for patients undergoing rehabilitation. But they were too close to the Pacific division of OWI for Gloria and Thierry.

Now that the Frenchman had his American woman, he was only desperate to escape the heat. After his Mediterranean youth and years in the South Pacific, he thought nothing of jumping into San Francisco Bay. When Gloria refused to join him he assumed it was because she was worried about being seen with him near Chrissy Field. From an inconspicuous vantage point she roared with laughter when he bounded out of the surge almost as quickly as he had jumped in. She giggled as he shivered, his vanity requiring him to say that the bay was as warm as the Coral Sea, the involuntary clatter of his teeth revealing the truth.

Gloria took a room at the Fairmont Hotel after calling her mother to say she would be working too late to catch the last train. The terrace level pool on Nob Hill was her favorite retreat in the city, made popular by guests like Ronald Reagan who had been a lifeguard before going to Hollywood. Now that every US industry was pouring money into neighboring bases and factories, the hotel was filled with visitors who demanded luxury. The pool at the Fairmont was busy enough in the early fall that one more couple was unlikely to attract much attention.

In her swimming suit, Gloria looked like a less angelic version of Esther Williams. When they were barefoot on the pool deck, Thierry was unbothered by being the shorter lover. In stature he resembled a Polynesian warrior; she had assumed he was a mixed-blood Caldoche before learning about his Algerian heritage. In the pool he was a stronger if less graceful swimmer than Gloria. The water refreshed them both, their cheerful voices merging with those of the other swimmers. The light of Indian summer gleamed through the arched windows and shimmered off the surface of the water and the deck.

After their swim, to minimize the risk to a married woman in a city where her family had many friends, they ordered room service. There was a steak and a lobster to share, a loaf of sourdough bread, an assortment of cheese that Thierry found disappointing, and a bottle of champagne from Guerneville, of all places.

"You know," Thierry said, "this is a pleasant wine. But it cannot be called champagne."

One of the conceits of Frenchmen who were young enough to have avoided the Great War was that their fathers fought the Germans for Champagne-Ardennes. Gloria raised her glass to toast Thierry, then mocked him.

"Wilson may have agreed to the Treaty of Versailles but the Senate never ratified it. We can call our sparkling wine whatever we want."

"In that case, we should drink it all."

The wine went to Gloria's head even faster than she intended. It was still exciting to abandon her last few lines of defense to a man who was so attracted to her. She had begun to wonder whether Hank made love to her because he desired her or because he felt a sense of marital obligation. Worse, before he left for Arabia, she feared her husband wanted another child that she had not agreed to have.

At the Fairmont, Thierry and Gloria shared nothing more or less than an enduring infatuation. The Frenchman was far more intoxicating than the champagne and she indulged herself wholeheartedly. Again that night Gloria was not a wife or a mother or a daughter. She was a woman who desired a man as much as he desired her. There was no war and afterwards there was a kind of peace, Gloria's best sleep since Hank left for Ras Tanura.

Ras Tanura, 24 November

Aramco celebrated Thanksgiving on Friday. American workers gathered for the traditional meal while Arab workers were off for Al-Jumu'ah, their day of communal prayer. The season brought the best weather since Hank arrived in the kingdom. He had a lot to celebrate in the Dining Hall, which was full of roast turkeys, hams, and all the other American-style dishes flown in for the occasion.

With many caveats, SAG had signed off on Aramco bringing in the Italians from Eritrea. An immigration process that the British and the Saudis were making up as they went along began to take shape. (The bureaucracies liberated in Rome began to assert themselves as well.) Once Hank had British exit visas and Saudi entrance visas for the first group of Italians from Eritrea, he spent most of November dealing with his counterparts in Payroll, Contracting and Legal.

A few months had passed since the last sinking of a Liberty Ship. U-boats were no longer being sighted in the Arabian Sea. As a result, Hank was making headway with his day job, working with Vukovich on the construction of the marine terminal. Although the process of unloading steel was still inefficient, it was more of a comedy than a tragedy. The maze of pipelines connecting the new refinery, the tank farm, and the marine terminal was growing every day. The stills for the new refinery were now the tallest structures in the Eastern

Province. The tank farm was growing on the flats near the pier like a pumpkin patch. Product lines for gasoline and fuel oil were beginning to appear. On the edge of the desert a village of steel was rising by the sea.

As the refinery complex grew, reports on operations multiplied. Department managers in Dhahran needed to share figures for barrels of crude oil moving from drilling sites to stabilizers, from stabilizers to storage tanks, from storage tanks to stills, and from stills to product lines. Products, byproducts, and contaminants needed to be accounted for in gallons, tons, atmospheric pressure, and cubic feet. Since crude oil came out of the ground hot and needed to stay hot to be efficiently moved through miles of pipelines, temperature and pressure readings were needed for myriad instruments in the propagating grid.

Words mattered as much as numbers. Hank spent half his time in Ras Tanura writing reports to counterparts in Dhahran, Manama, Al-Khobar and elsewhere. Some reports had to be co-written with Vukovich. Others had to reviewed by Ferguson before they could be shared with headquarters or Bechtel. There was another tier of reports intended for Standard and Texaco executives in San Francisco, Houston, New York, and Washington.

Ammar was indispensable when Hank was anywhere but his office. For every American worker in Ras Tanura there were three or four Arabs. But Ammar was useless when it came to writing, filing or retrieving Hank's burgeoning paperwork. As fluent as Ammar was when speaking English, he was hopeless spelling it. Common phrases he used effortlessly in conversation defeated him when Hank asked him to write them down. Aramco also used a variation of the Dewey Decimal System for categorizing documents by subject. Documents were also indexed by date and company division. But for Ammar, the papers that flowed across

Hank's desk were like grains of sand in the Empty Quarter, impermanent and individually meaningless.

The Jordanian was less troubled than Hank by his shortcomings: the assistants to Aramco executives were getting their own assistants.

As the burdens on English-speaking clerks from other Muslim countries grew, a younger class began connecting far flung offices. California Arabian had opened its first school for its Arab-speaking workers in 1940 out of necessity. The closest public school was in Al-Hofuf, a hundred miles inland. Few new hires from the Eastern Province could read or write their own language. In the beginning, the concession offered night classes in Arabic, English and basic math for its most promising local workers. As the concession ramped up in 1944, demand for teachers as Arab students increased. The Jabal schools, named after an early classroom between Dhahran and Al-Khobar, began a new program for the concession's youngest employees - office boys - who spent their mornings with teachers and afternoons with clerical staff like Ammar.

Ali bin Khalid Al Bahri looked like an early adolescent to Hank. But it was useless for Americans to guess the age of any undernourished male, young or old, from the impoverished gulf. It was common knowledge that Arab boys as young as twelve were working as office boys as demand for labor grew. In a land where the bedu began to herd their animals as children (and where slavery was still legal) there was no angst in Aramco about underage workers and little more in Riyadh.

Ali was a fatherless boy from a pearl-diving village near Half Moon Bay that had been devastated economically by cultured pearls from Japan. He proudly claimed to be *maybe eighteen*. When Hank discovered that Ali could find files and reference data that Ammar couldn't, he stopped worrying about how old he was. As bright as he was, Ali wasn't certain about the date or year of his birth nor why his father Khalid had died.

Despite the meager diet in Saudi Camp, Ali began filling out within weeks of his arrival. When the new office boy smiled, the corners of his upturned mouth almost touched his prominent ears. Ammar looked out for Ali as if he were a brother. His English wasn't as polished as Ammar's but his intuitive grasp of mathematics was miraculous. Ali's hunger for knowledge of any kind made Hank feel like he had been a slacker as a kid.

Like most engineers, Hank only trusted his own figures. He received the reports on volumes of crude oil and product flowing into the tank farm and out through the submarine pipeline to Bahrain. His standard practice was to verify the most important metrics with his own slide rule. Ali was fascinated by the mathematical tool which Ammar had ignored. Hank hadn't seen Peter for months. He was happy to spend his free time training Ali to do calculations. Within a few weeks, Ali could accurately do all of the calculations for the marine terminal on his own. Hank stopped rechecking the figures from the tank farm. Ali became as reliable at quality control as a journeyman twice his age.

Ras Tanura, 27 November

The prewar submarine pipeline to Bahrain was back online. Because Aramco was exporting much larger volumes of crude oil, new royalty tanks had been built near the marine terminal. Few things were more important to SAG than the tonnage of petroleum leaving the kingdom. Mac visited to inspect the royalty tanks and conduct a tutorial with Hank as they walked on the terminal, stretching farther into gulf every day. He began magnanimously.

"For every dollar we invest in oil exploration or production, we'll spend another dollar for roads, schools, hospitals and housing in the concession. We're making up for a thousand years of isolation and poverty, Hank."

"They need every penny, Mac."

The oilmen continued walking slowly on the new superstructure, one scalloped wave after another bouncing off the concrete footings beneath them.

"What do you know about CalTex, Hank?"

"Just that it's a joint venture of Standard and Texaco."

"When Standard sold half of the Saudi concession, the cash that Texaco contributed was symbolic. The real cost to Texaco was assuming fifty percent of the capital risk for developing Arabia. Rieber, the old pirate, had come up as a tanker captain. After building up markets for Texaco products in Africa and Asia, he convinced his board they needed the Arabian Layer."

It was difficult for Hank to imagine a project too big for Standard. But on their journey from the States, Mac had echoed something he had heard his father-in-law say: the rich got richer with other people's money.

"Standard contributed Bapco, our concession in Bahrain, to the joint venture. Texaco contributed all of its downstream business east of the Suez. But it's important for you to understand, Hank, that the Saudis have nothing to do with CalTex."

Hank had spent years learning to refine crude oil and control product flow. But as they admired the new pipeline to Bahrain, Mac was teaching him on how revenue flowed. Like an eager student, he phrased his answer as a question.

"So we close the books on the Saudis when we pay royalties on the crude leaving Ras Tanura?"

The Aramco VP smiled. "That's right, Hank. Whatever happens downstream from Ras Tanura is strictly between Standard and Texaco. The Saudis have no contractual right to look at the CalTex books."

While they were still somewhere between Cairo and Dhahran, Mac had explained the nexus of the agreement that Standard negotiated in 1932. Aramco was still paying the same royalty per ton to Abdulaziz twelve years later. The only variable, as serious as it had become, was the exchange rate between US dollars and British sterling. But the war had radically increased global demand for petroleum. And the end of the war would drive it farther.

Mac and Hank found themselves on a scaffolding nearly half a mile offshore. Three stories beneath them, the green waves from the gulf continued into the bay on a rising tide. From a tender, Vukovich used a bullhorn to yell at them to head back towards shore. The Aramco VP waved at Bechtel's project manager like a lost tourist before turning around. Hank invited him for lunch. Heavy cranes and scaffolding around the new refinery towers loomed beyond the other end of the terminal.

"CalTex is about to become more profitable than Aramco, Hank. The sleight of hand requires us to keep SAG focused on royalties increasing along with the tonnage of exports. But all of the feed you're pumping through this terminal will be worth more by the time it arrives in Bahrain. When the war ends and foreign markets are restored, CalTex will be able to raise prices without sharing the gain with Abdulaziz."

* * *

The royalty tanks vexed Hank in multiple ways. The political challenge that Mac laid out was vulgar but straightforward. Because the tonnage in the tanks determined the royalties due to him, the king's finance ministry needed to verify the amount of petroleum in each tank. Ohliger and Mac both pressed Hank to make sure that the Saudi officials had confidence in their own measurements.

The technical aspects of the royalty tanks were more demanding than their politics. The displacement of the tanks was always more than the volume on which royalties were due. Inside containers made from concrete and steel, the interaction between dozens of suspended hydrocarbons varied with hundred-degree swings in the temperature on Tarout Bay. Crude oil from the limestone formations of the Eastern Province contained water as well as other impurities. Natural gas and more dangerous hydrogen sulfide needed to be accounted for as a third phase of tank volume. Many measurements had to be done before calculating the tonnage of crude oil each time the royalty tank was refilled. Since each royalty tank held tens of thousands of barrels, differences of only a few grams per gallon imputed to thousands of shillings in sterling.

Since Aramco was paying royalties on tonnage instead of volume, each royalty tank had a unique value. Petroleum was like any other liquid in nature. Crude oil from different deposits within the Arab Layer had different amounts of each hydrocarbon, like barrels of muck from different parts of a swamp. Just as it could be sweet or sour with hydrogen sulfide, it could have different amounts of natural gas and water suspended within it. The weight and density of petroleum depended not only on its origin in Al-Hasa but its location within a royalty tank, the heaviest components on the bottom, the lightest on the top. The device used to measure the variation in specific gravity at index levels was called - unfortunately - a thief.

Manama, 4 December

Tottenham finally transported the first group of Italian workers on a British freighter from Eritrea to Bahrain. To attract less attention, the eighty-eight new workers were booked as employees of Bapco: the Bahrainis were more receptive to non-Arab visitors than the Saudis. The plan was for the Italians to arrive from Manama with as little fanfare as possible at Al-Khobar, the busiest port of entry on the gulf. But the morning they arrived in Manama, Hank received a cable from Pedani in the Bapco offices: the concession's liaison was urgently needed there.

The barges that made the twenty-mile crossing took all day. Hank was able to talk the harbormaster at Al-Khobar into spots on a highspeed launch for Ammar and himself. They raced down the coast in the old Ford with the American behind the wheel to make their noon departure. The weather in early winter on the Persian Gulf was downright pleasant. The seas between Al-Khobar and Bahrain were calm, the air wrapping around the launch refreshing. The open water was dotted with the triangular sails of dhows. Hank had never seen Ammar so relaxed, liberated from the unforgiving terrain of Al-Hasa, no longer an exile in his homeland. But Hank remained troubled by the last-minute crisis on the other side of the strait.

Pedani had mentioned the *caporegimes* in his cable without referring to any of the leaders of the tradesmen by name. During his second trip to Asmara, Hank had met them face to face. The experience had been like being across the table from the union leaders in Richmond. Each of the capos ruled their tradesmen by fear and favor. Pedani's official authority as chief engineer had ended along with the colonial regime. Once Eritrea became a British protectorate, Pedani's only power was his ability to competently negotiate in English for military contracts on behalf of all the trades. Most of the Italian workers had little formal education and all of them abided by the ancient system of patronage enforced by the capos.

Tottenham flagged two of the trade leaders as suspected war criminals. At that first meeting, Hank could have picked them out on his own. Squalo, the leader of the crane operators, had dark, wideset eyes, a jutting chin, and too many teeth. Bruno, the leader of the longshoremen, looked like a brown bear, more German than Italian in demeanor. They were the kind of men who could be counted on to carry a concealed weapon. Both admitted to being in the expeditionary forces that brutally overran Ethiopia. Berglund suspected they had been non-commissioned officers in the Blackshirts rather than the innocent conscripts they claimed to be. But Tottenham couldn't prove that Squalo and Bruno were war criminals and Pedani couldn't mobilize the crane operators or the longshoremen without them.

The speedboat carrying Ammar and Hank slowed as it neared the port of Manama. Compared to Al-Khobar, the multi-story Moorish buildings along the waterfront looked like Venice. The ruins of the Portuguese Fort reminded the American that other nations had come and gone before Standard struck oil on Bahrain. He found the Italians in an unhappy crowd outside Bapco headquarters. Most of them were staring at copies of their employment agreements.

Others were sullenly smoking in silence. Many of them had been POWs until Mussolini was deposed the year before. The rest had endured four years of British rule in their former colony before finding themselves in Bahrain, another British protectorate. It had been even longer since any of them had seen their families.

Squalo's nickname meant "shark" in Italian and he seemed to sense blood in the water around Manama. He gave Hank a cunning glance and followed the Aramco liaison through the heavy wooden double doors. Pedani was in the quartermaster's office, watching Bruno wave the employment agreement in the face of an exasperated Bahraini clerk.

Pedani nodded at Hank as the capos converged on the American. Squalo spoke first. "Why should we pay for food that your Arab workers get for free?"

"We discussed this in Asmara. The only meal we provide the Arabs is their lunch. It's usually just a bowl of rice and a piece of bread."

Bruno spoke next. "But we will be paid less than the Arabs after you deduct the cost of the same meal."

Squalo spit in the direction of the Bahraini clerk. "We will not work for less than the Arabs."

Hank watched the clerk sidestepping towards the door, then addressed the capos. "You'll be making more than the Arabs, not less. Our agreement with the king says we have to pay foreign workers on the same scale as the Arabs. But all of you have skills the Arabs don't have! You'll be paid at higher levels on the scale. That means that the average Italian is going to make more than the average Arab, hour for hour!"

Bruno and Squalo weren't persuaded. The capos were conveniently forgetting their first conversation with Hank in Asmara - neither had objected when he explained that the cost of their food would be deducted from their pay. But somewhere between San Francisco and New York, a corporate lawyer had opined that the Italian labor agreement would only be valid under international law if they could read it in their own language. Bruno and Squalo were trying to use the printed section about payroll deductions as leverage.

Hank stood his ground without saying more. Drillers over the concession were complaining that it took a dozen Arabs to do the work of a five-man crew in the States. The skills and experience of Italian tradesmen would compound the disparity. But acknowledging that would strengthen the capos' argument and weaken Pedani's position with the workers Aramco desperately needed for Ras Tanura.

Standing beside Hank, Pedani raised both hands and gazed at the capos in a beneficent fashion. "Give us a few minutes."

Without waiting for Bruno and Squalo to respond, Pedani backed into the hallway, waving for Hank to follow him. When they were outside, he raised his voice to be heard over the restless crowd of tradesmen from Eritrea.

"*Dacci qualche minuto!*"

Pedani waded through his countrymen and headed for the harbor. Hank followed him along with Ammar. Behind them, Hank heard Bruno and Squalo shouting at them from the entrance of Bapco's headquarters, telling Pedani where he could put the employment contract. Pedani and Hank ignored the epithets. When they were too far away from the other Italians to be heard, Pedani spoke.

"We need to give the men something - *una concessione.* Without it, Bruno and Squalo will continue to try to turn the other capos against me."

Hank concurred as they passed the severed head of a camel hanging in a butcher's stall. The vendors in Manama offered much the same inventory that he had seen in the markets of Al-Khobar: dates, rice, flour, fragrant spices, and the catch of the day from the gulf. Ammar trailed them through the souk to ward off pickpockets. The American, Italian, and Jordanian made their way through passages crowded with Bahrainis.

There was a promenade of battered stone along the waterfront. In the harbor they passed an odd assortment of watercraft: the wooden dhows of the fishermen and pearl divers, a flotilla of commercial vessels building the new submarine pipeline from Ras Tanura, and British gunboats. Farther out, one of His Majesty's destroyers was at anchor in the bay. In Asmara, Hank had felt the deep sense of loss among the Italians stranded in East Africa. Even though the British had defeated them, the Europeans shared the same colonial mindset. Right or wrong, Bruno and Squalo felt superior to Africans and Arabs - as did their tradesmen.

"Let me see if I can make the mid-day meal free, like it is in Saudi Camp."

Pedani nodded agreeably as he walked. "*Il compromesso*."

"I'll need to check with Dhahran."

They returned to the Bapco offices. Ammar showed Hank a back entrance where they wouldn't be spotted by the Italians outside. Inside, there was a private telephone line for between Bapco and Aramco. Rather than going straight to Ohliger, Hank called Mac. The oilman's Scottish accent sounded thicker across the strait.

"What can I do for you, laddy?"

"There's a hitch with the first boat of Italians and I need a favor. Aramco needs to cover the cost of the mid-day meal for the men in Italian Camp."

"You know there's no such thing as a free lunch, laddy!"

"Pedani's men are hung up on us feeding the men in Saudi Camp for free."

"They're lucky to be out of Eritrea. There's no work to be had there!"

"Mac, all I'm asking for is a bag of rice and a case of spam. There's less than a hundred men here in Manama!"

"Not for long, laddy. There'll be a thousand Italians in Ras Tanura in a few months."

"Not if the capos here refuse to sign on, Mac. These men know the Americans working for Bechtel are making a lot more for the same work. But they won't take less than the Arabs. Can you explain this to Ohliger for me?"

For a moment there was only static on the submarine telephone line. "Pigs get fed and hogs get slaughtered, I suppose."

Hank thanked Mac and got off the line before the money man could change his mind. Within an hour, Ohliger cabled his approval to Bapco: the mid-day meal in Italian Camp became a benefit instead of a debit. Hank let Pedani announce the good news to the tradesmen before Bruno and Squalo could claim victory. It took another hour for the Bahraini clerk to amend eighty-eight copies of the employment contract. Most of the men seemed happy to be on their way to Ras Tanura; the trouble-making capos were the last to sign.

After the Italians boarded the barge that ferried them to Al-Khobar, the wind dropped on the strait and the gulf turned glassy. Most of the tradesmen were lulled to sleep during the slow crossing. But Pedani admired the sun setting over the kingdom from the bow, with Hank and Ammar standing alongside.

Dhahran, 5 December

After months at the *Albergo Italia* in Asmara, Berglund's accommodations in Dhahran left a lot to be desired. The US consular branch at Aramco headquarters was half of a prefabricated box that doubled as his sleeping quarters, with only a swamp cooler to remind him that he was on the winning side. The OSS officer had agreed to camp out in the concession until he could work through the details of the international payroll for the Italian families. He knew as well as Hank and Mac that the challenges went far beyond the first eighty-eight souls languishing at Ras Tanura. And he wasn't sure he had enough gin from Eritrea in his diplomatic pouch to last until his return to Jeddah.

Berglund dressed to join a senior staff meeting in the administration building. The concession's business attire didn't meet his usual standards. Ohliger expected his senior managers to wear suit pants but coats stayed on hangers unless dignitaries - not including junior diplomats - were visiting from the States or Riyadh. Worst of all, Ohliger permitted short-sleeved shirts if they were white and worn with a knotted tie. Thus, Berglund arrived better dressed than any of the Aramco executives: a lightweight cream-colored double-breasted suit, a crisp white shirt with French cuffs, and a silk tie. The oilmen greeted him in a perfunctory manner, like a brother-in-law who sold used cars.

Berglund's boss arrived a few minutes later, the older man leaning on a cane adorned with ivory and brass, an inscription in Arabic wrapped around the handle. His grey suit was wrinkled after flying from Jeddah on the Aramco C-47. Barger, who had driven him over from the airfield, wryly announced his arrival.

"Gentlemen, I would like to introduce Colonel William Eddy, minister plenipotentiary of the United States to Saudi Arabia."

Mac and Ohliger greeted Eddy more warmly than they had Berglund. After hearing so many of the OSS adventures in North Africa over drinks in Asmara, Hank was dazzled to meet Eddy in person. The oilmen viewed the new minister as a vast improvement over Moose, the first US envoy to the kingdom. Neither Eddy nor Berglund underestimated their hosts. Aramco had its own intelligence sources in Jeddah, Riyadh, and Washington: most of FDR's oil advisors were from Standard, its sisters in New Jersey and New York, or Texaco. But everyone in Dhahran seemed confident that Eddy would convince Abdulaziz that Roosevelt was more trustworthy than Churchill.

As planned, the group split into two separate meetings. Eddy wanted to brief Ohliger and Barger on the push-pull between the Saudi ministers, the British ambassador, and the US government. Everyone in the room was in an awkward situation: Eddy's new superiors in the State Department wanted a military base in Dhahran more than the War Department; Aramco wasn't keen to expand its airfield unless their government was willing to pay for it. Negotiations between the Saudis and the US were shaping up as a new round of poker, with the British claiming their bases obviated the need for an American military presence in the Persian Gulf.

Berglund was on point in the lower-profile meeting with Hank and Mac. The Scot looked like he regretted being cut out of the conversation with Eddy. But he was savvy enough to understand why the US minister needed to be at arm's length from what Aramco was cooking up in the SS-controlled provinces of Italy. Mac led Hank and Berglund down the hallway to his office.

"As a general rule," Mac confessed, "I don't like Wall Street lawyers."

"Think of me as the military attaché, then."

"Just skip all that Ivy League mumbo jumbo."

"I'll do my best, sir."

"Call me Mac, my boy." His office was less distinguished than Ohliger's but Berglund knew better than to judge an oilman by appearance or education. Mac gestured to a pair of matching chairs as he settled into the padded one on the other side of his desk.

"*As you know*, John Junior has been the largest shareholder in Chase National Bank for some time."

Berglund smiled agreeably, as if everyone from his old law firm, Sullivan and Cromwell, was on a first-name basis with each of the Rockefellers.

"Standard controls a number of entities with international accounts at Chase National. But getting payroll from Bahrain through France to Italy will be difficult."

"The Vichy branches of Chase are no longer relevant," Berglund asserted.

Insulted, Mac sat back in his chair, silently demanding an explanation if not an apology.

"The Allies landed near St. Tropez - of all places - in August and advanced rapidly up the Rhone Valley. The Vichy government collapsed like a desert tent. The Swiss have the largest unaligned army in central Europe and they're aggressively protecting their French border. But smaller Swiss units are crossing their Italian border at will. The SS only control the populated areas and the railways. Cooperation between American and Swiss military intelligence is better than with the *partigiani* - commies mostly. It won't be hard to find Italian bankers who will be happy to tell us what's happening to the only hard currency flowing through their branches."

"In that case," Mac said, "We should probably route Italian payroll through our merchant bank in Istanbul. The Turks and the Swiss are both used to meeting the needs of the Germans."

Berglund agreed. He didn't mention that the Allied advance had improved the flow of information between Bern and London, the OSS hub in Europe. Allen Dulles, the chief of the OSS station in Bern, had helped recruit Berglund when they were both still practicing law at Sullivan and Cromwell. Private sources that Dulles had been cultivating for years were paying off in spades. Other than the identities of their account holders, there were few secrets the Swiss wouldn't share with American contacts. Berglund offered one nugget to Hank and Mac.

"The Swiss banks are no longer extending credit to the German banks. The SS in northern Italy may be more eager to accept sterling for exchange against the lira than you think. The top Nazis are sitting on huge piles of loot that are hard to transfer. They need liquidity for their personal exit strategies through Portugal and Spain."

Berglund enjoyed the looks of surprise on the oilmen's faces. The end game in Europe was turning Aramco payroll behind enemy lines into child's play for the OSS.

Ras Tanura, 8 December

Hank was awakened by cannon fire. By the time he heard the second report he was outside the trailer. It was coming from the east and north, where the Italian Camp had just gone up. He hopped in the old Ford and hurried to the beach.

It was embarrassing to see the British Army surplus tents again. Hank thought the rotting canvas had been burned after they finished the bunkhouses for Bechtel workers in August, when even the drilling crews were pounding nails. But temporary shelters deemed uninhabitable for Bechtel workers were now home for Pedani and his men. Intended to protect troops from winter weather, the fixed flaps made it impossible to ventilate the tents in the Persian Gulf.

Hank was afraid that veterans of the Italian expeditionary force had rejoined the Axis. But Pedani's men were in high spirits. Somewhere between Manama and Al-Khobar, one of them had acquired a small cannon from an armed dhow. Piracy had been more important than pearl diving on the gulf before the discovery of oil. The Trucial Coast owed its name to the nineteenth century accord between the sheiks and the British Navy.

Hank asked what the hell was going on. Pedani waved back in peace.

"*Buon natale*, *Anka*." Gesturing at his merry band, he said, "The men are celebrating *L'immacolata Concezione*."

The Advent season began in Rome with a round from the cannons of Castel Sant'Angelo. Pedani's men had only been in Ras Tanura a few days, but long enough to have procured enough blasting powder to announce the beginning of the year-ending holiday season.

A lonely guy missing his own family began to go soft. As a boy, Hank had gravitated to the Italians because of the joy they took in small things, and each other. Most of all, Giulia had warmed the place inside him where his mother's love was supposed to be. As a teenager, he had been curious about the Immaculate Conception. Teachers in public school didn't explain the virgin birth of Mary. But by the time of their first holy communion, the Catholic girls could explain it with legalistic detail, even if they were hazy on the biology. When he had asked Giulia about the Blessed Mother, she had simply said that Mary was qualified to bear the Christ child because she was untainted by sin. Hank could imagine such a woman because of Giulia's generous heart and peaceful soul.

A truckload of Jiluwi's soldiers arrived. The platoon leader hopped out of the cab, pistol in hand.

Hank raised his arms and began walking slowly in the direction of the truck. He called out, "*Hasananaan, hasananaan*," then repeating in English, "Everything's okay!"

It was just as well that Hank's Arabic was limited and Ammar wasn't there to translate. It would have only made things worse if the Saudi soldiers heard that the infidels who had just arrived from Africa were celebrating the Immaculate Conception. Hank could hear Barger and others during his orientation, warning new hires that they were prohibited from practicing any religion but Islam.

The platoon leader, more annoyed than angry, inspected the cannon. Hank was glad that it was pointed out to sea. Fortunately, the Italians had already used up the blasting powder they pinched from Bechtel. There were no cannonballs or signs of other weapons that might incite the soldiers of the Emir. As was often true in the kingdom, a cultural coincidence worked in favor of Aramco. Bedouins liked to fire their long rifles during celebrations as much as the Italians loved their ceremonial cannons.

"*La 'akthar*," the platoon leader said. *No more.*

In unison, Hank and Pedani obediently shook their heads. "No more," they agreed, "*Hasananaan.*"

The platoon leader waved to his men to get back in the truck. The Italians stood in place until the soldiers were well down the dusty road back to Ras Tanura. Then Pedani beckoned for Hank to follow him to one of the tents near the cannon. He pulled back the flap to reveal another fond memory. Most of the fishermen in Martinez were from Campania or Sicily, where Nativity scenes appeared on the eighth of December as well. *Presepes Napoletano* were more entertaining than the somber religious depictions seen in most of America. In addition to Mary, Joseph and the animals in the manger, Italians populated their Nativity scenes with whimsical contemporary figures.

Even Squalo was light-hearted. He grabbed Hank by the elbow and said, "*Guarda qui, Anka.*"

Squalo pointed at a professorial figure in a long white coat, slide rule in hand, standing behind the empty cradle. Hank could see the resemblance in the handmade figure. His Italian was a little better than his Arabic at that point.

"*E Pedani?*"

Eighty-seven Italians - everyone but the figure's pained inspiration - howled in glee, hopping up and down, slapping each other's backs.

"*Si, si!*"

"*Il professore!*"

"*Professore Pedani!*"

Palo Alto, 16 December

If she couldn't be a better wife for the holidays, Gloria was determined to be a better mother. She had written Hank about getting Peter his first bicycle for Christmas and he had sent back his endorsement. After sleeping in on Saturday, she went to the same bike shop on University Avenue where her parents had taken her as a child. She remembered an assortment of models and sizes for boys and girls and her father's impatience when she couldn't decide on a color. Now, to her astonishment, she was the harried parent, one of many on the sidewalks trying to finish their holiday shopping. The familiar-looking decorations crisscrossing University were worse for wear after years of wartime service.

Because of its proximity to Stanford, the bike shop usually had a steady stream of customers. Gloria was unsettled to find she was the only one when a bell on the door announced her entry. There was one row of adult bicycles spaced to create the illusion of variety. All of them had the same thin wheels, flimsy tires, and desultory fenders. There were no adornments to inspire a child that was big enough to ride them. All of them were painted the same a color that wasn't a color at all, an amalgam of browns and greys blended into a non-hue. Gloria imagined that the gloomy feeling was like shopping in Petrograd. The store's owner, whose rimless bifocals she remembered from when she was no older than Peter, was behind the counter.

"Can I help you ma'am?"

"I'm looking for a bicycle for my son. He's only five. None of these will do."

"I'm sorry, we only have the one size. The government took over the design and production of bicycles after Pearl Harbor."

"Yes, I remember. Victory Bikes?"

"The Production Board and the Price Administration can't seem to get along. A lot of manufacturers have gone out of business. There's only a few companies left to build the official design and their quotas have been dropping every month."

"But that's absurd!"

Forlorn, the bike shop owner beckoned at the identical bicycles.

"They stopped making them entirely in September. As far as I know, these are the last bikes I'll get until the war's over, ma'am."

"That's outrageous!"

The store owner shrugged and said, "If it weren't for repairs, we'd be out of business too."

"But what am I supposed to get my son for Christmas?"

The owner's expression lightened. The holidays were still about hope and the next miracle was only nine days away.

"Maybe you can find an old one. People keep bringing in bikes they find in the garage for us to recondition. We'd be happy to fix one up if you can find one!"

Gloria was still out of sorts when she arrived back at her parents' home without a bike. There were too many other presents under the oversized tree, decorated with all the same ornaments she had grown to hate as a child. Her father, wearing his red cardigan, was crooning along with his favorite carols on the radio. The holiday spirit was like gravy he poured over his rotting marriage. It was an ugly if familiar *folie a deux*; her parents had everything but enduring affection for each other. That was why they lived so close to where they met; it was easier to remember when they were in love.

Holidays notwithstanding, her father's personal regime prohibited more than two cocktails a night. But her mother made up for his moderation. The first year that Hank spent the holidays with them, she had to explain that (for her mother) the Twelve Days of Christmas meant one more drink each day than the day before. In January, when her father insisted that everyone in the house abstain from alcohol, her mother would become even more dreadful.

Gloria stayed upstairs with Peter until they were called to dinner. By then her mother had consumed enough alcohol to be ruthless at the table with everyone but her grandson who, in the absence of Christ, was her Messiah. As usual, the first words out of her mouth seemed innocuous and vaguely maternal.

"Phil Sorensen is home for the holidays, Gloria."

"That's nice."

"He's making a fortune in Portland. Aluminum seems so much more interesting than petroleum, don't you think?"

Gloria frowned and glanced at her father. Both of them knew better than to challenge the family inebriate.

"His mother says he still asks about you every time they speak. I hope you'll be able to join us for dinner the day after tomorrow."

"Mondays are usually busy at the New Caledonia desk."

Her mother stared spitefully at Gloria. She had never forgiven her daughter for not dating the boy next door. That Gloria found Phil boring had never mattered to her mother. Now that he was on his way to his first million, she would never be allowed to forget it. The next words out of her mother's mouth sent a chill through Gloria.

"Can't Thierry cover you at the Presidio?"

Was it possible that she knew about her affair? Even if she didn't, her mother's sodden expression hid another secret: she didn't expect her daughter to be any more faithful to Hank than she had been to Gloria's father. Drunk or sober, that was her mother's point. If her father had disappointed her as a husband, her daughter shouldn't be surprised if she took another lover. And if her mother had never wanted Gloria to marry Hank, then it was never too late to abandon him. As usual, her father came to her defense.

"You know that Gloria's irreplaceable, darling."

"But the Sorensens are our oldest friends. Phil and Gloria haven't seen each other for years!"

"Gloria's a married woman, dear." He turned to his grandson and said, "Your mother's serving her country - like your father, Peter. Would you like another slice of roast? We've got to put some muscle on you!"

Not to be outdone, her mother put a dollop of mashed potatoes on her grandson's plate. She gave her daughter a withering glance, reminding Gloria that Peter was now the family's most prized possession. As soon as her son finished his dessert, Gloria took him upstairs to get ready for bed.

After reading the chapter about the Little Prince tending his Rose, Gloria curled up beside Peter until he fell asleep. Her mind continued to race as the little boy's breathing became more peaceful. She heard her father lock the doors, turn off the lights, and guide her stumbling mother up the stairs. For as long as she could remember, her parents had slept in separate bedrooms. When the only sound in the house was her mother's snoring, Gloria crept into her own room and dressed for bed, putting a warm robe over her last decent pair of silk pajamas. Knowing that she couldn't sleep, she took a pentobarbital and sat in an overstuffed chair until she was drowsy enough to get under the quilted satin bedspread.

Looking through the window at her husband's convertible, its top up for the winter, Gloria promised herself that she wouldn't be trapped in Palo Alto for the holidays. Her first choice would have been to take Peter to the Sierras. But Sugar Bowl, the first ski area at Lake Tahoe with a chair lift, was closed because of the war. She was infuriated that gas rationing could keep her son from playing in the snow while his father was pumping millions of gallons in Ras Tanura.

There were other attractive holiday destination like Monterey and Pebble Beach. But if she couldn't be certain she could get somewhere and back on one tank of gas, she crossed them off her unwritten list. In the iconology of the season, Thierry was Satan. Outside of work hours at the Presidio, Gloria wanted to be as far away from San Francisco as possible. The Frenchman was more tempting with proximity and, under any circumstance, could never meet Peter. As she fell asleep Gloria decided to spend Christmas in Martinez, as far from her lover as she could get on half a tank of gas in her husband's car.

Ras Tanura, 24 December

Winter on the Persian Gulf was kinder than summer. Days were seldom hot and evenings were cool, chilly if the wind came up. The most punishing winds out of the northwest - *shamals* - weren't expected until later in the spring. Unlike summer, when the gulf was like a hot bath, the waves on the beach at Ras Tanura were refreshing. As the end of 1944 approached, nearly all of the building material and new equipment had finally arrived. Pedani's men were allowing Bechtel to begin catching up with construction on the refinery and the marine terminal. Project timelines for Aramco were improving.

Although Ohliger discouraged fraternizing across camps - even between Bechtel and Aramco - Hank's responsibilities as liaison gave him many reasons to visit the Italian Camp. He hadn't been able to talk Ferguson out of putting up barbed wire around the compound, but it had been laid out to accommodate thousands of workers. That meant there was still a vast amount of sandy space inside the perimeter for its first eighty-eight occupants. And the location - east of the refinery complex rising on Tarout Bay, north of American Camp - left the new arrivals with miles of empty beach to themselves, giving Italian Camp the feeling of a rustic resort.

Hank's final agreement with Pedani had weekly overtime pay for the Italians delivered as silver shillings - like the

Arabs. Most of it was going for food. In his wisdom, Pedani had brought the best cooks in Asmara with the first wave of workers. The simplest meal always seemed to taste better to Hank in Italian Camp. If the Chinese who cooked for Aramco and Bechtel concentrated on quantity, the Italians focused on quality - the best grain, spices and produce available in the souks of Al Qatif and Al-Khobar. If the food prepared by the Chinese cooks in American Camp was *cha bu duo*, then the motto of their Italian counterparts was *un po' meglio*.

Pedani insisted that Hank join his men on Christmas Eve for *La Vigilia*. In Martinez, devout Catholics had fasted during the day and then gathered for a holiday meal they called the Feast of the Seven Fishes. For the occasion, the Italian workers in Ras Tanura had commandeered enough plywood and sawhorses to sit at one long table on handmade benches. Most of the ground was barren but the holiday table was set up under a hardy cluster of date palms that was older than the Third Kingdom. A few steps away, the hardpan gave way to the sandy beach and the rhythmic surge of whitewater.

Pedani invited Hank to sit beside him. On his other side was his closest friend, Dr. Scarcella, the head of the medical clinic. The first course in Italian Camp was one of the American's favorites, deep-fried calamari.

Up and down the table, the men sorted themselves out by affection and region rather than trade or rank. Squalo sat among the other Neapolitans in the middle of the table. Bruno sat at the far end among the northerners. The second course was gently sauteed clams on the half-shell. The Italians could afford to eat their fill because they were forbidden for Muslims.

The feast included whitefish from the gulf that were salted and cooked whole, like Giulia's cod when Hank was a kid. There were fresh sardines that were seasoned and oiled, an eel soup, even handmade pappardelle with sauce made from precious tins of tomato. Hank's contribution was four cases of beer from the American Camp. Most of it was gone by the time he rose to make a toast.

"*Questo è il miglior pasto che ho mangiato dall'America!*" The men looked at each other before their laughter spread up and down the table. Hank looked at Pedani in confusion. "But it really is the best meal I've had since I left America!"

Pedani shook his head like a patient teacher. "You said it was the best meal you've had from America."

Embarrassed and defeated, Hank settled back into his seat. Pedani rose in defense of their liaison.

"*Anka stava cercando di dire che questo è il miglior pasto che ho mangiato da quando ho lasciato l'America!*"

The Italians laughed even louder, toasting his illiteracy. Without comprehending every word, Hank could hear the murmurs. *America. Aramco. Americano.* Then he bolted to his feet to make another toast.

"*Viva l'Italia!*"

All eighty-eight men rose as one. "*Viva l'Italia!*"

Most of the men were somewhere between drunk and drowsy when Hank heard bagpipes. Two of the pipefitters appeared, dressed in goatskins and rough cloaks, *zampognari* descending from mountain villages to celebrate the birth of Jesus. The beer, barbed wire, and bagpipes made some of the Italians cry. The rest of the men tried to console them.

Hank's mind began to wander. Gloria had written that she was taking Peter to Martinez for the holidays. He thought of his mother preparing for Christmas with Giulia. Most of the boarders would be joining them: waifs and strays from the refineries not unlike the men in Italian Camp.

Martinez, 24 December

On Christmas Eve, there were few cars in either direction on the tollway between the peninsula and the east side of the bay. Gloria gripped the steering wheel, only able to see a few car lengths ahead of her in the heavy fog. The private causeway was only a few yards above the bay and it was cold inside Hank's convertible, even with the top up and the heater on.

An Army truck headed in the opposite direction disappeared as fast as it had appeared, startling Gloria. Less than halfway across the seven-mile span, she regretted taking her father's advice. When he had given up on trying to talk her out of taking Peter to Martinez for the holidays, he recommended the short cut. Few drivers had ever been willing to pay the hefty toll just to get from San Mateo to Hayward. With gas rationing, the causeway would have been empty if not for military vehicles and holiday travelers.

Beside her, Peter screeched every time he saw another cargo ship or naval vessel looming in the fog. Gloria feigned excitement, even though she knew the armada was far larger and more terrifying than her little boy could imagine. Before the war, the lights on both sides of the causeway would have stayed on during bad weather for safety. Instead, the first lights she saw were flashing red as they neared the shipping lane transecting the causeway. Gloria sighed and turned off the engine. Whatever time she had hoped to save was lost as soon as the five steel sections of the causeway began to lift ahead of them. At first, Peter was ecstatic to see barge after barge loaded with materiel pass in front of them. But by the time they were on their way again, the little boy had fallen asleep. Heading up the east side of the bay, the factories and naval bases and warehouses blurred. Gloria thought back to the first time Hank had taken her home to Martinez.

* * *

When they reached the weary Victorian on Alhambra Avenue, he had parked his jalopy off the street and held her hand as they climbed the exterior stairs on the back of the boardinghouse. His mother had opened the door to their private quarters before they reached the landing. If not for the strong facial features they shared, Gloria wouldn't have believed that the little woman could have given birth to Hank. Her hair was greying and she wore an aging sweater over a plain dress. As her son leaned down to give her a peck on the cheek, she had looked at Gloria as if he had won the grand prize in a raffle.

"Who is this, Henry?"

"This is Gloria!"

Dorothy Simmons had folded both hands around hers. For a moment, Gloria didn't think she was going to let go.

"Call me Dot, dear. How lovely to meet you."

Dot was the antithesis of Gloria's mother, a teetotaler whose son wrongly predicted would be dour. The small sitting room in their suite was filled with the best pieces of furniture left from what had been a grand first floor, with lace covering every threadbare arm. The wall above the couch was dominated by a framed photograph of Henry Simmons, Sr. Dot had been charming. Without saying so, she seemed surprised that her son had won Gloria's heart. As Hank sat in silence, his mother chatted about her parents, their home in Palo Alto, and her travels in Europe and the South Pacific.

175

She approved of Gloria's every word, as if their engagement would unlock the door to a life that Dot had always felt she deserved.

Sitting next to him at that first meeting with his mother, Gloria could feel Hank's hands grow cold as his expression froze. She had fallen in love with a bespectacled giant, affable and upbeat with people from all walks of life. But being in the same room with the Simmonses was strange. It was if Hank was Clark Kent and Dot was his kryptonite, despite her best intentions. Sitting beneath the portrait of Hank's fleshy namesake, done when the Twenties were still roaring, seemed to cast a pall over his widow and his son. When his mother called her fiancé Henry, Dot might as well have been referring to her husband.

She didn't seem to understand that every mention of his father made Hank feel abandoned again, even though her husband's suicide had been just as devastating for Dot. Without malicious intent, she had yoked Hank with his father's name. Her son's presence would never make up for her husband's absence. Nor did it seem that Hank's accomplishments would ever make up for her husband's failures. Everything that they had lost and everything they had overcome was embedded in *Henry*, a burden his mother seemed to want her son to bear alone.

Gloria could see that Dot was as intelligent as Hank but had had few opportunities, like most women of her generation. If she had been unfair to her son, he was the exception to a life that had generally been unkind to her. Their misfortune was that neither seemed able to take pleasure in the company of the other. On subsequent visits, as Gloria's mother made their wedding plans impossibly complicated, Hank's childhood came into focus. After his father died, the life that Dot and Hank had lived on the second floor of the boardinghouse was devoid of color. She kept their accounts in order, read the News Gazette, and did needle point. He did his homework, played sports year-round, and read his way through the public library. With rare exception, the only voices heard in their home were on the radio. At any age, it was never very long before Hank found a reason to go to the kitchen, Giulia's undisputed domain.

* * *

Peter was awake by the time Gloria passed Richmond and headed east. Refineries and tank farms stretched out on the Carquinez Strait. Ocean-going vessels and local tenders stretched upstream from the naval shipyard at Mare Island. Hank's hometown was no longer a fishing village surrounded by orchards and ranches. For better or worse, the war had brought prosperity to Martinez and the boardinghouse on Alhambra Avenue. Dot waved at her grandson as Gloria parked next to the garage. Peter bolted out of the Olds and into her arms, lingering in each other's embrace. Gloria was happy that Hank's mother could enjoy being a grandmother more than being a widow with a son. While Dot showed Peter the Christmas tree in the parlor downstairs and the Victory Garden in the back yard, Gloria slipped off to find Giulia.

Even though Hank would never admit it to his mother, the first time he brought Gloria to Martinez had been to meet Giulia. Hank needed to show the woman from Isola delle Femmine that he could love someone as truly as she loved him. The gleam in Giulia's eyes that day had been the only validation Gloria needed to marry Hank. Blessed with a quiet mind, Giulia trusted her instincts and her feelings. There were no irrational needs, no distractions from her old-world beliefs. Giulia was simply the kindest person that Gloria had ever met. All Hank needed as a little boy was a mother's love, nourishing meals, and a little attention. Giulia had provided them all, turning him into the biggest kid in town - and a better man.

The aroma in her kitchen was as close to heaven as Gloria expected to get. Naturally, it was Giulia who had answered her prayers for Peter's first bike. The small frame handed down from one Amalfitano to the next was still tucked away in the cellar on Alhambra. When Gloria offered to pay for a local bike shop to restore the beat-up bicycle for Peter, the two women had insisted on splitting the expense.

On Christmas Eve, she found Giulia chopping basil and slipped her arms around the ample waist of the older woman. Giulia turned around to hug Gloria and then lead her down the steps to the cellar, where Peter's gift was hidden between a shelf of preserves and a stack of kitchen utensils. The bike shop in Martinez had worked the kind of miracle that Gloria had been promised in Palo Alto. The two women returned to the kitchen before they could be missed. Then tears appeared in Giulia's eyes.

"It was Tommy's bike, you know."

Gloria was instantly overwhelmed. Giulia's oldest son had passed through New Caledonia before the Marines landed at Guadalcanal. The day that Giulia was notified that he had been killed in action was the worst day of the war for both families. The thought of Peter riding Tommy's first bike touched both women deeply. They were crying on each other's shoulders when Peter came into the kitchen. Giulia used her apron to wipe her tears away and then beamed at Gloria as she hugged Hank's son.

Martinez, 25 December

On Christmas morning, Peter was up before everyone but Giulia. When he saw the red bicycle that Santa had left for him, his exuberance woke his mother and grandmother and drew Giulia out of the kitchen. Apart from lubricants, only the paint and the streamers on the handlebars were new. But the little boy was oblivious to the bike's hints of rust and hard use before he was born. Gloria embraced Dot and Giulia. Then all three of the women doted on Peter, sharing his happiness and innocence with each other.

By the time the hubbub died down, the boarders had gathered in the dining room for Christmas breakfast. Gloria was touched as she watched them digging into the spread that she and Dot had helped Giulia assembled. She imagined what the occasion was like on the other side of the world in Ras Tanura. The hardened faces of men without families softened as they passed around Dot's irrefusable fruitcake, a platter of scrambled eggs, thick slices of glazed ham, another platter of bacon, and rounds of *Panettoni*, the traditional sweetbread that Giulia baked in coffee cans the night before.

When their bellies began to fill, Peter showed off his new bicycle as Gloria poured fresh coffee. When Dot helped Giulia clear away the plates, Gloria giggled as the boarders hurried a pint of whiskey around the table to spike the coffee.

179

After breakfast, some of the boarders took turns helping Peter learn how to ride his new bicycle. They took advantage of the gentle downhill slope of the boardinghouse block of Alhambra towards the strait. At first they let the little boy coast, walking beside him as they braced the stem of his saddle. When they got to the corner Gloria shouted at them to turn around: Dot and Giulia were both watching from the front porch. Peter's mother had to laugh as he labored on the pedals up the gentle incline, then turned too abruptly at the top of the block, a boarder catching him before the bike tipped. On his second trip down the block, he wobbled on his own, a boarder trailing behind him on either side.

Peter was delighted when he began to feel the balance of the bicycle in the wide handlebars. The refinery workers tired before the little boy but took turns chasing him up and down the block as he gained confidence. The only time he stopped was when Gloria took a picture, half a dozen refinery workers standing behind him, honorary uncles for a day.

Ras Tanura, 31 December

Everyone in American Camp felt like they had permission to get smashed on New Year's Eve. The only women to dance with in the compound were the two married nurses. Alcohol, on the other hand, was plentiful. There were cases of American, British, and surprisingly good Indian beer. Name-brand booze was still hard to come by; otherwise-corruptible customs officials in Al-Khobar drew the line at fine spirits.

By year's end Ras Tanura was home to some of the best young chemists and engineers in the kingdom. Nor were the new towers of the world-class refinery the only stills in the Aramco compound. After hours, amateur craftsmen from Purdue and Texas A&M turned to the construction of alcohol-producing stills from an expanding inventory of spare parts. Back home, booze was divided into clear products, like vodka or gin, and whiskeys, like Scotch or Bourbon. But the distillers of Ras Tanura simplified their offerings to white or brown. One operation hidden from the emirs fermented sacks of sugar to produce the clearest moonshine in the Middle East. The other converted all the canned corn in Ras Tanura into the first batch of mash whiskey produced outside Dhahran.

Everyone hoped that 1945 would bring the end of the war. That night, only men like Ohliger and Ferguson were dreaming about producing half a million barrels of crude oil.

181

For everyone else, there were three time zones between Ras Tanura and Greenwich, the longest midnight of Hank's life. He wouldn't remember when the BBC announced that 1945 had finally arrived in England. For all of the Americans who weren't lucky enough to catch a dance with one of the nurses, the existential question remained, white or brown? For most of them, to their detriment, the answer was both.

At first light, the call to Fajr ringing from the minarets were like knives in both sides of Hank's head. Abstinence, as required by the Prophet, seemed like an idea whose time had come. Most Mondays would have been the third day of the Aramco work week. In his wisdom, Ohliger had declared the first day of January as a company holiday. Whatever setbacks in construction or production might occur were less risky than misadventures due to hangovers. The Arab workers didn't mind because it was a paid day off; something they would expect more often as production increased. For most Americans in the Eastern Province, Monday would have been a sick day without Ohliger's forbearance.

The sun was too bright for Hank to stay outside for long, even though the winter weather remained mild. He stayed in his bunk until he couldn't stand listening to Lanier snore. There was a coffee pot in the office end of the Airstream at the marine terminal. He used the afternoon to catch up on paperwork. Ammar wasn't there to watch his hands shake. In the evening, after a bland dinner and a glass of milk, Hank re-read Gloria's last letter to him, which she had posted in the middle of December. Then he wrote her his first letter of the new year.

As happy as he was that Peter was getting his first bicycle, he was sad that he wouldn't be the one who taught him how to ride it. He was glad that she was taking their son to Martinez for Christmas, even though he shared Gloria's disappointment that she couldn't take Peter to the snow. It was too bad that the Southern Pacific no longer stopped by Sugar Bowl.

Hank had fond memories of Gloria teaching him to ski when they were still at Berkeley. She was an accomplished skier, graceful and rhythmic. He had been lucky not to break one of his legs when his skis crossed in the snow. He could still hear Gloria laughing at him as he lay on his back, his head pointed down the slope. When she tried to help him up, she wound up falling on top of him. Her lips were wonderful when she kissed him. He fell asleep remembering the heat of their bodies and the softness of the snow.

San Francisco, 1 January 1945

New Year's Day was a Monday, the first day of another working week for the Pacific branch of OWI. It was already Tuesday in New Caledonia and the Far East. Nearly all of France had been liberated by the Allies and the Caldoche were growing impatient with the US forces remaining around Nouméa. The challenge for Gloria and her colleagues was reminding the French colonial government that the war against Japan was far from over, even in rear areas.

When Gloria looked at the bloodshot eyes and puffy faces of the other passengers on the train to San Francisco, she was glad that she had been responsible the night before. The only inspiration she needed was watching her mother drink feverishly before her father locked up the booze the next day. She was grateful that Giulia had sent her back to Palo Alto with a packet of her lentil soup - one of Hank's favorite traditions - ready to be prepared on New Year's Eve.

Even when they were engaged, Gloria hadn't fully grasped the importance of Giulia to Hank's upbringing. Several months passed between their graduation and their marriage. Once he went to work for Standard, he would make her breakfast if she slept over. If she dropped by his apartment unexpectedly in the evening, he would make her dinner. But it wasn't until they came back from their honeymoon in Carmel that she understood how Giulia set the tempo for

Hank's daily life. She hadn't taught him how to cook; she taught him how to live. In the best sense, Hank lived from meal to meal. Shopping was to be done daily, if possible. The freshness of produce was as important as the best cut of meat. For Giulia (and therefore Hank) making a meal wasn't an obligation. It was an opportunity to leave the rest of the world behind. The simplest food was meant to be prepared thoughtfully and shared with those one loved.

When Gloria arrived at the New Caledonia desk on New Year's Day, some of her co-workers were missing in action. Others should have stayed in bed. When Thierry arrived, he looked as if he hadn't slept at all. They had been lovers long enough for Gloria to know that he always carried a freshly laundered shirt in his briefcase, along with his toothbrush and spare underwear. The practice was as important for a con man as a paramour. As usual, he was circumspect with Gloria in the presence of their co-workers. But she could smell another woman on Thierry as surely as she knew the fragrance on his coat wasn't Jean Patou. Despite his hangover and lack of sleep, he greeted her triumphantly.

"*Bonne année, Gloria!*"

"*Bonne année, Thierry.*"

The moment she had always expected had arrived at the most predictable time. Her anger with herself lasted far longer than her anger with her lover. The rest of the day she felt as numb as her co-workers who couldn't remember the night before. When Thierry followed her downstairs on the Presidio grounds and offered to accompany her to the Transbay Terminal, she declined. Then she pushed him away when he tried to kiss her farewell; the Frenchman smelling riper at the foot of Lovers' Lane than he had that morning at the New Caledonia desk.

On the train back in Palo Alto, Gloria found herself sitting beside a younger woman who she had seen before, another commuter who had often passed time looking at a photo of her husband, a freckled sailor with too many teeth. On New Year's the younger woman, a blonde dressed in black, was still staring at the photo, crying quietly as the train continued down the peninsula, long after her tears had run dry. Neither woman knew the name of the other; they had only smiled at each other in the past when they found each other on the same coach.

Gloria forgot about Thierry as she sat beside the blonde in black, far too young to be a widow if not for a world that men had driven mad. After the younger woman put the photo of the dead sailor in her purse, Gloria rested her hands on hers. The space between them gave way as they sobbed, sharing their anonymous grief.

When they reached Palo Alto, the women embraced wordlessly and set off in different directions. Gloria began walking home in the rain which had been coming down all day. That time of year, Hank usually wielded his umbrella like a shield when they were together. Because of the length of his arms - and because he was the kind of husband who didn't mind getting drenched - Gloria could walk beside Hank without the rain touching her head. But on the first night of 1945 she was soaking wet by the time she reached her parents' home, shivering with a sense of loss far deeper than the cold night.

Ras Tanura, 6 January

The twelfth day after Christmas, *Le Epifania*, was the day of gift-giving for Italians in Arabia, as it had been when Hank was a kid in Martinez. He called the payroll office in Dhahran and asked for a copy of the first cycle of payroll for Pedani and his men. The bookkeepers in Dhahran referred Hank to Manama, where the accounts for the Italians were handled by Bapco. But the only photostat machine in the region was at Aramco headquarters in Dhahran. The equipment and supplies were expensive. The only authorized users were the top men in operations and government relations. The primary consumers were senior executives in Aramco's offices in New York, Washington, and San Francisco. After numerous calls and the unauthorized use of Mac's name, he finally got the photostat he needed of the payroll report from Bahrain.

When Hank arrived at the Italian Camp, Nando was dressed as an old woman wearing a mask of *La Befana*. The female version of Santa Claus brought gifts to the children of Italy on the day that Catholics celebrated the arrival of the Three Wise Men in Bethlehem. It was a light-hearted moment being shared by men who were more than three thousand miles away from their families. The gifts were simple, a bar of soap, a package of shaving cream, a pair of socks.

Hank handed an envelope with the payroll report to Pedani. The most important column showed the name and address for next of kin for each of his workers in Italy. The next two columns showed the Italian bank account and the number of shillings being deposited. It was the first time that Hank saw the countenance of the civil engineer lose its usual reserve. With tears in his eyes, Pedani thanked the American and shook his hand. Then he passed the document to the lead doctor, Scarcella, who passed it on to Squalo. One by one, men hardened by war and depredation looked at the document, found their family name and stared at the amount of cash deposited in a bank in their hometown. Silently, the document passed through the hands of all eighty-eight men from Asmara. The levity of La Befana on the beach was replaced by relief, then longing for home.

The men hugged each other, tears flowing freely. On the night of Le Epifania, Hank was thanked by many of the men of Italian Camp. As they shook his hand, few of them could say more than *grazie*. Some of them couldn't resist planting sloppy *bacetti* on both sides of his face.

Hank's own wife and son were even farther away than the families of Pedani and his men. But for the first time since he arrived in the Eastern Province, he felt at home. They had each other at a moment when they could only think of places and people beyond their reach. Each of them was overwhelmed with thoughts about loved ones without knowing when they would see them again. Despite the tranquility of the waves lapping on the sand on a mild night on the gulf, every family on the list was suffering through a winter of hunger and loss, even in the southern provinces that had been liberated. In the northern provinces, fear and death still reigned amidst ice and snow. The newspapers from home were reporting the brutal retreat of the SS from Milano and Torino.

Pedani and the other northerners shared the moment with each other, cheered in some inexplicable way while invaders and nature threatened everyone they loved. A war that had gone on too long and cost too many lives was drawing to a close. Aramco's silver would provide comfort for their families, the means to hang on.

That night the men in Ras Tanura weren't Arabs or Americans or Italians. They were human beings trying to outlast the isolation they were all enduring. Even those in Saudi Camp were separated from their families. All of them needed to believe they could build a better future. The natural wealth of the kingdom might make Al-Saud rich. It might make Standard and Texaco more profitable. But Ras Tanura would fuel the planes, ships and trains that would someday reunite the men in all three encampments with their families.

Dhahran, 12 January

Near the end of the hour between Ras Tanura and Dhahran, a gust of wind hit the side of Hank's Ford like an angry bull. The sky was full of grit blown all the way from Syria. As bad as shamals were in the summer, in winter they were bone-chilling. He hurried to reach his meeting before the coast road disappeared under the sand. Berglund had flown in with personnel files for hundreds of Italian workers arriving by freighter the next day. But he was meeting Hank and Mac to share information that was too confidential for telephones. The military attaché began with the good news.

"The Bank of Italy's commissioner in the Social Republic let your latest batch of transfers from Switzerland go through. You can tell Pedani that the families are getting their money."

Mac crossed his arms and leaned back in his chair. "What's the bad news?"

"As you know, inflation is a big problem in Europe. It's easier to print money than produce anything of real value. Even in the southern provinces where the real Bank of Italy is operating, the exchange rates between the British pound and the Italian lira are pretty awful."

Not to be outdone by Berglund in front of his best student, Mac gave Hank another lesson in international finance. "With rapid inflation there's always a lag between what banks use as exchange rates what real people have to pay merchants. They

190

profit from the difference between what a pound actually buys and what they're willing to pay in local currency to their account holders."

Berglund went on. "The Nazis forced the countries they conquered to trade in Reichsmarks. If the Germans bought more goods than their vassals, the central banks in places like Holland had to make it up by using surplus marks to buy more German stuff, whether they wanted it or not."

Mac chortled. "The sterling zone works the same way in the British Empire."

"Lately the Nazis have been stealing all the hard assets on their way out of eastern Europe. Now they have huge stockpiles of gold and silver piling up between Germany and Switzerland."

Outside, the sandstorm at concession headquarters was becoming more intense. The pebbles hitting Mac's windows kept getting bigger. "Get on with it, Berglund."

"General Wolff, the commander of German forces in northern Italy, was a banker before he joined the SS. Now he's like a bad guy in the Wild West with his own gold mine."

"Aramco, Berglund."

"Wolff's partner in crime is Rudolf Rahn, the head of the Nazi civil service in Italy. He's the one looking over the shoulder of Mussolini's bank commissioner. Wolff and Rahn are letting the Swiss branch of your Turkish bank transfer deposits into the northern provinces they control, but they're using a peg between the lira and the pound that goes back to the pre-war era, before inflation really kicked in."

Hank was a fast learner. "So most of the money that Pedani's men earned is getting skimmed off the top?"

Berglund nodded mordantly. "The British get their cut when Aramco buys sterling with dollars. The rate's higher in Bahrain than New York or London. The Turks get their taste between Bahrain and Basel. And then the SS are really hammering what's left before it hits accounts in the north."

As Hank sank into despair, Mac asked a more practical question. "How much of the money is getting to the Italian families in the provinces under Allied control?"

"In the south it's not too bad - maybe sixty percent of what British sterling is worth on the black market in Rome. But up in the Social Republic, we think it's more like thirty."

Hank got out of his chair and began to pace. Dust making its way through the windows and the swamp cooler was becoming visible in the air around him. "Holy Blessed Mother of Christ! The Italians who can't stand being paid on the same scale as the Arabs are actually getting far less?"

"War is hell, Hank," Berglund said. "Wolff's gang is using your payroll to turn their loot into cash they can get out of Switzerland. OSS Bern thinks they're all brushing up on their Spanish and Portuguese before moving to South America."

Hank collapsed back into his chair. After months of effort, he and Berglund had succeeded in adding the Italians to the APO system in the concession. Once their letters cleared military censors in the region, they were going to be able to communicate with their families for the first time in years. He laid out his dilemma for Mac.

"Before long, our workers with families in the south are going to be getting letters back from their relatives. The lira they're receiving isn't going to square with the shillings we're supposedly paying them."

Mac was gazing out his office window. His brow furrowed as the oil rigs on the Dammam dome were swallowed by the shamal. He jumped when a crack appeared in the glass. The room went dark as the sandstorm blocked the sun. Then the power failed in the building. Flaws in the Italian payroll scheme were the least of Mac's concerns.

"We have no choice but to acknowledge the facts on the ground in the south. Aramco didn't start the war, laddy."

Hank thought about Pedani and the other men from the northern provinces. There was nothing to gain from revealing what Berglund knew about the SS. As much as Hank hated subterfuge, honesty in Italian Camp wouldn't make anyone's family safer. Nor would the truth help get the talent in Eritrea needed to complete the project in Ras Tanura.

One of the Pakistani clerks rapped politely on the door before Mac waved him into the office. A cloud of dust from the hallway billowed around him. "Excuse me, Mr. Ohliger would like to speak with you, Mr. MacPherson." As Mac rose from his chair, the clerk turned to address their official visitor. "Captain Berglund, your flight to Jeddah has been delayed."

Outside, it sounded as if the metal roof was being torn off Aramco's headquarters. After Mac left his office, Berglund sulked in the darkness while searching for a cigarette. Hank got out of his chair and grabbed the kerosene lamp stored for such emergencies. Berglund lit his cigarette with a match and then used the cigarette to fire up the old-fashioned lamp that Hank placed on the desk. The light seemed warmer than the incandescent bulbs had been. Rockefeller's first million had been made refining kerosene from crude.

"There's another thing I wanted to tell you."

Loathing every second that followed, Hank slowly settled in his seat.

"The ship that's bringing the next five hundred Italians from Eritrea is a Soviet freighter."

"They're still on our side, right?"

The military attaché crossed his legs and shook his head. "Every Russian vessel has a political officer, sometimes several. I guarantee you that the freighter's taking the scenic route across the Arabian Sea. If the Russians didn't already have agents in Eritrea, they will by the time the Italians arrive in Ras Tanura. At a minimum they will be reporting our progress. At worst they may try to disrupt the refinery or exports from the terminal."

"Then why would Tottenham allow the Russians to transport the Italians to Ras Tanura?"

Berglund scoffed at Hank's unsophistication. "The British aren't going to just hand over the Persian Gulf to the American oil industry. They still think of this as their pond."

"You're saying our closest ally is trying to sabotage Aramco?"

Berglund took another puff of his cigarette and shrugged. "The British intentionally brought smallpox to Plymouth colony. The disease was better at killing the local tribes than the Pilgrims were. Infecting your concession with communists is no different. The Crown owns a big chunk of the British oil industry. Other than getting Hitler, there's not many things that Churchill would like more than labor disputes between the Saudis and Aramco."

"That's crazy!"

"Anglo Persian and IPC think they've inoculated themselves against labor problems by paying their Muslim workers for their communal day of prayer. They also added an inflation adjustment to their pay scale to keep their best workers. Send me a postcard when Aramco follows suit."

Berglund tapped the ash off the tip of his cigarette. Hank watched it disappear into the sand swirling across the floor.

Ras Tanura, 29 January

The construction of the marine terminal was no longer Hank's project to supervise: it belonged to Pedani.

The ranks in Italian Camp increased by the week. Every ship from Massawa brought hundreds of men who were put to work by Aramco or "leased" to Bechtel; the Italians working for Vukovich outnumbered the Americans. That created leverage for Pedani if not equity. The chief engineer was demonstrating his excellence as a project manager, just as he had in colonial Eritrea and again for the British and American military after the Italian surrender.

Hank had pangs of jealousy when he realized that the Bechtel superintendent was only coming to his trailer to be polite. By the time he knocked on the Airstream's door, Vukovich had already worked out every interpretation of the project plan with Pedani.

The Italian had established dominion on the pier, where his men built a shack overlooking Tarout Bay. No more than ten meters square, it owed more to the Arab barastis than the prefabricated offices of Aramco managers. The roof was corrugated metal, supported by galvanized pipe that Pedani's welders fabricated to his specifications. All four sides were open so that the generalissimo caught every whiff of breeze off the sea. The focal point was a drafting table built by

Pedani's carpenters. There was an adjustable lock that he preferred at an angle suggesting an artist's easel.

From his station, Pedani could see his men working throughout the marine terminal as well as the gangs crawling up and down ladders and ramps of the refinery complex. All of Pedani's men could see him. They came and went with questions about the blueprints done by industrial engineers in San Francisco. All matters of timing and priority between the Italian trades were resolved by audiences before *il capo dei capi*. Pedani ruled the construction zone with the same hands-on beneficence that Abdulaziz used in the rest of the kingdom.

Pedani listened patiently to all comers. When too many men spoke at once he would show them the palm of his hand, like a traffic cop in front of the Pantheon. He never raised his voice and he seldom spoke more than a few words when he gave advice or orders. The more foremen and supplicants who surrounded his throne, the more serene he appeared. Whether the challenge was an interpersonal conflict between Squalo and another foreman, an aesthetic quandary that would never trouble the American oilmen, or the most complex engineering formula, Pedani had a clear vision of how Ras Tanura would look and how it should work.

From his trailer, Hank could watch the Renaissance unfold through a window. The Italian punctuated his working hours with sips of tea from a thermos that kept it hotter than the sun on the bay. He had a pipe which looked Bavarian and indulged himself with the finest Turkish tobacco he could procure in Al-Khobar. Most of all, Pedani liked to think as he walked. As Vukovich's multi-national crew pushed the marine terminal farther into the bay, Pedani would pace it off, stopping occasionally to gaze at the sea. It was as if Columbus was building a bridge to the New World instead of sailing on the Santa Maria.

Hank had to rethink the best use of his own time. For the first few weeks, he would wait for moments when the queue shortened before Pedani's throne, then ask the Italian to update him on the progress of construction. When it became clear that the Italian had faultless command of the Aramco design as well as Bechtel's project plan, Hank made fewer pilgrimages.

As the pace of construction picked up in the refinery and the marine complex, its manager fine-tuned the flow of crude oil through the original submarine pipeline to the Bapco refinery. The new submarine pipeline needed to be operational before either of the new stills. Then Hank focused on Aramco's upstream plans: new feeder lines from drilling sites to the expanding tank farm, pulling naval fuel oil off the bottom of one of the new stills, enhancing octane levels from the aviation fuel in the higher reaches of the other.

Ras Tanura, 1 February

Hank and Pedani developed a new routine. Most of their meetings occurred after hours, when neither of them were as likely to be interrupted by the staff they supervised. Since men from American Camp and Italian Camp were not encouraged to fraternize, the two managers would meet after dinner and walk the beach north of the point. Thursday evening – the end of the work week in Al-Hasa - Pedani asked if Scarcella, his closest friend, could join them as they strolled along the sand.

The doctor had been among the first eighty-eight from Asmara. Hank had had few occasions to speak with him since his clinical duties kept him in Italian Camp. Because there were more than ten men in Eritrea for every position Aramco needed to fill, the British doctors had screened out the colonials who were the most contagious or had wasting diseases. As a result, the health status of the Italians was better than the Arabs. But the men Scarcella attended in his clinic were not as healthy as the Americans, who arrived in Dhahran like a fattened herd.

Scarcella had a long face, thinning hair, and melancholy eyes. He was taller than Pedani but stooped, the kind of physician who assumed the suffering of his patients. He relaxed in the company of his friend and chatted affably with Hank, whose Italian was better than the doctor's English.

198

Then Scarcella looked at Pedani quizzically and spoke in a whisper that Hank could make out in the surf.

"*Perché suona come un siciliano?*"

Pedani laughed and translated his friend's joke. "Luigi thinks you sound like a Sicilian, *Anka.*"

Like his old friend, Scarcella was a northerner. Hank did his best to explain growing up in Martinez among the fishermen who immigrated from the south. The doctor was touched when he mentioned the importance of Giulia in his childhood.

The moon rose as they walked in single file on the compact border of the ebbing tide. Pedani was on point, followed by the doctor, with Hank at the end of the line. The smoke from the master builder's pipe wafted behind him. Scarcella glance back at the tall American and then called out over the sound of the waves to his friend.

"*Assomigli a Sua Altezza.*"

"I look like His Highness?"

Pedani stopped to explain, the surge wrapping around his feet.

"The Viceroy of Italian East Africa, the Duke of Aosta, was almost two meters tall. He was the first cousin of the king, a great gentleman. We called him His Highness as a term of affection and respect."

"Where is he now?"

Scarcella's face grew longer and sadder. "*Morto.*"

"He died soon after he surrendered."

Haunted, Scarcella said, "Amba Alagi."

Pedani stopped and put his arm around his friend. "Luigi was in practice in Asmara until Mussolini declared war on France. The coward hesitated until the Nazis had driven the British into the sea at Dunkirk. All men in Eritrea of fighting age were drafted. I was spared as director of public facilities but Luigi was not. *Il Duce* didn't permit - how do you say - *obiettori di coscienza.*"

"Conscientious objectors?"

"Yes, thank you. Luigi was forced to serve. At the beginning of the campaign, Aosta had a quarter of million African troops - *Ascari* - and a hundred thousand Italian soldiers and sailors, including the Blackshirts."

Scarcella added, "*Cinquecento aerei!*"

Hank tried to imagine where five hundred Italian planes - and pilots - had gone between the beginning of the war in East Africa and his arrival in Asmara, when the only ones in sight were British.

Pedani continued, "When the duke surrendered, nearly all the Africans had deserted or been killed. And there were less than five thousand Italian troops left."

Scarcella was gazing at the moonlight on the gulf, the whitewater reaching his knees. "*Follia...follia totale.*"

Pedani tried to regain his friend's attention. "*Andiamo, Luigi.*"

The former POW was sinking into the wet sand, surrounded by ghosts. Pedani began walking up the beach again. Scarcella fell in line behind him. Then Pedani continued.

"Aosta fought alone for a year after he was cut off from supplies and reinforcements. Many of us believe that Mussolini didn't want the duke to survive. The people might have called for Aosta to restore our constitutional monarchy and reject *Il Duce.*"

Scarcella muttered, "*Il capo del comando supremo.*"

"Typhus and dysentery killed more Italians than the British."

Hank was confused. "Didn't Italy fight on the side of the British and the Americans in the last war?"

Pedani nodded, "That was before Mussolini, before King Immanuel sided with the fascists over the socialists. Sua Altezza went to school in Surrey. He liked to play polo and fly airplanes. Women loved him. Even the Ethiopians

200

respected him. He ended slavery and left a letter for the British in his palace in Addis Ababa, asking them to protect the women and children from looting and rape. Before Mussolini declared war on them, he dined with the British generals in Cairo and Khartoum. They even told him about their plans to invade our colonies from Sudan and Kenya and the Red Sea. They trapped him when he retreated into the mountains between Ethiopia and Eritrea. When he finally surrendered after a long siege, they gave him full military honors."

In derision, Scarcella said, "*Onori de Guerra.*"

Pedani continued, "After the monsoons, the duke led his men out of the caves in a parade down Amba Alagi. They were starving, wearing filthy rags. But the British played their bagpipes and cheered. They let the duke keep his pistol and his sword. Then they put him and Luigi and the rest of the survivors in a prisoner of war camp in Kenya. Luigi stayed by the side of Sua Altezza until he died from malaria and tuberculosis."

"*Nessuna medicina,*" Scarcella said, still outraged. "*Niente!*"

Hank thought about Scarcella's medical clinic in the Italian camp. He feared it was little better than the POW camp in Kenya. He felt guilty about his lack of honesty about the Nazis skimming the hard-earned wages of Italians from the north, like Pedani and Scarcella. The Americans and the Saudis were only being less blatant than the Germans in the way the treated the Italians. Then a chill went through him, as if Pedani and Scarcella had grabbed him by his arms and were shaking him violently. But Hank could see them standing a few steps away, alarmed by the uncontrollable shivering in his limbs and torso.

The American dropped to the sand. The whitewater surged around him, only adding to the feeling that he was freezing from the inside out. Pedani and Scarcella dragged him up the beach. The doctor felt his forehead and his cheeks, then took his pulse. He looked at his friend gravely and said, "*Malaria.*"

Ras Tanura, 2 February

Pedani and Scarcella had to help Hank as they walked back down the beach. It was past midnight by the time they reached American Camp, where a Saudi soldier guarded the gate. The Italians bowed their heads and said *Salaam*. The guard offered them peace in return and watched impassively as they half-dragged the big American to the medical clinic, one of the new structures put up by Bechtel. The door was locked and there were no lights inside. Scarcella knocked on the door while Pedani circled around the single-story structure.

The medical staff lived nearby in a new duplex. Pedani knocked on the door with a small placard that read "Dr. and Mrs. Vogel." He appeared in a light robe thrown over his undershirt and boxers. After Pedani apologized and explained, Dr. Vogel returned in a white tunic and white pants and followed him back to the entrance, where Hank was slumped on a bench. Vogel recognized Scarcella, shook his hand, and then unlocked the front door to the clinic.

Hank staggered through the reception area to an exam room. The other three men helped him lay down on an adjustable bed. Vogel examined his patient while Scarcella spoke through Pedani.

"Luigi thinks that *Anka* has malaria. He was okay when we began walking, then had shaking chills that lasted for an hour."

Vogel nodded as he drew a small sample of blood and said, "We'll see what the thick smear looks like."

Mrs. Vogel appeared with clean linen and cotton blankets. Weak but no longer shivering, Hank thanked the nurse. While her husband prepared a slide for the new microscope in the clinic laboratory, Scarcella surveyed the room. Aramco had purchased the best equipment available for the new clinic in Ras Tanura. While modest in scale, it exceeded the standard of anything in Eritrea that had survived the war. Envy and jealousy competed for control of the Italian doctor's emotions.

Malaria was as much a problem in the marshlands of Italy as it was in the oases of the Eastern Province. Several species of the parasite that infected human blood were transmitted by mosquitos whose eggs depended on standing water. The more people within a region were infected with the protozoa, the more likely others were to be infected by the mosquitos who thrived on their blood. In many cases, the protozoa were visible in the specially stained smears of infected red blood cells.

Vogel returned from the laboratory and shook Scarcella's hand again. "You were right."

He turned to look at his new patient. "You've got malaria, Hank. We've got plenty of quinacrine now. I'm going to give you a loading dose, then you'll need to take it every day until we get the infection under control."

"How long before I can go back to work, Dr. Vogel?"

The American doctor shrugged and said, "We'll see. Maybe a couple of weeks. I want to keep an eye on you here until morning, make sure you tolerate the medication. After that, I want you to rest up. Before the war, we would have treated you with quinine but the Japs overran the plantations in the

Dutch East Indies where its extracted. Then the Nazis took over the laboratories in Holland where it was manufactured. Luckily, we've been able to produce quinacrine since last year. The biggest problem is getting the boys to take their medicine."

"Whatever it takes, Dr. Vogel. I've never felt so bad."

The American doctor gave him a pat on the shoulder and told him to rest, then thanked the Italians again. Before Aramco made him an overwhelming offer, Vogel had been one of the medical missionaries who earned the trust of the people of Al-Hasa, as well as Abdulaziz. The Saudis permitted the Lutherans to save as many lives as they were able, so long as they didn't challenge the teachings of the Prophet.

Pedani gripped Hank's upper arm, a look of concern still on his face. *"Buona notte, Anka."*

Scarcella stood beside his friend, looking even more worried. *"Dormi bene, Sua Altezza."*

Hank thanked them repeatedly. *"Grazie molto. Mille grazie."*

Pedani was embarrassed, Scarcella only fatigued by another unscheduled patient. They inched away from Hank's bed, bowing politely to the Vogels.

"Non era niente."

"It was nothing."

Mrs. Vogel gave him two aspirin and put a pitcher of fresh water beside his bed. After she turned off the clinic lights and returned to her quarters, Hank lay awake in the dark, his feet dangling off the end of the bed. A swamp cooler hummed nearby, out of his sight. At first he felt too exhausted to sleep, then drifted off.

For the rest of the night, he was lost in the worst kind of dreams. He found himself in the mountain caves of Amba Alagi, fighting alongside the Duke of Aosta. Their opponents were not British or African but ghouls wearing Aramco overalls. Then he found himself in another American Camp, unguarded and abandoned, left to die of thirst in an uncharted desert.

When he was awakened by the muezzins, he was drenched in sweat, as were the sheets on his bed in the clinic. He wanted to repeat the words of the Fajr prayer and thank Allah for sparing him. The light shining through the window blinds in the clinic lessened his bewilderment.

Palo Alto, 4 February

Gloria could hear soft rain falling when she awoke on Sunday morning. Sometime during the night - probably when the rain was falling harder - Peter had crawled into her bed. She looked at his tousled hair and listened to his peaceful breathing, amazed again that she had brought such a wonderful creature into the world.

On the nightstand beside her were two telegrams. The first had arrived on Thursday while she was still at work. By the time she returned home her parents had already opened it, fearing the worst. Her father had been impressed that the telegram was from an Aramco VP, a ridiculous feather in his son-in-law's cap. *Hank has malaria but under care of our excellent doctor, (signed) James MacPherson.*

Gloria had sat up most of Thursday night after getting Peter ready for bed. In all the years she had known him, Hank hardly ever caught a cold. The thought of him alone in a hospital on the other side of the world filled her with sadness and guilt. Her mother had insisted that she speak with their family doctor whose reassurances matched the ones she heard the next day at the Presidio. *Malaria was common in war zones and very treatable with modern medication.* She began to wonder if Hank's illness would be a convenient pretext for his return.

Gloria had spent Saturday with her family in Palo Alto. Even before the bad news about Hank arrived, she had only seen Thierry away from work once since the year began; a moment of weakness and want. But the thought of never seeing the Frenchman again made her feel like her mother on New Year's Day, knowing she had to choose between drinking and her husband when life without either was unthinkable.

The second telegram on Gloria's nightstand had arrived on Saturday. *Getting better on quinacrine, love you and Peter very much, (signed) Hank.* At first she had been annoyed that both Hank and Mac had only managed to send ten words, as if there was a quota on telegram length, like everything else in the concession. But by that night, comforted by the hope of Hank's recovery and return, she was able to get some sleep.

When the rain stopped on Sunday morning Gloria was tempted to open the window and let in the delicious air. But she stayed in bed until Peter awoke.

"I'm hungry."

Any other day of the week Gloria could have sent Peter to the kitchen to tell her mother's cook. But Sunday was her day off. Pillow talk with a hungry little boy wouldn't work as well as it would have with his father. She touched a lock of his hair, the same color as her own. "What would you like, dear?"

The little boy's eyes widened. "Pancakes!"

"You'll have to show me how to make them."

"Okay!"

"Give me a few minutes and I'll meet you in the kitchen."

As she freshened up and put on a robe, Gloria took stock of her culinary skills. Since marrying Hank she had learned how to boil eggs, toast and butter bread, and make coffee. She still relied on the skills of others for everything else. By the time she had gone downstairs, Peter had found a bag of flour, a dozen eggs, a gallon of fresh milk that had been delivered the day before, a glass mixing bowl, and a whisk.

"You are your father's son."

Peter looked at her quizzically. "Will Daddy be coming home soon?"

"I hope so, dear."

Gloria was better qualified to teach Peter to read than cook. She posted Hank's telegram on the corkboard by the kitchen calendar and found a pencil, underlining her son's name and Hank's love. Her husband was the kind of man who could forgive her past sins without an inquisition. But in his absence, Peter was more demanding.

"You need to put the flour in the bowl and then mix in the eggs."

"How much dear?"

Peter pointed to the mid-point in the bowl. Gloria dutifully added the flour. "How many eggs, dear?"

"Two!"

Gloria obliterated the first egg; most of the yolk oozed over the rim of the bowl. After cleaning up her mess, the next two she cracked made it into the flour along with a few bits of shell she picked out with her fingers.

"Is that all, dear?"

"You forgot the milk."

"How much should I put in?"

"Just a little, then mix it all up."

Gloria obliged, whisking the contents into lumpiness. Peter grappled with an iron skillet from a shelf under the counter on his way to the stove.

"Who taught you to make pancakes, dear?"

"Giulia."

"Of course."

Gloria's first pancake was a soggy mess that Peter threw away. His father would have been kinder about her failure. She scorched the second so badly that she tossed it in the trash. Then her son impatiently accepted the third, drowning it in maple syrup. She poured him a glass of milk as he smiled through her fourth. Making coffee, she began to think of herself as a happily married woman.

San Francisco, 5 February

By the end of the weekend in Palo Alto, Gloria had made up her mind. The longer she allowed Thierry to remain in her life, the more she would hate herself. Whether Hank was home in a week or a year, she was going to reunite with her husband. With any luck, the war would end too. Thierry had already proven himself to be as untrustworthy as she had always known he would be. Peter needed his father as much as she wanted to believe that Hank still needed her. Only a fool would bet the rest of her life on a man like Thierry. Whatever else she might be, Gloria was not a fool.

When she arrived for work at the Presidio, Gloria slipped a note to Thierry instructing him to meet her on Lovers' Lane. Then the speech she had prepared was delayed by rain. As soon as it stopped, she left the New Caledonia desk without looking at him. For the first time since she started working for OWI she felt like a spy. She despised the thought of her affair being revealed on the same day she planned to end it. And she didn't want her co-workers to see her walking with Thierry on the first naked section of the trail by their office.

Gloria had always preferred to walk Lovers' Lane alone, her respite from the night-and-day turmoil at the New Caledonia desk. Through her father's mother, she felt connected to Spanish soldiers who had walked the footpath to Mission Dolores for generations. After California became a state, the

US Army planted thousands of Tasmanian blue gum trees to prevent erosion on the sandy headlands. The ridgeline trail was now covered by a pungent canopy that reached hundreds of feet into the sky. She loved to walk it even more after it rained, when the wind off the ocean carried the aroma of eucalyptus. As she waited for Thierry, Gloria felt a kind of solace she hadn't felt in the most hallowed churches in Europe before the war.

Halfway up the slope, near neat rows of townhomes for married officers, Gloria watched as Thierry approached. They both wore heavy coats and scarves. The air was cold enough for them to see each other's breath long before they were close enough to embrace. Even though the rain had stopped, their faces were anointed with fragrant droplets from the trees above them. Standing face to face, Gloria still wanted Thierry as much as her mother wanted her whiskey. But she had made up her mind.

"My husband has malaria."

Thierry shrugged with polite indifference. "I am very sorry." Malaria was a rite of passage for European colonials, insufficient grounds for ending a mutually satisfactory arrangement.

"I'm hoping he will be coming home soon."

"I see."

"We need to stop seeing each other."

The corners of his mouth turned down slightly, as if he was in pain. But it was just as easy for Gloria to see the pleasure in his eyes.

"*Je t'adorerai toujours.*"

Gloria was flattered by the lie: *I will still adore you.* If she were to deny that they had ever had an affair, Thierry would deny that it had ever ended. Neither of them had many illusions before they became lovers. He only seemed troubled that her husband was still in Arabia, taking the best medicine that

American oilmen could buy, while they were still in one of the most beautiful cities in the world.

Lovers' Lane was a good place to say goodbye. As Thierry moved from cheek to cheek to cheek - *trois bise* - their lips were close enough to meet. In the lonely months that followed, she would remember when they did. She would also remember when he took his hands - strong, cold, bare - out of the pockets of his overcoat to kiss hers - gloved in umber suede - before starting back down the trail without her.

Ras Tanura, 10 February

After ten days of quinacrine and resting in his quarters, Hank was feeling better. His fevers were gone, along with the shaking chills. The nightmares about Gloria and Peter had been replaced by his usual waking worries about them. Although his strength hadn't returned, he could work in his office for a few hours at a time. Ammar was attentive, bringing meals and handling his mail and calls. Ali had kept his files in order, allowing him to catch up with reports he had missed during his illness.

Hank ventured out to see how much progress Vukovich and Pedani were making with construction. Bechtel's ocean-going crews had finished the new submarine pipeline to Bahrain. Before the feed from drilling sites proliferating in the concession could be pumped to the Bapco refinery, a team needed to be trained for its new stabilizer. Vukovich had finished the unit - a miniature still that burned off unwanted vapor pressure and toxic gases - near where the new pipeline disappeared under Tarout Bay.

The crude oil from the early strikes was "sour" because of its high concentration of H2S. The feed line smelled like rotten eggs, one of the contaminant's better qualities. H2S corroded pipes it flowed through. It was poisonous enough to have been used as a weapon in the Great War. Homer Whitlow was the Texaco specialist assigned to run the stabilizer unit at Ras Tanura. Somehow Hank wasn't surprised that he was one of the most toxic Americans in the Eastern Province.

The scrawny son of an Oklahoma sharecropper, Whitlow had been working in refineries around the Gulf of Mexico and the Caribbean since he was fifteen. He was the kind of man who hated blacks, mestizos, and indigenous tribes with equal irrationality. The Arabs assigned to his stabilizer crew were destined to be another colored race that disappointed him. In the Dining Hall, Whitlow was the exception who made Hank hate the unwritten rule of the Hundred Men, who recognized no distinctions between blue-collar and white-collar workers in the American Camp.

Whitlow was proud of his rank as regional treasurer in the Ku Klux Klan, Inc. But the Internal Revenue Service had forced the Klan into bankruptcy the year before. Feeling persecuted by FDR and Morgenthau, his Treasury Secretary - *a Jew, of course* - Whitlow had signed on with Aramco because his foreign earnings would be exempt from federal taxes. As racists went, he was magnanimous in Ras Tanura, keeping his low opinions of his Arab crew to himself on the job. But on his own time, in his ignorance, he assumed that all the Americans in Arabia shared his views. Soon after Hank felt well enough to take his meals in the Dining Hall, Whitlow sat down on the other side of his table.

For what seemed like a long time, Hank could feel Whitlow looking at him. Finally he said, "You're *yellow*."

It was true. Hank had been alarmed at first, looking at himself in the mirror in his trailer. He had made an extra trip back to see Dr. Vogel when he realized his skin was the same color as Giulia's lemon custard. The doctor had peered at Hank's eyes and then smiled when he was satisfied they were as white as ever, except for the blue irises. *It's nothing, his doctor had said, just a side effect of the quinacrine.* When Hank asked Vogel why he hadn't warned him, his matter-of-fact answer

215

was that he didn't want to give him a reason not to take his medicine. His doctor assured him that his skin would clear when he no longer needed the medication. Hank didn't want a relapse that would force him to leave before Ras Tanura was done.

Whitlow continued to stare at Hank, as if he owed an explanation for the color of his skin to all the white men in the concession.

"I had a touch of malaria. My shade of yellow is just a side effect of my medication. I'm not contagious - unless you bite me."

Whitlow snorted before tearing into his meatloaf and mash potatoes. As his belly filled, he resumed what he considered to be ordinary table talk.

"I hear the King and his cousin, the A-mir, have black slaves."

"They're personal bodyguards. They hold them in high favor, trusted warriors who have proven their loyalty in battle."

Whitlow was silent for a few moments. Sharecroppers had seldom been slave owners. But owning other human beings included the presumption that some were more valuable than others.

"Them niggers they gave me don't know the difference between propane and kerosene."

"They're not *negroes*, Homer. Most of them are Bedouins whose tribes have lived in the desert for generations. And there were no schools in Arabia, except for what we call Sunday School, until we opened our own. As long as you can teach your crew how to monitor the temperature in the cooler and the pressure in the gas separator, it doesn't matter if they know one hydrocarbon from another."

Whitlow snorted, "Them ragheads don't even know how to piss. Did you know they squat like women? Won't even touch their peckers to pee."

"That's part of their religion."

"Goddam A-rabs don't have religion."

"Sure they do. Christianity and Islam are both Abrahamic."

"Like Lincoln? He got what he deserved."

"No. Like Abraham. In the Old Testament."

Stymied for a moment, Whitlow charged off in the direction of another indignity. "I can't believe Aramco makes us stop work five times every day just so they can heel down like dogs."

"They're praying, Homer. It's in the concession agreement. We're guests in the kingdom, but only as long as we respect the teachings of the Prophet."

Whitlow was enough to make Hank skip the cherry cobbler. But as he got up from the table, Whitlow raised his left hand. Abrupt even when polite, he asked if Hank's assistant, A-mar, could help him translate the next morning. He had to do H2S safety training for his crew. It was the most reasonable request Hank had ever heard him make.

Before Ammar met Whitlow, Hank gave him a short course on hydrogen sulfide. It was insidious. Even when Saudi crude was not as sour as the first strike in Dammam, H2S was a toxic byproduct of many refinery processes. Although it was a gas at normal temperatures, the compound was slightly heavier than the atmosphere. It settled in closed spaces at sea level. Worse, one of its first effects was to dull the sense of smell. Anyone who failed to notice the odor of rotten eggs would soon be overcome. The stabilizer separated the poison from less volatile components of the feed line that could then be safely sent to the Bapco refinery in Bahrain.

Managers in Ras Tanura worried that H2S was their biggest technical risk. Not only because of the sour nature of Dammam crude, but because of the Saudis' lack of formal education or experience in the oil patch. Basic H2S safety training was strictly enforced throughout the refinery, tank farm and marine terminal.

Like a high school principal, Hank dropped in Whitlow's session with his Arab crew. Beforehand, he had made a special request for Ammar to filter as much of Homer's profanity as he understood. The session went well, the Arab men following Ammar and all the movements acted out by Homer as if they were part of a KKK ritual. Blankets were stored in every enclosure. Victims were covered until they could be safely moved. Rescuers pulled suspected victims out of the enclosures where they were typically found. Most importantly, refinery workers were trained to do mouth-to-mouth until oxygen was available.

Rescue breathing had been proven in England before the turn of the century. The Royal Humane Society promoted mouth-to-mouth by giving out yearly awards for the most dramatic salvage after drownings or mining accidents. Hank was pleased to see that Arab men who thought nothing of holding the hand of male friends or relatives showed little hesitation about mouth-to-mouth training. Ammar explained that they were replacing bad air with good air in victims. The stabilizer crew nodded like learned scientists. Every man from the seaside villages knew at least one pearl diver who had drowned.

Dhahran, 11 February

The concession's headquarters had the best communications in the Eastern Province. At times their capabilities only added to Tom Barger's sense of isolation. It had been months since Ohliger had received a cable from New York announcing the return of the first group of senior staff wives. Kathleen Barger - the love of his charmed life - had been sending Tom letters, postcards, and telegrams for weeks on their way from the States.

Since the Allies were still bearing down on Germany, he wasn't surprised that the women had been delayed in Lisbon and then Cairo. As usual, the brunette who grew up on a dude ranch was attracting all the attention along the way. Barger hadn't seen Kathleen since the attack on Pearl Harbor. The Italian bombing of Dhahran was trivial by comparison, but it forced California Arabian to evacuate all of the women and a handful of children who lived in American Camp. Kathleen's plans to join her husband in Arabia had been put off four years.

Barger was startled by the overlapping calls of the muezzins in Dammam to the Asr prayer. There were only a few hours of daylight left for the pilots of the ATC flight carrying the senior staff wives.

The airfield in Dhahran didn't have electric lights. Visual flight rules applied for Aramco and the Army Air Force, which was still negotiating with Abdulaziz. Nor was there any radar to assist pilots.

The only airfield nearby equipped for night landings was the RAF base in Bahrain. That winter more than one jumpy ATC crew had diverted there before dusk. Kathleen might spend her first night in Manama instead of their bed in American Camp. It would take the better part of the next day before the women could reach Al-Khobar by boat. Barger had lived like a monk for too long. He was determined to spend the night with his wife. The director of government relations hopped in his car and headed to the airfield to see what he could do.

The airfield was little more than a ribbon of desert that had been scraped by road equipment. A maintenance crew had applied a fresh coat of oil to keep down the dust for the women's arrival. Barger was happy to see Bill Eltiste in charge, the most resourceful of the Hundred Men. The materials manager had collected dozens of five-gallon jerry cans and filled them with his own blend of kerosene and crude oil. The men spread the makeshift lights to outline the runway as sunset approached.

Barger knew that Kathleen would be begging the pilots of the C-47 not to divert. He had yet to meet a man who could resist her charms. A decade had passed since he returned to his alma mater as part of the engineering faculty. Barger had known it was a mistake the first day he stood in front of a class. But then he was beguiled by Kathleen. The most beautiful girl at the campus mixer was also brilliant, filled with empathy and energy, a heavenly spirit who miraculously fell for a mining engineer with few prospects and no money.

Barger watched Eltiste and his men light the canvas wicks they had placed in the jerry cans. As the sun disappeared in the west, the plane circled the field and landed, to the delight of everyone on the ground at headquarters.

Kathleen spotted Barger from the top of the ramp. When she waved a card with a red heart above her head, he worked his way to the last step in time for her to fall into his arms. A happy crowd of oily strangers and tidier managers applauded as the Bargers kissed.

That night in the Dining Hall, at every tableful of lonely men, the chatter was the same. *If one planeload of wives could make it to Dhahran, then so would many more.*

Part 3 – Victors and Thieves

12 February - Jeddah

An American destroyer was anchored in the harbor, the first time the US Navy had ever made an official call on the kingdom. Abdulaziz happened to be visiting the ancient port after holding court in Mecca. Berglund had been busy for days in the US legation assisting Colonel and Mrs. Eddy with the details of both entourages. Commodore Keating and Captain Smith of the USS Murphy had come ashore to pay their respects to the king at his palace. His second son, Prince Feisal, the viceroy of the Hejaz, and another local emir, the governor of Jeddah, had also welcomed the Americans. Afterwards, the Eddys hosted all the officers from the destroyer and twenty Americans who worked in Jeddah, including all of the local staff of the oil concession. For such occasions, the US legation still needed electricity generated by *Bait Americani*, a crumbling villa that Aramco had renovated nearby. The previous owner was St. John Philby, English adventurer, advisor to Abdulaziz and (secretly) Standard.

Berglund had worried that such a large gathering would overtax the legation's new facilities, the only flushing toilets in the walled city. During the rooftop party, the military attaché took pleasure in knowing the rest of the diplomatic community could see the American destroyer. His counterparts in the British consulate thought of the Red Sea as part of their empire, the southern entrance to the Suez.

That afternoon, Abdulaziz gave orders to break the Saudi encampment that had followed him from Riyadh through Mecca. Scores of his personal vehicles were packed for the rough drive back over the mountains of the Hejaz to the capital. Then something remarkable happened, without warning or fanfare, surprising even Berglund. For the first time in his fabled life, Abdulaziz left the country that he battled to create. The smallest imaginable retinue - only two of his younger sons and his most essential ministers, servants and slaves - stepped onto naval launches, motored across the harbor, and boarded the destroyer.

Eddy informed Berglund at the last moment, amidst the furor at the king's palace, where hundreds of his family and courtiers had been left behind. The US minister was still a spy at heart and loved keeping secrets almost as much as he loved his wife and children. The junior OSS officer hadn't seen such a twinkle in the old man's eyes since Tangier.

"I'm going to be pretty busy the next few days on board the Murphy. Would you like to come along and give me a hand?"

Berglund eagerly agreed.

"Don't forget your typewriter."

Typewriters were causing serious legation problems in Jeddah. Within a few months, the humidity rusted them until they seized up. The plenipotentiary was powerless to maintain the ordinary flow of documents from the new US outpost. Special budget requests had to be made to Washington DC. Explanatory letters to justify the additional expense had to be written. Backup typewriters had to be borrowed or stolen from the regional bureau in Cairo.

Berglund dashed to the legation and grabbed the best of the machines available. Unfortunately for him, the Underwood he took from the vice consul, Merritt Grant, was also the heaviest. Then he raced back to catch the last launch headed for the Murphy, his field pack on his back, the typewriter like a cast iron sink in his arms.

The colonel had resigned his commission in the Marine Corps when FDR appointed Eddy to be his minister to the kingdom. In either case he was only a guest on board the Murphy. For the next two nights and one long day, Eddy interpreted for Abdulaziz and defused confrontations between the Saudis and the crew of the destroyer. The king was accustomed to being the ultimate host. He had insisted on bringing on board enough food for the crew as well as his own party. Bags of rice and spice were easy enough. But Eddy had to mediate between the Murphy's captain and the king's ministers over how many sheep could be loaded on the destroyer. Muslims were only permitted to eat freshly butchered meat, so the king had brought a herd of one hundred for their journey. The captain assured his guests that the ship's cold storage had more than enough frozen meat for them all. The Saudis thought it was ludicrous that their king should eat anything other than the finest livestock prepared by Muslims skilled in the requirements of *halal*. Eddy's compromise was that only seven animals would be brought aboard ship. According to custom, the first was being sacrificed and skinned on the fantail as the Murphy was getting underway.

Three large suites below decks had been made ready for the king, his sons, and his ministers. But Eddy knew the king would only be happy on deck, where he could see the coastline of the Hejaz from the starboard side. The captain finally agreed to set aside the foredeck for their guests. The sailors put up canvas in lieu of the royal tents and the king's servants rolled out rugs that went everywhere with the court.

The crew demonstrated their deck guns and depth charges to the delight of Abdulaziz. Special American meals had been prepared for the king and his party. He took great pleasure in his first apple and even more in apple pie *a la mode*. Eddy oriented the officers to the five times each day that Abdulaziz would lead his party in prayer. The ship's navigator used

Islamic criteria to calculate each Salat prayer, courteously updating the king on the tangent of Mecca as they continued north. After confirming times and coordinates with his own astrologer, the king kneeled among his subjects on the foredeck, despite legs and feet battered by advancing age and many battles.

14 February - Suez

Eddy remained tight-lipped about their destination until the second day, after the Murphy entered the Suez Canal. Its heart was a natural body of water, the Bitter Lake, that the English and French had connected to the Mediterranean and the Red Sea. The broad passing lane for ships between the East and West was oddly empty. In the distance, Berglund could see the rocky shelves of the Sinai Desert. Then he saw an American cruiser, the USS Quincy, at anchor with the presidential flag flying below the Stars and Stripes. After two nights and a day of orchestrating the Saudi court and the Murphy's crew, Eddy winked at Berglund as the destroyer came alongside the cruiser.

"Roosevelt decided to meet the kings of Arabia and Egypt and the emperor of Ethiopia on his way back from Yalta."

Berglund was stunned for a moment. After haggling with Stalin about the future of Europe, FDR was showing Churchill (and De Gaulle) that America wasn't going to just hand back North Africa or the Near East. No US president had ever met directly with the puppet rulers of the European powers. And Abdulaziz was as ferocious as Churchill or Roosevelt about the independence of his kingdom.

The Quincy might as well have been the White House, its crew lining the deck in dress uniform. Overhead, Berglund could hear a squadron of US fighters patrolling the cloudless sky. A carpeted gangway connected the two American vessels. Having seen the difficulty with which he moved about his palace in Taif, Berglund held his breath as Abdulaziz carefully descended the steep ramp to the Quincy's deck. Eddy gestured for the king's younger brother, his body man, to follow him along with two of the younger Saudi princes and his ministers, Yassin and Suleiman. Another dozen emirs crossed from the destroyer to the cruiser and lined the foredeck. Like the Murphy, part of the deck of the Quincy had been carpeted for the first meeting of the king and the president. Roosevelt was already in place in a plush leather chair, his wheelchair nearby. He beamed as Abdulaziz approached and Eddy introduced them. No one knew better than Berglund how well-cast his boss was to carry their conversation. Eddy was another wounded warrior, another raconteur, one of the few Americans with the insight to make the first meeting of men from different worlds a success. His sons helped Abdulaziz settle into the other leather lounge. Eddy slowly eased onto one knee between the president and the king and waved at Berglund to take his cane.

Though they were similar in age, it was obvious to every Arab and American on deck that the Saudi king was bigger, stronger, and more robust than his host. Abdulaziz had been unaware of the president's handicap but, like any Arab, looked upon his polio as the will of Allah. FDR was the first to acknowledge his disability.

"You are luckier than I because you can still walk on your legs and I have to be wheeled wherever I go."

"No, my friend," Abdulaziz answered, "you are more fortunate. Your chair will take you wherever you want to go and you know will get there. My legs are less reliable and are getting weaker every day."

Roosevelt grinned and said, "If you think so highly of this chair I will give you its twin as I have two on board."

Berglund watched as the order passed from the president's staff through Admiral Leahy to the crew of the Quincy. While the heads of state continued to make each other's acquaintance, two sailors carried the spare wheelchair up the gangway to the Murphy. The custom-made chair was too small for Abdulaziz, but the gesture was magnificent, as were the king's gifts to the crew of the Murphy. Before leaving the destroyer, Abdulaziz had announced that each petty officer would be given fifteen pounds sterling and each sailor ten. (More than one crewman had asked Berglund how big their tip was in dollars.) The Murphy's officers received golden daggers and Arab costumes suitable for his court. Eddy insisted that everyone accept the ceremonial gifts: offending Abdulaziz would have been worse for their country than violating naval regulations.

Like any Arab guest, the founding king allowed his host to lead their conversation. As he had for three terms, the president focused on the welfare of the most vulnerable in Arabia. "The reports of drought in your country have troubled me greatly. I hope that our assistance through Lend Lease has helped you feed your people."

Berglund had to suppress a smile: Congress had only appropriated funding for democratic governments like the UK. Roosevelt had been forced to add the kingdom to the program through executive order as a 'strategic ally.'

"We are very grateful for your generosity," Abdulaziz said. Berglund glanced at Suleiman and Yassin, who seemed less appreciative.

"And the experimental agriculture station at Al Kharj?"

"Your experts have shown us how to modernize ancient systems of irrigation. We will soon be able to feed our own people."

FDR pointed his chin a little higher. "If we can grow vegetables in the Arizona desert, so can you!"

"You and I are really twins - old men with grave responsibilities for our people, but farmers at heart."

As FDR regaled the king about the life of a gentleman farmer at Hyde Park, Berglund leaned against the turret of one of the guns. As history unfolded, Eddy gritted through the pain on one knee. Then Admiral Leahy informed the president that their luncheon below deck was ready. The social hour was about to end; the private meeting of Abdulaziz and Roosevelt was scheduled to begin in a cabin after the meal. The founding king, on only the second day of his life outside his own kingdom, asked his first question since meeting FDR.

"The British prime minister has asked to meet with me. As your guest, I will not do so if it would offend you."

Eddy had shared the scuttlebutt with Berglund when they were on the Murphy: Roosevelt hadn't informed Churchill that he was meeting the three monarchs until the day he left Yalta. Churchill was outraged that the US president would meet with the rulers of their protectorates, Egypt and Ethiopia, without British chaperones. The Crown's foreign service had been feverishly arranging for Churchill to meet with Farouk, Selassie, and Abdulaziz in Roosevelt's wake. Like any Arab with good manners, the founding king didn't want to offend his host by accepting Churchill's invitation without the president's approval. From a few feet away, it was hard for Berglund to tell which of the new friends savored the moment more.

"Why not? I always enjoy seeing Mr. Churchill and I'm sure you will like him too."

Admiral Leahy wheeled the president to an elevator; Eddy escorted the king to another. Berglund caught up with the Saudi party at the luncheon. As the minutes passed they became impatient though Abdulaziz remained the face of equanimity. Eddy whispered to Berglund to see what was holding up FDR. He found the other elevator just as its door opened. A billow of cigarette smoke filled the passageway. (Abdulaziz refrained from tobacco as well as alcohol.) Roosevelt had held the elevator until he could smoke two cigarettes, one after the other. He looked at Berglund dismissively, like a sixth former at Groton caught smoking in a dormitory by a fourth former. Berglund saluted and stepped aside.

15 February - Suez

By the time Eddy joined Berglund at Bayn Field and boarded an Army Air Force C-47 back to Jeddah, both men were exhausted. The day before - after the three-hour meeting of Roosevelt and Abdulaziz - they had been up most of the night drafting a memorandum of the conversation for both rulers to sign. In their private session on the Quincy, Eddy had continued to interpret for the president as well as the founding king. Berglund took lawyerly notes for the American side while Yassin did the same for the Saudis. While Abdulaziz and Roosevelt viewed the conversation as an opportunity to establish their relationship, every word they spoke had meaning for both governments.

As Eddy had expected, the founding king never mentioned American aid or oil. Once FDR had convinced him that the Allies would win the war in Europe, Abdulaziz only asked for assurances that the US would honor the independence of his kingdom. But the defender of Mecca was adamant on the question of Palestine. The year before, the president had campaigned for a Jewish homeland. Each time that FDR raised the subject, Abdulaziz became terser. In the end he would only paraphrase the words of the Prophet: *The victims should be compensated by their oppressors. They should be offered the best land in Germany. Palestine is only one of fifty on the winning side, a tiny country that shouldn't have to do more than its fair share for the Jews of Europe.*

Apart from affirmations of mutual respect and future cooperation, the final version of the memorandum was reduced to two promises that Roosevelt made Abdulaziz: *as president, he would take no hostile actions against the Arabs, and the US government would take no action on Palestine without full consultation with both Arabs and Jews.*

The only serious conflict occurred late in the afternoon when the captain of the Quincy announced that the meeting had to end for the ship's security. Abdulaziz was incensed. He gave Eddy a tongue lashing for not informing him that he wouldn't be able to host the president for a meal aboard the Murphy, his temporary home. Eddy was only spared because he could truthfully say the timing of the Quincy's departure had been kept from him as well. Even if the Germans were losing, the Bitter Lake was still in reach of their bombers. The diplomatic crisis was averted when FDR agreed to have the king's own attendants, in their finest dress, serve tea and coffee according to Arab custom.

Afterwards, Berglund typed up the English version of the memorandum while Eddy and Yassin worked on the translation in Arabic. Abdulaziz signed both copies after his meeting with Churchill, who the king felt was rude and obnoxious. The following morning, Eddy hopped on a float plane to Alexandria, where the Quincy had docked after passing through the Suez Canal. Before leaving the cruiser with FDR's signature, Eddy was asked to go through crates of elaborately crafted gifts from the king with the president's daughter. The minister had also been entrusted with a jewel-encrusted sword for Roosevelt himself.

Eddy slept longer than Berglund on the flight back to Jeddah. The C-47 was far less comfortable than the one that Aramco used to shuttle the military attaché between Asmara and Dhahran. By the time his boss woke up, Berglund's curiosity had gotten the best of him.

"So what was Roosevelt's gift to Abdulaziz?"

The old spy beckoned to the unadorned fuselage. "One of these - the civilian version, a DC-3 - plus a ground crew trained by OSS Cairo. We made some modifications to the toilet. From now on, we'll be able to monitor the king's effluents. If he gets diabetes or kidney failure or internal bleeding, we'll know."

Berglund smirked in admiration. Nothing in the kingdom was more important than the health of Abdulaziz. The crown prince, Saud, was a dullard and a drinker, an unworthy successor. Eddy favored Prince Feisal, the second-born, who lacked his father's charm but was his equal as a thinker and defender of the faith. The problem for the OSS was that the founding king had more than thirty sons by many wives. A lifetime of alliances through marriage would give several tribes legitimate claims to the throne.

The sun was setting over the Red Sea when their plane began its descent into Jeddah. For Berglund and Eddy and the American officials who followed them, the dilemma would remain the same: the third kingdom of Al-Saud could fall apart as easily as the first and second. If so, the entire peninsula could devolve into another millennium of competing sheikdoms. The largest oil reserves in the world could go untapped or, worse, fall into the hands of America's enemies.

Ras Tanura, 15 February

Dr. Vogel had allowed Hank to reduce the dose of quinacrine enough that the yellow cast of his skin was concealed by his deepening tan. The days were growing longer and the sun stronger. Weeks were passing quickly. The new submarine pipeline to Bahrain had been online for a week. The checklist between Aramco and Bechtel before firing the first still was down to a few pages.

Despite his illness, Barger had begged Hank to release Ali from his duties as the marine terminal's office boy to assist Rashid with the royalty tank audits for SAG. For the first time in months, Hank was spending hours confirming figures in reports that were beyond Ammar's mathematical grasp.

The emergency claxon sounded on the submarine pipeline stabilizer. A jolt of adrenaline went through Hank's body that made the muscles in his back and limbs ache and burn. He ran in the direction of the alarm, looking for signs of smoke or fire as he went. As he climbed the stairs to the control room of the stabilizer, another kind of alarm went off in his head: the strength and endurance he had taken for granted as a young man were gone. After weeks of bedrest to combat malaria, he was in the worst shape of his life. But he was still the first American to reach Whitlow. Hank found him sprawled on the floor of the control room, unconscious.

One member of the stabilizer crew was on his knees, doing mouth to mouth on the former Klabee of the Greater Houston KKK. The other Arabs on the crew were beseeching Allah to be merciful. After a few minutes, another man took over. Each of them offered their own advice in Arabic about the rescue techniques of the others. All of them were doing well enough with Ammar's training that there was no reason for Hank to take over. As terrifying as the moment was, it pleased him that the Arab men that Whitlow held in such low regard controlled his fate. Hank tried to fight off the unkind thought that they might not be able to save him.

The gangway became overloaded with Arabs and Italians who had heard the claxon. Hank began to send them away before it gave way from the weight. He ordered another foreman to shut down the feeder line bringing the crude oil from the production sites to Ras Tanura. Somewhere in the stabilizer or the feeder line there was a problem. Crude oil would begin to fill one of the many new tanks near the refinery. The operators hated the refiners when they shut down feeder lines.

But it was the only way to protect the rest of the workers in Ras Tanura until they had time to inspect the feeder lines and the stabilizer.

Whitlow's arms and legs began to stir. He took his first semi-conscious gasp.

Whitlow's men rejoiced, arms raised, praising Allah and embracing each other.

"*Allah akbar!*"

"*Allah rahim!*"

Hank didn't need Ammar to translate. *Allah was great. Allah was merciful.*

Ammar arrived after fighting his way onto the ramp. He asked, "What happened?"

"They must have found him on the ground. They did everything you taught them to do. They pulled the alarm.

They threw blankets over him. They dragged him out of the control room. They took turns doing mouth-to-mouth until he began breathing on his own."

Mrs. Vogel arrived from the clinic. She carried a small tank of oxygen with tubing and a mask she placed on Whitlow's face.

Hank shook hands with each member of Whitlow's crew, fighting off the urge to grab them with his left hand as well. His Arabic would have to do as he expressed his gratitude and shared his sense of triumph.

"*Shukraan lak.*" Thank you. "*Shukran jazilaan lak.*" Thank you very much.

All of the stabilizer crew smiled back at Hank. Their faces were filled with joyous befuddlement. They laughed at the strangeness of what they had witnessed. Turning to Ammar, they sounded deferential.

Ammar translated, "They say that they only did what we taught them to do. The rest was the will of Allah."

In a moment when Americans might congratulate each other or even take credit, the Arabs praised their Creator. That Allah would save a man like Whitlow - who any god could see was unworthy of salvation - was an even greater wonder to Hank. He helped Mrs. Vogel move Whitlow into an upright position to ease his breathing.

When he finally opened his eyes, Whitlow asked, "What happened?"

"Your men saved your life, you dumb Okie!"

The oxygen just beginning to reach his brain, he muttered, "Hell they did."

237

Ras Tanura, 20 March

The first day of Spring had little meaning to Hank. The days were growing longer and the heat penetrated deeper into the darkness. The gulf was turning back into a bathtub in a boarding house on a Saturday night. Both of the new stills in the refinery towered over the tea kettle, though months remained before they went online. Americans hired by Bechtel to build Ras Tanura continued to leave. The same was true of many of the drillers, mechanics and refiners hired Aramco.

Oilmen were used to drilling dry holes. It was the nature of the business. The price of petroleum was always marked up to cover losses. But it was harder for the concession to recover when skilled workers left without fulfilling their agreement. Ferguson pounded on his managers to pick up the slack. Hank and Lanier and Vukovich pushed back. There was only so much that Aramco and Bechtel could do with half of the skilled workers they were supposed to have by early 1945.

Construction at Ras Tanura had progressed to individual product lines in the new refinery. Heavy derivatives like the Navy's fuel oil came off the bottom. Lighter ones like gasoline boiled off the middle of the two new towers. Volatile products like natural gas came off the top. The industrial design called for welders and pipefitters with real skill to direct the flow of each product to royalty tanks. There was simply no way that Arab workers could be trained fast enough to finish the job by the end of the year. Only Anglo-Iranian and Iraq Petroleum had built facilities on the scale of Ras Tanura in the gulf. As Berglund predicted, British oilmen weren't inclined to help their American competitors as the war wound down.

Mac didn't have to explain to Hank how Ohliger and Ferguson got hooked on the Italians. They had the education, experience, and cultural fit that the Saudis lacked. Pedani's men could be imported from Eritrea for next to nothing. Even better, Aramco only had to pay the Italians a third of what they were promising Americans. Within a few months, the number of Italians in Ras Tanura had jumped from a hundred to nearly a thousand. Nor were they only welding pipes and bending metal. A lot of them were driving trucks and pumping gas, entry-level jobs that Saudis were beginning to think of as their own.

Ras Tanura was looking more like an Italian project than an American one. But Italian Camp looked and smelled like it was for POW's. The perimeter of barbed wire fences expanded as the number of workers increased. The humidity was rising as the season advanced. The wind off the gulf laid down, as if the air were getting too heavy to move. The stench rising from the open latrines was overwhelming. The rows of rotting tents grew longer.

The only part of the camp that wasn't getting bigger was the medical section, Scarcella's clinic only became more pathetic. There was no electricity to refrigerate medications or supplies that had to be protected from hundred-degree heat. Fresh water was hauled in by tanker truck from an Aramco well. If they used it up before the next truck arrived, patients couldn't be bathed and the staff couldn't maintain basic hygiene. The conditions guaranteed that the Italians became infected with the endemic diseases of Al-Hasa: dysentery, dengue, and malaria. Aramco had hired every nurse and doctor that they could find in Asmara. But Scarcella and his staff were of little use to their countrymen without proper equipment and supplies.

Scarcella snapped one afternoon after examining a truck driver who was brought in by co-workers. The ruts in the secondary roads around Ras Tanura dated back to camel tracks. They could loosen fillings and jar the spines of older men. But the young Neapolitan had excruciating pain in the right side of his lower abdomen after every bump on a quarry run. His friends couldn't explain it to their doctor. The trip had been no worse than any other. Yet the truck driver told the doctor in Italian Camp that it was the worst pain he had experienced in his life.

Scarcella examined the young man, who was vomiting and had a low-grade fever. It was easy enough to conclude that he had appendicitis. But when his doctor realized he had no more ether or even iodine to scrub his abdomen before surgery, Scarcella assigned his patient to an attendant and marched to the marine terminal. He barged to the front of the line waiting to consult with Pedani and then grabbed the chief engineer by the sleeve, dragging his friend to the trailer shared by the Aramco managers.

Hank jumped out of his chair when the Italian doctor pounded on his office door. The American had never seen Scarcella so overcome by frustration and rage. He demanded that Hank and Pedani follow him to the Aramco clinic in American Camp.

Ammar followed his boss and the two Italians. Scarcella pounded on the door and demanded to see his counterpart, Dr. Vogel. His wife appeared first in her white uniform, shielding her husband from attack when he appeared behind her.

"Quanti americani ci sono a Ras Tanura?"

Pedani said, "I'm sorry...Dr. Scarcella is asking how many Americans there are here."

Dr. Vogel looked at Hank before saying, "About three hundred."

Pedani turned to his friend and said, *"Trecento."*

Scarcella nodded, behaving more like a lawyer in a courtroom than a doctor preparing for surgery. *"Ci sono novecento italiani!"*

Pedani said, "Dr. Scarcella says there are nine hundred Italians here."

"Quante lattine di etere hai?"

Pedani said, "He wants to know how many tins of ether you have."

Dr. Vogel frowned at Hank, glanced at his wife and then answered, "We have three I think, maybe four."

"Non ne abbiamo. Prenderò due delle tue lattine di etere!"

"Dr. Scarcella says we have none in our clinic. He would like two of your cans of ether."

"Mi scusi. ne prenderò solo uno ora poiché non ho modo di tenere l'altro."

Scarcella's sarcasm didn't need to be translated. Pedani stared at his friend with displeasure.

"The doctor excuses himself. He will only take one can now because he has no facilities to keep the other refrigerated in his clinic."

Dr. Vogel had had enough. "What's this all about, anyway?"

Pedani answered, "Dr. Scarcella has a patient with appendicitis who needs emergency surgery. But the clinic in our camp lacks the necessary supplies and equipment. My friend is very upset because he has made many requests that Aramco has ignored."

The Vogels encouraged each other in a glance. "Then bring the patient here. I'll assist Dr. Scarcella and help in any way I can."

Pedani translated Vogel's offer. Scarcella's long face reverted to its usual melancholy,

mixed with relief and remorse. Mrs. Vogel headed for the Italian Camp with a stretcher. Hank and Ammar and Pedani grabbed the other three corners. Vogel invited Scarcella to scrub for the surgery. Once inside its gleaming interior, the Italian doctor kept apologizing to his American colleague.

"Perdonami...Mi dispiace molto...Grazie mille."

Ras Tanura, 23 March

The truck driver from Naples was eating chicken soup from the Dining Hall in American Camp. His recovery under the care of the Vogels continued. But for Pedani, Scarcella, and the rest of the leaders of Italian Camp, a compassionate exception only proved how much more Aramco could be doing for its workers from Eritrea. Now that most of their country had been liberated, the men in Italian Camp were receiving mail from home. Friends and relatives who had been POWs in the States had been freed. 'Italian Service Units' were being paid, housed and fed better by the US government than ex-colonials employed by Aramco.

From their walks on the beach, Hank knew that Pedani was losing control of the Italian Camp. The arrival of so many of their countrymen meant that Squalo, capo of the crane operators, and Bruno, the capo of the longshoremen, spoke for hundreds. Italian workers had been unionized long before Mussolini came to power. The journalist elected as a populist after the Great War didn't become Il Duce until his Blackshirts used violence against unions supporting other parties. Squalo and Bruno were eager to assert their power in Ras Tanura. The rest of the Italian political spectrum - royalists, socialists, and communists - were all well-represented as Italian Camp grew.

Whatever goodwill Hank had earned among the Italians was exhausted. Only a fraction of them knew how hard he had worked to get the families in the northern provinces paid. The rest took for granted that American oil companies could do as they pleased. It didn't matter that Berglund said the German forces in the Social Republic were retreating to alpine strongholds. Wolff's Group C was being pinned down by leftist partisans. Tito's irregulars were within reach of Trieste. The Red Army was over-running Hungary and Austria. Hank was afraid of the day when everyone in Italian Camp knew how much of their payroll had been skimmed by Nazi bankers - and wanted to know when Aramco knew.

Pedani led a contingent who met with Hank to address the deficiencies in shelter, hygiene and food in Italian Camp. Squalo and Bruno looked like they wanted to tear his trailer apart. None of the problems in Scarcella's clinic had been solved. But Hank had no authority beyond the marine terminal. He took Pedani and the trade group to meet with Ferguson but the project manager for Ras Tanura wasn't even polite to the Italians. His answer to every request was the same in English and Italian - No.

Being Aramco's liaison in Asmara no longer looked like a promotion to Hank. He was doing no better than the labor council with Ohliger. Barger told him that it was politically impossible to improve Italian Camp without doing even more for Saudi Camp. The Arab workforce was growing faster everywhere in the concession than the Italians were in Ras Tanura. Nothing was more important to Abdulaziz than improving the condition of his people; few things were of less concern to him than how Aramco treated their foreign workers.

Pedani and Scarcella warned Hank on their evening walks on the beach, away from the eyes and ears of their countrymen. The Italian Camp was breaking into political factions that mirrored their homeland. There were communists and anarchists who had been sent to Ethiopia as cannon fodder by the fascisti. There were veterans like Squalo and Bruno who hated the British and the Americans almost as much as they hated the Arabs. Ammar had told Hank about the atrocities committed by earlier generations of Italians during the conquest of Libya. The British had been investigating crimes committed during the retreat from Ethiopia while the Duke of Aosta was still fighting in another corner of Italian East Africa.

Across the political spectrum in Italian Camp, all of the workers that Hank helped recruit agreed that Aramco was treating them like slaves.

"We just need a little more time," the American promised. "Once the refinery starts production and the crude oil is filling tankers, there will be more revenue to support better food, better housing and better pay."

"*Sempre un po' di tempo*," Scarcella muttered, shaking his head. For workers in any regime, the answer was always a little more time.

That night, before going to bed, Hank re-read Gloria's letters. Something had changed since he contracted malaria. Week after week, his wife was pleading with him to come home. Even though he was feeling well on quinacrine, with the construction project back on schedule, he was sorely tempted. It was bad business for Ohliger and Ferguson to treat their best workers as poorly as the men of Italian Camp. Hank was beginning to doubt that the problems in Italian Camp were about business at all. He remembered the first time in Martinez he heard one of their boarders call Giulia, the kindest person he had ever known, a Wop. A lot of people in his hometown looked down on his Italian classmates. Long before the war, there were doors that never opened to the immigrant community of Island Hill. For men like Whitlow - if not Hank's bosses - the war and the gulf were just excuses to justify their worst tendencies.

To escape his own thoughts, Hank strolled along the marine terminal. At low tide Tarout Bay reminded him of Port Richmond. He could feel the fog rolling into San Francisco Bay. The sound of his son laughing echoed in his head. Most of all, he ached for his wife's embrace. Even if Standard didn't hire him back, he knew he could get a job. The post-war economy would be fueled by petroleum. Few people were more qualified than Hank. But the idea of quitting anything as important as Ras Tanura was unimaginable. He thought of the marine terminal as his own: not Pedani's, not Vukovich's, not even Aramco's. The impossibility of leaving before the project was completed finally allowed Hank to fall asleep.

13 April - Riyadh

The king opened the mosque within his palace in Riyadh every Friday to lead his followers for Al-Jumu'ah. Yousuf Yassin, his Syrian minister, knew that Abdulaziz would disapprove of him listening to the radio during the day of communal prayer, even though the king loved his Marconi sets. Just as the king's most trusted slave stood guard behind him as he prayed, the Syrian couldn't protect his kingdom without listening to the news on the BBC. *The American president they met only a few weeks before had suddenly died.* Yassin had never heard of Warm Springs, Georgia, but understood why Roosevelt needed a refuge from his duties and detractors.

Yassin re-read a letter that had just been delivered to Abdulaziz from the US legation in Jeddah. Only a week before, Roosevelt had written to say how much he enjoyed meeting the king and affirming the promises he had made on board the Quincy: he would never take hostile action against the Arabs and he would consult with both Arab and Jewish leaders before taking any steps on Palestine. Yassin had informed Abdulaziz, who regarded the president's word as more important than the letter. Now that Roosevelt was dead, neither the founding king nor Yassin expected his successor to keep either promise.

Yassin chose to wait to tell his king the bad news. He asked for permission to speak to him after Abdulaziz went to his private apartment. Yassin did so with trepidation, knowing that this was a time when the king would be alone with one of his harem favorites. (It wouldn't have surprised the king or his minister that the president died in the company of his mistress.) Yassin considered Roosevelt's passing as he waited outside the gold-clad doors of the king's apartment. Like most Saudis of his generation, Abdulaziz cared little about the day of his birth or his death. That was for Allah to decide.

When the door opened, Abdulaziz was in good spirits. *As he should be,* Yassin thought. The king's three great pleasures were coffee, perfume, and the company of women. Another secret that Yassin had kept from the king was that his physician had forgotten the chest that contained his aphrodisiacs during their journey north on the Red Sea. Yassin and Eddy had gone to great lengths, along with the officers of the Murphy, to find it before Abdulaziz boarded the British battleship for his return to Jeddah.

The smile disappeared from the king's face when Yassin delivered the news about Roosevelt. Despite his cataracts, the king could easily see the wheelchair the American president had given him. It would remain in his private apartment for the rest of his life. For a moment after Yassin's news, the king seemed to be elsewhere, perhaps back on the deck of the Quincy, enjoying his memories of his great friend in the very chair that now sat empty in a corner.

"Allah has been merciful to him," the king said. "He suffers no longer. Many great burdens have been lifted from his shoulders."

Yassin bowed and begged forgiveness for having delivered such bad news. Few things were more important to the Saudi king than his relationship with other rulers. Neither Yassin nor Abdulaziz knew what to expect from the new president, who was said to be a little man. Both doubted that Truman would be as gracious or as honorable as their host on the Bitter Lake.

Palo Alto, 13 April

On the train home from San Francisco on Friday evening, Gloria did something unheard of: she fell asleep. The last thing she remembered before the conductor bellowed *Palo Alto* was passing San Mateo.

The day before - even before the death of President Roosevelt was announced - the Pacific branch of OWI had been funereal. Their primary mission had always been to win the hearts and minds of Japanese civilians. The China desk came next; French Polynesia was a distant third. But the beginning of the Battle of Okinawa made it clear that the imperialists in Japan were still winning the propaganda war.

For Gloria's co-workers at the Presidio, it wasn't just that hundreds of military pilots were turning into *kamikazes*, damaging Allied naval vessels by the dozen. It was that their willingness to sacrifice their lives for the Emperor made Americans wonder if the war would ever end. Colleagues in the hallways of the Pacific branch were whispering things that wouldn't stay out of US newspapers much longer.

Thousands of Okinawan boys are being turned into soldiers. Japanese soldiers are using Okinawan women and children as human shields. They're telling the Okinawans that Americans will rape them before killing them.

Once Gloria collected herself and stepped off the train, she appreciated the pleasant evening air. The rain that passed through earlier in the day had stopped and the trees on the peninsula were beginning to blossom. Gloria decided to walk to her parents' home to clear her mind and stretch her legs. By the time she reached the front door, she had almost succeeded in getting hundreds of thousands of Okinawan civilians out of her mind.

She found her parents in the den listening to the radio, just as her co-workers - apart from Thierry - had all day at the Presidio. Her father looked somber in his black cardigan and grey flannel pants. Her mother, after cocktails and wine with dinner, was somewhere between giddy and grotesque.

"I can't believe we're sitting here listening to the networks celebrate a dead socialist! They're covering every train stop between Atlanta and Washington."

Peter was sitting on the hearth playing with Ranger. He popped up long enough for Gloria to give him a hug and a kiss. Her father seemed desperate to keep Peter from thinking his grandparents were being unkind about the president's death. He got up to give Gloria a peck on the cheek.

"Would you like something to drink, dear?"

"I don't think so."

Gloria took off her shoes and reluctantly took a seat beside her pie-eyed mother, who stared at her and said, "I hope they make Dewey president now!"

Her father ignored her mother and gave his grandson, a kindergartener, his first lesson in constitutional law.

"That's not how presidential elections work, Peter. Since the incumbent, Mr. Roosevelt, defeated Governor Dewey last November, his running mate for vice president, Mr. Truman, takes over the executive branch."

He avoided his wife's withering gaze and looked at Gloria with resignation. Both of her parents revered Herbert and Lou Henry Hoover, early graduates of Stanford who built a modern mansion on campus long before his election. The Hoover House had become a shrine for a certain kind of

Republican when they returned to California after his loss to FDR. The last time Gloria had seen her mother mourn with sincerity was when Mrs. Hoover died suddenly a few months before Hank left for Arabia. Both her parents thought it was tragic that Herbert was living alone in his penthouse at the Waldorf Astoria in New York.

Gloria's mother erupted again. "Do you really think that two-bit haberdasher can beat the Germans and the Japanese? He won't even be able to stand up to the British, let alone the Russians!"

"Let's hope so, dear. He's Commander in Chief now."

Her mother snorted and then turned sullen as the rest of her family listened to the radio. A military band somewhere in the South was playing the Star-Spangled Banner. Her father hummed along in a solemn baritone. Gloria surrendered to melancholy, her thoughts drifting between the funeral train, her husband in Ras Tanura, and burning villages in Okinawa.

"Are you sad, Mommy?"

"Yes dear, I am. Mr. Roosevelt was the only president I can really remember. I was just a schoolgirl when he was elected."

"Does this mean Daddy will be coming home soon?"

As Hank recovered from malaria, it had become painfully clear that he was going to remain in Arabia until the refinery and marine terminal were finished. Gloria tried to hide her disappointment from her son.

"No dear, I don't think we'll see your father until the war is over."

"I miss him."

"We both do, dear."

Roosevelt's death was making Gloria feel like her situation was even more impossible than before. In Hank's absence, her parents were making her feel like a cross between a war widow and an unwed mother. She had already given notice to her tenants in Montclair that she wasn't going to renew their lease. But summer would be over before she and Peter could move back into their own home.

As much as she had grown to hate the New Caledonia desk, the OWI was already talking about transferring her to the Indochina group. The French colonies occupied by the Japanese were also home to a communist insurgency, the Viet Minh. France itself was fully liberated but deeply fragmented. Last but not least, Gloria had kept her promise to herself about staying away from Thierry. But the end of their affair only added to her sense of loneliness and emotional isolation. She was afraid to think about what her life would be like without her son.

Gloria's mother got up from her chair to change the radio station. When she realized they were all covering the death of the president, she turned it off in a huff and headed for the bar. It was Gloria's cue to escape with Peter - at least as far as her parents' kitchen.

"I'm getting hungry, dear. What is there to eat?"

Peter grabbed his mother's hand and eagerly dragged her out of the den.

Jeddah, 2 May

As the end of the war in Europe approached, the cable traffic in the US legation in Jeddah increased. So did the encrypted messages from the OSS stations in London, Bern, and Cairo. Berglund learned that Italian partisans captured General Wolff in late April before he was "rescued" by Swiss intelligence officers aided by OSS agents. A few days later, Wolff formally surrendered to American and British forces, citing a "communist uprising" in northern Italy as the rationale. The military intelligence services debated whether the Nazis were more afraid of the Red Army near the Austrian border or Tito's irregulars surrounding Trieste.

Earlier in March, the OSS station chief in Bern - Allan Dulles, Berglund's associate at Sullivan and Cromwell - ignored an order from the White House to include the Soviets in the secret negotiations between Wolff and the Swiss. After the Nazis in northern Italy surrendered, Stalin and Molotov were furious. Nor were the Soviets showing much interest in the first meeting of the United Nations in San Francisco. The cold war was underway, even if it wouldn't be called that until Berglund was back on Wall Street.

The military attaché forwarded the highlights of his dispatches to Parker Hart, the young foreign service officer who opened the consular branch in Dhahran. The lucky bastard had been assigned to the Saudi delegation traveling to San Francisco. The oilmen from Standard in Jeddah and Dhahran had had a few laughs briefing Hart on the best brothels for Prince Feisal, the leader of the UN delegation. The year before, Feisal and the crown prince, Saud, had toured the States on a private train as guests of FDR, earning a randy reputation with the FBI. Eddy had foisted the political appointees from the State Department on Berglund. Washington was worried about journalists catching the princes with their pants down in San Francisco. It was hard for Berglund to explain to diplomats next door to the White House that bad press had no meaning in the kingdom.

Earlier in the week, word reached the US legation that the Italian partisans had also captured Mussolini on Lake Como. Berglund had little doubt that some of the details of the treatment of the bodies of Il Duce and his mistress in Milan reached Hitler's bunker in Berlin. Then German national radio announced that Der Fuhrer had "fallen" in a final battle with the Bolsheviks. No one in the OSS believed their nemesis had died a hero's death.

On the other side of Arabia, Hank would be happy that the SS wouldn't be taking bites out of payroll for Pedani and his men. But Berglund's counterpart in Aramco was still a babe in the woods when it came to international finance. The exchange rates in Bahrain, Turkey, and Switzerland would get worse as inflation accelerated after the war.

But the grandest larceny of all in the concession would continue to be that the men in Italian Camp were being paid on the same scale as the mostly illiterate, nearly unskilled men in Saudi Camp. Pedani's tradesmen were earning a fraction of what they would have been paid if they lived in American Camp.

As a Wall Street lawyer, Berglund had to admire the terms of Aramco's agreement with the Saudis. The concession's labor practices were legally defensible; the kingdom only permitted foreign workers to do jobs that Arabs weren't trained to do. The best financial crimes weren't illegal: Hank's superiors were doing business beyond the reach of US regulators and within the bounds of international law obliterated by war.

In sight of Berglund's office in the US legation, the Red Sea was coming to a mid-day boil. The military attaché was proud of his small part in Victory in Europe, even though his accomplishments in Africa and Arabia remained secrets among gentlemen. His next mission in Jeddah would be extracting as much gin from the British consulate as he could get for a hundred pounds of American ice.

Ras Tanura, 8 May

VE-Day called for celebration on Tarout Bay, regardless of whether one worked for Bechtel or Aramco. For a few hundred Americans on the wrong side of the world, it was the best possible excuse for getting drunk. For moonshiners throughout the concession, it was another hurry-up, white-or-brown moment. That night in the Dining Hall, the only Americans in Ras Tanura who weren't smashed were a table of upstream Mormons who still acted as silly as their co-workers. A record player hooked up to the public address system in the Aramco compound blared big-band music by Dorsey, Ellington and Goodman all night long. The nurses obliged as many men who had to dance as they could before their feet gave out. Mrs. Vogel even accepted a few patriotic embraces until one of the red-blooded builders took things too far.

Like everyone else, Hank spent the evening clinking glasses, shaking hands, and acting foolish. The more he missed Gloria, the more he drank. Around midnight, he staggered out for some fresh air. The evening was pleasantly warm, the air as balmy as Miami or Havana. He passed the Emir's soldiers, who seemed to be getting the beat. The faraway war that had caused so much suffering was over.

Hank found himself wandering - staggering, really - on the road to the beach. It took him past Italian Camp, which was strangely quiet and dark. The men on the other side of the fence weren't sleeping. They were sitting or standing in long shadows cast from the bright lights of American Camp. They smoked cigarettes and sipped stolen beer, somberly watching the drunken celebration in the distance.

Intoxicated as he was, it was impossible for Hank to think of the men from Eritrea as anything other than what they were: losers. Pedani, Scarcella and the rest of the Italians, now well more than a thousand in Ras Tanura, weren't just on the wrong side of the war. Mussolini and his National Fascist Party had wasted a generation in their homeland. Even if they had survived the Blackshirts and the Nazis, it might take another generation before Italy recovered. Unlike the men in American Camp, their homeland was in ruins. Families that were thousands of miles away from them remained in tatters, their cupboards empty. Nearly all of the Italians knew an American by name who was making three and four times as much as they were for the same work in the same department. Hank felt powerless to do anything that would make a difference.

In the darkness he continued to the beach, the raucous noise coming from American Camp fading, wavelets from the gulf lapping at low tide. Hank's head was spinning again. This time it had nothing to do with the sun. He had been careful to only drink the brown stuff on the rocks, mash whiskey, depleting the concession's supply of canned corn again. He wondered who was dancing and drinking with Gloria. He could imagine her in San Francisco celebrating while her parents looked after Peter in Palo Alto. Then he shook off the thought, a drunkard holding onto his own puke.

The stars in the night sky seemed bright, glimmering in time with the horn section in the distance, "Take the A-Train" by Ellington, the other duke.

Two figures - maybe three or four - were approaching Hank at the water's edge.

"Sua Altezza Americano!"

It was Pedani and Scarcella, heading back down the beach. The chief engineer flashed one of the smiles that stood for other men's frowns. The lead doctor regarded Hank more clinically, estimating his impairment from the choppy movement of his long legs as the waves wrapped around his feet.

Hank tried and failed to think of the right thing to say. As his friends stopped a few steps from him, he uttered the only words his sodden brain and thick tongue could agree on.

"We won!"

Scarcella shook his head gravely. Pedani said, *"You* won, *Anka."*

Hank nodded. They faced each other for a long uncomfortable moment. The Italians were too sober to contend with him. The moon above the gulf was a waning crescent. The starlight bounced off the calm sea. Back in American Camp, they were playing the version of "Poinciana" that had outlived Glenn Miller.

The American was remembering his first flight with Berglund from Massawa to Asmara. The miraculous tramway that Pedani had designed and built would have stretched from Ras Tanura to Bahrain and back again without touching the water. That it ascended seven thousand feet from the Red Sea to the colonial capital seemed incomprehensible - even when Hank wasn't drunk. He thought about the churches that Pedani and his peers had built in Asmara, an ecumenical triumph.

Hank looked at Scarcella and imagined him at the bedside of the Duke of Aosta as he wasted away in a POW camp in Kenya. *Sua Altezza* was only one of hundreds of thousands of Italians and East Africans sacrificed to the monumental ego and ineptitude of *Il Duce*. Hank was ashamed that the Italian doctor had had to beg the Vogels for anesthetics and a proper operating room for the truck driver with appendicitis.

He considered his own complicity in tens of thousands in British sterling that the Nazis had skimmed off the top of Aramco payroll. He had never told Pedani or his men what happened to most of the money that he had promised to send to the families in the northern provinces. The crime's numerator was thousands of hours of grueling labor in Ras Tanura.

VE Day was only the end of thievery by the Germans. A more sophisticated form of theft by Standard and Texaco was only beginning. Standing on the edge of the Persian Gulf, Hank knew that Pedani and his men were no closer to home - or economic equality - than they were before Wolff surrendered.

Scarcella was murmuring in Pedani's ear. Hank was too drunk to make it out.

"Luigi says that if we leave you here, you may pass out and drown when the tide rises. Walk back with us. We have water for you to drink, a little bread to eat."

Scarcella took Hank by the arm and gave it a pull, like a rider leading a horse who was too lame to ride.

"Viene con noi, Anka."

Hank didn't move, not so much resisting as lacking dominion over his too-tall, too-drunk carcass. The doctor nodded for the engineer to grab his other arm.

"Viene con noi, Sua Altezza Americano."

Hank followed Pedani and Scarcella back to Italian Camp, feeling as stupid as the Frankenstein monster in the movies. There was nothing more that he could say to them, even less that they were willing to hear. Humanity remained a mockery in the middle of the twentieth century. The second world war wasn't even over while men like Berglund and Tottenham were ready to start another. Hank felt more like a loser than a winner, though the losses on the other side were beyond measure. The pathetic ebb and flow of mankind continued.

When they reached Pedani's tent, Scarcella spread a blanket on the ground. It took both Italians to help the American lay down without falling. The doctor gave Hank a cup of water that he dutifully drank as he sank onto his left shoulder. Pedani offered him a chunk of bread that he was too tired to eat. Hank was unconscious before Scarcella rolled up another blanket and placed it under his head.

San Francisco, 8 May

The end of the fighting in Europe was not a cause for celebration very long at the Presidio. The war in the Pacific hung over the base as heavily as the seasonal fog. With exceptions like Gloria, everyone on the post had seen the war up close, were preparing to confront the enemy, or were caring for the wounded at Letterman Hospital. Everyone lived in dread of the untold lives to be lost before the Japanese surrendered.

From the windows of her office, Gloria watched each day as patients with life-changing injuries were transferred from Letterman to the long-term care facility at Fort Miley. In a way, she was most alarmed by the men being transferred to the Department of Veterans Affairs without visible injuries. Thierry asked to speak to her at Land's End before VE Day was over. In a borrowed jeep, they drove west through the hilly forest until they were outside the Golden Gate. Ambulances passed them on the winding road that connected the Presidio with Fort Miley.

Though Land's End was spectacular on a clear day, it was shrouded in heavy mist that felt as somber as the Presidio. The government had made the mistake of thinking that Fort Miley could be decommissioned after the first world war. Now soldiers were guarding a series of batteries that were being expanded on the bluff above the unseen ocean. Thierry slowed as they approached the VA. Gloria recognized the New Deal design, the same as public hospitals built in many American cities before WWII. After parking the jeep, they walked in silence interrupted by the waves breaking at the bottom of the rocky bluff.

"You wanted to talk to me, Thierry?"

"I wanted to tell you that I will be leaving soon."

Gloria nodded attentively and waited. Since the end of their affair, they had become more civilized; congenial workers who didn't see each other away from the Presidio. Their audience in New Caledonia had become more receptive to the OWI as the war in the Pacific moved farther west and north. Like San Francisco, most of the military personnel in Nouméa were in transit from one place to another. The ex-lovers still shared a dark sense of humor about the futile tendency of US officials to appeal to French consciences. De Gaulle's appointees still disliked the Americans, even if they were only staging the wounded or running warehouses in New Caledonia.

"Our friends in the OSS want me to go to Saigon. I am unknown there."

Like a vendor in a souk, Thierry made a flourish around his head. Gloria, the anthropologist, had always thought his features were distinguished by their brutality, more Berber than European, dark curly hair combed back with pomade, wide nose flattened by violence, the color of his eyes muddled by generations of invaders. In some ways, Gloria admired him more than when they met: Thierry would never be defeated by life's cruelties or any disappointment in himself.

"You're not going back to Nouméa?"

He shook his head slowly. She nodded in accord. They had spent years trying to speak neutrally to factions in the French colony that opposed each other more because of the American presence. The indigenous Kanak were Melanesians who thought the US Army treated black soldiers better than the French treated them. They hoped (in vain) that the US would liberate them from their oppressors after the war. The Caldoche, French colonials who had lived in the islands for generations, wanted to protect advantages of race and class that the US preferred to ignore.

Thierry was one of many newer immigrants from the collapsing empire who would never be embraced by either. There was a pejorative term in Nouméa for Frenchmen like Thierry who were more interested in Pacific francs than birth rights. She indicted him with a smile. *"Zozo!"*

Thierry's eyes twinkled as he confessed. *"Zozo."*

A new set of waves crashed boisterously on the rocks below. They peeked over the edge of the bluff to watch the dark green surge bubble before returning to the sea.

"What about going back to Algeria or France?"

"I considered that. But neither the left nor the right will trust me now that I have worked for the Americans. The OSS want to set me up as a merchant with a new identity. They don't think they can rely on the French to be truthful about the Viet Minh, once the Japanese are gone."

Gloria knew that Thierry would leap at the opportunity to get rich with other people's money and someone else's name. Saigon was the perfect place for a handsome scoundrel. She stopped for a moment on the trail so she could gaze into his eyes, offering her left cheek and then her right with understated formality - *seulement deux bise.*

Their friendship had survived their intimacy but stood little chance of lasting any longer than their time at the Presidio. Gloria only wanted to wish Thierry well.

"Bonne chance en Indochine."

"Bonne chance en Aribie."

Thierry took Gloria's hand on their way back to the jeep. She knew that he was still baffled by her devotion to Hank, who seemed to love his work more than Gloria, the only unforgiveable sin. While Thierry felt no shame in strengthening his lover's marriage, it afforded him little satisfaction. His parting words were a friendly warning.

"Les américains sont leurs pires ennemis."

Gloria had to agree: Americans (were) their own worst enemies.

Ras Tanura, 9 May

Hank woke up on the ground in Italian Camp, wondering how he got there. Shaking, he got to his feet and headed back to American Camp as the eastern sky turned red. He washed up and found his way to the Dining Hall, where the line for coffee was longer than the one at the bar the night before. After his third cup, Hank went to his office to hide out, feeling like Gene Krupa was playing "Drum Boogie" on the top of his head.

When the phone on his desk rang, he grabbed it before the second ring. It was Barger, sounding cheery after dancing all night with his wife in Dhahran.

"Top of the morning, Hank."

"Morning, Tom."

Barger kept chirping. "I hate to bring it up, but there's still a war in the Pacific. We've got to pump a lot of product through your marine terminal."

"Right."

The night before Hank had been ashamed to be an American working for Aramco. Barger was trying to make him feel like he was back in the starting five on fraternity row.

"I haven't forgotten how helpful you were with the royalty tanks. How is Ali, the future president of Aramco?"

"Top of his class at the Jebel School in the morning, doing all the royalty tank calculations for the finance ministry in the

266

afternoon. I'm the only one who's unhappy: he doesn't have time to manage my files anymore."

Barger laughed. "We all have sacrifices to make, Hank. You know what they say: *whatever it takes.*"

Omar al Rashid, one of the many sons-in-law of the founding king, had been appointed to measure the tonnage of crude oil flowing through Ras Tanura for the finance ministry. The oilmen's dilemma was that the process was immensely technical and the Rashidi had only attended a Wahhabi school, a *madrassa*, for a few years. Mac had warned Hank that Aramco didn't want to simplify the process, which involved variable amounts of gases, water, crude oil, and contaminants in the tanks. The Saudis were still being paid royalties based on the price of a ton of petroleum in London in 1933.

When Hank had tried to train the king's son-in-law, he had been as haughty as his grandfather, the last Rashidi sheik of Riyadh, who Abdulaziz had beheaded. Hank had solved Barger's political problem by training his office boy, Ali, a gifted orphan, to do the measurements and calculations for the royalty tanks. (Ali loved the primary instrument for measuring the density of liquids, which was called – unfortunately - a thief.) Omar was happy to stay at the palace in Riyadh while the most significant transactions between the oilmen and the finance ministry were handled by Ali, who was looked after by Ammar, Hank's assistant, in Saudi Camp.

As Hank's head continued to throb, Barger got to the point. "Ferguson and Lanier are haranguing me about stolen tools and material in Ras Tanura. Truth is, it's a problem everywhere."

"Agreed."

In the bad old days, construction had been disrupted sporadically when the *Monsun Gruppe* bagged a Liberty Ship. Lately, as Bechtel tried to catch up, a steadier stream of building supplies that had been logged into warehouses in Ras

Tanura weren't there when Vukovich went looking for them. Now that the marine terminal was so vast, Pedani was suspicious about what Bruno's longshoremen were doing a kilometer offshore. So far, Arabs were getting caught in the act far more often than Italians. Then Barger said something that made Hank think that Mac was winning his private war against Ohliger, the other VP in Dhahran.

"*As you know*, piracy and banditry used to be ways of life in the gulf sheikdoms. Stealing from infidels or rival tribes was fair game. The problem for my department is that we have no police power under the concession agreement. Even raising the subject of thievery by Arab employees would offend the king's ministers. More to the point, the Eastern Province is the responsibility of its governor, Jiluwi. Ohliger wants me to lead a delegation to Jiluwi's palace in Al-Hofuf. I'm calling to see if I can talk you into going along with me. You can explain how serious a problem thievery is for Ras Tanura."

"Sure, Tom."

"The third kingdom is hardly any older than the concession. Abdulaziz has to maintain a delicate balance between the other major tribes and Al-Saud. His ministers all have their own agendas too. As much as possible, the concession needs to have one - and only one - approach. The bigger Aramco gets, the more important it will be for our relationship with SAG to be clear and constructive. I don't have to tell you we have a ways to go. Standard and Texaco don't necessarily agree on the details of our strategy or our tactics."

Dhahran, 10 May

Hank was excited about being part of the Aramco delegation until it assembled at headquarters. Then he saw Lanier in a linen suit and a Panama hat, chatting up Barger. Lanier was anything but a diplomat. He looked flattered but flustered about the audience with the Emir in Al-Hofuf. Hank wondered if his presence was a clue about what Barger was juggling in government relations. His Bahraini assistant, Saleh, introduced himself, looking more like a middle-aged merchant than an interpreter.

Few roads had been built into the interior of the province that weren't directly related to drilling sites. Barger predicted it would take most of the day to cross more than a hundred kilometers of open desert to the ancient capital of Al-Hasa. The morning was already hot, a hint of the gulf wafting through Aramco's headquarters. They loaded up a newly imported Ford power wagon equipped with four-wheel drive and balloon tires for traction in the sand.

Government relations was only one of Barger's projects, according to Mac. The VP thought of him as Aramco's rising star. Standard had been drilling four years without making a buck before he arrived. A mining engineer by training, he had helped survey an uncharted concession the size of California. In his rookie year, Barger established the kingdom's border with the sheikdoms of the Trucial Coast. The Dakotan had trekked with Bedouin guides, his first tutors in Arabic. Because of his skill as a marksman, the bedu always had oryx to eat. Like his mentor, Max Steineke, the geologist who solved the limestone's riddle, Barger was an adventurer at heart. But Duce, the VP of government relations in DC, had a stake in Barger too. After his first hitch, he had spent time on Bush Street selling the top brass on Steineke's analysis of the Arab Layer. Before Mac and Duce left Standard for the Petroleum Administration, Barger was back in the Eastern Province, holding down the concession for the rest of the war.

Barger, Mac said, was the kind of man who assumed the best in others without illusions about their tendencies. Somehow, Hank wasn't surprised when Barger offered to give him his first off-road driving lesson on their way to Al-Hofuf. Hank had rarely ventured west from Ras Tanura and had never been farther south than Dhahran.

After swapping seats in the power wagon, Barger chuckled when Hank froze behind the wheel. "With me riding shotgun, what could possibly go wrong?"

Most of the way to Al-Hofuf, they wallowed along an old camel track. Occasionally they had to cross stretches of windswept dunes. Barger told Hank to follow the top of the ridgelines. A globe-shaped compass was mounted on the dashboard between them. He was supposed to keep heading south by southwest, though his instructor barked if Hank's eyes didn't stay focused on the meandering crest of the dunes. The first time they side-slipped off the top of a sandhill, Hank thought they were going to roll. Lanier was petrified in the back seat. Saleh laughed along with his boss. Barger showed Hank how to hit the gas instead of instinctively hitting the brakes. He started to get the hang of steering into ridgetop turns with the four-wheel drive and the souped-up engine.

Barger's favorite terrain was *dikaka*, hardpan shaped like wind waves on the strait between Martinez and Benicia. Going directly across them was like driving over washboards. Barger taught Hank the trick that Steineke had taught him: crossing *dikaka* on a wide angle, like a sailboat tacking off the wind. The driving student was exhausted by the time they reached their destination, the largest inland oasis in the world.

After months of unrelenting sun on Tarout Bay, Hank drove through shaded groves of date palms tended by Arab men of all ages. Barger and Saleh bantered about which variety of dates came from each grove. It was the first time Hank had seen fields of grain since arriving in the Eastern Province. Rice paddies that reminded him of the California Delta appeared. Donkeys circled water wheels that irrigated open ditches in the groves and fields. They passed through village after village of low structures built from stacked mud bricks. Saleh said there were sixty villages scattered over thirty thousand acres of oases, the provincial capital, Al Hofuf, being the largest. Tribes from all over the region spent at least part of each year in the wadis. As they neared the palace, Barger cautioned Hank and Lanier.

"Let me do most of the talking. Don't expect Jiluwi to be in a hurry to get to the point. There's no such thing as a business meeting with the Saudis. We are guests of Abdulaziz and the Emir will feel obliged to treat us as his guests too. He won't have much to say outside of pleasantries. But Arabs in the province are his informants as well as his subjects. You should assume he knows more about what's going on than we do. And he will be offended if we accuse his people of being thieves without proof."

Hank could see a walled fortress looming above the homes and shops. Americans weren't the first foreigners to put up consequential structures in the Eastern Province. The Ottoman Empire had built the Ibrahim Palace in the sixteenth century to house the garrison that ruled Al-Hasa.

Barger said, "When Abdulaziz and Mohammed Al Jiluwi were young warriors, they took Riyadh with a handful of their tribesmen. Mohammed saved the life of the future king during the attack. Jiluwi's spear is still in the wooden doors they breached to enter the quarters of the last Rashidi sheik. You know the story, Hank. That was Omar's grandfather."

Hank looked out the window of the Ford power wagon. The turrets at the corners of the fortress were curved. The walls were three or four stories high. He could see the white dome of a mosque rising above the fortress walls. The Emir's African guards allowed them to enter. Across the sprawling parade grounds Hank could see a graceful expanse of whitewashed archways surrounding the palace. He could feel his heart pounding and his breathing become shallow, imagining Ottoman life. Four centuries before, the Ibrahim Palace had been larger and grander than anything the British or French built in North America.

Lanier pointed out the unmistakable shape of a desiccated human appendage nailed beside the fortress gate.

"What's that?"

Saleh said, "The hand of a thief."

Barger explained, "Sharia law calls for a thief to lose a hand after a third offense. Everyone in the province knows not to mess around with Jiluwi."

In the rear-view mirror, Hank could see a look of disgust mixed with dread on Lanier's face.

Hofuf, 10 May

As the oilmen got out of the power wagon, Barger said, "Remember your Arabic. Don't worry about being perfect. They'll appreciate you making the effort to speak their language - and Arabic *is* beautiful. Otherwise just smile when I smile, use your right hand if they offer to shake, and do what I do."

In the Spanish-speaking Americas, *jefe* transliterated as "chief" but doubled more widely as an honorific. In the kingdom, *emir* was much the same. Hank met a half dozen emirs that day. However, there was only one Emir, Saud bin Mohammed Al Jiluwi. Like his father, who had died in the early days of the concession, he ruled Al-Hasa under the authority of his father's ally and cousin, the founding king. Any solution to Aramco's ongoing property losses would have to be defined and enforced by Jiluwi.

One of the lesser emirs, Hassan, an administrator who dealt with Barger and Ohliger in Dammam, came out of the palace to greet them. Barger waved to the older man, who had been an advisor to Saud's father. They approached each other with well-practiced smiles and shook hands.

Barger began, "*Salaam aleikum.*" Peace be with you.

Hassan answered, "*Wa aleikum es salaam.*" And peace to you. They were still shaking hands in an unpressured way.

Barger asked, "*Kayfa halakum?*" How are you?

273

Hassan tilted his head and allowed, unconvincingly, "*Iinaa bikhayr.*" I am well.

Barger raised his left hand without touching Hassan, saying "*Alhamdulillah.*" Praise Allah.

Hassan then turned his gaze to Lanier, repeating the greeting. Lanier was close to Hassan's age but looked less weathered, with baby skin compared to the emir. His Panama hat did less to block the sun on his head and neck than Hassan's *keffiyeh*. They offered each other the same courtesies. Since Lanier was from east Texas, his accent in Arabic sounded deep-fried. Cautious if not suspicious of each other, their pleasantries were not repeated.

Hank's turn came next. Hassan looked up at him in amusement, like an uncle who had missed a growth spurt. As he shook the American's hand, he asked Barger, "*Hal hu eimlaq?*"

The African guards standing on either side of the heavy wooden doors to the palace were even taller than Hank; they still laughed at his expense.

Barger grinned as he shook his head and said, "*Iinah 'iinsan.*"

It wasn't the first time that Hank's stature had been the subject of a stranger's joke. He laughed along, looking to Saleh for help. He said, "The emir asked if you were a giant. Sahib Barger said you were only a human being."

Hassan laughed even louder once Hank was in on his joke. It took a few more minutes for Hassan to repeat the cycle of pleasantries, three times before he seemed satisfied. *How are you? I am well. Peace be with you. And peace to you.* Warmth passed between them that had been absent between Hassan and Lanier. The longer Hank was in the kingdom, the more he believed that Americans and Arabs shared the same sense of humor; one of the reasons the Saudis preferred them to the British.

Hassan led the Aramco delegation into the palace. They entered a large salon that was furnished only with cushions around the perimeter of the squarish room. There was no artificial light, high windows without glass allowed a light breeze and some late afternoon sun. The Emir sat in a low divan on the far side of the room. Hassan was one of five functionaries who greeted the Americans as Jiluwi watched. *Peace be with you. And with you. How are you? I am well. Praise Allah.* As they moved from host to host and guest to guest, the phrases were often repeated, as if the words themselves brought the Arabs joy.

Barger and Jiluwi knew each other well. It seemed that fewer words passed between them than had passed between Barger and the other emirs. On the long drive across the desert, the director of government relations had warned Hank and Lanier that Jiluwi was more taciturn than most Arabs, befitting his position and influence. Then the Emir waved for the tea to be brought in.

A male servant in simple dress poured the first cup of tea. According to custom the small cup was first offered to Barger, who waved it off in favor of the Emir. The Emir waved it back, and Barger accepted it gratefully. The Emir accepted the next cup of tea. Tea was then given to Hank and to Lanier before Saleh. The servant then served tea for the other emirs in attendance, Hassan receiving his first as a sign of the Emir's respect. Hank's cup was strong and sweet; he waved off camel's milk.

Before they had arrived, Barger had given Hank and Lanier a short course in table manners in the kingdom. They slurped their tea as guests were expected. But Saleh looked at Barger with worry when they weren't served a third round of tea, an indication that they weren't truly welcome by Jiluwi. His servant rushed through the preparation of the ceremonial coffee like a short order cook on a busy night. Barger watched in consternation as another servant hurriedly rinsed the teacups before they were used again for their coffee.

Again, the first cup was offered to Barger. Again, he waved it off in favor of the Emir, who waved him off in turn. When everyone else had been served, Hank sipped the coffee. It was the first time he had ever smelled or tasted cardamom - complex, aromatic, smoky and minty. The seeds from which it was made were native to India. Hank's mind wandered, imagining Arab sailors and Indian merchants trading spices through antiquity.

Barger looked relieved when their coffee cups were not refilled to the brim; a full second cup would have been a sign they were no longer welcome in the Emir's palace. In English, he began to explain the reason for their visit, with Saleh translating into Arabic for the Emir. Jiluwi nodded but said nothing until Barger was completely through explaining Aramco's problem. The director of government relations began to describe the steady loss of tools and materials in Ras Tanura and elsewhere in the concession.

"Your excellency, most of these things are small things. Each of them alone would not be a matter to trouble the Emir. But taken together, they are precisely what we need to pump more oil and begin refining. Then we can turn your petroleum into gasoline and many other products that will bring great blessings to your people. Without these things that are being stolen, it will be much longer before we can greatly increase the kingdom's royalties.

"For as long as we fought the war, there could be little exploration or development of Al-Hasa. Our company can't afford to advance more against future royalties. We need your help to find the thieves who are stealing our tools and building material. We would be most grateful for any help you can provide."

The Aramco delegation Waited for the Emir to speak. He would have made an excellent poker player, despite what appeared to be a lazy eye. He looked from Barger to Hank and then from Hank to Lanier. Finally he spoke.

"The Prophet teaches that no man is permitted to take that which belongs to another."

Hank and Barger glanced at each other. Lanier seemed oblivious to Jiluwi's allusion, which could be applied to Aramco ignoring the King's decree about seven day's pay for six days work as easily as it could to Arab employees stealing from the concession.

Then the Emir told Barger what he wanted to hear. He would do what he could to prevent further thievery, Allah willing. The servants brought incense to punctuate the end of the encounter.

Barger thanked their host. Having the verbal commitment that he hoped for, he didn't press Jiluwi for details. Another cycle of pleasantries began.

Lanier squirmed, uncomfortable on his pillow, unable to keep his legs crossed as long as the occasion required. Saleh tried to calm the refinery manager like a father quieting a child in church, worried that Jiluwi would take note.

Hofuf, 11 May

By the time their meeting with Jiluwi had ended, it was too late in the afternoon for the oilmen to return to Dhahran. The desert in darkness would have been unsafe for the power wagon. The Emir invited them to spend the night in the palace. But neither Jiluwi nor Hassan joined Barger, Hank, and Lanier for dinner. It was the first time that the managers from Ras Tanura had been guests at a traditional feast, a whole lamb, roasted with herbs, along with heaping piles of rice. But Barger was worried after their delegation ate alone with his Bahraini assistant. He was concerned that the Emir was more troubled by their accusations about stealing by his subjects than he had revealed.

Hank was glad that Saleh was the only Arab to witness him trying to eat for the first time while only using his right hand. Lanier grumbled about bringing his own knife and fork the next time he was a guest at the palace. Hank practiced burping as his stomach filled, another sign of good manners according to Saleh. Barger demonstrated his polite eructation, practiced over countless meals in camps and palaces. But he seemed troubled as the Emir's servants took away the platter and then brought scented water to cleanse their hands. More tea was served. They sipped in silence.

Hassan had appeared out of the shadows to whisper to Barger, who was relieved that Jiluwi had asked to meet with him privately. He unwound his legs from his cushions, nodded to Saleh to join him, and followed Hassan out of their quarters.

Tired, full, with the taciturn Lanier as his only company, Hank had stretched out on a low platform bed covered with a thin mattress. There were several cushions decorated with silver thread and dense geometric colors. When Hank put his head on one, it smelled like it had belonged to an officer in the Turkish garrison. Hank turned off the last of the kerosene lamps. As far as he could tell, there was no electricity in Ibrahim Palace. In the darkness, the Isha call echoed through the palace from the many villages of Al-Hofuf. After an exhausting day, Hank had soon fallen asleep - even with Lanier snoring like a pig on the other side of the room.

When he awoke, Barger and Saleh were already up, preparing for their return to Dhahran. The head of government relations shared little with the other Americans on their way home. His late-night meeting with Jiluwi had robbed him of his usual light-heartedness. Only the lesser emirs bid the Americans farewell, though the well wishes between Hassan and Barger were as lengthy and sincere as their greetings the day before. Their farewells to Lanier were more perfunctory, before their then struck a fonder note with Hank, the friendly giant from *Merica*.

The date groves and the green fields of Al-Hofuf gave way to the open desert. Barger seemed to enjoy the distraction of Hank's second driving lesson. As his student's confidence behind the wheel grew, the instructor spent more time gazing absently at the terrain, already rippling under the sun.

As he drove, Hank imagined that everything between Al-Hofuf and the Persian Gulf could be underwater, the sandy floor of a larger sea. The sun beat down on the roof of the power wagon. They drove with the windows down, neither trusting the air conditioner.

Barger remained distracted on their way to Dhahran, saying little until the early afternoon, when he saw Hank's head swim. He began asking his driving student questions, trying to keep him alert in the throbbing heat.

"You married, Hank?"

"Yes. I met Gloria at Berkeley."

Barger smirked as his student concentrated on the road ahead. "With all you guys from Cal and Stanford, it's hard for a lowly miner from North Dakota to feel at home in Arabia."

"Gloria works for OWI, one of the French specialists in the Pacific branch."

Bemused, Barger whistled out the window.

"We have a son named. Peter. They're living with her parents in Palo Alto."

"Someday soon, we'll get them out here, Hank. Our kids can play together and our wives can complain about how much time we spend on the job."

As happy as Hank was to hear the head of government relations say so, there was something unconvincing about the tone of Barger's voice. The road to Dhahran flattened and widened as they approached the concession's headquarters. Hank looked away from the wheel long enough to see the expression on Barger's face. But it was his instructor's turn to nod off, giving into the heat and humidity and a sleepless night after Jiluwi's harsh criticism.

Al-Khobar, 16 May

Jiluwi staged a reprisal after Barger complained about Arab thievery. Unlike his father in his youth or his father's cousin, the future king, it didn't involve swords or long guns.

The Emir met regularly with the customs officials who controlled the growing port of Al-Khobar. His outpost was another Ottoman monument, smaller than Ibrahim Palace. There was no mistaking its design - a fortress to repel invaders from the sea. Its location was perfect for its function, blocking traders and pirates from Bahrain or the other sheikdoms. Jiluwi invited Ohliger and Barger to meet him in Al-Khobar. Since Aramco headquarters were nearby, it was a reasonable request. More to the point, it would have been impossible for the Americans to decline without offending the Emir of the Eastern Province.

Ohliger and Barger were greeted by Hassan, who was gracious but more reserved than he had been a few days earlier. Along with their translator Saleh, the Americans were led to a room on the upper floor that only had three walls. The fourth was open to the harbor and the sea beyond. Because of the seasonal wind and the sand it carried, Bahrain was not visible. The roof projected several meters farther than the floor of ornate tile. Like the reception hall in the Ibrahim Palace, it was furnished only with plush pillows that lined the white walls. The sun had already passed overhead and the entire room was in shade. Sea breezes gusted by Ohliger and Barger; curtains flew through portals on the inland wall.

As the Americans waited for the Emir, it was easy to imagine the commander of the fortress keeping watch over Al-Khobar and the rest Al-Hasa. The implication was the same for the guests of Saud bin Mohammed Al Jiluwi. The concession could not have been developed without his family's cooperation. The Emir could just as easily shut Aramco down, provided he had the king's approval.

Jiluwi arrived and thanked his guests for coming. The ritual progression through rounds of tea and coffee followed. The Americans found their host to be even less fulsome than usual. In moments of awkward silence while they were being served or sipping from hand painted cups, the loud banter between Arab captains and longshoremen rose from the docks below. Barges and dhows ferried cargo from larger ships anchored nearby. Farther off but more relentlessly, a steam-powered piledriver was expanding footings in the harbor. Aramco's plans for Al-Khobar were even more ambitious than the marine terminal at Ras Tanura.

Because of commercial shipping on the gulf, there were few secrets among the sheikdoms. The slightest nuance in payroll schemes or royalty arrangements traveled with the wind and tide. In 1942, when the production of crude oil in Iraq and Kuwait had been vital to the British war effort, the Iraqi Petroleum Company increased compensation for its Arab workers. At the urging of the Kuwaitis, IPC began to pay for seven days of work instead of the customary six. This effectively made every Friday - when the devout rested and prayed Al-Jumu'ah - a paid holiday. Abdulaziz, whose kingdom was struggling without revenue from the *Hajj*, his people starving because of drought, passed a law that mirrored his neighbors. Saudi workers would also be paid for seven days instead of six. With the backing of bean counters from Standard and Texaco, California Arabian had ignored the royal decree. Ohliger had repeatedly pointed out to Suleiman, the finance minister, that compensation for Saudi workers for six days was higher than Arabs employed by IPC, even with seven days of pay. But Suleiman was as tenacious as he had been in 1933 when the concession was finally signed. For Ohliger, who had been in the kingdom for more than a decade, it was no surprise that the Saudis had not conceded the point.

After their first round of coffee, the Emir returned to his parting question to Barger in their late-night meeting at the Ibrahim Palace. Saleh translated, a hint of terror in the voice of the Bahraini, as much an interloper as the Americans in the seaside fortress of Al-Jiluwi.

"If Aramco paid its Arab workers fairly, wouldn't they be less likely to steal from the concession?"

Ohliger opened with his usual argument on the Saudi labor law. "Aramco is already paying more than the British, even if their payroll standards are different."

The Emir showed little interest in whether Aramco could prove they were paying more than the British. Barger understood while Saleh was still translating for Ohliger.

"It's not a matter of how many shillings are paid to Arab workers. You, as holders of his concession, have dishonored the king by not obeying the law and paying his loyal subjects for their day of prayer and rest. The king is the protector of the holy cities and the servant of his people."

Barger tried to remind the Emir how many projects Aramco was already engaged in to improve the daily lives of Arabs in the kingdom. He spoke in English, trusting Saleh to convey his feelings.

"We are providing health care to our workers. We are opening schools so that bright young Arabs can train for better jobs in the concession. Our drillers have found new sources of sweet water all over the kingdom to help end the drought. Soon we will begin working on the railroad between Al-Khobar and Riyadh, just as the king envisioned."

Jiluwi nodded in the direction of the harbor without leaving his perch in the corner of the room before he began to speak. Saleh took notes until the Emir settled back into angry silence.

"One ship carries a hundred times more than you say the Arab workers have taken from the concession. The scraps and tools they borrow for their barastis are nothing compared to the houses you are building for Americans. I have heard too many times that Aramco is failing to feed its workers properly, as you have promised."

Ohliger reminded the Emir, "The best solution for everyone is to increase production of crude oil in the kingdom. But Aramco needs the help of Your Excellency with petty thievery so we can afford to continue all of the projects you desire that aren't part of our agreement with His Majesty. Aramco can't advance royalties any more without increasing production."

Jiluwi was unmoved. He nodded at his servants to fill the cups of the Americans with coffee to the brim. Ohliger and Barger glanced at each other, silently alarmed by their host's insult. The Emir bowed indifferently at his guests as he left the room, a final gust filling his lightweight thobe. Hassan escorted them back to their company car, parked outside the gates of the fortress.

On their way back to Dhahran, Ohliger and Barger were both troubled. Barger, behind the wheel of his Ford power wagon glared at his boss in the seat beside him.

"I've been telling you for two years that we need to do this."

"You don't have to convince me," Ohliger said. "The problem is the board."

Barger knew the boards of Standard and Texaco wanted to use as much local labor as possible for overseas production.

Even if they were less efficient, it was cheaper than paying American crews to produce the same barrel. But the emirs who dealt with the concession were no fools. Despite Ohliger's protests, without including the cost of exchanging dollars for pounds, the Americans were paying their Arab workers less than the British.

Ras Tanura, 17 May

The only muezzin in Ras Tanura called the Fajr prayer, marking the dawn of the last day of the work week. Unlike the larger encampment in Dhahran, Muslims from all over the world lived together in Saudi Camp in Ras Tanura. As the light came up over the Persian Gulf, the new village of steel loomed over the bedu tents and barastis.

Even before Ali became the hero of the royalty tanks, pleasing the Americans as well as Al-Saud with his calculations, Ammar had looked after the orphan in the Arab encampment. But Ali's brilliance didn't earn him special treatment from Mohammed, who had been hosting Ammar since he arrived in Saudi Camp. When Ammar asked his fellow Jordanian to allow the teenager to stay with them, the pudgy clerk hadn't protested. But that didn't keep Mohammed from rousting Ali when he hadn't stirred in his bed by the end of the Fajr prayer.

Ali rubbed his eyes and carried two empty pails to the water tank on the other side of Saudi Camp. The Jordanians as well as their Pakistani neighbors expected the youngest of the five Aramco clerks to fetch enough water for all of them to cook and wash before they went to work.

The Pakistanis, Tariq and Wahid, had been educated by British colonials and worked in their oil industry. They considered themselves more worldly than the Arabs in Saudi

Camp. Before Ammar arrived in Ras Tanura, the Pakistanis had told Mohammed, a trusting sort, that they were brothers. They resembled each other only in the most general way: wiry young men with shocks of black hair they left uncovered, unlike the Arabs in Saudi Camp. Ammar suspected that they were related only by the depth of their affection for each other. It was easier for Muslim men who were lovers to live together while working overseas, far from disapproving wives arranged by their families.

When Ali returned with the water and they were all bathing, Ammar kept a close watch on the teenager, as he always did in the presence of the Pakistanis. But Tariq and Wahid remained preoccupied with each other and their sense of injustice as foreigners in the kingdom. Oddly, they retained the British sense of superiority over the American oilmen in Ras Tanura. The Jordanians spoke no Urdu and the Pakistanis spoke only enough Arabic to get by. As they prepared for another Thursday, they voiced their complaints in English, the language of empire.

"I wish Al-Jumu'ah were today and not tomorrow," Tariq said.

"What good is a day of rest when we have nothing to eat and there is nothing to do but pray?" Wahid retorted.

Mohammed was equally forlorn about the food in Saudi Camp. "It has been a week since we had wheat to make bread."

"I am sure there is plenty in American Camp," Wahid said.

Mohammed started to boil rice over a small fire made with wooden scraps discarded by Bechtel. He offered the Pakistanis dates from a nearby village.

Tariq nibbled one as Wahid brandished another. "These don't compare with the Aseel dates in Karachi."

Ammar and Mohammed felt equally unwelcome in the kingdom but had grown weary of the Pakistanis' complaints about Arab food. Ali seemed to be the only one interested in their conversation as they ate rice seasoned with bitterness.

"At least the British would pay us tomorrow for Al-Jumu'ah, our day of prayer," Tariq said.

Wahid agreed with his beloved. "We should be paid as well as our brothers in Basra and Abadan."

The Pakistanis worked in the payroll office for Saudi Camp and considered themselves authorities on compensation. "The British are also paying an adjustment for inflation in Iran and Iraq," Tariq noted.

Ammar understood why the Americans valued oil from the Persian Gulf less than the British. Standard and Texaco controlled large reserves of petroleum in the US, while the UK only held coal. But there was nothing to be gained from explaining this to the Pakistanis.

Mohammed repeated a common refrain in Saudi Camp. "They say the Americans are paying the Italians more."

Having heard Hank speak about it for months, Ammar was more pragmatic. "The Italians are being paid more because they have more skills than most Arabs."

Wahid pointed in the direction of Italian Camp. "Then why are they fighting with Arabs to drive trucks?"

Mohammed sided with the Pakistanis. "And why would they refuse to be paid in silver?"

"It is obvious," Tariq said, "the Italians are Christians like the Americans and the British. They all hide their money in banks run by the Jews."

Ali listened in awe, his ears seeming to stick out more than usual. Ammar gave him a brotherly shove. "Don't believe everything hungry men say."

After breakfast, Ali headed for the Jabal School for his morning classes with the other office boys. As was their custom, Tariq and Wahid held hands as they walked to the Aramco complex. At the gate, the dark-eyed Saudi guards looked as if they were ready to beat the couple. The

Pakistanis were easy to spot with their uncovered heads; the Jordanians had grown tired of watching them trim each other's hair. Ammar and Mohammed lagged behind, bowed reflexively as they passed the guards, and remained silent until their voices were drowned out by the riveters and welders and the diesel engines powering their tools.

The Bechtel men were climbing all over the new stills that towered above the refinery. Along each product line branching off from the stills, cylindrical holding tanks and spherical reservoirs were being connected with pipes as thick as a human torso. The American and Italian builders were developing a language of their own, all whistles and bellows and hand signals. As far as most of the Arabs were concerned, they might as well have been building rocket ships. Every day the walk between Saudi Camp and the Aramco complex became more extreme, the medieval past within a few hundred yards of an industrial future; the American world.

Because of the war (and because there was no oil in Jordan) Ammar and Mohammed were the only members of their families who were working. Neither felt at home in the Eastern Province. But like most of the men in Saudi Camp, they had many more mouths to feed than their own.

Ammar worried more than Mohammed about keeping their opinions about Al-Saud and Aramco to themselves. It was the only way to protect distant family members who were depending on them. In that way, the Jordanians were no different than the Italians. The important distinction, which Ammar understood better than Mohammed, was that foreign Muslims like Tariq and Wahid foolishly thought they had as much of a right to their opinions as the Italians.

After the Pakistanis entered the Aramco payroll office near the gate, the Jordanians continued to the trailer that Hank shared with Lanier at the marine terminal. Ammar felt the need to remind Mohammed about the reality of their situation.

"The Pakistanis are being foolish. They aren't protected by British colonial law in the kingdom as they were in Karachi."

Mohammed nodded somberly. "I understand. Here there is only Sharia. Even then, the law is only what the ulema and Al-Saud say it is."

"The Pakistanis don't know that Abdulaziz and the Ikhwan massacred thousands of Hashemites. And they don't know that the king turned against his own jihadis when it was time to bargain with the British and the Americans."

"Al-Saud pays silver and gold to the other sheiks to maintain their claim over Mecca and Medina, while they enrich themselves far more."

Ammar held his finger to his lips. Mohammed was too quick to give voice to their hatred of Al-Saud, who had displaced their fathers from the Hejaz. As Hashemites exiled to Jordan, their beliefs made them as vulnerable in the Wahhabi kingdom as the Pakistanis, who also practiced a more moderate version of Sunnism. Ammar had little doubt that Abdulaziz would side with the Americans over the Muslim foreigners in Saudi Camp, regardless of how faithfully they adhered to the Five Pillars. The lives of Tariq and Wahid were meaningless in the Saudi kingdom. And the Hejaz, the cradle of Islam, was no longer home to Ammar and Mohammed.

Ras Tanura, 30 May

Memorial Day was a working Wednesday in the concession, even though the American Way had never meant more than it had since the war in Europe finally ended. Most of the men in Aramco, including Hank, thought they were delivering a better way of life to their Arab workers. But the amenities in American Camp in Ras Tanura were becoming more than sources of envy among Arabs and Italians. They were becoming symbols of race and class. Hank could see it in the eyes of Ammar and Mohammed, as well as Pedani and Scarcella, even though the top brass were offering the Arabs and the Italians different excuses for the squalor they endured separately.

The segregation of workers into camps by nationality didn't keep them from finding out how differently Aramco was paying them. In a land where women were seldom seen, men from all over the world wanted to know which country's workers were being screwed the most by the concession. Intricate details of compensation and benefits were sexy topics and English was their language.

Arab workers spending time in Aramco's schools were multiplying rapidly. Once they learned simple phrases and numbers, the men from Saudi Camp wanted to talk about money with Americans. Men from Eritrea had picked up some English while building military installations for the

Allies on the Red Sea. Arabs and Italians had time to kill between loads of lumber, masonry, or pipe. Americans and Italians had nothing better to talk about while Arabs answered the call to prayer. Bechtel spiced the chatter with dozens of first-and-second generation builders who spoke Italian.

What the international workers could see with their own eyes was vivid as what they could taste and smell. As improvements continued around Tarout Bay, the sensibilities of anyone who wasn't from the States were offended.

The American Camp was closest to the fresher air by the sea as well as the Aramco complex. Ferguson already regretted putting the Italian Camp farther up the beach. Although it meant that Pedani and his men had farther to walk to work, it also meant that the Americans were downwind from the worsening stench of Italian Camp. The only toilets that flushed, septic tanks, and freshwater showers were in American Camp.

The Saudi Camp was to the west of the Aramco complex, where the tidewater turned marshy and the shamal carried a thicker layer of sand from the interior. In their wisdom, Aramco provided no buses for the Italians. As their workday and lunch break began and ended, they walked past the American Camp. When they got to the Aramco complex, the Italians could see the Saudi Camp. The Bedouin tents were more functional than the British surplus.

Soon enough, the Italians began competing with the Arabs for scraps of lumber and palm fronds to construct barastis with Mediterranean touches. In the colonial world before the war, Europeans looked down on Arabs and the Orient. Many of the workers in Italian Camp had occupied Ethiopia and Libya. In Ras Tanura they were constantly reminded how far they had fallen, surrounded by barbed wire, their encampment no better - if not worse - than Saudi Camp. The only electricity for the encampment was in the string of lights on top of the poles connecting the wire, as if the Italians were still POWs.

The Saudi Camp had no electricity at all. But the Arabs had deeper grievances. Shia from coastal villages had been persecuted by Al-Saud, who were Wahhabi fundamentalists. Most of the Sunni bedu were still in the desert, where infidels were less able to disrupt a timeless way of life. But the drought had lasted longer than the war, forcing thousands of nomadic Arabs to accept Aramco's silver.

On Memorial Day, Hank's patriotism was trumped by his frustration with the disparities in food, shelter, and medical care between the encampments. The US holiday had originally been intended to reunite a divided nation after the Civil War. Hank's growing fear was that the Japanese were the only thing keeping the Americans from starting a different kind of civil war in Arabia.

Ras Tanura, 11 June - Zuhr

Despite his threats, the Emir kept the promise he made to the Aramco delegation in Al-Hofuf. His guards began searching workers at the end of their shifts in Ras Tanura. There were more Arab laborers helping to build the refinery and marine terminal than Italian tradesmen. In theory, any employee of Aramco or Bechtel was subject to search. But Ammar could see that only the Arabs and Italians were being frisked by Jiluwi's slave-soldiers. Residents of both camps at Ras Tanura were inflamed by the heavy-handed searches. The Muslims regarded them as personal violations. The Italians despised the presumption that Africans were even allowed to touch Europeans.

It was obvious to Ammar that the Shia were suffering the roughest treatment by the Emir's men. Though many of the men in Saudi Camp were from Shia villages along the coast, the guards were Wahhabi, like their masters. Nor were the neediest of the bedu spared simply because they were Sunni. But it was rare for any Arab worker to be caught with more than a hammer or a wrench worth a few shillings, more often a pocketful of nails or fasteners worth a few pence in Al-Khobar. If the Italians were stealing (as Ammar and Hank suspected) they were too sophisticated to be caught by the guards at the gate.

Regardless of whether the offenders were Sunni or Shia, the legal punishment for petty crimes against Aramco was turning out to be less harsh than Jiluwi's guards. As more Arab workers were caught stealing, severe enforcement under Sharia law became less practical for the Emir. Ammar wasn't surprised that the ulema became more lenient in counting to three, even though some of the men from Saudi Camp repeatedly violated the law.

Muslim scholars knew that all but one chapter written by the Prophet began with the same words, *"In the name of God, the Merciful, the Compassionate."* Since the only victims of thievery in Ras Tanura were infidels, no severed hands appeared on the fences around the main gate. If all politics were local, the ulema seemed to care less about Arabs stealing from the Americans than they did about Aramco defying the Saudi decree on Al-Jumu'ah.

Every hungry soul in Saudi Camp knew that Aramco hadn't replaced the kitchen equipment that was lost on the cargo ship hit by the Germans. Nor had the Americans improved on the nutrition of its Arab workers. In the Persian Gulf, unless you could ship it in like the Americans, fresh meat and grain couldn't be found at any price. For most of the company's workers, the midday meal on the job was still the only one they could count on. The Arabs had been promised more than rice for months, without Aramco delivering.

That Monday, the third day of the Aramco work week, the muezzins announced Zuhr at the highest point of the sun. After their prayers, the Arabs went to their mess hall in Saudi Camp for Aramco's mid-day meal. A crowd gathered around the large pots over open fires.

It was easy for Ammar to find Tariq and Wahid. Because they worked as clerks and interpreters, they spent most of their time in Aramco offices equipped with swamp coolers. At the back of the crowd, their clean clothes and dry skin stood out. By mid-day, the hundreds of men alongside them in the crowd were covered with sweat and oily grime.

Many times, usually late at night, Ammar had listened as the Pakistanis amused themselves by mocking the Arab tribesmen in neighboring tents. They hated Sunni who spent their days squeezing oil out of the sand. They belittled Shia from villages a few kilometers who complained about how far they were from home.

None of the Arabs had ever crossed their own sea in a storm! How could Muslims who couldn't read or write their own name look down upon them, simply because they were foreigners? How could nomads and pearl divers who had never seen a foreign city dismiss their beloved Karachi?

The contempt of Tariq and Wahid for the Arabs was exceeded only by their hatred of the Americans, who claimed to be better than the British but were even greedier and just as ignorant!

Regardless of nationality or education, there was no semblance of a queue at mealtime in the Saudi Camp. As they all pressed closer to the Yemini cooks, the clothes of Hank's assistant and the Pakistani clerks were soiled by the rest of the crowd. Workers from other parts of Al-Hasa had little regard for the *hadhari* among them. Elbows dug into Ammar's side. Shoulders sought to cleave Tariq from Wahid. Soon even the hands and faces of the Aramco office workers were as dirty as the rest of the men pushing their empty bowls forward.

Until they reached the front of the crowd, Tariq and Wahid didn't know they were being served rice again. The only things that united the Arabs and the Pakistanis - other than their belief in Allah, who seemed to have forgotten them - was that they wouldn't stand for another day without grain or lamb, even fish! They were all proud men who were trying to support their families, their flesh roasting in the early summer sun, underpaid, underfed and far from home.

First Tariq and then Wahid threw their bowls at the kitchen staff. The Yemenis stared back as if the clerks were not merely a different race but another breed. Fueled by their frustrations and their hunger, the crowd spontaneously erupted, joining the revolt started by Tariq and Wahid.

Ammar was frightened by the intensity of the riot as soon as it began. He found Mohammed cowering at the edge of the mob and retreated to their barasti as the men from Saudi Camp swarmed the perimeter of the main encampment and the gate guarding American Camp and the road to the refinery and marine terminal.

Ras Tanura, 11 June - Asr

Hank didn't see the first rock being thrown. But he heard one hit the metal roof of the Airstream. He went outside and saw hundreds of Arab workers lined up outside the storm fence surrounding the marine terminal. They were throwing rocks, stray bricks, even their sandals. It was rare to hear anything over Bechtel's riveters in the refinery or the piledriver extending the marine terminal into the bay. But the shouting of angry Arabs went through Hank like a shotgun blast. Some of them used their hardhats like discus throwers. Others removed their keffiyeh and used them as slings to load with rocks.

Tiersen, the tank farm manager, happened to be crossing from one of the new stills in the refinery to the machine shops near Hank's office. Like a startled deer, he stopped to stare at the Arab workers yelling on the other side of the fence. The rock throwers aimed at him. He turned to run but stumbled and fell. A rock split open the back of his head. Blood spurted. Tiersen went limp. Other Americans dragged him into the closest of the machine shops. They closed the heavy door behind them. The rocks continued to bounce off the corrugated metal of the door and walls of the building.

Three Arabs appeared in the mob with burning sticks of wood they had pulled out of the open fire used to boil the rice. Hank knew a fire could destroy the entire complex. Most of the tanks were as combustible as bombs. Hundreds could be killed. When the three torch bearers broke the windows out of an Aramco flatbed truck and tossed in the burning wood, he was almost relieved. The truck was parked away from the refinery and the tank farm. The Italian firemen who were always on duty would have a chance to put it out before the flames reached the truck's gasoline tank.

Reinforcements arrived. Three companies of Saudi soldiers joined the Emir's guards. They attacked the protesting workers with their rifle butts. But there was no gunfire and relatively little bloodshed. The Saudi forces pounded the strikers into submission, driving the unarmed Arabs back into Saudi Camp. Then the Emir's guards surrounded the protesters, trapping them inside their own fenced compound.

Within an hour of the first rock being thrown, the Aramco complex in Ras Tanura was eerily silent. Tiersen was attended to by the Vogels at the clinic. The strikers who were too battered to run away were attended to as well. No one died. The only shots fired were warning rounds from the Saudi troops over the heads of the rioters. But the illusion of harmony between the Americans, the Saudis, and the foreign workers was destroyed along with the ad hoc kitchen in Saudi Camp. Through it all, the firemen in the Aramco complex were the only Italians to leave their perches on the cranes in the marine terminal and the gangways connecting the towering stills, condensers, and cooling tanks in the refinery.

The Dining Hall filled early in American Camp. Workers from Bechtel and Aramco gathered to protect themselves as if they were in Fort Apache. Saudi troops were guarding the refinery, the tank farm, and the perimeter of the marine terminal. Hank and Lanier spent the afternoon inspecting tanks and pipelines with Aramco security officers, looking for evidence of sabotage or stray missiles that untrained eyes would miss. There were so many high-pressure points that could have blown. There were so many invisible ways that an

American lighting a cigarette could still get killed by an unseen jet of natural gas.

Conversations in the Dining Hall between old friends or new acquaintances repeated themselves:

I sure as hell didn't sign up for this. I thought these ragheads were on our side. That rock missed me by (holding up fingers or hands) this much.

When Tiersen went down, I thought he was dead.

Do you think the Arabs will show up for work tomorrow? I won't go near them if they do.

Did you see the looks on the faces of the Italians? Those mothers were enjoying the show while we got pelted. They were sitting on their keisters the whole time!

I think I saw an Italian throwing a rock. They throw like girls.

Those A-rabs are damn good with their slings. Just like David and Goliath.

What do you think is going to happen tomorrow? Hell, what do you think is going to happen tonight?

Are we safer here or the main camp in Dhahran?

Maybe we should hop on a launch and head for Bahrain. The British will protect us.

The hell they will. They'd like nothing better than for us to go home.

I'm putting in my resignation first thing in the morning.

I'm getting on the first ATC flight with an open seat.

I could be working for the same money or better in (Louisiana, Oklahoma, Texas). I could be sleeping in my own damn bed. Or sleeping with (wife or girlfriend).

The motor on one of the freezers had taken a direct hit. All of the best cuts of meat were cooked up and served that night, as if everyone in American Camp was on Death Row. Their bellies full, the men settled down after dinner.

Ferguson got up in front of several hundred employees of Aramco and Bechtel. A few steps away from him was the head of Ras Tanura's security department wearing a sidearm.

They stood on the same podium where the music had played on VE Day.

"Men, I've just come from the medical clinic. I want you to know that Tiersen is going to be okay. There were no other serious injuries. But we got a scare today - a surprise attack, I'd say.

"The Emir's men have established a secure perimeter. The refinery and the marine complex and the tank farm - knock on wood - were untouched. The Saudis have promised us that they'll round up the offenders - God help them! Jiluwi will deal with them more harshly than our own government would if this happened in the States.

"As far as we can tell, this was just about the food in Saudi Camp. I don't have to tell you that it's hard to get enough fresh food - quality food - in the gulf after so many years of drought and war. The Nazis sank the Liberty Ship that had their kitchen on board. We'll have to make amends for that, and we will.

"The main thing I want you all to understand is that what happened today doesn't change one damn thing in Ras Tanura. We're going to finish the new facilities. And we're going to be processing fifty thousand barrels a day by the end of the year. You have my word on that. And we're going to be pumping half a million barrels a month through the pipelines to Bapco and the tankers that are going to start lining up on the new marine terminal in a few months.

"There's still a war going on. We're not going to let our country down because the Arabs are tired of eating rice. Our boys in places like Okinawa are fighting Japanese who would rather blow themselves up than surrender. We're not backing down in Ras Tanura because of a few goddam rocks!"

Steve Bechtel followed with his own steely affirmation for his construction crew. The beer and the liquor stayed locked up. Every cigarette in American Camp got smoked. Nobody wanted to risk leaving the Dining Hall for their beds.

Everyone in Aramco met everyone in Bechtel before the men got talked out, found a quiet corner, or wrote a letter home as if it might be their last. When the call of the Isha prayer came from the muezzins in the minarets outside their encampment, the Americans all looked at each other, mixing expressions of disgust and fear. A lot of the men slept on the floor in the Dining Hall. Some slipped out, one by one, and crept through the shadows to their bunks. The rest were like Hank, who couldn't sleep at all.

Ras Tanura, 12 June

Ali had been at school when the mid-day riot broke out in Saudi Camp. When he tried to enter the Aramco compound, he had been herded back to their encampment by the Emir's soldiers. Neither Ammar nor Mohammed would explain what had happened to Ali. When Tariq and Wahid tried to speak with him the night before, Ammar told them to leave the Arab teenager alone.

The next morning, as Ali was returning with fresh water from the storage tank. a truck pulled up with a platoon of soldiers. Before Tariq and Wahid could finish the Fajr prayer, Jiluwi's men dragged them away.

The Pakistanis screamed at their friends for help. Ammar and Mohammed sat and watched in silence as the soldiers bound and gagged Tariq and Wahid before throwing them into the back of the truck. Hundreds of men in Saudi Camp watched grimly as the truck gathered speed on its way south on the coast road.

Only Ali seemed surprised. "Where are they taking them?"

"They will lock them up in a jail somewhere between here and Dammam," Ammar ventured.

"But only after they have beaten them," Mohammed promised.

Ali was still bewildered. "What will happen to them?"

"Tariq and Wahid will be deported," Ammar said, trying to reassure his young assistant.

"If they are lucky," Mohammed added. "The Emir may simply kill them. It would be cheaper than shipping them back to Pakistan."

"But why?"

"Because they are fools," Mohammed said.

Ammar became impatient with Ali's questions. "Tariq and Wahid are foreigners. The Americans and SAG consider them untrustworthy. But you, Ali, have a bright future in the kingdom. Allah has blessed you in many ways. But you must never speak against Al-Saud. And you can never speak against the Americans if you want to keep your job. Learn as much as you can. The wiser you become, the better you will understand our warnings."

As intelligent as Ali was in many ways, he didn't entirely understand the fear and anger of the Jordanians he lived with in Saudi Camp. But he knew enough to heed their warnings, continue his studies, and serve Omar Al Rashid at the royalty tanks. When Ammar and Mohammed left for work in the Aramco compound, Ali returned to his school in the village.

That day, the Emir's soldiers rounded up as many of the clerks from Iraq and India as they could find. Everyone else went to their jobs in the Aramco complex as if nothing had happened. The guards at the gates searched everyone arriving from Saudi Camp, which before they had only done at the end of the day.

Ammar and Mohammed were late by the time they reached the office that Hank shared with Lanier. They apologized for being tardy as they stepped inside. Lanier was nowhere to be seen. Hank looked at the Jordanians as if they were strangers. Then his sense of decency broke through the uncertainty he shared with the Arabs.

"Are you okay, Ammar?"

"Yes."

"What about Ali?"

"He is okay," Mohamed said. "He went to school this morning."

"I hope you two had nothing to do with the riot."

"We did nothing wrong," Ammar said. "When the others began to make trouble, we stayed in our barasti."

"The food may be bad," Hank offered. "But the riot was worse."

"The soldiers took away the Pakistani clerks this morning," Ammar said.

Mohammed seized upon the convenience of Tariq and Wahid. "The riot began when the Pakistanis threw their bowls at the cooks."

Hank glanced at Ammar, who was less eager than the other Hejazi to point fingers. There was nothing more that Hank could say with any real conviction. There was little more that Ammar was willing to volunteer. The psychological damage to the international workforce of Ras Tanura was far worse than the destruction of Aramco's property. Trust would have to be rebuilt - if it had ever really existed. The worst of summer was yet to come. And none of the problems between the Americans, the Arabs, and the Italians had been resolved.

Ras Tanura, 16 July

Hank was on the road to headquarters before the sun came up, Ammar sitting beside him. They said little to each other on the way. Both had slept poorly. It had been months since Ras Tanura was comfortable at night. Since Hank had had his swamp cooler running full blast in the trailer, he didn't complain to his assistant, who slept on the ground in Saudi Camp. Ammar dozed off as Hank drove with the windows down in the Ford. The air wrapping around the American at sixty miles an hour dried the sweat clinging to him like a shroud.

Ohliger had met with his top operators every Monday morning since the food riot in Ras Tanura. The administrator feared wider strikes by Arab workers and wanted regular updates from every corner of the concession. He knew that the quality of food was an issue. But it wasn't just a problem for the concession. The war had disrupted food supplies in the gulf for years. For a pioneer like Ohliger, the mystery was why the locals were complaining when their daily lives had never been better.

Aramco's Arab workers were grumbling about living in barastis while the Americans slept indoors with their swamp coolers. Men in Saudi Camp who had washed from buckets their entire lives complained about not having showers. There was growing outrage about not being paid for their day of prayer. Ohliger was openly second-guessing his decision to fire the only American doctor who attended to Arab workers. She had refused to leave an unstable patient in Dhahran to evaluate the vague complaints of one of Jiluwi's wives in Dammam. Wounds were festering and broken bones unset in Saudi Camp.

Most of the Aramco managers agreed that outsiders had to be agitating their Arab workers. Ohliger had been warning the men around the table not to put the most sensitive intelligence in writing. Lanier was not the only manager beginning to question the loyalty of the kingdom's own clerks and translators. The senior staff in Dhahran were perplexed. The ramp-up amounted to a privately funded New Deal for the province. Nearly everyone was working for the concession, directly or indirectly. Merchants and traders were getting rich because of the boom in building and production.

One of the few things that the two VPs - Ohliger and his nemesis, Mac - agreed on was that they were paying Arab workers more on an hourly basis for six days per week than the British were paying for seven. Conveniently, they also agreed that the cost-of-living adjustment that IPC had been paying the Iraqis for wartime inflation was irrelevant in the kingdom.

The only American in the executive conference in Dhahran every Monday who openly questioned the conventional wisdom was Cochrane, the quirky geophysicist.

"It's not how much we pay. It's how different we are."

"What the hell does that mean?" Ohliger demanded.

Cochrane was lumpy, pale, and prematurely grey, one of a handful of Anglo-Saxons from MIT in the kingdom. He went outdoors even less often than Ohliger, doing most of his stratigraphic analysis from his office in Dhahran. His misfortune was that he understood Einstein's theories of general relativity and quantum mechanics better than the engineers. A few weeks later, he would be the only man around the table who wasn't surprised when atomic bombs started going off.

"Everything is relative, sir. The Arabs know that we pay ourselves at rates that are a magnitude greater than the scale that we - and the British - are using for local labor."

Ohliger was incensed. "That's a standard practice throughout the industry, Cochrane."

"Yes sir. But it's not just about the money. They sleep under palm fronds while we're in cinderblock buildings. It doesn't matter to them if they are making more than they ever made. They're disturbed because they see us living in ways that were beyond their imagination."

"Bollocks," Mac said. "We are delivering the highest standard of living in the history of the Arabian peninsula."

Cochrane shrugged, lonely in defeat.

Hank pitied the geophysicist: most of the men around the table didn't like him. He didn't drink and he didn't smoke. He didn't even seem to miss American women. Some said he was probably too smart to be working in the concession - too different himself. Sipping frosty bottles of Coca-Cola during a break earlier in the summer, Cochrane had confided to Hank that he regretted accepting Texaco's offer when he was a underpaid professor. Away from the table, there were side bets about how many months would pass before Cochrane boarded an ATC flight back to the States.

The real problem, as most of the senior staff saw it, was that the Arabs of the Eastern Province had so little education or experience. Importing skilled laborers from the British side of the oil patch had been unavoidable. Then drillers from Iraq had been the first to complain about wages, housing and food. In response, Ohliger had asked the Emir to deport them all. But the Iraqis had already infected the Saudi drillers they trained. On the twelfth of July, more than a hundred of the best Saudi drillers had gone on strike for benefits and pay equal to the Americans. They demanded to meet with their supervisors.

Ohliger had refused to allow negotiations of any kind. Instead, he had sent Barger to meet with the local emir to warn him that a wider strike could be coming. Hassan had been receptive to the request from the head of the concession's government relations. Like most Arabs, the kindly old man was always more likely to say yes than no. But Ohliger and Barger remained uncertain whether Jiluwi would help Aramco put down a strike.

Hank knew the head pioneer could feel the other VP in the room breathing down his neck. Standard and Texaco had sent Mac to Dhahran to find out - after pouring millions and millions into Arabia - when they were going to break even. Most of all, the owners of Aramco wanted to raise production. The riots and the strikes were exactly what Ohliger didn't need. In his mind, the friction between camps didn't make any sense. Arabs in the province were finally leaving the wadis and coastal villages for a better life working for Aramco.

Mac had explained his side of the oil patch to Hank while they were on their way to Dhahran.

"The way I see it, Hank, everyone in this business is either a missionary or a mercenary. The missionaries only care about opening up new countries or developing new industrial processes. The mercenaries only care about getting the oil out of the ground and selling it for a profit. I'm a proud member of the latter fraternity. Ohliger - God bless him - spent his first five years here telling the board how mysterious the Arab Layer was and the next five kissing the king's ass."

Dhahran, 16 July

Hank and Ammar arrived outside the Aramco complex in Dhahran. They saw hundreds of angry Arab workers blocking the gate, trying to keep hundreds more from Saudi Camp from going to work. The police from Dammam had already joined the guards. Blood was flowing freely for the first time since Americans arrived in Al Hasa in 1933.

Hank saw Barger try but fail to quell the violence between the Arab workers and the Emir's police. An older Arab man had his front teeth knocked out by the rifle stock of one of the guards. The leaders of the strike were dragged off by the police and thrown in the back of a flatbed truck. Employee 4733, Hamad Abdallah Adhayf, the old man whose front teeth had been knocked out, remained on his hands and knees, searching for them in the oil-covered hardpan at the gate.

Hank waved at Barger from the other side of the mob. Barger hopped over the fallen workers on his way back. When he made it to the Ford he told Ammar to follow the police to their station in Dammam.

Jiluwi and Hassan were waiting when their police arrived. They threw eleven strikers out of the back of their truck. The Emir ordered them to their feet. The rifle butts found the backs of the workers who were too slow to rise. Jiluwi demanded that the leader of the strikers come forward. The bloodied men looked at each other. Finally, one took a step closer to the Emir.

He spoke too quickly in Arabic for Hank to follow. In the striker's hand were the handwritten demands of his peers, already familiar to Aramco managers: seven days' pay for six days of work, housing like American Camp, food like American Camp, and a new hospital for Saudi Camp. Ammar translated for Hank as the striker spoke to Jiluwi.

Since we are all equal, none of us is the leader. These are our demands, which are no more than requests to be treated as well as you, as Emir, have told us we could expect from the Mericans.

Jiluwi looked impassively at the lesser Arab. Hank didn't need Ammar to translate his order to the soldiers. They began to beat the striker with their rifle butts. He soon fell to the ground.

Another striker stepped forward. *Since we are all equal and our demands are just, you will have to beat us all.*

Jiluwi nodded to the soldiers. They descended on the second striker. Within a few seconds he was motionless on the ground.

Barger approached Jiluwi and extended his right hand. The Emir didn't hold it as long as courtesy required. Barger was begging the Emir to stop the beatings. Remembering his manners, Hank stepped forward and respectfully greeted Jiluwi. The Emir glanced up at Hank and touched his hand even more perfunctorily than Barger's.

Jiluwi gazed at Barger and then Hank. Ammar still flanked the Americans. Hank could see the rage in the eyes of the young Hejazi, a Jordanian only because his family had been exiled by Al-Saud, in whose name Jiluwi ruled. The Emir seemed to dare Ammar to give voice to the anger visible in his countenance. Instead, Ammar bowed with the obeisance Jiluwi expected, then touched his heart with his open right palm. The Emir seemed satisfied if unmoved by Ammar's gestures of loyalty.

Jiluwi nodded at Hassan, who then commanded the rest of the strikers to return to work at the Aramco compound. The police threw the strikers back in the truck. The two men who had stepped forward remained on the ground. Barger tried to speak again to Jiluwi. The Emir was even less responsive than he had been before the beatings. Barger retreated to the Ford and told Ammar to follow the truck back to the concession headquarters.

The Arab workers in the back of the truck stared sullenly at the Americans as the Ford followed them. Hank had never seen the concession's rising star look so close to despair.

"What did Jiluwi say, Tom?"

"He told me that he will maintain order in Al-Hasa as he sees fit."

"What did you say?"

"I told him we would never interfere again."

Ammar heard everything and said nothing as he drove, the only one of the three men in the Ford who didn't seem surprised by what they had seen. Hank thought about Barger's speech during his orientation the year before. The concession's leading authority on the kingdom had been shown to have no influence within it. Dominion belonged to Al-Saud and their relations in the Eastern Province, Al-Jiluwi. One thing that Hank remembered Barger saying during his orientation had been proven. *They were all guests in the kingdom.* Both of the Americans were worried that they were wearing out their welcome.

When the police arrived back at the front gate to the Aramco complex, their commander spoke to the crowd of Arab workers who were still waiting there. *They would be beaten if they didn't return to work.* Slowly, the men from Saudi Camp began to disperse. Little was accomplished the rest of the day in Dhahran or the wells. Even the Americans were relieved when the muezzins called the Asr prayer.

Jornada del Muerto, 16 July

While the sun was setting in the Persian Gulf, another American encampment secretly detonated the first atomic bomb in the high desert of New Mexico. Nuclear fission instantly surpassed petroleum as the ultimate source of power. The secret was horribly revealed a few weeks later in Hiroshima.

Part 4 – Concessions and Betrayals

Ras Tanura, 20 July

For Dr. Scarcella, Friday wasn't a day of prayer as it was for the Muslims in Saudi Camp. Nor was it a day of rest as it was for his countrymen in Italian Camp. In the outermost circle of Hell, he cared for dozens of men with dysentery or malaria or typhus. Like every other day that summer, there wasn't enough fresh water to quench their fevers or bathe them. Nor was there enough medication to relieve their pain or treat their infections. Everyone else in the encampment had eaten dinner by the time Scarcella joined Pedani, as they did every Friday.

The two men had been friends since they were university students in Torino. They fondly remembered summers when they had nothing to eat but polenta and winters when they took turns wearing their heaviest coat. They had always shared whatever they had with each other, including the barasti that Pedani commissioned on the beach in their encampment. That Friday evening, as soon as Scarcella appeared, Pedani stepped into the surf and returned with a basket of sardines that he had hidden from thousands of men. Then, like a magician, he dipped into a satchel and presented the doctor with a loaf of Arab flatbread.

"*Pesci e pani!*"

"*Tu sei il mio Salvatore!*"

Pedani's re-enactment of the miracle of the fishes and loaves wasn't entertaining because they were both atheists. That was only part of the philosophical construct they had agreed upon as young idealists. The doctor was amused because he knew the engineer would do anything to lighten his heart. Part of the old Scarcella had died in the British POW camp in Kenya. And no one missed him more than his oldest friend. Pedani waded back into the surf, this time returning with two bottles of Indian beer. He offered them beatifically to his weary friend. Scarcella held up his hands in prayerful gratitude before accepting the bottles.

"*Grazie, Santo Spirito!*"

The doctor opened the beers as the engineer started the small fire that he had prepared while his friend was toiling in the clinic. Then Pedani set a battered pan of Arab brass on the fire and added palm oil from a small tin, followed by the sardines, pepper, and sea salt.

"*Bravo, Alberto.*"

Pedani saw the faint smile appearing on Scarcella's long face. "*Bravo, Luigi.*"

The doctor sipped his beer with contentment. Wavelets from the calm sea lapped like a sleeping child's breath. The aroma from the pan sweetened the turbid air. Depending on the direction of the wind, the smell of the latrines could be overwhelming as the encampment grew. Pedani took the pan off the fire and placed it between them on the sand. Scarcella tore off a piece of the loaf and handed it to his old friend. They feasted with the sardines in one hand and the bread in the other.

As his stomach filled, the doctor began to speak to the engineer more freely. Since their youth in Torino, the strength of their friendship had always been reflected in the passion of their disagreements. When they were both enthralled by the Comintern, Scarcella had subscribed to Trotsky's purism while Pedani favored Lenin's pragmatism.

316

But the failure of Italian politics between the wars had destroyed the careers they strived for. After they were exiled to Eritrea, the engineer had accused the doctor of being a hopeless idealist. The doctor had scolded the engineer for losing faith in his fellow men.

"The electricians are ready to strike with the doctors and nurses and engineers."

Pedani didn't approve of the multiplying factions of the labor council who thought a work stoppage would improve their conditions. He had a mocking name for Scarcella's coalition.

"*L'intellighenzia* grows stronger then."

"Perhaps when the Arabs and the foreign workers join our fight for better pay, better housing, and better medical care you won't think we are so ridiculous."

"Only *l'intellighenzia* see this as an international class struggle. The *fascisti* will insist on better terms than the Arabs!"

"We shall see."

"But Luigi, can't you see that a strike would be futile? We are trapped in a feudal state. The Americans offer the only decent work in the region!"

"You are too cynical, Alberto. You only care about building monuments to your own ego! What about the common man?"

"We have no rights in the eyes of the Saudis. The Americans say they share our values but they won't share their wealth. For once, Luigi, be realistic!"

Scarcella shook his head sadly as he looked at his old friend. "My life is meaningless if I am only a slave to the Americans and the Saudis!"

"Perhaps, but you are also a fool if you think they will ever nationalize the oil concession for all Arabs to share equally!"

"Luigi, you have become a tool of the capitalists and a ruthless king!"

Pedani sighed as he stood up and began walking up the beach. Scarcella followed him. The tide was dropping and the moon was a growing oval. The evening was still sultry but the breeze off the gulf cooled the sweat on their brows. Neither Pedani nor Scarcella could stand to be angry with the other for very long. As usual, the engineer was the first to rebuild the bonds between them.

"You should know by now, mio amico, that the world is a dangerous place. Bruno and Squalo would rather kill you than join the Arabs."

"But what if I can get the Americans to arrest them?"

Pedani stopped to look back towards the encampment to be sure that no one could overhear Scarcella. "What are you saying?"

"Squalo and Bruno are not who they claim to be. They are Blackshirts who committed genocide in Ethiopia before they were captured by the British. I took care of the real Squalo and Bruno before they died in Kenya. The capos assumed their identities when we were released after the armistice."

"Why didn't you tell Tottenham?"

"Because I couldn't prove it. All the records of the original conscripts in Asmara were destroyed by the British bombers. Once we started working again in Eritrea, I was afraid the capos would kill me if they found out I was an informant!"

"Let me think about it, Luigi. It would be almost as dangerous to tell Berglund as Tottenham."

Ras Tanura, 29 July

One of the unintended consequences of Aramco segregating workers by nationality was that there were no Arab eyes or American ears at the secret meetings of the labor council in Italian Camp.

After another searing day in Ras Tanura, the leaders of the tradesmen gathered in a barasti near the center of the sprawling encampment. Pedani was alarmed when he stumbled upon the capos: it was the first time that he had not been invited. Even Scarcella had concealed the gathering from him. The lead doctor glared at the chief engineer as he took a seat without the capos offering him one. For some time Pedani listened carefully without speaking. They were debating a strike vote that the entire labor council knew he would oppose.

Pedani understood their predicament as well as any of the tradesmen. They had stood by during the food riot in Saudi Camp even though the meals that Aramco provided them were no better. When the anger of the international workforce shifted south, the labor council had received secret updates from Italians building the airfield in Dhahran and the port in Al-Khobar. Longshoremen and truck drivers were offloading intelligence in Ras Tanura. The capos knew the first Arab strike in Dhahran had petered out the week before. None of them were surprised when the emirs sided with the

319

Americans against their Arab workers. In colonial Africa, economic power and brute force had always gone hand in hand, just as they did in Italy.

As crowding and living conditions worsened in Italian Camp through the vicious summer, Pedani had observed an emerging hierarchy. Squalo's crane operators and Bruno's longshoremen and the general laborers had been ready to strike for weeks. The men at the bottom of the oilmen's day labor scale had the least to lose economically. As more workers arrived from Eritrea, they were competing against Arabs for the least skilled positions in the concession. The innate hatred of working-class Italians for the men in Saudi Camp was inflamed by their fascist leaders.

Nando's pipefitters and Guggiana's welders remained ambivalent. Their politics matched their moderate status. Bechtel and Aramco prized their skills and their pay was considerably higher on the so-called D scale. Most of them had traditionally voted for royalists in the Italian parliament before the pope and the king were co-opted by *Il Duce*. The better-skilled tradesmen in Italian Camp dreamed of being employed directly by Bechtel and earning the higher pay of their American *paisans*.

Pedani had warned Scarcella about the political impracticality of an alliance between Saudi Camp and Italian Camp. But his old friend had always been dedicated to treating his patients to the best of his ability, regardless of race or means. The sentiments of the fascists and royalists in the barasti was quite different than *l'intellighenzia*. Most of the men in Italian Camp still felt superior to Africans and Arabs. Even if the strike of all of the non-American workers in the oil concession was successful, most of the Italians would only be happy if their conditions, as Europeans, were ultimately better than the men in Saudi Camp. After listening to the others squabble over details and dead ends for an hour, Pedani finally spoke up.

"If you will permit me, I would like to ask you all a question. Since the governor's troops took the side of the Americans against their own people, what makes you think Jiluwi will not beat you into submission as well?"

Predictably, the military veterans, Squalo and Bruno, said they were not afraid to fight for their rights.

Pedani puffed on his pipe. "Aren't you afraid of deportation?"

Nando and Guggiana, the royalists, challenged the others. "How will we support our families if we are returned to Eritrea?"

Pedani knew Squalo had been waiting since their arrival in Bahrain for another chance to diminish him in the minds of the other tradesmen. He chose the strike vote as his moment.

"Why do you take the side of the Americans, Pedani?"

From the other end of the rough table, Bruno pressed the point. "Are you a traitor, as some say?"

Pedani chuckled, his teeth clenched around his pipe, the smoke lingering between him and the fascists.

"I am only stating the obvious. The Americans have the support of the king and his government."

Pedani glanced at Scarcella, both men knowing they had waited too long to share their secret with Berglund. If either of them went to the US consular branch before the Italians struck, the rest of the labor council would know who had betrayed Squalo and Bruno. There were other Blackshirts hiding in Italian Camp who would kill the engineer and the doctor if the capos were arrested. Ras Tanura was the most dangerous place in Al-Hasa: the new stills were the most flammable structures in the province and the marine terminal stretched a kilometer out to sea.

Then Scarcella spoke up. Pedani instantly knew his old friend was trying to protect him while furthering his own cause.

"We should demand an arbitration by the US government. We can direct our grievances to the consular branch in Dhahran."

A communist ally of the doctor sneered. "What would be the point? The American diplomats will only take the side of the capitalists!"

Pedani could see the inspiration in Scarcella's idea. "By addressing your demands to the US government, you take them out of the hands of the king and the oilmen."

Guggiana nodded. "My nephew was a prisoner of war in America. When Italy surrendered, he was released and paid to work. The food in his camp is so good he got fat! For the first time in his life, he could take a hot shower every night. Even though he fought for the *fascisti* the government treated him better than Aramco is treating us!"

As the discussion continued, everyone seemed happy except for the fascists, who didn't trust Pedani or Scarcella or the Americans. Then an evil smile appeared on Squalo's face.

"I propose that our brilliant leader, the chief engineer, present our demands to the American government."

Pedani looked at the approving faces of the rest of the labor council. Only a few hours before, they hadn't trusted him enough to invite him to their secret meeting. But the price of regaining their respect would be very high. If he refused to give voice to their legitimate grievances, Squalo would be the first to say it proved that he was a *traditore*. If he delivered their demands, Aramco would fire him and have the Saudis return him to Eritrea as surely as they had deported unruly clerks to India and underpaid drillers to Iraq. But standing alone in the middle of the encampment, Pedani knew he was nothing without the men who helped him build Asmara and Ras Tanura.

"It would be my honor to represent you. I only ask that your colleague, Luigi Scarcella, join me."

The doctor was too touched to speak for a moment. Before he could agree, the labor council was gathering around Pedani and Scarcella to congratulate them. As the meeting ended in the barasti, the old friends embraced. After surviving two world wars and the political infatuations of their youth, their estrangement had lasted less than a week. After being banished from Torino and building a new world in Asmara, they were happily reconciled in Arabia. But as they exchanged bacetti, they both knew that the labor council was about to make them martyrs, after all.

Ras Tanura, 30 July

Hank was up after the Fajr prayer, trying to see as much of the construction as he could before the sun dominated the bay. By 8:00, he expected the Italians to be working at the refinery and the terminal. Instead, he heard the Italians - sixteen hundred in all - singing as they marched from their encampment towards the Aramco complex. He didn't recognize all the words as the masons, welders, and crane operators approached, but he could hear:

"Alla mattina appena alzata o bella ciao bella ciao bella ciao, ciao, ciao alla mattina appena alzata in risaia mi tocca andar."

Each verse had a faster tempo than the last. Among the men were a handful of musicians playing accordion, trumpet, and clarinet:

"E fra gli insetti e le zanzare o bella ciao bella ciao bella ciao ciao ciao e fra gli insetti e le zanzare un dur lavoro mi tocca fare."

Hank had never heard Bella Ciao; Berglund would later opine that it was the anthem of the Italian partisans. To intelligence officers, the implication was that all the Italian strikers were socialists or communists. Pedani and Scarcella would argue that the men were singing the original version: the lyrics ringing out on the oil-covered road between the Italian Camp and the Aramco complex were first sung by the strikers' grandmothers in the Po Valley.

The Arabs watched in confusion as the Italians marched with more order than they had ever shown on the job. There were three times as many Italians as Americans working at Ras Tanura. Most of the latter did their best to be invisible, still traumatized by the Arab food riot. It was as if the Italians had won the war instead of the Allies. The upbeat protest sounded triumphant, as the pace picked up with each verse:

"In the morning I got up oh bella ciao, bella ciao, bella ciao, ciao, ciao
In the morning I got up to the paddy rice fields, I have to go.
And between insects and mosquitoes oh bella ciao, bella ciao, bella ciao, ciao, ciao
And between insects and mosquitoes a hard work I have to work."

As the march approached the marine terminal, Hank could see some of Vukovich's men mouthing words they had learned as the children of immigrants. Paisan builders couldn't take their eyes off the parade, their heritage in conflict with Bechtel, which was using hundreds of men from Italian Camp.

At the front of the march, Squalo carried the Italian green, white and red tricolor flag. Hank had seen the flag flying in Asmara, where Tottenham disapproved of it as the colors of the Nazis' rump republic. But the tricolor was about to become the official flag of post-war Italy. Some men waved flags that were half black and half red, the standard of the anarchists and communists who fought against Franco's royalists. Aramco had succeeded in angering the political spectrum in Italian Camp into rare unity.

Lanier appeared at the entrance to the complex, where Jiluwi's soldiers stood guard. The refinery manager had a cigar sticking out of the right side of his mouth, arms akimbo, ready to take on the Eye-talians. Hank stood beside him, along with Vukovich. The other Aramco foremen were agog, picking out their men in the parade of strikers.

Scarcella stepped forward to read the official statement written by the trade leaders. As Scarcella read their demands in Italian, Pedani stood beside him, translating them into English. The anger and indignation in Scarcella's voice disappeared into the even-tempered words spoken by the chief engineer.

"We, the Italian nationals who freely chose to work for the Arabian American Oil Company, demand that the company immediately correct the following offenses against common decency and violations of our contracts.

"Number one - the company must provide us fresh water that is fit to drink twenty-four hours a day."

On cue, after waiting for Pedani to finish translating Scarcella's words, sixteen hundred men shouted their angry agreement.

Scarcella and Pedani continued, "Two. The company must provide us with bread that is fit for human consumption."

The Italians shouted again, some grumbling to those around them about the weevils in the bread imported from Basra.

Scarcella and Pedani went on. "Three. The company must provide hot water in the camp kitchen and in the washrooms."

Each affirmation from the Italian workers was louder and angrier than the last.

Scarcella and Pedani: "Four. The company must install lighting so that men are not falling into open latrines that are filled with disease."

As the list of demands lengthened, Lanier frowned around his cigar.

Scarcella and Pedani: "Five. The company must eliminate the filthy conditions in the clinic that are making sick men even sicker. They must provide clean linen, bedding, and medical supplies to the same extent as the clinic in the American Camp."

The Italians brought men on stretchers that they had carried all the way from their camp to the gates of the refinery complex. There were twenty-nine of them, their faces drawn and dehydrated, their clothing filthy. They looked too much like pictures the Americans had all seen in magazines of prisoners liberated from Nazi concentration camps. Hank could feel his stomach turn and his throat well up. Standing beside Lanier, he tried to hide the shame he felt as an Aramcon.

Scarcella and Pedani continued. "Six. The company must pay to transport men with serious medical conditions to their homeland for proper medical care."

Some of the sick men on the stretchers raised clenched fists. Others pressed their hands together, beseeching the Americans to send them home.

Scarcella and Pedani: "Seven. The company must provide free transportation to and from our work to our camp for lunch, so that we are not exhausted by prolonged exposure to the sun."

The Italians roared in agreement, bathed in sweat at summer's peak on the gulf.

Scarcella and Pedani: "Eight. The company must provide us with housing that is as comfortable and safe as the American Camp."

The Italians sought the eyes American builders and refiners looking down from the catwalks that ran through the refinery. Others were hanging back on the far reaches of the marine terminal, trying to stay out of harm's way. The Italians pointed them all out, swearing at each of them. Every American was sleeping under a roof with a swamp cooler, even if they were bunking two to four men to a room. Every Italian in the crowd was still camping in rotting British surplus or barastis they had built with their own hands.

Scarcella and Pedani: "Nine. The company must pay us for seven days of work instead of six, as it pays its oriental workers."

The Italians shouted louder than before, filled with outrage. Hank caught the phrase that Scarcella used - nativi dell'Oriente. He knew that some of the Italians hated the Arabs, unwanted reminders of the Africans they dominated before the war. The rumors of seven days' pay for six days work had reached the ex-colonials, though they didn't know that Aramco was still resisting the Saudi labor law.

Pedani waved at their men to quiet them as they reached the end of their demands. Scarcella took a deep breath and spoke more deliberately.

"*Dieci. Non continueremo a vivere come animali in gabbia. La compagnia deve immediatamente abbattere il recinto attorno al nostro campo!*"

The Italians roared in fury. Even Lanier took a step back in fear. Pedani turned and waved both arms above his head until his men calmed down enough for their demand to be heard in English. Then he turned to face Hank and Lanier and Vukovich and the rest of the foremen. Hank could hear Pedani's voice shaking for the first time.

"Ten. We will not continue to live like caged animals. The company must immediately take down the fence around our camp."

The men roared again. Thousands of Arab workers stood motionless, watching in grave silence. Scarcella and Pedani turned to calm their countrymen again. Scarcella waved his notes in the air to remind them they had a final demand. The other leaders, even Squalo and Bruno, tried but failed to silence their own tradesmen.

Scarcella and Pedani gave up as the shouting continued, stepping close enough to Lanier to be heard. The words were familiar enough that Hank understood them as Scarcella spoke. Hank watched Lanier's jaw go slack as Pedani repeated them:

"We demand the immediate intervention and arbitration of the United States Consular Branch in Dhahran. Until representatives of the American government have completed their inspection of our working conditions, and the company has complied with all of the recommendations of the American consul, we will not return to work in Ras Tanura."

Scarcella tried to hand a copy of the demands to Lanier, who refused to accept them. His eyes welling with tears, Scarcella turned to Hank. *Was he just another American, an Aramco boss, or a human being?*

Hank didn't see the doctor standing before him. He saw his whole life: crossing the Carquinez Strait with his father, the shotgun missing from the rack in his den, fighting with lodgers from the refinery for the last biscuit on the table, the smell of Giulia's lemon pie, the sound of her lilting voice in the kitchen, the wonder he felt when she let down her hair at the end of a long day, his hunger for Gloria's embrace, the look in her eyes the first time their tongues met, the sound of Peter laughing when Hank made silly faces, the invisible punch in the nose when he first stepped off the C-47 in Dhahran, the taste of gelati as he walked the streets of Asmara with Pedani.

The Italian physician came back into focus before the younger, more fortunate American. As surely as Scarcella had been the first to tell him he had malaria, Hank knew the indictment in Scarcella's outstretched hand was true. He wanted to address every demand. Pedani looked on hopefully. All three knew what Scarcella was thinking after countless hours walking together on the beach north of Italian Camp. *Was the young American another human being, like the good doctor and the chief engineer, or was he another builder of empires and oppressor of his fellow men?*

When Hank reached out and took the demands from Scarcella, the Italians cheered. The doctor looked up at him, relief in his weary eyes.

"*Grazie, Sua Altezza.*"

Hank felt redeemed even as Lanier spat at Pedani's feet. The chief engineer ignored the refinery manager and offered Hank a cryptic smile. Their demands delivered, the Italians turned around and marched back to their camp, singing the remaining verses:

The boss is standing with his cane oh bella ciao, bella ciao, bella ciao, ciao, ciao

The boss is standing with his cane and we work with our backs curved.

O my god, what a torment oh bella ciao, bella ciao, bella ciao, ciao, ciao.

Oh my god, what a torment as I call you every morning.

And every hour that we pass here oh bella ciao, bella ciao, bella ciao, ciao, ciao.

And every hour that we pass here we lose our youth.

But the day will come when us all will work in freedom oh bella ciao, bella ciao.

Jeddah, 31 July

Berglund had received an urgent cable at the main US legation while the Italians were still marching back to their encampment. Ohliger had little choice but to comply with the Italian demand for arbitration. Eddy was in the mountains above Beirut with his wife, who couldn't physically tolerate summers on the Red Sea. Berglund was on point; fuel for the American military was in his official portfolio. Aramco dispatched its C-47 to pick him up in Jeddah. Once onboard, he had time to review the diplomatic traffic between Dhahran and Jeddah.

Most of the communication was from Parker Hart in the consular branch at Aramco's headquarters. Hart had already helped one American keep his head: Powell, the wildcatter who stabbed one of Bechtel's builders at the end of their orientation. The FSO had hidden him in Bahrain until Dr. Vogel saved his victim's life, eliminating the worst-case scenario: beheading the driller under Sharia law. Hart negotiated Powell's deportation after ten well-deserved, face-saving days in a Dammam jail.

Hart envied Berglund in a good-natured way, knowing the military attaché was an OSS agent. The young diplomat had spent the better part of a year trying to transfer from the State Department to active duty. But Hart was even-tempered, spoke several languages and had degrees from Dartmouth,

Harvard and Geneva. The evaluations in his personnel file at the legation in Jeddah might as well have been stamped "Future Ambassador." His idea of a good time was to borrow a weapons carrier from the American airmen to visit Al-Kharj, an oasis south of Riyadh that US agronomists were transforming into the first belt of modern farming in the kingdom.

Berglund was sure that Eddy (as well as Aramco) would have wanted Hart to serve as arbitrator with the Italians. But he had earned a stateside holiday after attending the first meeting of the UN with the Saudis - the lucky bastard. In an unfortunate turn of diplomatic machinery, the acting vice consul in Dhahran was Walter Birge Jr. Berglund had known him since he crewed for Princeton and Birge for Harvard. The son of a wealthy industrialist, he was the sort of dilettante that self-made American oilmen hated in the foreign service.

Instead of a cool hand like Hart, the most sensitive international incident since Eddy's appointment fell to Birge. Berglund had received a look-out call from his OSS counterpart at the US embassy in Istanbul. Birge, for no discernible reason, fancied himself as the bane of the Nazi spy network on the Bosporus. Like many pre-war hires by the State Department, Birge's strongest qualifications for foreign service were his trust fund and an assortment of tuxedos.

Berglund was greeted by Birge at the airfield in Dhahran. The diplomat looked huskier than when they were crewing as Ivy lettermen. Only his moustache was thin, his linen suit lumpy with humidity.

Heat rose from the tarmac like a giant hotplate as Berglund crossed to the hanger. They waited briefly for the rest of the concession executives. Birge was accompanied by Barger, whose assignment seemed to be to keep the vice consul away from the Italians until Berglund arrived. They were soon joined by Ohliger, Mac, and Ferguson, the project manager for Ras Tanura.

Eddy had explained the dynamic between the American factions in Jeddah, Riyadh and Dhahran when Berglund took his post. Aramco executives viewed their own country's diplomats as a necessary evil. There hadn't been an official American legation in Jeddah until 1943, when estimates of the Arabian oil reserves drew the attention of the Pentagon and the White House. Hundreds and soon thousands of US citizens needed services from the consular branch on the other side of the kingdom. The port at Al-Khobar and the airport in Dhahran were becoming busy gateways to the kingdom. Entrance and exit visas had to be obtained from Saudi officials. US passports had to be issued, replaced, and stamped. Someone other than Aramco executives, who officially denied ever paying baksheesh, had to address the transactional requirements of Saudi bureaucrats holding up American work and travel.

On the hour-long drive between Dhahran and Ras Tanura, Ohliger waved highlighted pages of the employment agreement at Birge and Berglund. Every Italian had signed off on hair-raising disclosures about the working conditions in the kingdom written by concession attorneys, some of them associates of Berglund's at Sullivan and Cromwell.

The concession administrator assured Birge, "They all knew what they were signing up for. We only hired tradesmen who had spent years in East Africa. Conditions there were just as harsh, if not worse."

Ferguson was up in arms as well. "All we're doing is giving the Italians a chance to get out of the British protectorate, where there's no work at all, and earn the prevailing wages here in the Persian Gulf."

By noon, the caravan of Aramco sedans and wagons arrived in Ras Tanura. Hank and Lanier were barely speaking to each other but standing side by side to greet the VIPs. Ohliger introduced Birge to the managers of the refinery and marine terminal.

Looking up at Hank as they shook hands, Birge tried to win a needless strength contest. Being named arbitrator between Aramco and the Italians seemed to have activated Birge's animal spirits. Hank looked at Berglund for help as the vice consul mangled his right hand. As much as he wanted to bear down on Birge, he knew it wouldn't help the concession. Standing behind his fellow diplomat, Berglund mouthed a warning to Hank. *Ass. Hole.*

Ras Tanura, 31 July

After a long night in Italian Camp, the labor council had been waiting all morning in the Aramco conference room. When the delegation from Dhahran entered, Pedani was admiring the best swamp cooler in the complex. The others were smoking cigarettes and chatting. Lanier had been drowning them with coffee and orange juice and stuffing them with bacon and eggs. But men who lived without running water smelled no better after breakfast in American Camp. Birge choked on the stench of the Italians as he came into the conference room. Hank introduced Pedani to the vice consul, who took for granted the chief engineer's gentility. Then Pedani introduced the vice consult to Scarcella, Squalo, Bruno, and the rest of the labor council. The Harvard man with the vice-like grip didn't want to touch a single Italian.

They all sat around the conference room, the labor council on one side, the Aramco staff on the other, Birge looking self-important at the head of the table. Berglund sat at the opposite end, ballast for a top-heavy vessel. Pedani calmly reviewed the list of demands for the vice consul. Scarcella, who understood more English than he was willing to speak, provided *soto voce* translation for the rest of the labor council. Birge tried to take notes on a yellow legal pad with a fountain pen that was sputtering after the hot sandy drive. Ohliger and Ferguson interrupted Pedani frequently for points of order.

335

They showed Birge flag after flag in the contracts the Italians had signed. Before Hank's first trip to Asmara, Berglund knew the concession lawyers in New York were already drafting whereas upon whereas.

Birge heard Mac, Ohliger and Ferguson repeating each other's arguments.

Aramco had disclosed the harsh conditions its new workers could expect in the Eastern Province. The Italians who had endured captivity and deprivation in East Africa should have known what to expect when they were free agents in Asmara.

The concession agreement prohibited them from paying the Italians more than the Arabs. American pay was irrelevant because top dollar in the States hadn't been enough for Aramco to fully staff the Ras Tanura project.

The accommodations in Italian Camp might not be up to European standards but they were better than those of the indigenous population of the Eastern Province.

There was still a war going on: proper food and medications in the Persian Gulf were as hard to come by for the Americans as they were for the Italians.

Birge spoke little before leaving to inspect the Italian Camp. In fact, he didn't seem to want to breathe in the same room as the Italians. Whenever he wasn't taking notes or looking at documents, Birge held a fresh kerchief over his nose and mouth. But he did raise one question that he asked Pedani to translate. Looking down the table at the labor council he asked, "Gentlemen, don't you understand how important Ras Tanura is to the Allied war effort?"

At the other end of the table, Berglund winced at Hank. The acting vice consul was asking the vanquished why they weren't enjoying slave labor.

After Pedani repeated the question in Italian, Squalo let out a guttural laugh. Bruno and most of the others joined in. Only Scarcella and Pedani were able to keep a straight face as they looked back at the American official.

Taken aback, Birge shifted back to their demands. The list of disputed facts grew as the first meeting dragged on.

Berglund knew that Birge had been stationed briefly in the US embassy in Baghdad after Istanbul. He suspected that the Harvard man was being passed from station to station like a bad penny. But he seemed to have a passing familiarity with the British oil facilities around Basra. Unfortunately for Aramco, Birge's questions reflected what he had been told by British diplomats in Baghdad. The vice consul seemed to believe that IPC was doing a better job of housing and paying their workers. When Ohliger went on about the concession's version of six versus seven days' pay for hourly wage-earners, Berglund could see Birge's eyes glaze over like a young drunk at closing time in a Boston dive.

The Italians invited the vice consul to tour their encampment. Everyone in the conference room joined the Aramco caravan. Squalo and Bruno took special pleasure in riding in an American sedan. As the delegation drove through the gate of the Italian Camp, the Emir's guards remained at attention as the infidels passed by.

Some of the Italians were swimming just offshore from where the waves hit the beach. Others were smoking and chatting in their mess hall, which was little more than a series of wooden benches shaded by canvas tarps. Scarcella led Birge to the latrines, which were downwind from the long rows of surplus tents. The system was no more complicated than digging a trench out of the sand, building toilets from rough planks along the perimeter, and then refilling them with sand as putrefaction set in.

Mussolini had referred to Libya by its Roman name, Cyrenaica. Berglund had toured the coast after it was liberated by the Allies. The sewer system in its first-century ruins were designed better than the Italian Camp. An unearthly number of flies and mosquitos attacked any human being within twenty feet of the latrines. The trenches were filled with ground-born larvae and insects crawling over the human waste. The trailing end of the latrines remained swamp-like long after they had been filled in.

Birge was unnerved by the flying insects. He covered his mouth and nose with a white handkerchief, waving them away from his eyes. Before Ras Tanura, the worst experience of the vice consul's life had been hazing by upper classmen at Deerfield. But it was Scarcella's next stop, the infirmary, that hurt Aramco the most in the arbitration.

The sick men who had been carried to the refinery complex during the march were back in their rotting tents. The air was only a little less dense with flies and mosquitos than the latrine. It smelled more like a morgue than a hospital. Scarcella ran down some of the statistics as the chief medical officer in the Italian Camp, with Pedani interpreting for Birge.

"More than sixteen hundred men have come here from Eritrea in the last eight months. Three hundred of them have contracted malaria. Nearly half of them have had dysentery. Another three hundred have had dengue fever. Nearly all of them have required treatment for at least one skin infections. Two hundred more have been treated for heat stroke. Some have had broken bones that could not be properly treated."

Scarcella mentioned the young man who would have died from appendicitis without emergency surgery that couldn't be safely done in his own clinic. Hank was the only American who knew Pedani was dialing down his friend's anger and bitterness as he translated.

Scarcella walked Birge past the rows of ill-looking men on crude straw mattresses without clean linen. He beckoned to what passed as the hospital kitchen. Cans of fruit juice had exploded in the heat. There was no way to refrigerate the scanty medicines. The only water was in an open basin that had to be refilled by hand – too warm to refresh the thirsty but not hot enough to kill bacteria. The only way to boil water was over an open fire.

Birge had switched from his balky fountain pen to a pencil to take notes. His hands were shaking, overwhelmed by what he was seeing. The boy raised in a mansion in Greenwich with European servants had sat out the war in embassies in Turkey and Iraq, untouched by war. The brahmins in the State Department still expected foreign officers to approach their employment as public service, an obligation of the privileged few. But nothing seemed to have prepared the vice consul in Dhahran for Italian Camp in Ras Tanura.

The vice consul stuck his head inside a couple of the threadbare tents, their dank interiors dark despite the late afternoon sun. He declined the labor council's offer for coffee or tea. Back into the Aramco vehicles, back into the swamp-cooled conference room in Ras Tanura, everyone could hear Birge vomiting before spending another five minutes washing up in the restroom reserved for senior managers. He regained his composure after three glasses of lemonade on ice and saltine crackers.

Then Birge asked for the rest of the day to review his notes and draft his recommendations. Ohliger and Pedani agreed. The angry room emptied without sidebar discussions between the Americans and the Italians, who remained silent until they were out of sight of each other.

Ras Tanura, 1 August

After a night in guest quarters in American Camp, Birge reconvened with the Aramco executives and the Italian labor council. Wearing a clean shirt without his dirty suit coat, the vice consul worked his way through the list of the Italian demands. Across the table, Pedani translated as Birge spoke.

The vice consul acknowledged that the prevailing pay scale in East Africa was referenced as the compensation standard in the agreements all the Italians had signed.

Watching Pedani react more rapidly than he could translate, the labor council began to frown.

The vice consul accepted Aramco's argument that their agreement with the Saudis didn't allow the concession to pay the Italians more than the Saudis.

The labor council began to stiffen. Ignorantly, Squalo began to glare at Pedani, as if the translator who opposed the strike was in control of its outcome.

The limitations on shelter and housing were clearly defined in their signed contracts as well.

The royalists who were the last to endorse the strike cast accusatory glances at the *fascisti* and *l'intellighenzia*. They, in turn, avoided each other's eyes. Arbitration or not, the strike was being crushed.

Then the room began to turn. The concession executives began to stir, as if they were somehow losing a game they had paid to rig.

The vice consul sided with the Italians on their demands for better food.

The royalists looked at the *fascisti* and *l'intellighenzia* more approvingly. After money, few things were more important than a good meal.

The vice consul sided with the Italians on their demands for clean water and better medical care.

Scarcella and his allies shook each other's hands. The health care professionals could declare victory.

The vice consul agreed with the Italians that Aramco should pay for the repatriation of all workers who were too ill to fulfill their contracts.

Most of the labor council congratulated each other; Pedani remained reserved. Hank recognized the rueful expression on the face of the chief engineer that he had seen at their first meeting in Asmara. The labor council could declare victory in Italian Camp but Birge had sided with the concession on the most important issues on legal technicalities.

The capos began to gather around Birge to thank him. He seemed to be receptive until they were close enough to smell. Ohliger was ready to give the vice consul the bum's rush out of Ras Tanura. Barger pleasantly offered to drive him back to Dhahran. The vice consul didn't seem to want to stay in Ras Tanura any longer than necessary.

The labor council headed back to Italian Camp. Without asking permission from the American oilmen, they were giving themselves the rest of the day off to celebrate. On his way out of the room, Pedani offered Hank a wry shrug.

The last three men in the conference room were Hank, his boss in Ras Tanura, Ferguson, and his boss's boss, Ohliger. They both stared at him bitterly, as if the arbitration could have been avoided if Hank had simply refused to accept the written demands of his Italian friends.

"You got us into this mess, Simmons," Ferguson said, shoving his copy of Birge's ruling into Hank's hands. "Now you can get us out of it."

"Call me when you figure out how much this is going to cost," Ohliger said.

After the top brass headed back to Dhahran, Hank walked alone on the spit of sand that separated the American Camp from his trailer at the marine terminal. The sun beat down on his head, covered by a *ghutra*. The gulf wallowed on both sides of the construction zone. His long slow strides kept time with the sound of Vukovich's piledrivers offshore. Being the liaison between Aramco and the Italians had become a curse rather than an honor. But as he neared the Airstream, Hank had to laugh, darkly.

The men in Ras Tanura who had done the most to prevent the strike - Pedani and Simmons - would now be expected to implement the arbitration for their opponents. Worse, the agreement was being imposed on Aramco by the US government. *Sua Altezza Americano* knew that would appeal to the Saudis as much as it did to his Italian counterpart.

Ras Tanura, 2 August

Because the top brass agreed to delegate the concession's response to the agreement to Hank, they all felt entitled to call his office to lament the arbitration. Ohliger was annoyed that Birge had taken the side of the Italian workers over Aramco. Mac was boggled that their vested partner, the US government, was impeding their progress. Ferguson was stunned that the vice consul thought that they weren't doing enough for men who were better off than when they had been British POWs.

Hank kept his own suffering to himself. Somehow, he had managed to let down his company as well as his best friends. Scarcella was heartbroken by another reminder that most men weren't as decent as he was. The rest of his coalition would never see the nationalization of the oil concession. Pedani had handled the complexity of Ras Tanura as well as he had in Asmara, only to be outdone again by bad politics. Some of their mutual adversaries in the Italian Camp still seemed worthy of contempt. Squalo and Bruno were still full-blooded fascists after the demise of Hitler and Mussolini.

If nothing else, Hank had a blank check to remediate Italian Camp. Ohliger was like most oilmen, willing to spend whatever it took to get the US government out of his hair and the strikers back to work. But Mac, a bean counter at heart, groaned about new revenue disappearing into overhead before it was even produced.

Every time one of his superiors in Dhahran called him, Hank tried to paint a brighter picture. Exports continued to increase through the new submarine pipeline to Bahrain. He was about to fill the first Armadillo with naval fuel oil from the new marine terminal. Drillers were hitting massive amounts of crude all over the concession. *Higher production funneling through Ras Tanura would cure every illness in the kingdom.*

But the future couldn't come fast enough for anyone, Hank least of all. He was sitting in his office, penciling out estimates for the new shuttle between Italian Camp and the refinery complex, when Vukovich burst through the exterior door.

The swamp cooler had barely been keeping Hank comfortable by mid-morning. And Vukovich was even hotter than the steamy furnace that followed him into the Airstream.

"Why didn't you tell me that Pedani was being deported?"

Vukovich might as well have kicked Hank. "What are you talking about?"

"Jiluwi's men just arrested him on the job and took him away!"

"Where did they take him?"

"They threw him in the back of a truck with the other capos and headed for the airfield in Dhahran."

Hank grabbed his keys and brushed past Vukovich on his way out. He got behind the wheel of the Ford and sped off to Dhahran. Both sides of the road were crowded with trucks and tankers. After a thousand years of stagnation, industrial activity was in crescendo across a vast swath of Al-Hasa. He passed one heavy vehicle after another as others headed to Ras Tanura barreled towards the Ford. Arab and Italian truck drivers honked their horns and threw up their hands as Hank caused one close call after another.

The heat and humidity began to sap his anger but the adrenaline in his bloodstream allowed him to think more clearly. The Aramco brass had cut Hank out of the most important decision about the arbitration he was supposedly implementing. Ohliger was doing damage control on the concession's relationship with SAG. Their own government had humiliated the American oilmen by siding with their foreign workers in the arbitration. Now the Italian labor council was being sacrificed as Aramco tried to limit the damage with the Saudis. And the concession's liaison to Eritrea was the last to know.

The ATC hangars and Quonset huts at the airfield had tripled since Hank's arrival the year before. A company of Saudi soldiers stood guard around the section of the airfield restricted to the Army Air Force. There were several C-47's lined up on the tarmac. But there was only one C-54 with red crosses on the fuselage and wings. The military version of the four-engine airliner could ferry more troops than the C-47. The one loading the sickest of the Italians for their return to Eritrea was configured like a flying hospital.

Hank found the labor council crowded in the shade of a small shed. The healthiest Italians were being loaded last. Hank recognized one of Jiluwi's slave soldiers guarding Pedani, the African towering over the impassive engineer. When he saw Hank, a genuine smile appeared on his face.

"*Anka*! How nice of you to see us off."

Scarcella remained mordant, a prisoner again in a different kind of war. Squalo looked like he would have taken a swing at Hank if it weren't for the soldiers ready to lop off his head.

"I didn't know, Alberto. I swear I didn't know."

"I believe you. We are both innocent, *Anka*."

"*Innocente*," Scarcella muttered.

"I am so sorry," Hank said. "This is terrible."

Pedani reverted to his basal stoicism. "It is not so terrible, *Anka*. We only agreed to come here for a few years. Arabia was never very - *ospitale*. If we are no longer welcome, we will be safer in Asmara."

Hank nodded in consolation. "It will be cooler there. The food will be better."

"Of course," Pedani agreed.

Scarcella looked at the American ruefully. "*Presto ti verrà detto di lasciare il Oriente.*"

Pedani tipped his head towards Jiluwi's soldiers.

"Luigi is right, *Anka*. Soon enough, the Arabs will tell the Americans to leave too. None of us is truly welcome here. One foreign flag over a colony is no better than another - even in America, eh?"

Hank was startled by the doctor's prediction. It had the ring of history if not truth. In the long run, why should Americans think they would fare any better than Europeans in Africa or Asia?

The call to the Zuhr prayer echoed around them. The sun was its peak over the Eastern Province. In the control tower, the air temperature was 114 degrees Fahrenheit. The heat radiating off the asphalt made it look like the US military aircraft in the distance were all melting.

"I feel like getting on that plane with you," Hank said. "I want to go home too."

Pedani shook his head. "No, *Anka*. You must finish Ras Tanura. It is important for you. It is important for the Arabs. But you must never forget that this is their world. You will teach them how to get the petroleum out of the limestone, how to refine it, how to transport it. They have a lot to learn. But when they do, the Arabs will get rid of you - just like us."

An ATC sergeant appeared. It was time to load the passengers who could walk for the flight to Asmara.

Pedani was the first man to stand. Squalo was the last. Jiluwi's soldiers used their bayonets to prod him and Bruno to the front. As the rest of the labor council shuffled into single file behind them, Scarcella offered Hank bacetti. The American felt the doctor's tears as their cheeks touched. One of the guards shouted at the doctor. As he moved on, he looked at his ex-patient with affection.

"*Arrivaderci, Sua Altezza Americano.*"

It was Hank's turn to cry. He looked down at the chief engineer in dismay. Pedani reached for Hank's hand and pulled him closer as they clasped. The American could smell the Turkish tobacco on the chief engineer. Pedani's lips brushed against his left cheek, then his right. The guard brandished his rifle and the Italian raised his arms in surrender. He offered Hank the same look of bemusement he had at their first meeting in Asmara; a survivor of the Old World who always knew the New World would fare no better.

As he crossed the tarmac, Pedani cast no shadow in the blinding midday sun. The fourth engine of the C-54 turned over, adding to the moment's rage. But all Hank could hear was the echo of Scarcella's penultimate words. *Soon enough you too will be told to leave the Orient.*

Riyadh, 3 August

After the arbitration, the political dilemma for Barger was that every improvement won by the Italians would inevitably have to be extended to their Arab workers. If Ohliger waited to approve the additional expenses until SAG demanded them, the concession wouldn't earn any good will for maintaining parity as their agreement with Abdulaziz required. The witless vice consul in Dhahran had effectively committed Aramco to building a new Arab hospital by mandating better medical care for the Italians. Because the Arab encampments were larger and more numerous, Birge's call for fresher water and better food in Italian Camp would ultimately cost far more when extended to Saudi Camps throughout the concession.

Ohliger and Barger headed for Riyadh, hoping to meet with the king before he left for the milder weather in the mountains of Taif. Even Abdulaziz needed to escape the worst part of summer in the kingdom's interior. The concession executives flew from Dhahran without securing a firm commitment for an audience from Yassin or Suleiman. Both ministers were unhappy with Aramco after the Arab strikes in Ras Tanura and Dhahran turned violent. Word of the partial victories for the Italians from US arbitration only added to their dissatisfaction with Ohliger. Saleh, Barger's most reliable Bahraini translator, accompanied them.

Abdulaziz was hosting the final *Majlis* before his departure. Barger recognized the old man whose teeth had been knocked out in the riot at Dhahran in the queue of petitioners. A truck from Al-Khobar to Riyadh carrying Aramco Employee 4733 had beaten the company's plane. Barger whispered to Ohliger as the old man reached the front of the line before the gilded throne. The freckled face of the concession administrator turned pale.

Abdulaziz smiled at the sight of another elderly bedu. When the old man smiled back, his lips were still swollen and his gums bloody from Jiluwi's soldiers. His words whistled through the jagged edges of his fractured incisors.

My name is Hamad Abdallah Adhayf, and I have come all the way from Al-Hasa to tell you of the great injustices which are happening there.

Since the beginning of the year, I have been forced to work for the Mericans. The wadi where my people have lived for generations has gone dry and most of my animals have died. My back aches because of the bricks that I carry every day. I am forced to live in their encampment because it is too far to return to my home every night. The camp is a foul place with no water, little more than rice to eat, and the filth of too many men asked to live too close together.

We tried to present our grievances to Saud bin Mohammed Al Jiluwi. I fought with his father to rid the province of the Turks. Now, many of us are forced to work for the infidels you have permitted. But they won't provide us decent food, potable water, or medicine.

We also asked that the Mericans pay us for Al-Jumu`ah, our day of rest and prayer, as you decreed three years ago. Even the British, as ignorant and insulting as they are, understand the teachings of the Prophet well enough to respect our beliefs and pay for Al-Jumu'ah.

For our troubles, I lost the last of my teeth when I was struck by one of the Emir's soldiers. Other tribesmen were taken to the police station in Dammam and badly beaten by the police.

I have come not for myself, since Allah spared my life, but for all the citizens of Al-Hasa who depend on your protection.

As the old man spoke, the king listened carefully, never once looking in the direction of Ohliger or his own ministers. In that moment, Abdulaziz had only one subject. Barger had to admire the old warrior as much as ever. His empathy for the less fortunate - and the defeated - were among the founding king's most important talents.

I am sorry for your troubles, father. I will ask my own doctors to attend to your injuries. This very afternoon I will speak to my advisors and to the foreigners. They are no more or less than our guests. They have promised to bring great blessings to this kingdom. Surely the oil beneath the sands of Al-Hasa is a gift from Allah. But it troubles me greatly to hear what has happened in Ras Tanura and Dhahran. I promise to address your grievances with the Americans, who are here even as we speak.

Stay with us tonight, father, and eat whatever you are capable of eating. Rest after your long journey and my ministers will speak with you again tomorrow.

As Ohliger watched in dismay, Adhayf thanked Abdulaziz profusely, apologized for any trouble he might cause the king or his government, and said again that he was asking for no more than the Emir and Aramco had promised their workers in Al-Hasa.

The *Majlis* ended. One of the lesser ministry officials approached the concession executives and asked for them to wait. It took half an hour for the last palace event of the season to wind down. Whether they were following the king to Taif or returning home to other provinces, everyone was happier than the Americans as they bid farewell to each other. Finally the reception hall was again a (nearly) empty room with carpets over the stone floor and curtains covering a few windows. An attendant still tended a brazier used to prepare the king's beverages. A coterie of ministers, emirs and princes dressed in the season's lightweight finery surrounded Abdulaziz.

Another attendant invited the Americans to approach the king. Tea was served. Pleasantries were exchanged. Coffee was served. For half an hour, the concession executives had the illusion they remained in the good graces of Abdulaziz. Yassin and Suleiman appeared no more dissatisfied than the oilmen were accustomed. Then Abdulaziz spoke. Saleh translated, Yassin and Suleiman listening carefully to the king's every word as they slowly migrated from Arabic to English.

Ohliger, I have treated you like my own son for many years. You have been of great assistance to my kingdom in many ways. For these things we are grateful. But you have made many promises that you have not kept. I am too tired to discuss them with you again, though you are welcome to consider your obligations with my ministers. There is only one thing that I must tell you before I leave for Taif.

I will not allow our dealings to come between my countrymen and its government. Whatever disagreements you have with your workers and my emirs must be settled between you. I will always expect you to do what is right and what is just. I will honor our obligations to you in the agreement just as you must honor our laws and respect my administrators. If this is not acceptable to you, then we will have to reconsider our agreement.

The chanting of the muezzins across the capital began to echo through the palace. The hour of the Asr prayer had arrived. Mohammed and Mansur, the young princes who accompanied their father when he met the American president, stepped towards his throne and helped him to his feet. They held his walking sticks as Abdulaziz wrapped his gnarled hands around their upper arms, the power of his grip still evident to his guests. As the king was about to leave the hall and lead the palace in prayer, he offered his final words to the concession administrator.

May Allah grant you wisdom, Ohliger. May you treat our men as well as you treat your own.

Ras Tanura, 4 August

For weeks, Hank had walked the marine terminal every morning as the sun rose over Tarout Bay. If he passed men from the night shift, he would say that he was inspecting the progress of Vukovich's builders. But the real reason he walked nearly a kilometer to the end of the platform was for solace. Being surrounded by the sea made him feel closer to home. The length of the marine terminal was only a little less than the width of the Carquinez Strait. The smells of the refinery in Ras Tanura were beginning to resemble Martinez. At the end of the pier on Tarout Bay, he could be in Benicia, looking back at his childhood home.

After another bad night in his trailer with little sleep, he savored the light breeze off the gulf. The illusion was disturbed by the distant call of the muezzins for the Fajr prayer. Bechtel's graveyard shift was doing the final welds for the tanker pipelines. Arc lights illuminated the entire length of the pier. The briny humidity of the gulf and the ozone given off by the welders combined like smelling salts that cleared Hank's head. Because he had walked the pier so many times with him, he could still feel Pedani's presence as he stood alone at its end. It was the first moment of peace he had felt since the labor council had been deported. In the distance, he could see the silhouette of a Navy tanker waiting for the tide and the sun to rise before approaching the terminal. There was still a war going on, thousands of miles away in the Pacific. British and American military vessels - as well as merchant marine tankers - were still forbidden from using their running lights at night, even in the Persian Gulf.

Usually the Aramco complex came alive as Hank walked back. Saturdays were the first day of a new work week in the concession. Ordinarily, Arab workers returned from their day of rest and communal prayer refreshed. But that Saturday morning was eerily quiet. Americans - only a fraction of the workforce - were the only ones working. Foremen from Aramco and Bechtel waited for the general laborers to arrive from Saudi Camp. Captains of barges waiting to load or unload at the marine terminal paced impatiently. The stevedores and truck drivers from Italian Camp were nowhere to be seen. The cranes looming overhead were motionless. The bright lights of the terminal seemed to pin the empty trucks in place.

Hank returned to his office after passing through an industrial ghost town. A handful of Americans were wandering around, looking for the departed. His own countrymen could accomplish little in the Aramco complex without foreign workers. The general strike that Ohliger had feared for weeks had finally begun. Even the SAG contingent at the royalty tanks were absent. The Ras Tanura complex was Fort Apache again, waiting to be attacked. Unlike the earlier demonstrations, the police of the local emir and the soldiers of Jiluwi were as absent as the striking workers.

Finally, the telephone on Hank's desk rang for the first time. He was near the top of a telephone tree. The word came from headquarters in Dhahran that a general strike had begun. As Aramco managers throughout the concession answered, the extent of the crisis became clear. Not a single worker who wasn't American had shown up at any of the drilling sites or installations throughout the concession, nearly ten thousand men in all.

The sun beat down on the leaders of dozens of crewless projects reaching from the twin refinery towers to sea around the marine terminal. The scale of the construction site made the lonely foremen look like Lilliputians in the illustrated book Hank read to Giulia as a child. Every sweating American knew they would never finish Ras Tanura by themselves.

Ras Tanura, 5 August

The resolve of the men in Saudi Camp was stronger on the second day of the general strike. Every minute that passed without the police appearing in Ras Tanura was encouraging. Rumors were spreading that Jiluwi would not intervene against the striking workers.

The concession schools continued to hold classes. The teachers - bilingual foreigners, for the most part - took the position that they worked for their Arab students. For Ali, living with Ammar and Mohammed in Saudi Camp, it simply meant that he didn't have to meet Omar Al Rashid at the royalty tanks. Like an older brother, Ammar made sure that the office boy spent the first afternoon of the strike on his homework. As brilliant a mathematician as Ali was, it was a relief to Ammar (intellectually) that he still needed help with his English lessons.

Early that afternoon, the Jordanian was helping Ali with his writing. One of the few advantages of Ammar being left-handed was that it was easier for him to write neatly in Arabic from right to left. Ali, like most people, was entirely right-handed. He had only learned to write in Arabic with great care to avoid smudging the ink as he wrote. Starting a new line in English on the left side of his lined notebook should have been an advantage. Instead, Ali was discovering it was almost impossible to command his right hand to form letters into words and phrases in English. They were both laughing at the ridiculousness of the language shared by the Americans and the British when Ammar heard a stranger calling him by name.

A rush of dread went through the Jordanian's body when he saw the man wearing the red and white *keffiyeh* favored by the Saudis. He was going from tent to tent, asking for the clerk from the marine terminal. As the stranger found his way, Ammar fought for control of his instinctive fear. Soldiers of the local emir had asked for the Pakistani clerks by name before they were arrested and deported. The stranger seeking him was dressed like a minor functionary in the Saudi government, wearing little more than a summer thobe. Ammar got to his feet and acknowledged himself before the Saudi arrived outside their tent.

The official, who was about the same size and age as the Jordanian, beckoned for Ammar to follow him without explanation. Mohammed looked up anxiously at his friend, still sitting cross-legged alongside Ali. Ammar told them to wait for him without any confidence that he would return at all.

A Lincoln Continental was parked outside the gate of Saudi Camp, so dusty that its color was difficult to discern. The functionary who sought out Ammar proved to be its driver. He opened the back door and motioned for the Jordanian to enter. The driver then circled around the Lincoln, opening all of its doors to allow the fresher air between the gulf and the bay to pass through.

Ammar found himself sitting beside Hassan, the emir of Dammam, who was as gracious as the kindly old man had been when he met Hank in Al-Hofuf.

"You are the giant's assistant?"

"Do you mean the American who runs the marine terminal?"

"Yes, that is the one! Are you not frightened that he might step on you?"

Ammar could see that the old man was trying to amuse him as they became acquainted. He answered the emir's jest with one of his own.

"I try to walk one step behind him rather than beside him."

Hassan laughed. Ammar nodded at the mess of humanity on the other side of the fence.

"During Ramadan, he fed the men in this encampment in darkness who worked too hard or fasted too long during the day."

"He is a blessing then. Allah is greater."

"How may I assist you, emir?"

"I have come on behalf of Saud bin Mohammed Al Jiluwi. The governor of the province wishes for you to help your fellow workers by serving on a labor council that the king has directed him to create. You will be joined by representatives of our government, such as myself. We will negotiate with the Americans for better pay and better conditions for Arab workers."

Ammar was incredulous. "I am Hejazi, an exile until recently. I was raised as a Jordanian even though I was born in the kingdom. Why would Al-Saud want me to represent the Arabs of Al-Hasa?"

The elderly emir smiled, the wrinkles deepening around his eyes. "Allah has changed the world. The days of thinking of each other as members of one tribe or another, one province or another - these are things of the past."

Ammar nodded at the fence surrounding Saudi Camp. Tens of hundreds of men now lived in a jumble of tents and barastis. A few of them, with nothing better to do on the second day of the strike, were staring at Ammar, curious about the limousine and the emir.

"Most of these men think that I am *hadhari*. They will question why the governor would choose a man they

357

consider a foreigner, who is not bedu, to represent them. The rest of the men in the camp are Shia. They will question if a Hashemite can honor their beliefs and uphold their interests."

Hassan nodded. For a moment he was silent. They both knew that everything Ammar had said was true. Then the emir spoke.

"My mother was Shia, like many of the people in the villages along the gulf."

Ammar was confused. In his manner and dress the emir looked like any other elder of Al-Jiluwi or Al-Saud.

"My father divorced my mother soon after I was born. He came to believe in the teachings of Muhammad bin Abd Al Wahhab. He waged jihad alongside the father of Jiluwi, the old Emir. I was raised to believe what my father believed. But Allah blesses the devout and the generous, whoever they may be. You are Sunni, my son. You understand these things. All of us pray in the direction of Mecca."

"If that were true, emir, my passport would say that I am a citizen of the kingdom. Instead, my family has suffered in exile for my entire life."

Hassan nodded. "I am sorry, my son. But we are all Saudi now. We must work together for the good of our people. Otherwise the Americans, like the British before them, will use our differences against us, to keep their hold over us."

Ammar sat in silence. Trust did not come easily, even if he wanted to believe everything that the elderly emir was saying. Hassan placed his right hand on Ammar's.

"You are held in high regard by Omar Al Rashid, who remarked to me how intelligent you were in his training for the royalty tanks. Others say you have tamed the American giant. Everyone knows that you were well educated in Amman and Beirut before the war."

Hassan gazed at the growing line of striking workers on the other side of the fence in Saudi Camp, then continued.

"Most of your fellow workers, whether they are bedu or not, can neither read nor write. They know nothing of the world beyond this fence. The king and his ministers have come to believe that our best representatives are those with the most understanding of the foreigners and their business. The oil beneath us belongs only to the faithful. But only those who can learn what must be learned from the Americans can assure the blessings of Allah will flow to our people."

The longer that Hassan and Ammar spoke, the deeper the crowd of workers watching from inside Saudi Camp became. The emir waved at them through the open doors of the limousine. Ammar felt his right hand rising, as if it were waving itself. Allah was greater. Even if he couldn't believe everything that Hassan was saying, it would be foolhardy for Ammar to refuse a direct request from Jiluwi, the Emir of Al-Hasa, a man who was far more powerful and ruthless than Hassan.

Ammar smiled at the emir of Dammam for the first time. He placed his right hand over his heart for all the onlookers to see.

"It would be my honor to represent my fellow workers, and an even greater honor to serve the king."

Dammam, 6 August

On the third day of the general strike, concession executives met with the labor council assembled by Jiluwi. The king had made their negotiations a requirement for his subjects to return to their work in Aramco. The meeting was in the offices of the local emir, Hassan. The government building was a lesser holdover from the Ottomans, two weary floors of mud bricks. The only comfort it afforded was that its thick walls and flat roof kept some of the stifling heat at bay. Electrical power and lighting had been installed during the war, courtesy of the concession's generators in nearby Dhahran.

Heavy wooden tables had been arranged in a row that extended across the square reception hall. On one side sat Hank, Ohliger, Mac, Barger, and Ferguson. On the other were Jiluwi, Hassan, Rashid, and another local emir. Ammar and four other Hejazi clerks were interspersed between the Saudi government officials. The other Hejazi clerks all worked in the offices of the concession executives in Dhahran.

Mac, Ohliger and Ferguson were incensed by the sight of their own assistants on the other side of the table. The Saudis had handpicked Arabs with the most inside information on the concession's finances and operations. Jiluwi had also insisted that the negotiations be done in Arabic. Sitting beside

Barger was his Bahraini translator, Saleh, looking like a man on trial.

The meeting began without the traditional service of tea and coffee. The absence of Arab hospitality had a stifling effect on the stuffy room. Ohliger objected before they could begin.

"We do not feel that the clerks are a fair representation of our Arab workers. The vast majority of our local workforce are day laborers or drillers."

Jiluwi responded tersely. The Americans waited for Saleh to translate. The Bahraini was terrified, trapped between Al-Saud and the American oil men.

"The Emir says that it is not for your company to choose. All of the Arab workers are subjects of Abdulaziz Al Saud. The king has asked for Saud bin Mohammed Al Jiluwi to select them, since he governs the Eastern Province on his behalf."

Defeated, Ohliger and the rest of the Americans listened to the familiar demands. They were the same as the Italian demands, with more emphasis on discrimination by the foreigners against the kingdom's own workers. Hassan asked for the Hejazi clerks to each read one of the demands of the strikers.

All Aramco workers want to have the same standards for food as those in American Camp, so long as they are also halal.

All Aramco workers want to have the same standards for hot and cold running water as those in American Camp.

All Aramco workers want to have the same standards for sanitation as those in American Camp.

All Aramco workers want to have the same standards for medical care as those in American Camp.

Ammar avoided eye contact with Hank, who sat across the table from him, until he read the final demand.

All Aramco workers object to the concession ignoring the king's decree since 1942 and call for seven days' pay for six days work, with Fridays free for the Muslim workers to gather for communal prayer, Al-Jumu'ah.

Hank felt like he was in a bad dream, back in the role he had played for Standard at the refinery in Richmond. Across the table, Ammar looked no more comfortable between the Saudi officials. The American and the Jordanian watched each other as they listened to senior concession executives strike familiar notes.

The concession had done more to raise standards of living in the Eastern Province in a dozen years than had occurred for centuries.

At its own expense, the concession had drilled well after well that produced potable water for most of the population of the Eastern Province.

Because of the war and the drought, most foodstuffs were either unavailable or prohibitively expensive in the amounts needed for the concession's rapidly expanding workforce.

Before the concession brought in full-time nurses and doctors, the only medical care available in the Eastern Province had been from occasional American medical missions and traditional Bedouin healers.

The only reason that the concession hadn't followed the king's 1942 labor law was that its compensation for six days pay for workers exceeded what the British were paying for seven days of comparable work in the region.

While there was not as much scripting as the Arab side, each of the Americans had roles to play. Ferguson focused on the mutual benefits of ramping up production and revenue. Barger was there to remind the emirs how much the concession had already done at its own expense during the war and the drought. He was even more passionate about its plans to improve education, housing, and medical care for the concession's workers in the future. Hank was the expert on the concession's plans to extend the Italian wins on water, sanitation, and health to Saudi Camps. Mac was the numbers man, making a complicated (and inaccurate) case for why

British and American pay standards in the Persian Gulf couldn't be compared.

Ohliger, after a long day that only established an even longer list of grievances, lost his composure. Saleh struggled to keep up his translation for the Arabs on the other side of the table.

"I have a few remarks to make in closing. First, we only agreed to meet with you as a precondition for our employees returning to work.

"Secondly, we are deeply disappointed by the lack of loyalty being shown to the concession operators and owners, who have done more for this province than anyone who came before us.

"Thirdly, the owners of the concession, Standard Oil of California and the Texas Company, are losing patience. We must remind the king and his ministers and emirs that we have already advanced millions upon millions to the kingdom. We are only legally obliged to pay these large sums when we achieve our production goals. To be frank, the advances are really charity unless we are allowed to export very large amounts of crude oil. That will require the full cooperation of our workers and the Saudi government - neither of which we are receiving, at present.

"Finally, I have dedicated the last decade of my life to the concession and the province. I strenuously object to the notion that my fellow Americans or I have discriminated against the Arab people in any way, shape, or form!"

By the time he finished haranguing the Hejazi clerks and the Saudi emirs, they were staring at Ohliger as if he were unwanted, an infidel ready for slaughter. Saleh was trying and failing to kowtow to Jiluwi while delivering the administrator's final volley in Arabic.

Hassan, their host, insisted on rounds of tea and later coffee before they adjourned. The distance between the Americans and the Saudis receded. Barger had opportunities between pleasantries to celebrate their mutual interests and affection. A few smiles began to appear among the Hejazi clerks who, by prior agreement, would return to work for the Americans on the other side of the table the following day. But Hank and Ammar both observed a growing polarity between Ohliger and Jiluwi. The freckled administrator and the provincial governor were aligned only in their anger and contempt for each other. The bond between the pioneering oilman and the powerful emir was broken. As the rest of the Americans and the Arabs offered each other platitudes, Ohliger and Jiluwi were silent.

When Hassan finally adjourned the meeting, Hank and Ammar found each other between the table and the door opening on a dusty street. Each had spoken less than the more strident personalities on their side. An American and an Arab who had treated each other as equals when they were strangers were uncertain how to treat each other as adversaries in the Aramco labor dispute. Hank almost welcomed his company losing control of one aspect of its Saudi concession. But he sensed that Ammar was struggling with how rapidly he was gaining influence among rivals he had always viewed as persecutors of his own tribe.

"Will I see you in the office tomorrow, Ammar?"

"Yes, Hank. I will see you in the morning."

The two men shook hands and separated, Americans with Americans, Arabs with Arabs. Hank was feeling uncomfortable among his fellow concessionaires. Ammar, along with the other Hejazi clerks, basked in the attention of the government officials. The Arabian American Oil Company, without intention, was making every tribesman - Sunni or Shia, Hejazi or Rashidi - feel like a Saudi.

Dhahran, 7 August

None of the concession executives or the labor council knew that the US had detonated an atomic weapon over Japan before their meeting. By the time the White House released a statement, most of the Arabs and Americans in the Eastern Province were asleep. As the strikers returned to work the following morning, the truce between Aramco and the Saudis was overshadowed by the summary event in the Empire of the Rising Sun.

Jeddah, 9 August

Berglund had spent another insufferable day at the legation waiting for Eddy to arrive from Riyadh. Abdulaziz had summoned the US minister to a private meeting in his palace. His boss may have retired from the Marines, but the military attaché could imagine his salty response to the urgent request from the king. Eddy had been enjoying a summer holiday with his wife in the mountains above Beirut, refreshed by the milder climate of the Mediterranean. Berglund could hear Eddy cursing in three languages as he left the comforts of Lebanon at summer's peak in the kingdom.

While Berglund waited in Jeddah, a cable from Cairo reported that the Army Air Force had dropped another atomic bomb. Nagasaki became inevitable when the Emperor refused to surrender after Hiroshima.

When Berglund was still an undergraduate at Princeton, Albert Einstein accepted a lifetime appointment to the Institute of Advanced Studies. Stone cold sober, he had attended a colloquium featuring the winner of the Nobel Prize. Einstein still lost him after the first few minutes of his introduction to quantum mechanics. Now hundreds of thousands of Japanese were dead, the only proof of particle physics that Berglund needed. He only wished that tens of millions of people didn't have to die before Truman gave the order. As far as he was concerned, the military high command in Japan were the only ones to blame for the second mushroom cloud.

As he waited for his boss's plane to arrive from Riyadh, Berglund pondered the other consequences of his government's secret program. Abdulaziz might still reign over the Arab Layer, but the strategic value of petroleum had been discounted by nuclear fission. It pleased the OSS agent to think that America was emerging from the second world war as the only super-power. He wondered how close the Nazis had come to developing an atomic bomb and he worried about the Soviets having their own. But it would be years, if not decades, before nuclear power could be harnessed for domestic use.

In the meantime, the Swiss were already using natural gas to generate electricity. And the US oil industry would make billions on fuel and lubricants for every internal combustion engine that moved people and things by land, sea, and air. If they were lucky, the British might even make enough in the Persian Gulf to recapitalize the Crown. But no matter how many sons the founding king fathered Al-Saud would be the richest family in the region. He shuddered at the thought of them gaining direct control over their reserves.

Eddy arrived and offered Berglund a terse greeting on his way to the cabinet where he kept his Old Harper. He followed his boss into his office, waiting for him to throw down his first shot of his favorite bourbon. As Eddy was refilling his glass, Berglund asked his first question.

"Did you hear about Nagasaki?"

"The co-pilot told me after we took off from Riyadh."

"What was on the king's mind?"

"The Aramco strike. He summoned me to pass along his vote of no confidence in Ohliger."

"Really?"

"It was extraordinary. No interpreters, no ministers. He insisted that I tell no one in Aramco. But he obviously expects me to pass the word along to Washington."

Berglund was boggled by the idea of Abdulaziz speaking to Standard and Texaco through the US government. "Communication has broken down between the oilmen and SAG?"

"Quite. My sense is that his ministers want him to tear up the concession agreement and open up bidding with the British. I think our friend is trying to preserve his relationship with the American oil industry. The king has never trusted the British. And they didn't help their cause by locking up his advisor, St. John Philby, for insurrection."

"I thought Suleiman and Yassin hated Philby more than the British?"

"That's beside the point. Abdulaziz is setting up Ohliger as the sacrificial lamb to preserve the Aramco concession. That's in our national interest, nuclear energy be damned."

Berglund couldn't help thinking about the first animal slaughtered on the fantail of the Murphy. He was amazed by how quickly the kingdom was changing. The Saudis were learning while the rest of the world was fighting. After twelve years of Aramco executives standing in for the US government, Eddy and FDR – rest his soul - had convinced Abdulaziz that the most important American oilman was whoever occupied the White House.

Even though they had been deported for their trouble, the Italian labor council had shown the Saudis how to pit the US government against the titans of its oil industry. Birge had unwittingly mixed facts, figures, and foul-smelling aromas in a Washington-style negotiation, handing a moral victory to the war's less-offensive losers. Then the Saudis, smarting for years after Aramco refused to honor the king's decree on pay for communal prayer, added officials from their own government officials to the Arab labor council, along with the concession's savviest clerks, even though they were Hashemites. The American oilmen had no chance against a team of Arabian all-stars when only money was at stake.

Eddy was still dressed like a sheik after his meeting with Abdulaziz. He took off his ghutra and began to reconcile himself to being back in Jeddah. Without saying so, they both knew that Aramco was too unstable for Eddy to return to Lebanon for his summer holiday with his wife and daughter.

"We have to get a classified cable out to the State Department. Help me draft it before you encrypt it."

"Yes sir."

Berglund was sending as many encoded messages from Jeddah as he had before the invasion in Tangier. The British consulate was around the corner in what passed for the embassy district in the crumbling port. They still controlled the only telegraph system on the Arabian peninsula. It wouldn't do for the British oil industry to learn about Ohliger's dilemma before Aramco.

The infighting between the Allies for control of the Middle East had been ferocious before the US entered the war. He had still been practicing law in New York between the fall of France and the attack on Pearl Harbor. The most effective intelligence operation in town had been British, not German. Monitoring trade between the US oil industry and Germany, Spain, and Portugal had been a top priority for Churchill and his spies in Manhattan. Berglund knew that someone in the State Department would share Eddy's report on the crisis in Dhahran with James Terry Duce, the Aramco VP based in Washington. Even after he left the Petroleum Board, Duce remained in the loop on nearly every discussion in the US government about oil in the Middle East.

The night after Nagasaki was a long one at the US legation in Jeddah. Eddy's doctorate from Princeton was in English literature. The report on his private meeting with the founding king was drafted and redrafted until the professor was satisfied. Then Eddy showered and changed clothes while Berglund transmitted their encoded cable to the US legation in Cairo. Afterwards the two OSS veterans took another ration of Old Harper to the terrace on the legation's flat roof. Like the hottest nights in North Africa, it was the best place to sip whiskey and pray for a gust of sea air.

Their conversation continued as they settled into Adirondack chairs that Mrs. Eddy had imported. Berglund did his best to imagine they were in New England, whiling away the season by a mountain lake. The fetid air of Jeddah intruded on the illusion. At least the night sky was clearer than it was during the day, when the Red Sea boiled over. The waxing moon shimmered on the harbor. Then the senior officer interrupted their respite.

"What's Rentz going to do when OWI shuts down next month in Cairo?"

George Rentz Jr. was the most accomplished Arabist in the Office of War Information. The scuttlebutt was that the Pentagon and the White House planned on folding OWI to appease Democrats as well as Republicans in Congress. Domestic propaganda was about to revert back to peacetime politics.

"I believe George is taking a position on the faculty at the American University in Cairo this fall."

"Damn fine family."

George Rentz, Sr. had been a chaplain in the US Navy, a graduate of Princeton's divinity school who gave up his place on a life raft after the USS Houston was torpedoed in the Pacific. Eddy knew that the young Arabist was a friend of Berglund's. But he didn't know that Rentz's namesake was a notorious hellion on the Nile.

Eddy said, "I'm going to recommend that Aramco hire Rentz. Ohliger's foreign translators have let him down. His successor will need men who understand the nuances of Arab culture - trustworthy Americans who can read minds as well as they speak and write Arabic."

"Good idea, sir."

Berglund imagined the line forming at Aramco's headquarters as US military intelligence mustered out agents all over North Africa and the Levant. As if he was counting sheep instead of spies, the military attaché's eyelids grew heavy. Eddy began to snore, the old war horse slumping into his Adirondack after an epic day.

Before Berglund could slip off, as he usually did that time of night, he too fell asleep. Neither stirred until the muezzins announced the Fajr prayer. By then, the rest of the legation staff was napping around them in the terrace's fresher air.

San Francisco, 14 August

After the bombings of Hiroshima and Nagasaki, everyone in the Pacific division of OWI thought it would be madness for the Japanese to continue fighting. But it still took a week for rationality to prevail. The blood of fanatics was still drying outside the Imperial Palace when Emperor Hirohito's speech was broadcast in Tokyo. Linguists stationed at Pearl Harbor, the Presidio, and Treasure Island carefully reviewed every word of the pre-recorded broadcast to be sure that the Japanese had accepted the Potsdam Declaration without errors or omissions.

Because of the International Date Line, the whispers reached the New Caledonia desk the day before the announcement in Japan. Gloria hugged the men and women she worked with but said little. For the government's propagandists, nothing was real until they read or heard it in media they didn't control. There was always a radio on somewhere in the OWI offices at the Presidio, no matter how much she wanted to concentrate on translations at her own desk. Someone who outranked her always insisted on listening to how the American press was spinning their messages. But that afternoon, the only thing that mattered was when Truman confirmed the Japanese surrender. When he did, every siren, bell, and whistle in San Francisco drowned out the national radio coverage.

Gloria and her co-workers gave up on trying to congratulate each other with words, laughing as their ears rang with the city's tintinnabulation. Hundreds of ships carrying more than a million men rumbled and whistled nearby. The prospect of an all-out offensive against the Japanese homeland had terrified them all. As horrific as the atomic bomb blasts were, the OWI staff had a lot to celebrate, including their own unemployment. There was little doubt that Congress would defund the agency, whose unpopularity at home overshadowed its success overseas.

For Gloria, the thought of being out of a job was a relief. She watched from the windows of her office as the patients from Letterman Hospital, still dressed in their pajamas and robes, merged with uniformed men and women on the streets of the Presidio. Everyone from the New Caledonia desk joined the celebration. Gloria let any patient who could catch her kiss her. The walking wounded were turning back into boys who were forgetting they ever thought they were going to die fighting the Japanese.

The location of the VJ Day party became the last serious project for the Pacific branch. San Francisco had been standing room only before Hirohito's announcement. Liquor stores were emptying out faster than the vessels at half a dozen Navy bases. One of the domestic writers knew Mel Melvin from MGM. The studio's top set designer had spent a million at the Fairmont converting their indoor pool into a Polynesian bar. As silly as the notion seemed to Gloria, the VJ plan was ingenious. The fire marshal hadn't signed off on the Tonga Room. The OWI was added to the guest list for the private preview when Melvin's buddy tracked him down at his suite at the Fairmont.

One of Gloria's favorite co-workers, a blonde Québécoise named Elaine, talked a sergeant from the motor pool into a ride. The bellmen outside the vaulted entrance of the hotel on Nob Hill didn't know what to do when the troop carrier came to a stop. Gloria hopped out after Elaine. Then the bellmen helped down the rest of the women, leaving the male propagandists to fend for themselves.

The transformation of the pool where Gloria swam with Thierry was almost as surreal as the Japanese surrender. A thatched village of exotic hardwoods had been built on stilts over the terrace level. A portion of the pool was still visible as the tropical lagoon. The bar in the center of Melvin's design appeared to float. Somewhere between her first and second drink, the celebration was interrupted by automated thunder followed by a tropical indoor shower. Every incredulous VIP in the room erupted with laughter.

The cocktails kept coming and the chatter drowned out the house band dressed in Hawaiian attire. The Tonga Room was still hampered by the acoustics of the terrace pool and the alcohol began to have a paradoxical effect on Gloria. Some men were still fighting on jungle islands while other Americans couldn't wait to make a buck. The military graveyard at the Presidio had been full before Pearl Harbor and the new one on the peninsula was filling up fast.

Three years in the OWI seemed like a lifetime that Gloria regretted. A lot of the people at her table who weren't spooks had written for radio or the movies before the war. All of the Hollywood types were talking about their prospects in the civilian wing of the American dream machine. Gloria felt like the only one who wasn't trying to figure out how to get rich now that the war was over. The rest of the Pacific branch looked up in disbelief when she was the first to leave.

All Gloria could think about was a husband who might still love her and a son being raised by her mother. Even though Thierry was gone, she still hated herself for adding to the distance between her heart and Ras Tanura. She wished that she had never moved out of the bungalow in Montclair. Hank wouldn't have a place to call home for another month, when she and Peter moved back in. The rest of her life had to be different. It would begin on the next train to Palo Alto.

Even for the bellmen at the Fairmont, trying to find a cab was impossible. The sun had gone down and everyone in the city was out for the evening celebrating. The taxi drivers were out of their cabs along with their fares. Gloria took off her high heels at the corner, thankful that most of the way to the Transbay Terminal was downhill.

Before she could enter the crosswalk, a drunken marine barreling down California in a Plymouth sedan ran over a sailor and his girlfriend crossing from the other side of Mason. Gloria screamed but didn't stop as bystanders gathered around their bodies, a wedding bouquet rolling farther down the block.

Sobbing as she ran down Mason, she turned left on Bush and continued downhill. Every sailor in town seemed to be headed for Market. Most of them looked like teenagers who had never been so drunk, grabbing any woman who was younger than their mothers. Some of the girls in saddle shoes were foolish enough to play along. Other women couldn't escape the crowds of men (in and out of uniform) spilling into the streets. Gloria heard muffled screams as she passed an alley echoing with the profanities of several men.

Half a block above the headquarters of Standard Oil of California, someone dropped a metal trash can filled with water from an upper floor and killed an old man on the street below. On the other side of Bush, Gloria passed the smaller building of the Arabian American Oil Company, where local hooligans were smashing the windows.

At the bottom of the hill, a naked madwoman had her legs wrapped around one of the bronze men on the Mechanics Monument, egged on by the leering crowd. Gloria needed to cross Market to reach her train but her path was blocked by thousands of revelers. Young drunks had climbed on the roofs of every streetcar and truck for blocks. Through the windows of city buses, she could see the faces of older women who looked petrified and older men who simply wanted the insanity to end. Traffic lights cycled automatically even though vehicles couldn't move through the raucous throng. Gloria saw a streetcar conductor changing cars get bashed in the head by a sailor with an empty bottle.

She lost count of how many men in uniform tried to get a kiss from her. There must have been twenty of them between one side of Market and the other. The ugliness of the experience would be with her for the rest of her life. If men tried to put their arms around her she gave them an elbow. Repeat offenders got a knee to the groin.

It took forever for Gloria to push her way down First to the Transbay Terminal. Her only luck was that the delays in San Francisco allowed her to catch the last train of the night down the peninsula. By the time she got to Palo Alto, her feet were throbbing from being stepped on repeatedly by the mob. She called her father from a telephone booth to pick her up. There were still tears in her eyes when she slipped into the front seat of his Cadillac and clung to him for the first time since she was a young girl.

At first he was befuddled that Gloria wasn't happy about the war being over. She tried to explain the scene downtown until he begged her to stop. Then they held onto each other until she allowed him to drive her home. When they reached the house where she grew up, Peter came running out to meet them. She grabbed the little boy and clung to him as she kissed him. Peter was the only thing she was truly proud of, the only part of her life that wasn't broken or spoiled. Best of all, when Gloria nuzzled his ear, he smelled like Hank fresh out of the shower.

"Mommy, does this mean you don't have to go to work anymore?"

"*Exactement, mon amour!*"

"What about Daddy? Will he be coming home too?"

376

Gloria gazed into Peter's eyes. Her son resembled her but was his father through and through, tender-hearted and bright. She squeezed him even tighter. "I hope so, dear."

Dhahran, 16 August

The day after Japan surrendered, a dozen managers gathered at Aramco headquarters looking worse for wear. Hank watched as concession veterans congratulated each other. For a relative newcomer, it was still hard to imagine what it was like for the Hundred Men when Rommel dominated North Africa and Dhahran seemed as vulnerable as Tobruk. But the mood in the room wasn't as ebullient as VE Day had been. World War II might have ended but the battle between Aramco and Al-Saud was just beginning.

The question that the concession's top men were asking each other was why they were reconvening on the day before Al-Jumu'ah. Ohliger had held his usual weekly meeting with them three days earlier. For those in charge of distant sites like Abqaiq, the round trip was eating up a day they would rather have nursed their white or brown hangovers at home.

Most of the drillers and operators took their usual seats. A few hopped spots to catch up with someone from another corner of the concession. Soon enough, the only vacancy was at the head of the table. Mac, the last kibitzer, stood behind Ohliger's empty chair. He grabbed a gavel that the previous administrator had seldom used and tapped until he had the attention of the table.

"I must tell you that Floyd has been asked to return to the States for consultations with senior management. As the only other officer in the kingdom, the board has asked me to carry on with the day-to-day administration."

The room fell silent. Old hands glanced at each other. The longer Mac's fact-finding mission had gone on, the more obvious it was that the Hundred Men who defended the Arabian concession during the war didn't control it anymore. The general strike had been the last straw. During the first few weeks of negotiations, Ohliger had appeared downtrodden as Aramco accepted one Saudi demand after another. Now the man who had been in the kingdom longer than all but a few of the Hundred Men was packing his bags. None of the managers relished the thought of being back in the States if it meant facing Davies and the Aramco board. The violence that preceded the general strike was too fresh in their minds. Even though the workers from Saudi Camp were back on the job - along with the Italians and the rest of the foreign workers - tensions were still high. Yet Mac was as upbeat as Ohliger had been glum.

"Gentlemen, I want to begin by congratulating you on our final victory. I know some of you spent most of the bloody war here, far from home and - for a time - without hope of reinforcements. Despite all the threats and obstacles you faced, we have made tremendous progress this year. It's a credit to each of you and your dedication to the concession.

"Some of you may be thinking we are losing the battle here in Arabia. I just want you to know, on behalf of Standard and Texaco, that we are poised for victory. We are sitting on top of the largest oil reserves the world has ever seen. Now that the war is over, everything with wheels is going to run on derivatives of petroleum.

"The best thing that could happen to this concession is for the Saudis to think they won our labor negotiations. We're going to deliver better food, housing and medical care and all the rest to the men in Saudi Camp. And we're going to make Abdulaziz the richest king since Croesus.

"Do you know why? I'll tell you. For every shilling we pay the Saudis, we will produce nearly two barrels of crude oil. That's less than our competitors anywhere in the world. In a few months, when we fire up both of the new stills at Ras Tanura - along with our new refinery in Bahrain - Aramco and CalTex will be sending more product downstream than anyone east of the Suez. Our own government is begging us to build a pipeline to get Arabian crude to European markets. The world is our oyster, lads. We may be making the Saudis rich but we'll be making ourselves richer!"

Mac guffawed at his own bluster, slapped the backs of Barger and Ferguson, and led a score of men around the table in three hip-hip hoorays. Hank and Mac grinned at each other - no one else could be as corny as the Scot and get away with it. The piper had found his way to the front of the parade.

"Standard and Texaco want us to produce half a million barrels of oil a month. While I'm minding the store, that won't be our ceiling. That'll be our floor! Now that we've sorted out the Arab Layer, we are going to drill gusher after gusher. We're not stopping until the kingdom is the number one producer in the world!"

More applause followed. Mac tried to tamp down the fervor he had just stirred up.

"As you know, Floyd's motto was *'Whatever it takes.'* And I want you to understand, it still applies!"

The drillers, refiners, engineers, physicists, and operators all cheered. Mac went around the table and shook every man's hand. When he reached Hank, he winked like a poker player holding a full house.

Ras Tanura, 19 September

The Stars and Stripes were streaming from every pole in the new refinery complex. But wherever they flew, the green and white flag of Saudi Arabia waved alongside. Only a few of the Americans present could read the inscription in Arabic above the flag's sword. *There is no god but Allah...Muhammad is the Messenger of Allah.*

A series of rectangular canvases had been suspended between the marine terminal and the refinery. From the other side of Tarout Bay, they looked like the sails of an ancient ship. A long line of American sedans were backed up on the rocky spit between the point and the new complex, bringing dignitaries from all over the Eastern Province. All of the men who built it had been given the day off. Thousands of them were resting in Saudi Camp or Italian Camp, happy to be out of the heat and humidity of late summer. But hundreds were on hand with most of the Americans to witness the ceremonial firing of the first still of the new refinery.

The men of Ras Tanura sat or stood on every perch in the complex, some of them ten stories above the churning gulf, watching the guests being directed to their seats under the canopies. A number of the wives of Aramco executives had been driven up from Dhahran for the occasion. Most of them were as dowdy as their middle-aged husbands. But the men on the catwalks lusted after Kathleen Barger, who was wearing an elegant sun hat and a shapely red dress with white polka dots. The Americans whistled; the Italians were more outspoken.

Che bella! Bella figura! Baciami piccola! Sposami! Bella figura! Che bella che sei!

In bemusement, Tom Barger waved his arms to quiet them before their Muslim guests could take offense.

When the first tanker called at Ras Tanura in 1939, Abdulaziz himself had opened the valve for the crude to flow. Though the celebration lasted for days, the royalties slowed to a trickle a few months later when the Nazis invaded Poland. In 1942, to stave off hunger among his subjects, the founding king had decreed that all workers should receive seven days' pay for six days' work. But three more years passed before Mac capitulated on Al-Jumu'ah. Even then, the concession's new administrator delayed the effective date until the beginning of 1946. Al-Saud, understanding the need for the American oilmen to save face, didn't object. It was the precedent that mattered in the kingdom. Standard and Texaco had bowed down to the post-war reality: their production goals would only be achieved with the full support of SAG.

The firing of the first still should have been a bigger celebration than Ras Tanura's first tanker. But neither the Americans nor the Saudis were in the mood so soon after the Arab labor council prevailed. The muted honor of firing the still went to Gladys Ferguson, the wife of the hard-driving project manager, now Mac's second in command. The top brass from Aramco and Bechtel gathered around her under the center canopy. Lanier stood nervously beside Mrs. Ferguson, trying to make sure his boss's wife didn't blow up his brand-new refinery.

Steve Bechtel, the primary contractor, stood proudly beside his project manager, Vukovich, who looked exhausted and relieved. After making millions on Liberty Ships, John

McCone was busy unwinding his partnership with Bechtel in California. William Eddy, the US minister plenipotentiary, was attending to other matters in Riyadh, as were the founding king, his ministers, and the crown prince. The US legation in Jeddah was represented by Rod Berglund, the military attaché, wearing his naval dress whites. Since the American military were Aramco's primary customers, there was some logic if little majesty in Berglund taking his place among the VIPs. At Hank's insistence, the new leaders of the Italian labor council sat beside him in the back row.

The most senior member of SAG present was the Emir of the Eastern Province. Standing with Jiluwi was the ranking emir, Hassan, wearing formal Saudi attire. When the ceremony began, Jiluwi deferred to Hassan, his elder advisor, to speak on behalf of the king. Then Mac took a longer turn at the microphone, trumping the kindly emir as he explained the significance of the occasion. The afternoon heat swelled as the translations continued. Hank winked at Ammar when he caught him yawning in the next row. For weeks, the two men had been reversing roles constantly. When they were working on the marine terminal, the American was in charge and the Jordanian was his assistant. When they were sorting out the side agreements between Aramco and the Arab labor council, Hank followed Ammar's lead. Both sides relied on the pair to resolve the details of new housing, sanitation, and medical services for the concession workers.

When Mrs. Ferguson finally pressed the red button igniting the burners at the base of the still, every claxon in the refinery sounded. The Italians whooped and applauded with the Arabs and the Americans. Water trapped for millions of years in the crude oil feed had the lowest boiling point. Within a few minutes, it began to escape the highest tower in Al-Hasa as steam. Soon after, the faithful in the crowd were called to the Asr prayer. As the Muslims began to make their way back to their cars and encampment, the rest of the international gathering broke up as well. The oilmen graciously and patiently saw off Jiluwi, Hassan, and the lesser emirs.

Hank had arranged for a prodigious amount of beer and canned delicacies to be delivered to Italian Camp from Bahrain. By the time the Americans arrived in their own encampment, the post-graduate moonshiners were offering their products in the Dining Hall, along with the best spread anyone had seen for months.

After a couple of shots Hank stuck to Indian beer. Berglund found him in a corner, a lonely wallflower gawking at the Bargers, the most glamorous couple in Aramco.

Berglund stuck out his hand and waited for Hank to shake it. The liaison to Eritrea hadn't spoken to his OSS tour guide since the Italian labor council had been deported. He winced when Hank finally gripped his right hand.

"I just wanted to congratulate you, Hank. What you've accomplished in Asmara and Ras Tanura is really incredible."

"Sparc mc, Berglund."

"I'm being completely sincere. This project is crucial to rebuilding Asia and Europe. America's the greatest country in the world and you're a great American."

Hank stared down at Berglund, feeling less patriotic than the fake diplomat. He tried to change the subject. "Imagine what Arabia's going to be like."

"Exactly! You're helping them make up for centuries!"

"There's enough crude in the Arabian Layer for another hundred years," Hank said.

At the dawn of *Pax Americana*, Berglund was feeling expansive. "If we stick together - government and industry, I mean - we can do anything!"

"I'd settle for a month's leave."

An aging bachelor, Berglund was unsentimental about the homefront. He took another slug of bathtub gin and British tonic as he continued his pitch. "At the very least, we should be able to keep the Soviets out of the Persian Gulf."

Hank hated the way that intelligence officers were already gearing up for the next war. "If you say so."

Berglund tapped Hank's chest. "You just have to decide what side you're on."

"What kind of a crack is that?"

"I know you blame me for Pedani getting deported."

"We'll all be better off without Squalo and Bruno. But Scarcella was a great doctor and Pedani could have built everything we need!"

Berglund looked at Hank as if he was an idiot. "They're communists."

"What proof did you have?"

"We've been in Turin for months now. The records of their membership in the Italian communist party go back to their university days. Why do you think Mussolini sent such smart guys to Eritrea in the first place?"

"But they weren't a threat in Arabia!"

"*Au contraire, mon ami.* Al-Saud spent generations flipping the other sheikdoms. Long before the Prophet came along, wealth flowed through tribal leaders. They don't want anything to do with socialism."

Hank started walking away. "I need another beer."

Berglund blocked the bigger engineer. "Stay here while I get you one."

Hank stood in the corner as Berglund dashed to a fifty-five-gallon drum that had been cut in half, painted silver, and filled with ice and beer. The rest of the room was overflowing with Aramcons who were getting boisterous. Hank felt like everyone was happier than he was. He headed out to the grassless baseball diamond and took a seat on a wooden bench. In the distance, the lights in the refinery and the marine terminal danced on the bay. To his displeasure, Berglund found him, carrying two beers. The military attaché tossed the jacket of his dress uniform at Hank and resumed his political discourse.

"Why do you think the Saudis make such good business partners for Standard and Texaco?"

Hank didn't bother to answer. He had learned in Asmara that Berglund needed no encouragement after a couple of drinks.

"The oilmen and Al-Saud want the same things. All the money in the world and all the power that goes with it."

Hank took a chug of his fresh beer. "That's not what I want. I just want to go home."

Berglund shook his head in disappointment. "You may be a big boy, Hank, but you need to grow up."

It wasn't the first time that Berglund had pissed him off. But it was the first time that Hank couldn't control his anger. The memory of Pedani and Scarcella being marched off at the airfield propelled him. He gave Berglund a good shove, even though he knew the OSS had trained the lawyer to maim and kill. Instead, he defeated Hank by other means.

"Did you know your wife was fucking the Frenchman?"

A lot of men would have taken a swing at Berglund. But after working together for a year, they both knew that Hank wasn't one of them. He was too busy hurting.

"*Thierry*." All those nights when he wondered what Gloria was doing, it was always the con man from New Caledonia who had kept him awake.

Berglund became the aggressor. "The OSS signed off on him for OWI but Gloria turned up while he was being tailed in San Francisco."

"Fuck you, Berglund."

"I knew about the affair before we met in Washington. The only reason I didn't ask you about it was that Mac wanted to be sure you got on the plane."

Hank grabbed his antagonist by his shirt and pinned him on the hard ground. A few stragglers from the Dining Hall stopped to watch the fight. Hank wrapped his hands around Berglund's throat.

"I can't decide whether to strangle you or just break your neck!"

"Take it easy! She broke up with him months ago!"

Hank bounced the back of Berglund's head off home plate. "Shut up!"

Berglund tried and failed to free himself from Hank's jealous rage. "We're taking Thierry off your hands! We're setting him up in Saigon!"

"Fuck you, Berglund."

"War is hell, Hank. You either get killed or you get screwed."

"Leave my wife out of this!"

"I only mentioned her because you were about to ruin our beautiful friendship!"

Hank released him and got back on his feet. "We were never friends."

Berglund sat up on the ground. The onlookers seemed disappointed.

"Why are you so sore about the Italians? Pedani's family was waiting for him in Asmara. Scarcella's the best doctor in town. Tottenham says they still get together every Friday night for dinner."

"Leave me alone."

Hank wandered towards his trailer in the marine terminal. Berglund followed him at a safe distance.

"If you forgive your wife, you can still live happily ever after! But no one's going to forgive you if you side with the commies!"

Berglund watched Hank walk in and out of the shadows of the security lights in American Camp on his way back to the Airstream. Then the military attaché brushed off his pants, put his dress jacket back on, and returned to the party.

Ras Tanura, 4 October

Whenever Hank was alone at night, after completing every other obligation he pretended was more important, he re-read the letters that Gloria had sent from Palo Alto. As much as he wanted to believe that Berglund had been lying, the truth was between the lines. The author of Peter's bedtime story, de Saint-Exupéry, was right. Gloria may have deceived his eyes and ears, but Hank knew in his heart that he was already a cuckold when Aramco recruited him. Somewhere else in San Francisco, Gloria had been sleeping with Thierry. When he had begged her to let him transfer to Ras Tanura, she was already thinking about weekends with her lover in Montclair.

But when Hank re-read her letters, he could also see that Gloria's tone had changed before the war ended. The woman who used to think the New Caledonia desk was more important than her marriage was gone. She seemed to have abandoned Thierry months before the government folded OWI. Now all Gloria said she wanted was to reunite with Hank and Peter in Arabia or California. Her preference was still implicit: she had moved back into their home in Montclair with their son. Knowing that Gloria genuinely missed him made every day in Ras Tanura tougher, halfway through a three-year hitch that was beginning to feel like forever. Mac was dropping hints about giving him the month's leave that he was due but Ferguson always intervened. Few Aramcons were going anywhere before the refinery complex was completed.

The marine terminal was getting as busy as Port Richmond. For the first time, the Arabs and the Italians had simultaneously docked and loaded tankers at both ends of the T-shaped causeway. But Hank could no longer stand to watch the ships raise anchor and head for the Arabian Sea. The kid who dreamed of adventure had become a disheartened man on the wrong side of the world, like millions of displaced people who survived the war. The thought of another holiday season without Gloria and Peter was more than Hank could bear. As the firing of the second still neared, he felt defeated.

On Thursday afternoons, the end of another long work week, some Arabs simply disappeared after the Asr prayer. Others perfected the art of looking busy. The Italians were just as good at doing nothing in the last few hours before Al-Jumu'ah. Ordinarily, Hank was one of a handful of managers with checklists and timetables who tried to push on after Asr. But that Thursday, he found himself looking west across Tarout Bay. In the lengthening shadows, he saw the silhouette of a hilltop structure on Tarout Island that he had never noticed. He handed Ammar his binoculars and pointed it out.

"What is that?"

Ammar peered through the lens. "The castle. I have heard the villagers mention it."

"Let's go check it out."

Ammar looked at Hank as if he was unwell. Since the strikes had ended, the Jordanian had become accustomed to the American always having one more thing to do. Hank grabbed the keys to the Ford from his office and got behind the wheel. Ammar followed in amazement. They drove slowly north on the narrow spit of sand that connected the marine terminal with the main complex, then continued west through the guarded gate and the other encampments. The flow of heavy trucks between Ras Tanura, Al Khobar, and Dhahran was light. When they reached the crumbling village of Tarout, Ammar had to ask a fisherman for directions to the bridge connecting the island. Hank hoped that the creaking relic of the Ottomans wouldn't collapse under the weight of the Ford. He continued east across the flats until he reached the rocky promontory near the center. They passed few islanders but found an old man sitting at the edge of the ruins.

It was typical of Al-Hasa that the ragged guide didn't promote himself. Yet his livelihood was showing visitors the castle he had inhabited since he was a boy. Ammar got out of the car and gave him a few riyals. The old man rose from his perch on a limestone block and began to speak to Ammar in Arabic.

The ruins looked less impressive from the promontory than they had from Hank's office. He had only been able to make out two round towers from the other side of the bay. From the rear he could see three corners with tapered peaks that looked like they were built by Crusaders; most of the interior and a fourth tower had been destroyed in a forgotten battle. Hank had loved reading about castles since he was a boy. He looked at the irregular stratum at the bottom of the "modern" ruins and knew he was setting foot inside a structure more ancient than anything he had visited in Cairo.

Ammar began to translate for Hank. "The Phoenicians built a temple to Astarte here five thousand years ago."

When they were only lovers, Gloria had taught Hank about the goddesses of the ancient world. Astarte was known by many names. To the Mesopotamians she was Ashtar and Ishtar. To the Greeks she was Aphrodite. To the Romans she was Venus. Wherever civilizations took her, she was the goddess of love and power and war, surrounded by lions, horses, and adoring subjects.

"After the ascension of the Prophet, the temple was destroyed during the caliphate of Al-Uyuni. About five hundred years ago, Portuguese invaders built the castle we see today."

Hank ran his hand over the reddish mortar that covered the surface of the stacked wall of limestone blocks between the towers. Conquerors had come from all over the ancient world to claim Al-Hasa, only to have it wrested away by others with greater gods and stronger iron. When the old man continued around the promontory, Ammar and Hank followed. He pointed out an abandoned well. The slope around it was nothing but sand and rock. The closest living thing was hundreds of yards away, a single goat in futile search of grass. Ammar listened to the older Arab and continued to translate.

"The ancient ones built on this hill because it had the only freshwater spring on the island."

Hank nodded as he raised his binoculars to survey the bay. Tarout was a transliteration of Ishtar. He wondered if the Portuguese had been displaced by the failure of their water supply or the strength of the Turks. He gazed at the refinery and tank farm on the other side of the bay. The kingdom's oil reserves would fail as surely as the spring that fed the castle. Everything that the Americans built at Ras Tanura was destined to return to dust or the sea. He reached into his pocket and gave their guide another handful of riyals.

As Hank and Ammar returned to the Ford, the old man followed them in gratitude. *Shukran. Shukran jazilaan.*

Driving back to the Aramco complex, Hank's mind was a jumble of ancient goddesses and a living woman - the mother of his son - that he still worshipped. Ammar watched in bewilderment as his boss began to cry. Nothing mattered more to Hank than loving Gloria and Peter.

Ras Tanura, 5 October

On their day off, the new leaders of the labor council invited Hank to dinner in Italian Camp. His social equity had increased in the months following the arbitration. When the men ate bread that wasn't rotten, they knew they had *Anka* to thank. When the doctors in the clinic opened the new refrigerator that stored medications, they knew *Anka* had procured it. When men could use the latrine at night without falling in, they knew that *Anka* had arranged for the installation of the electric lighting.

As Berglund predicted, Aramco's two thousand Italians were moving on. After the deportation of Pedani, Scarcella, and the other *capos*, they elected new leaders who were less outspoken. As the encampment evolved, the hometowns of its residents were more meaningful than their skills. Most of the Italians lived alongside other men from birthplaces that none of them had seen for years. A few of the younger colonials who were born in Eritrea had never set foot in Italy. As *la madrepatria* recovered from the war and remittances improved, traditional foods were shared with benign provincialism. In Ras Tanura, the availability of regional cheese was more important than the future of Italy's constitutional monarchy.

As the only American who had been at the first Christmas in Italian Camp, Hank was happy to hear about their plans for the next holiday season. It would be the first year for *Perciavutta*, the Italian equivalent of early red wine in France, *Beaujolais*.

The Calabrians offered their guest - the chemical engineer - a taste of the Iranian grapes they were fermenting. Hank was terrified after one sip: heavy tannins and black ink that tasted like formaldehyde instead of ethanol. He complimented them and discreetly switched to Indian beer. After a course of seafood and another of pasta, the labor council got down to business.

Nando, the pint-sized pipefitter with forearms like Popeye, was the only original *capo* who hadn't been deported. Supply and demand still trumped politics in the gulf: master pipefitters were the scarcest tradesmen in a concession brimming with critical joints. In an unusual gesture of equanimity, Ferguson had decided that Nando was a follower rather than a leader of the revolt. He looked up at Hank and asked a serious-sounding question that the American didn't fully comprehend. The only thing that Hank could make out was *gratifica natalizia*.

"Nando wants to know when we will receive our holiday pay," one of the newer arrivals from Asmara at the table explained. Nando went on about Mussolini and *tredicesima mensilità* as the newcomer continued translating for Hank. "*Il Duce* made companies pay workers for a thirteenth month at the end of each year. Nando wants to know when Aramco will pay."

Mac's answer would be *never*. But like a good guest in Saudi Camp, Hank avoided a direct response. "Perhaps after the first full year of service - 1946."

Nando nodded stoically. In the lull that followed, the new capo of the carpenters introduced the craftsmen working on the encampment's Nativity scene. The figures were placed on the table for Hank's consideration. In addition to the biblical standards, *il Professore* was still part of the Presepe. As Hank fondly remembered Pedani, the carpenters presented their newest figure, *il Medico*, whose solemn countenance was unmistakably Scarcella.

Hank was touched but headed up the beach before the labor council could dredge up any more memories or make any more demands. Walking alone where he had walked so many times with Pedani and Scarcella, the American was tormented by his own conscience.

How could it be wrong for the Italians to demand things that Americans took for granted? How could the Saudis see the Italians as threats when they were the only tradesmen in Arabia with the skills needed to make them rich? Even in a kingdom that was still practicing slavery, how could Americans justify the treatment of free Europeans like prisoners of war?

Ras Tanura, 6 October

Hank was resolved. He wanted to be with Gloria and Peter in California. He wanted to transfer back to Standard. With a good word from Mac, he might even get his old job back at Port Richmond. As soon as Ammar appeared in his office, Hank asked to be driven to headquarters in Dhahran. He said little to his assistant, who was less talkative than usual. The road was busy, mostly flatbed trucks hauling material and men to Ras Tanura. Scattered clouds hung low over the gulf, the sun at an increasingly respectable distance. Just the kind of picture postcard Aramco needed to lure unwitting Americans.

Ammar finally spoke when they were halfway to Dhahran. "Have you met George Rentz yet?"

Hank hesitated. Mac and Barger had approval to create an Arab Affairs Bureau. The lead Arabist with OWI Cairo, George Rentz, had agreed to join Aramco. The conflicts with SAG and the strikes of Arab workers convinced the board that they needed a better understanding of the kingdom. Another failure to find common ground with Al-Saud or their local workforce would be fatal. As a courtesy, Barger had called Hank to let him know that Ammar was being considered for the new division. But he could honestly say that he hadn't met Rentz face to face.

"Not yet."

"Professor Rentz offered me a job. He wants me to work in the Arab Affairs Bureau. There are so many documents that must be translated from English to Arabic and vice versa."

Hank was amused by the studious Arab's use of Latin. The clerk who couldn't keep his files straight had been flawless in his negotiations with the concession executives. Now they were promoting Ammar after losing to him in the Saudi arbitration. It fit with everything that he had learned about Aramco. Ammar's hunger for equality had made him a leading voice among the Arab workers. But his grasp of the oil business was making him an acquisition target for the concession itself.

Ammar tried to reassure his boss. "I wouldn't start until after the first of the year. They are still looking for offices in Dammam."

Hank nodded, a card player with a middling hand. Berglund was the matchmaker who had talked Rentz into leaving Cairo. The military attaché was spending as much time at the legation branch in Dhahran as Jeddah. Nor was Rentz his only client. Berglund was helping place OSS and OWI veterans from all over North Africa and the Middle East in the Arab Affairs Bureau. Lanier, of all people, was up in arms about Mrs. Rentz. The Egyptian woman would be breaking the color barrier in America Camp. That she was a Coptic Christian who was active in the international community in Cairo mattered little to Aramcons with Jim Crow tendencies. Hank decided that the moment called for a little levity.

"Maybe I still have time to teach you my filing system."

Ammar's brow furrowed. He stared at the road as if it weren't dead straight.

"It was a joke, Ammar."

The Hejazi still had less of a sense of humor than most Arabs in Al-Hasa. "I have another offer," he said.

"Oh?"

"Emir Hassan has promised that the government will send me to the American University in Beirut to finish my studies."

"That's wonderful, Ammar!"

"At first he said that they would send me to Al-Azhar in Cairo. But I explained to him that it wasn't enough to study Sharia Law. Agreements between our government and your company will be based on international law. Do you think I should go law school to Harvard or Cornell?"

The American chuckled. "It sounds like I should be driving you!"

Immune to hyperbole, Ammar glanced at his boss impatiently. "Hank, I need your advice about which offer to accept. The government scholarship or the new bureau in Aramco?"

Hank took a deep breath. Ammar was posing another moral dilemma, whether to serve his country or the concession. The answer seemed clear. "There is nothing more valuable than a great education."

Ammar reached into the pocket of his shirt. "I forgot to show you something." He handed Hank a new passport emblazoned with the seal of the kingdom.

"Congratulations, Ammar!"

The Ford drifted in front of a tanker truck headed for Ras Tanura. The tanker's horn blasted. Ammar swerved to the right and almost rolled the Ford. For once, Hank was glad that the coast was flat.

"Keep your eyes on the road for Christ's sake!" Ammar put his Saudi passport back in his shirt pocket and slowly pulled back onto the coast road. Head-on averted, Hank didn't speak again until the monotony of the road took hold of him. "I'll be leaving Ras Tanura soon."

It was Ammar's turn to be incredulous. "Why would you leave when we are going into full production?"

Rather than disrupting Ammar's new sense of himself, the concession, and the kingdom, Hank simply shrugged. "I've had enough. I want to go home."

"Madness," Ammar said. "Mac won't let you leave."

Hank was surprised to hear Ammar refer to the new administrator by his nickname. But Mac's larger-than-life personality was what the moment required in the concession. He was making employees forget Ohliger, even though his predecessor was still sitting in an office in Dhahran. The board was still interested in the ex-administrator's perspective. But what was the point of being the VP of government relations when Ohliger had been shunned by the Saudis?

Dhahran, 6 October

When they reached headquarters, Ammar asked for permission to borrow the Ford to meet with Rentz. The Saudi labor negotiator wanted to thank Aramco's new Arabist personally before turning him down. Hank and Ammar agreed to meet again after the Zuhr prayer. When Hank arrived at Mac's office, he had to wait for a triumphant group of drillers to file out.

A shy young woman with freckles, curly hair, and thick glasses ushered Hank into Mac's office. He couldn't help noticing the absence of a wedding band on her ring finger. Mac pointedly ignored his new assistant; Mrs. MacPherson was a few blocks away. The purge of untrustworthy male foreigners from the clerical staff was leading Aramco to a new category that would have been unthinkable in California Arabian: single American women.

Mac's meeting with the drillers seemed to have gone well. The concession's new administrator was reaching for a fresh cigar, savoring the prospect of the kind of strike he liked.

"What can I do for you, Hank?"

"First of all, I want to thank you. It was a blessing to travel with you last year. I still learn something every time we get together."

As generous as he was when offering praise, the Scot was intolerant when receiving it. He frowned at Hank as he lit his cigar with a new butane lighter. "Get on with it, laddy."

"I've completed the project I was sent here to do. I want to go home as soon as we fire the second still."

Mac's mood darkened as he uncrossed his legs and leaned closer to Hank. "I won't hear of it. You're one of my best men."

"I don't think I'm cut out for work overseas."

"Bollocks. You've already done things in Arabia and Eritrea that a lot of important people said couldn't be done!"

"Thanks, Mac. Maybe you can put in a good word for me at Bush Street in San Francisco."

"I'll do no such thing!"

Hank said, "I never let the company down, Mac. But I feel like I may have let myself down."

"Bloody Hell. Is this about the Italians? Did you think we were going to let a few commies waste twelve years of development and millions upon millions?"

"Of course not."

"We're sitting on top of the biggest oil reserves in the entire world, Hank. And I'm not going to let anyone or anything keep me from proving it. You could be set for life by the time you're forty! You just need to decide if you want to be part of the team. If not, I'll find someone who is!"

In the distance, Hank could see natural gas flaming off of the new wells in the Dammam complex. It would be years before anyone bothered to capture it. But for the first time he could see his own career going up in smoke. Not working in Ras Tanura was one thing. Not working in the industry he grew up in was another. The kid who wore hand-me-downs from oilmen in his mother's boarding house couldn't imagine being blackballed by Standard and Texaco.

"I just want to be with my family. I've already missed too much."

Mac puffed on his cigar while his new secretary pounded out sixty words a minute in the next room. Hank knew he preferred carrots to sticks.

"What are we paying you?"

"Ten thousand a year."

"How does a thousand a month sound?"

"It sounds nice. But I'm not here to ask for a raise. I want to go home."

"What if you got the raise and I put you at the top of the list for family housing? Take your pick. Dhahran or Ras Tanura."

"I don't think Gloria would like it here."

"Nonsense. Your wife can live like a queen in Al-Hasa. What you need is a month's leave, first class. Next thing you know, Gloria will be having another baby!"

Hank had to laugh. Mac was doing his best to beguile him. And Hank was doing his best to forget that Berglund helped Mac shanghai him in DC. The Scot got out of his chair and circled around his desk. Still seated, Hank felt Mac place his fatherly hands on his shoulders. He could barely remember Henry Senior's.

"You've worked hard. I'm not surprised you're worn out. I feel guilty having my wife here when it's been more than a year since you saw Gloria. In fact, I'm giving you eight weeks off. That will give me time to arrange housing as good as California. You can live on the beach, just like a movie star! Make sure your wife knows that your housing allowance will pay for a houseboy. I'll find her a Filipino who speaks the King's English and cooks French cuisine."

Hank scoffed politely as Mac sat in the chair beside him. His boss gave his cigar a tug and then aimed it in the direction of the airfield.

"I want you to get on the next flight out of here. Kiss your wife. Take your son to a ball game. Go dancing at the Fairmont. Stay over for mimosas and eggs benedict. Then I

401

want you to bring them all back with you. Stop in New York and go to a show. Spend some time in Paris - Gloria will like that. Go to Rome if you love the bloody Italians so much. All I ask is that you sign up for another three-year hitch."

Mac sat back and crossed his legs again. He beamed at Hank as the smoke from his cigar swirled around the ceiling fan. Hank thought back to the Arabian tales he read to Giulia as a boy. His boss might as well have been a jinn.

What do you say?

Acknowledgements and Glossaries

The author would like to thank the staff of the University of Utah for their assistance with the Wallace Stegner Papers at the Marriott Library, which include the notes and drafts of his authorized history of the Arabian American Oil Company. Because of disputes with Aramco, the final version of *Discovery! The Search for Arabian Oil* that Stegner submitted to the public relations department on Park Avenue in New York in 1958 has never been published.

During a fast-paced tour of the Arabian concession three years earlier, Stegner interviewed a number of pioneers that had been selected by the PR staff. The most eager might have been Phil McConnell, one of the oilmen who remained in Dhahran after it was attacked by Italian bombers in 1940. McConnell later published a memoir of the war years, *The Hundred Men*, a primary source for some of the encounters of Arabs and Americans described in this work. Stegner's least productive interview was with Aramco's most accomplished Arabist, William Eddy, the senior OSS officer in pre-invasion Tangier and the US minister plenipotentiary to Arabia later in the war. But Stegner did have *FDR Meets Ibn Saud*, Eddy's account of the secret rendezvous of the founding king and President Roosevelt, published with funding from Aramco and the CIA, the source of many details in this work about their encounter.

Stegner's personal choice for "hero of heroes" was Tom Barger, a multi-talented mining engineer who arrived in Dhahran in 1937, surveyed vast tracts of the third Saudi state, and became a favorite of his Bedouin guides, his superiors, and the Saudi emirs. Stegner valued Barger's vivid letters home to his wife and parents, which were later published as *Out in the Blue*. Ironically, his hero had ascended to the presidency of Aramco by 1959 when the project was shelved, collateral damage in the eroding relationship between Al-Saud and the oilmen. Both sides spent the next several decades trying to conceal their disputes with the concession's international workforce in 1945, as later documented by Robert Vitalis in *America's Kingdom*.

The author is grateful for the assistance of Tom Lippman, who wrote Eddy's biography, *Arabian Knight*, as well as standards like *Inside the Mirage*, and Hugh Wilford, who wrote *America's Great Game*, a regional history of the CIA. The author is also grateful for the encouragement of Tim Barger, whose Selwa Press published many of the titles above, and Lynn Stegner, Wallace's literary trustee and the editor of this work. By intention, *Concessions and Betrayals* begins where the official version of the pioneer era of Aramco ended.

In part, this work is the imagined memoir of Henry S. Smith, who had worked for Standard Oil of California for several years and started a family before arriving in Ras Tanura in June 1944. The author's research into the beginning of Hank's career in corporate diplomacy for Aramco, Tapline, and Bechtel didn't begin until he and his second wife - the author's aunt - had passed away as gracefully as they had lived. Like many self-styled patriots in the oil patch, some of the secrets of the US intelligence services in the Middle East died with Hank. Among them were the details of how Aramco paid the families of the

Italians who built Ras Tanura during the climactic months of WWII, when many of their loved ones were still trapped in northern provinces controlled by the Nazis.

Ultimately, this historical novel is also a tribute to a lost tribe, the expatriates from Italian East Africa who helped transform the third Saudi state, only to be exiled a few years after the war; the end of one colonial era and the beginning of another; an ongoing series of catastrophes. Finally, the author is grateful to friends and family who endured multiple iterations of this work and - most of all - to Nadia, his protector and supporter on a long journey through appropriation, climate change, and quarantine.

Historical Arab Figures

Abdulaziz bin Abdul Rahman Al Saud - founding king of modern Saudi Arabia who negotiated an exploratory concession to Standard Oil of California in 1932-33.

Abdullah bin Suleiman Al Hamdan - first finance minister and long-term advisor of Abdulaziz, the founding king of modern Saudi Arabia.

Feisal bin Abdulaziz Al Saud - second son of Abdulaziz who outflanked and succeeded his older brother, Saud, to become the third king of modern Saudi Arabia. Assassinated by another member of Al-Saud in 1975.

Hussein bin Ali Al Hashimi - last Sultan of Mecca and king of the Hejaz before his lineage was displaced in 1925 by Abdulaziz and the Ikhwan, Al-Saud's army of Wahhabi zealots.

Saud bin Abdulaziz Al Saud - first-born son of Abdulaziz who is generally considered to have been unworthy successor to his father before being displaced by his brother, Feisal, with the support of most of Al-Saud.

Saud bin Mohammed Al Jiluwi - son of Mohammed Al Jiluwi, a kinsman and key ally of Abdulaziz, who succeeded his father as the governor of the Eastern Province, Al-Hasa, during the concession's rapid expansion.

Yousuf Yassin - Syrian-born advisor and minister to the founding king, Abdulaziz, and his successor, the crown prince, Saul.

Historical American and European Figures

Prince Amedeo - Third Duke of Aosta, first cousin of King Immanuel of Italy, who served as the Viceroy of Italian East Africa before he was captured by British forces and died in a prisoner of war camp in Kenya.

Thomas Barger - multi-talented engineer and executive who served as Aramco's director of government relations during and after WWII and went on to become the concession's chief executive and chair; widely lauded for improving the education, living standards and advancement opportunities of Arab employees.

Walter Birge, Jr. - Vice consul of the Dhahran branch of the US State Department in Saudi Arabia who arbitrated the labor dispute between Aramco and its Italian workforce in the late summer of 1945.

Fred Davies - engineer and executive from Standard Oil of California and its first subsidiary in the Persian Gulf, the Bahrain Petroleum Company, before becoming president and chair of Aramco.

Everette DeGolyer - pre-eminent geophysicist who developed seismography before serving in the US Petroleum Administration during WWII. His assessment of the oil reserves in the Middle East in 1943-33 correctly predicted the massive post-war shift of production from the Americas to the Persian Gulf.

James Terry Duce - British-born geologist and executive who served as Aramco's vice president for US government relations in Washington DC for decades, including war-time service in the Petroleum Administration.

Allen Dulles - chief of the OSS station in Bern who negotiated the surrender of the German forces in Italy and later became the director the CIA, a leading figure on Wall Street and Washington in the post-war era along with his brother, John Foster Dulles.

William Eddy - chief of the OSS station in Tangier before the Allied invasion of North Africa who served as the US minister plenipotentiary to Saudi Arabia in 1944-46 before becoming a consultant to Aramco and one of the architects of the post-war CIA.

Bill Eltiste - Pioneer driller who struck freshwater wells throughout the kingdom during the wartime drought; materials manager who helped develop a new class of Arab entrepreneurs as post-war vendors for Aramco, most famously Mohammed bin Laden.

Vic Ferguson - Aramco project manager for the refinery complex at Ras Tanura before becoming the concession's second in command under James MacPherson.

Parker T. Hart - Career diplomat in the US Foreign Service who opened the consular branch in Dhahran and went on to become the US ambassador to Saudi Arabia, Kuwait, North Yemen, and Turkey.

The Hundred Men - The pre-war employees of California Arabian who remained in the concession during WWII when the concession was largely cut off from North America and Europe, celebrated in a book of the same title by one of their own, Philip McConnell.

Owen Lattimore - director of the Pacific branch of the Office of War Information during WWII, a leading Sinologist who was prosecuted and acquitted on charges of being a communist agent during the McCarthy era.

T.E. Lawrence - British liaison to the Sultan of Mecca during the Arab campaign who was instrumental in the division of the Ottoman Empire after WWI and establishing Hussein's sons on the thrones of modern Jordan and Iraq.

James MacPherson - Scottish oil executive from Standard Oil of California who arrived in Dhahran in July of 1944 after service on the War Production Board and was appointed as concession administrator in late 1945.

James S. Moose Jr. - First official from the State Department to reside in the US consulate in Jeddah in 1943 who later became the first US ambassador to Syria.

Floyd Ohliger - a pre-war pioneer of California Arabian who served as the concession's administrator during the era of the Hundred Men and remained vice president of government relations after being replaced by MacPherson in late 1945.

St. John Philby - British military advisor to Abdulaziz during World War I who became a personal confidante of the founding king (and secret consultant to Standard); the father of Kim Philby, Soviet double agent in British intelligence before defecting in Beirut.

Franklin Delano Roosevelt - US President from 1933 until his sudden death in 1945, shortly after meeting Abdulaziz, the founding king of Saudi Arabia, in the Suez.

Max Steineke - California Arabian's leading geologist, who surveyed most of the Eastern Province during the early years of the concession and developed the core drilling techniques and stratigraphic analysis that correctly predicted the location of the massive crude oil reserves at extreme depths in sedimentary formations.

Orde Wingate - British Army officer, cousin of T.E. Lawrence and Sir Reginald Wingate, who trained the

Ethiopian and Sudanese guerilla forces who fought the Italians in the Horn of Africa in 1940-41 as well as Haganah, the precursor of the Israeli Defense Force.

Historical American Organizations

Office of Price Administration (OPA) - established by an executive order by FDR in January 1941, the agency had authority to set prices for consumer goods, subsidize agricultural commodities, and ration fuel oil, gasoline, and rubber for military use. The OPA continued to function until 1947, when it was finally dissolved by Congress.

Office of Strategic Services (OSS) - US military intelligence agency modeled on (and co- developed by) British Secret Intelligence, established in 1942 by President Roosevelt and terminated shortly after the end of WWII by President Truman. After a transitional period it was re-established as the Central Intelligence Agency in 1947.

Office of War Information (OWI) - US agency established in June of 1942 by President Roosevelt to coordinate the flow of news and information domestically and abroad. The agency's activities within the US were controversial in Congress. Its efforts overseas were more successful but overlapped with psychological warfare in the OSS. By 1944 the domestic activities of the OWI were defunded and 'white' propaganda was consolidated within the OWI, which was disbanded in September 1945, along with the OSS.

Petroleum Administration for War - Created by executive order of FDR in December of 1942 with Interior Secretary Ickes acting as administrator, coordinating the domestic and foreign production of crude oil and its derivatives for the US military. A number of oil industry executives, including Duce and Macpherson from Aramco, were on its staff within the Department of War.

War Production Board - Successor to New Deal agencies of the federal government that coordinated production of materials needed by the military and constrained or prohibited non-essential civilian production. Along with the OPA, rationed the non-military use of scarce commodities. Created by executive order by FDR in January 1942 and dissolved in November 1945.

Petroleum Industry Terminology

Arab Layer - After the British struck oil in Persia in 1908, the extent of the reserves around the Persian Gulf became a matter of intense interest in Europe and the US. The presence of crude oil in Saudi Arabia was confirmed in 1938 by the first Aramco strike on the Dammam Dome after several years of drilling. The impetus for accelerating the development of the Aramco concession was a report by DeGolyer which estimated the region's oil reserves at twenty-five billion barrels, dwarfing those in North America and the Caribbean Basin.

Aviation Fuel - During WWII, the fuel used in conventional Allied aircraft was 100% octane, while those of the Axis powers had lower octane ratings (and weaker performance). Refineries used a special distillation process to achieve higher octane ratings than regular automotive gasoline. As jet engines came into wider use after the war, modern aviation fuel has evolved to kerosene-based products that are stable under more extreme engine pressures, air temperatures, and altitudes.

Catalytic Cracking - The portions of crude oil with the highest boiling point are those with the highest molecular weight, such as fuel oil. In order to increase the amount of more volatile products that are in higher demand or more profitable, the thickest ("heaviest") components of crude oil fed into a still can be exposed to additional heat, pressure, and catalytic agents in order to break them into smaller molecules, such as gasoline (octane).

Crude Oil - The liquid phase of a large number of hydrocarbons derived from the breakdown of fossilized marine flora and fauna, primarily by anaerobic bacteria, after being trapped by subsequent geological layers during later periods of the Earth's history.

Diesel Fuel - A high molecular weight product of crude oil refinement which is used to power internal combustion engines at higher compression than gasoline engines; the properties of diesel are more like fuel oil than gasoline.

Fuel Oil - A broad category of hydrocarbons distilled from crude oil which share high molecular weight and viscosity, making them practical for use in furnaces to generate heat or power.

Gasoline - Liquid distillate from petroleum fueling automotive engines from numerous isomers of octane, often amended with other compounds to reduce engine "knock" due to premature firing of cylinders.

Hydrogen Sulfide - Because crude oil is based on the putrefaction of marine animal and plant life, one of its most dangerous contaminants is hydrogen sulfide. In addition to being a highly toxic gas, which lead to its use as a chemical weapon in WWI, H2S is also highly corrosive.

Natural Gas - The gaseous phase of petroleum, primarily comprised of methane with much smaller amounts of ethane, propane, and butane. Crude oil also contains variable amounts of carbon dioxide, nitrogen, and a liquid phase of natural gas (LNG).

Oil Patch - Can refer to either a geographic region where crude oil is produced or the petroleum industry but is often used to refer to both as a global domain.

Petroleum - often used synonymously with crude oil, an inclusive term for the gaseous, hydrous, liquid and semi-solid phases of hydrocarbons and other substances arising from the breakdown of prehistoric marine flora and fauna underground.

Product Lines - When heated, recycled, and reheated, heating towers (refinery stills) destroy or release unwanted contaminants - such as hydrogen sulfide and water - from petroleum end products. Because each contaminant and hydrocarbon has its own chemical structure and characteristics, the level at which they are isolated or purified in a tower can be controlled by manipulating the temperature and pressure inside the still and sequencing the elevation of the branches (product lines) on the tower.

Refinery Still - The primary heating tower in a refinery (the still) takes advantage of the differences in the temperatures at which each component of petroleum boils and vaporizes. Depending on their molecular weight, gases and liquids that are dissolved in air, water, or heavier hydrocarbons have unique characteristics when heated or pressurized that allow refineries to separate dozens of compounds in crude oil from each other.

413

Stabilizer - Before crude oil can safely be transported by pipeline or tanker, hydrogen sulfide must be removed. Stabilization refers to a number of chemical and industrial methods to separate H2S from the marketable elements of crude oil. The complexity of stabilization depends on the extent to which producers wish to preserve natural gas, principally methane.

Tea Kettle - For simpler systems designed to produce only a few hydrocarbons like gasoline and fuel oil, a smaller tower with fewer branching product lines is easier to assemble and control. A tea kettle was built in Ras Tanura for the use of the Saudi royal family and government before WWII. Importers of crude oil in emerging markets still use tea kettles, as do insurgents in oil producing regions.

Upstream - The petroleum industry can be described in three overlapping segments. Upstream refers to the specialists in finding and extracting petroleum from underground deposits: earth scientists, drillers, and operators of the equipment they employ.

Midstream refers to transforming crude oil into a wide array of gaseous, liquid, and viscous petroleum products, as well as transporting them closer to end markets through pipelines or specialized vessels.

Downstream refers to the processes required to distribute, finance, market, and sell petroleum products to end users.

About The Author

William Wesley Fields is a literature graduate of
the College of Creative Studies in Santa Barbara,
mentored by its founder, Marvin Mudrick.
He attended the Keck School of Medicine in
Los Angeles and trained in emergency medicine
at Harbor-UCLA before becoming an associated
clinical professor at UC Irvine, chairing a national
multi-specialty partnership (Vituity), and serving in
leadership positions for the American College
of Emergency Physicians.

The author has been published in a number of
peer-reviewed healthcare journals, co-founded
the Emergency Medicine Policy Institute
and collaborated on acute care studies by RAND
and the Brookings Institutions.

As William Wesley, his first novel, *Doctorcito*,
was purchased by Jeremy Tarcher while he was
a medical student at USC. His second novel,
Ghost Dancing, is a medico-legal thriller. His third,
Concessions and Betrayals, is based on a family legacy.

Early Praise for *Concessions and Betrayals*

"The story of the Italians in the Saudi oil patch has long needed to be told. Trapped far from home and forced to live in squalor, they nevertheless were essential to the development of the Saudi oil industry. Even readers who know Aramco's early history will learn a lot from this book's fascinating narrative"

Thomas W. Lippman, author of *Inside the Mirage*

"A stunning achievement: William Wesley has given us not just a riveting, page-turning novel full of character and color, but also the richest and most complete historical account yet of the fateful birth of the U.S.-Saudi alliance and the post-World War II world petroleum order."

Hugh Wilford, author of *America's Great Game*

Early Praise for *Concessions and Betrayals*

"A sweeping WWII tale set in a harsh, forbidding,
beautiful landscape, William Wesley's account of the
collaboration between American oil interests and
the nascent Kingdom of Saudi Arabia
is nothing less than epic.
To build a marine terminal on the Persian Gulf
that could refine and export only a few years
after the discovery of the greatest oil field
on the planet demanded an international team
of geologists, drillers, engineers, architects, oil men,
laborers, and of course, politicians.
This is their story, a story on the grandest scale,
exhilarating and surprising at every turn.
The innovations needed to surmount the staggering
challenge; the cultural clashes and quirks; the cast of
many, many thousands speaking different languages;
a founding king, a dying president, a young man
from California with a gal waiting back home -
it's all here - human, heroic,
and hugely engrossing."

Lynn Stegner, author of *For All the Obvious Reasons*